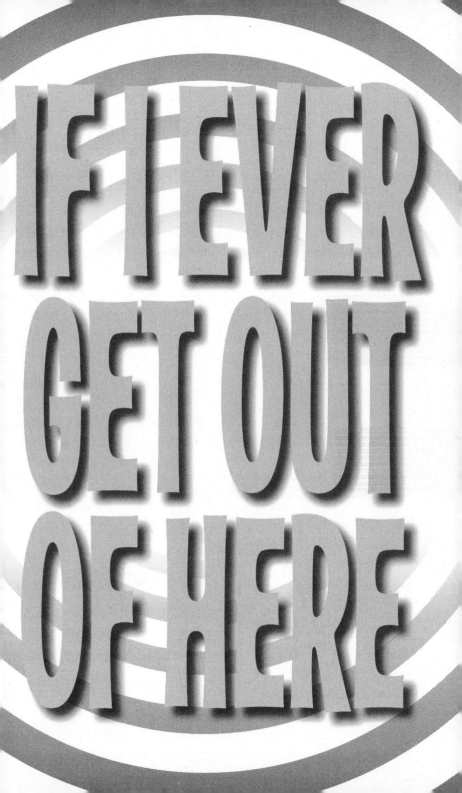

Library of Congress Cataloging-in-Publication Data

Gansworth, Eric L.
If I ever get out of here / Eric Gansworth. — 1st ed.
p. cm.
Summary: Seventh-grader Lewis "Shoe" Blake from the Tuscarora
Reservation has a new friend, George Haddonfield from the local Air
Force base, but in 1975 upstate New York there is a lot of tension and
hatred between Native Americans and Whites — and Lewis is not sure
that he can rely on friendship.
ISBN 978-0-545-41730-3 (hard cover : alk. paper) — ISBN 978-0-545-
41731-0 (paperback) 1. Tuscarora Indians — Juvenile fiction. 2. Families
of military personnel — Juvenile fiction. 3. Identity (Psychology) —
Juvenile fiction. 4. Friendship — Juvenile fiction. 5. Tuscarora Nation
Reservation (N.Y.) — Juvenile fiction. 6. New York (State) — Ethnic
relations — Juvenile fiction. 7. New York (State) — History — 20th
century — Juvenile fiction. [1. Tuscarora Indians — Fiction. 2. Indians of
North America — New York (State) — Fiction. 3. Families of military
personnel — Fiction. 4. Identity — Fiction. 5. Friendship — Fiction.
6. Race relations — Fiction. 7. Tuscarora Nation Reservation (N.Y.) —
Fiction. 8. New York (State) — History — 20th century — Fiction.] I. Title.
PZ7.G1532If 2013
813.54 — dc23
2012030553

10 9 8 7 6 5 4 3 2 1   13 14 15 16 17
Printed in the U.S.A. 23
First edition, August 2013

For the Bumblebee,
flying smoothly between
Venus and Mars,
and for Chuck Collins
and Jeff Ewing,
on their respective
planets

CONTENTS

Part One: If I Ever Get Out of Here · · · · · 1

Part Two: Moon and Stars · · · · · · · · 91

Part Three: Tragical History Tour · · · 235

Playlist & Discography · · · · · · · · · 353

Acknowledgments · · · · · · · · · · · 357

PART ONE

If I Ever Get Out of Here

1

With a Little Help from My Friends

"Cut it off," I yelled.

"Shut up, or my dad will hear you," Carson Mastick said. "He's not that drunk yet, and I'm gonna have a hard enough time explaining how you come down looking like a different kid than the one that went upstairs." For ten minutes, he'd been farting around, waving the scissors like a magic wand. Now he yanked the long tail of hair from my neck and touched the scissors an inch above my collar. "Is this about it? There's no turning back once I start chopping."

"Yup, that's it," I said.

"You think cutting off your braid is going to make those white kids suddenly talk to you?" Carson's cousin Tami said. "If you believe that, you need brain surgery, not a haircut. What do you care what they think anyway? You've had this braid since, what, kindergarten?"

"Second grade," I said. "If you'll remember, *someone* stuck a massive wad of gum in my hair that year and I had to cut it all off and start over."

"Was an accident," Carson said, the same thing he said

whenever he did something terrible that he secretly thought was funny.

"Give it to me," Tami said. "I got better things to do." She grabbed the scissors.

"Wait," Carson said, "I didn't —"

Suddenly, it was gone, the hair I'd grown for five years. Tami held it out in her hand and I turned around.

"You didn't fix it first," I said. Everyone on the reservation knew that when you snipped off a braid, if you wanted to save it, you had to tie off both ends before you cut. And since almost no one cut off a braid casually, you always saved it to remember the reason you had cut it. What Tami held looked like a small black hay bale. "What am I gonna do with that?" I yelled, and Carson made the shush expression with his face. "You can't braid it loose. It's not boondoggle."

"You could always do what I do," Tami said. "I have my stylist sweep it up for me, and then when I get home, I let it go in one of the back fields, so the birds can nest with it."

"Your stylist," Carson laughed. "*I'm* the one that cuts her hair."

In the mirror, my hair fell in strange lengths from Tami's cut. "Let me even this out," Carson said, but with each slice he made, my hair looked worse, like I was in one of those paintings at school where the person's lips are on their cheek and one eye sits on top of their ear.

I noticed something else in the mirror I hadn't registered before. "When did you get a guitar?"

"Last week," Carson said, picking it up and strumming it, then tossing it back in the corner. "I told my old man I wanted one, and he *knew* I was talking electric, but he brought this piece of crap home. Showed me a few chords, said if I'm still playing it in December, we'll think about the electric."

"Where'd it come from?" I walked over to pick it up, but he grabbed it away.

"Sorry," he said with a fake sad face. "The old man said no one else could touch it. We just got it on hock. Bug Jemison was hard up for some of his Rhine wine, so the old man bought him a few jugs 'til the end of the month, and we're holding the guitar hostage. If he don't pay up when his disability check comes in, the guitar's mine. But until then . . ."

"Can you play any Beatles?" I asked, hopeful.

"Beatles! They broke up and ain't never getting back together. Get over it."

I left a few minutes later, starting my long walk home across half the reservation, still gripping the hank of hair. I opened my fingers a little every few yards to let the August breeze take some for the birds. As I turned the corner at Dog Street, where I lived, I could see my old elementary school. The teachers would be in their classrooms now, decorating bulletin boards with WELCOME TO THE 1975–76 SCHOOL YEAR! in big construction-paper letters. They were going to be puzzled by the fact that the United States Bicentennial Celebration wasn't exactly a reservation priority, since *we'd* been here for a lot longer than two hundred years.

The sight of the school reminded me how I got in this situation in the first place. It probably started back in third grade, when I had become a novelty. When I told my ma I was going to be featured on Indian Culture Night as the only kid from my grade who could speak Tuscarora fluently, I thought she would be happy, since she was always talking good grades this and good grades that. But she laughed like she did when the case worker asked about my dad's child-support payments during our monthly visits to her cubicle.

"You're just the dog and pony show," Ma said. She spoke a couple of sentences in Tuscarora. "Know what I said?" she asked. I shook my head. "Didn't think so. They're looking for cash to keep the program going. Everyone wants to believe we can rebuild what the boarding schools took away from us. You're Lewis the Horse, the proof that it can be done, that kids could learn the traditional language. But I don't know who you're going to speak it to," she said. "No one your age speaks it, and no one out in the white world would understand you. Concentrate on subjects that are going to actually help you out."

She refused to attend Indian Culture Night. I walked to school myself and did my bit to amaze the teachers. Then I went home the same way I'd gone, on foot. I was known as a carless kid, but for that night, I was the smart kid, and I liked the change. I kept up my grades, moving into advanced reading with the fourth graders, a year older than me, and I kept up with the work, welcoming a change of identity.

So when Groffini, the reservation school guidance counselor, sent our names over to the county junior high at the end of fifth grade, they tracked me into what my brother, Zach, called the smarties section, the brainiacs. Trouble was, they apparently didn't think any of the other rez kids would make it in that section, so they tossed me in with twenty-two white strangers.

Maybe the fact that I'd been good at learning Tuscarora made them believe I'd be able to pick up the white kids' language easily. But with all my supposed brains, I didn't grasp that the way we talk to one another on the reservation was definitely not the way kids talked in this largely white junior high. On the rez, you start getting teased a little bit right after you learn to talk, and either you learn to tease back or you get eaten alive. One girl in my class, Marie, got stuck with the name "Stinkpot," courtesy of Carson, when we were in first grade. You can see how I was okay with "Brainiac" by comparison. You might also be able to see that if I thought calling someone "Stinkpot" was a good way of making friends, I was in for a fairly rough ride.

So the first week of sixth grade, I thought I'd come up with nicknames for two kids I wanted to hang out with, to show them I was Prime Friend Material. I tried an easy one first, calling Stacey Lodinsky "Spacey" instead, like she was an airhead. And Artie Critcher seemed like a friendly enough guy, so when I noticed that his hair curled out from the front and back like a dirigible, I made the obvious leap and started calling him Blimp Head.

Stacey maybe just didn't hear me, since she didn't say anything about the name. But when I said to Artie, "Hey, Blimp Head, you wanna sit next to each other in lunch?" he said, "My hair might have a funny shape, but at least I wash it every day. I don't want your dandruff in my soup, so no thanks." They both stopped talking to me shortly after that. Clearly, the only plan I had for forming friendships had been a spectacular failure. Maybe I needed a new nickname myself, something like "the Invisible Boy."

And then it got worse. For most of sixth grade, it was like I had a force field around me, like one of those Martian war machines in *War of the Worlds*, with a death ray waiting to blast the other kids if they made any sudden move in my direction. They just pretended I wasn't there as much as they possibly could. During lunch, we were required to sit with our class at two long tables. In every other section, the Indians gravitated to one another like atoms in some science experiment, but I sank to the bottom of my particular beaker, alone. Still, I had to eat, so I'd go to one end of our assigned tables, decide who was least likely to resist when I set my tray down, and inch myself onto the bench next to my reluctant seatmate, who usually gave up one butt cheek of room, sometimes even both. The force field kept me inside and everyone else out. I'd given up trying to make friends by Christmas break.

This year, I was going to make another shot at it. Thanks to my *zero* social distractions, I'd kept my grades up, so I remained among the brainiacs for seventh grade. I was hoping someone from a lower track had done well enough in sixth that they'd be bumped up to my class and might offer a new door to a friend. I wasn't crazy enough to think it would be someone from the reservation, so I thought the more I looked like everyone else in the class, the better chance I might have with someone who didn't know about my force field. I'd find out in a couple days.

Even though I'd turned on to Dog Street, I still had a long walk to my house, so I started eyeing whatever cars were going my way. One awesome thing about being from a tiny place where everyone knows everyone, and where everyone knows your family doesn't own transportation, is that you can usually snag a ride by just sticking your thumb out to hitchhike. Two vehicles later, I was climbing in a car's open trunk, already stuffed full of kids heading for a late-summer swim in the dike.

"What happened to your hair?" all of them asked me, shouting over one another.

"I bet it was lice," Floyd Page said, and they all backed away, exaggerating, pretending they were going to climb out of the trunk.

"Impossible," I said. "I wasn't using *your* comb."

Floyd rubbed my bristles as we laughed. In this way, we communicated in the language we knew best — hassling one another.

"You're in luck," my uncle Albert said when I got home. "She's not back yet, so you're not officially late."

He didn't seem to notice that my head looked like post-tornado TV footage. At that moment, my brother Zach's car pulled in the driveway to drop off my ma. The engine shut off, which meant he was coming in, probably helping with groceries.

"What the hell happened to your hair?" was the first thing Zach said. "You look like David Bowie on a bad night."

"I'nit tho," Albert said, laughing, registering my hair for the first time.

"Who's David Bowie?" I asked.

"That's a little later in your musical education," Albert said.

"So spill it. What happened?" Zach was not going to let me off.

"I cut it."

"It *looks* like you cut it," he said, sticking his fingers in my hair. "With a blindfold on."

Just then, my ma walked in, carrying a couple bags of groceries.

"What is this?" she said, staring at my hair.

"I cut my hair," I said. "I'm tired of not fitting in with my class. That two-foot braid just shouted, 'Reservation Kid Here,' so I got rid of it."

"Go get the buzzer," she said.

"What?"

"Either you're going to get it or I'm going to get it, but before we eat, we're cleaning that hair up," she said, grabbing a towel to pin around my neck. "You look like a Welfare Indian."

"I *am* a Welfare Indian," I said.

"You don't need to look the part," she said.

The buzzer was a garage sale purchase — a hair clipper that made more noise than it should have, grabbed your hair like it was mad at you, and sometimes gave off a burning odor while it did its job. She came at me. Five minutes later, the longest hairs on my head were in my eyebrows, and *they* survived only because they were behind my glasses.

"The next time you think about caving in to how you believe white people want to see you," she said, sheathing the buzzer in its holster, "you remember this."

She took the towel off me and I dunked my head in the washing pan. The water was cold, but I didn't want all those tiny hairs drifting down my shirt like a million little bugs.

"Nice look, G.I. Joe," Zach said from across the room, finishing the last of the spaghetti in the serving bowl before I had the chance to get any. "Too bad you don't have that patented Kung Fu Grip or you wouldn't need to worry about fitting in. You could just do a Bruce Lee on your enemies."

I peeked in the mirror. I looked exactly like what he said. My hair was buzzed to maybe a quarter of an inch, and it stood up straight, like dandelion fuzz that had been spray painted black.

When I went to bed that night, I grabbed the latest copy of *The Amazing Spider-Man*. Albert periodically supplied me with comics when he picked up his magazines, and I always hoped for Spider-Man. I was glad somebody's world was more complicated and lonely than mine, even if he was a comic book character in a blue-and-red bodysuit.

I reached behind me to pull my braid forward, as I had every night for years, but my fingers touched nothing but stubbly hair and skin. I shared a room with Albert, who lay a few feet away in his bed, thumbing through a magazine. He noticed my automatic gesture.

"Feels funny, isn't it? Like maybe a piece of you is missing?" he said. "You get used to it after a while." He closed his magazine. "Besides, if you don't like it, it grows back. They buzzed mine when I got drafted and shipped off to Vietnam. Now look at it." He flipped his long hair like he was in a shampoo commercial. "But you're gonna have to live with it for a while anyway. Hope it was worth it," he said, shutting off his light.

Man, We Was Lonely

When I got to class on the first day of seventh grade, homeroom was filled with most of the people I'd spent the previous year with. Despite my haircut, they were just as friendly to me as they'd been when I last saw them, which was about as friendly as strangers thrown together in a hospital emergency room late on a Saturday night.

I did register one new face, and a couple missing ones. The new guy looked like he was one of the kids off the local air force base. He was big, broad, probably buying his clothes in the men's department instead of the boys'. If we weren't smart kids, I might have suspected he'd failed a few times. As the only new person, he was my one potential shot at a friend.

We heard our Welcome Back to the School Year, a reminder about getting our personal business done in the five minutes allotted between classes, a politeness reminder, a suggestion about bus area safety, and the announcement of the various sports tryouts and the first activities night. Our new homeroom teacher, Mr. Franz, reaffirmed that the top three sections were more academically challenging than the other sections, but that the three were *equally* academically challenging; the three sections were organized around smart kids in chorus, smart kids in band, and nonmusical smart kids. Mr. Franz also stressed that the sections between four and eleven were all the same level too, and beyond eleven, those were kids who needed more support than the rest of us did. Then the bell rang for change of classes.

It turned out the new kid's locker was near mine. Before I could say hi, Artie Critcher was there. "George," he said to the new kid, "you see that girl there, the one who looks like an opera singer?"

"Summer?" I asked, to make sure. Summer Barnes was currently leaning over a desk in the hallway, gesticulating and telling someone else a story from her fabulous vacation.

"She's the one. Stay away from her. She's the vice principal's daughter, and she thinks her dad's power extends to her. Just means trouble."

"Thanks," George said.

Steven Lockheed suddenly appeared next to us. "And this kid?" he butted in, pointing to me. "Don't be fooled by the army haircut. This kid's an Indian. Stay away from him too. More trouble." He shook his head and then moved on down to his locker.

"So, you're the one, a real live Indian. I was wondering." George was suddenly shaking my hand.

"As opposed to a dead one?" I said. I understood enough about our history to get that a lot of people had preferred us dead, but I was kind of hoping that era was over.

"No, no. Of course not," George said. "My dad grew up around Indians, but I never had the chance to meet . . . Anyway, I met Artie here a couple weeks ago when my family relocated. When we discovered we were in the same section, he told me about some of the other kids, and said you'd probably still be in our class."

"Guy here likes the Wacky Packages too," Artie said. "He's got some on his folders, usually."

"So which ones do you have?" George asked.

Most kids I knew loved Wacky Packages — stickers that parodied popular household products. I named off a few, like Crust toothpaste, which seemed to show up in almost every pack; Ratz Crackers, a pretty rare one, pulled for the rat on it; Neveready batteries, where the cat has used up its nine lives; and *Playbug*, insect entertainment, featuring a bug in a skimpy bikini. "I put some *Yellow Submarine* stickers on my ma's vanity mirror a couple years ago," I said. "I didn't hear the end of that for months and months. So these days, any stickers I get wind up mounted on the headboard on my bed."

George nodded and gestured to Artie. "He stuck some Wackies in his room too, so I had to visit him to see his. Maybe I could come over to your place and see yours sometime."

That seemed really fast moving to me. I wanted school friends, but the idea of this kid coming to my crumbling house almost made my head explode. "So you just moved here?" I said, bringing the subject back to him. "Where from?"

"The island of Guam. That's where my dad was stationed the last couple years."

"Guam? Never heard of it," I said.

"Probably no reason you would, unless you're in the air force. It's in the South Pacific. I've got a scrapbook at home in Red-Tail Manor, if you'd like to see it."

"Could be cool." We lived between two Great Lakes, so it was cloudy nine months out of the year. I couldn't imagine living on a tropical island one day and then here in this gray, chronically dingy part of the world the next. "Are you in chorus?" I asked George.

"Yeah, I think they told me almost everyone in here was. What part do you sing?"

"First tenor," I said.

He sang the same part, so we sat together in class. It seemed like maybe my haircut was working after all, as this kid, who seemed cool, if a little bit pushy, actually wanted to hang out with me. Mrs. Thatcher, the seventh-grade chorus teacher, told us we'd be working through the lame songs from *Fiddler on the Roof, The Music Man*, and *The Sound of Music* that the school could afford sheet music for. But toward the end of the day, she peeked out into the hall, and ran back in to rock us out to choruses of the Beatles' "Hey Jude," promising we'd do that every so often to break up our bland diet of show tunes.

She also said we would spend the week before Christmas break listening to a taped radio program called "Paul McCartney is Alive and Well . . . Maybe," which was about the best news I'd ever heard in a classroom. When I was little, every time I asked about a song on the radio, it had been a Beatles tune, or one of their solos. Albert liked them, and knew all kinds of trivia, so he fed my interest. Paul McCartney had been one of the Beatles' lead singers and songwriters, and I knew of some crazy rumors that he'd been killed in a car accident and replaced by a look-alike to keep the band going for a few more years. Mrs. Thatcher told us there were all sorts of clues to this substitution in their albums, like McCartney's bloodstained, abandoned shoes in the *Magical Mystery Tour* album booklet and his bare feet on *Abbey Road*'s front cover. Then the bell rang, and we returned to homeroom for end-of-the-day announcements.

"That Paul McCartney thing sounds cool," I said to George. "I mean, I know he's not *really* dead, since he's in Wings now, but I always like conspiracies anyway."

"Yeah, even though it's clear he's still alive, you see this stuff all the time. Makes my dad laugh. He says he remembers it from the first time around."

"You like the Beatles?" I said. "We had pretty much all of their albums, but when my brother moved out, he took most of the later ones with him."

"We have them all," George said. "My dad's a huge Beatles fan. When we lived in Germany, he took me down to the Reeperbahn in Hamburg, because that's where they got their start. My *Mutti* about busted a blood vessel."

" '*Mutti*'? "

"Sorry, German, it's like 'mom.' "

"Why was she mad?" It was nice to know I wasn't the only one with a sometimes-grouchy ma.

"Those blocks didn't just have music clubs. They were also the place where all the hookers hung out."

"Hookers?" I asked, picturing a group of people with prosthetic arms.

He shook his head. "Did you grow up in a shoe box?"

"More or less. Wait a minute. I thought you came from 'the island of Guam,' " I said, imitating the formal tone he'd used to describe his old home.

"Germany was before Guam. Hey, you want to come over and listen to my dad's records? And then I could come to your place sometime and check out your Wackies."

"Aren't you going to take Steven's warning?" I asked. "Avoid the scary Indian?"

"Maybe Artie's right about that Summer girl," he said. "But I make my own decisions about who I hang out with."

We walked out to the bus platform together, saying good-bye when we reached his bus. The day seemed like a pretty decent beginning to my second year of junior high. As soon as I got on the bus, though, Carson and Tami jumped across the aisle from me.

"Who was that you were walking with?" Carson asked.

"Dunno. A guy from off the rez," I said.

"Duh! You think your magic haircut worked? Yeah, right," Tami said, laughing.

"He ever sees your house?" Carson added. "He'll be running for the border. And if I ever see you bringing some white kid home to visit?" I hated when Carson read my mind. "You and me? We're not friends anymore. I ain't having that oo(t)-gwheh-rheh stuck to my shoe."

"Your choice," I said. Carson, in the seven years I had known him, had always been blunt, and most often, he turned out to be right too. But I'd gone all this length to finally get a friend at school, and I wasn't letting these two hack my chance off like they had my braid. Anyone who would talk to me would have been good enough, but I genuinely *liked* George so far, with his strange European and tropical island history, and our both grooving on the Beatles. It was probably true that we'd be friends only at school, that it would take a natural disaster to crash around us all before he'd ever be able to come over to my house, but I didn't care. For the first time in over a year, I looked forward to the next day of school.

That night, as we filled our plates for dinner, Zach asked.

me, "Anyone talk to you at school today?" He lifted a sausage directly off my plate and ate it.

"Two kids, sort of."

"Being told to shut up doesn't count."

Artie hadn't exactly told me to shut up, but he had been his usual neutral self. "Okay, then one kid."

"From Red-Tail Manor?" I nodded. "Typical," he said.

"What's Red-Tail Manor?" our ma asked, suddenly interested. She wanted very much for me to be as integrated into the outside world as I could. Zach had made connections by playing lacrosse for the school, which most of the Indian kids did, but lacrosse was not in my path.

"Air force housing," Zach said.

"What's the deal with that anyway?" I asked, truly wanting to know. "How come he's the only person who might be interested in talking to me?"

"Can't say *why* he'd be interested," Zach said. "It is *you* we're talking about, after all. But I'd guess he's more *willing* because those military kids don't know about the reservation." He smiled. "All those others? Most of their parents have threatened them at some time or another with being dropped off here."

"Zachary, that's enough," our ma said. "There's more sausage here," she added.

"No, what do you mean?" I asked again. "Come on, I'm the one who's going to be dealing with this. What is it?"

"When some kids are bad in white families," my ma said, sighing, "their mas and dads say they'll dump them off among the wild Indians and let them find their own way home."

"The wild Indians? We're their punishment? You're making this up," I said. They were both sharp, and poking fun at each other is absolutely *the* way of life on the reservation, but my ma's expression told me they were serious and not just busting my chops.

"White guys on the lacrosse team told me after we got to know each other," Zach said.

"And none of you thought to tell me all of last year, even though you knew no one talked to me? What am I supposed to do?" All this time, I thought *I* had been the problem, not my address.

"Well, everyone else from here usually gets placed with a couple other Indians," Zach said. "That's who they hang out with until high school."

"Maybe you'll get to know some of the other singers better this year," my ma suggested. "Like this guy you just mentioned. This air force kid."

"You're in chorus?" Zach said, laughing. "The dorkiest activity. No other options?"

"No," my ma said.

"Not exactly true," I said when she went back to the kitchen to grab something. "In fifth, I scored high on those music tests, so I could have joined either chorus or band. That letter said I'd be a good trombone player."

"With your stubby arms? No way," Zach said.

"Didn't matter anyway. At Heavenly Music, a student-model trombone was three hundred dollars."

"Reservation translation: exactly one hundred dollars more than Ma's entire monthly income," Zach added, as if I didn't know that.

"Yup. That salesman said they had rentals or rent-to-owns," I said, remembering the salesman trying to cut a deal with my ma, while I looked at my own broke welfare face, distorted into a long horsey portrait in the trombone's gleaming brass, still playing my part in the dog and pony show. "But just like you said, that kind of money, even a rental price, wasn't going to work for us. So I turned us around and walked us out the door."

"Down to the budget again?" Zach said when I'd finished. "Glad my ass is out of here."

"Watch your language when you're home," our ma said, returning.

"*My* home is a single-wide trailer with one bedroom and a sweet Dodge Challenger in the driveway," he said, then looked at me. "Maybe you could fail some classes and get bumped down to the regular sections. Not the dummies, necessarily, just the average ones."

"Don't you even think of it," Ma said. "Your name is going to be associated with section three for your entire time in junior high, and don't you forget it. Get any homework?"

"Not on the first day," I said, then thought aloud, "Does anyone here know where Guam is?"

"Geography homework?" she asked.

"No, just curious. The kid I met today, the one who talked to me, moved here from Guam, and I have no idea where that even is. He said the South Pacific, but I thought that was only a lame musical we sang songs from in chorus. I didn't know it was a real place."

"Doesn't matter," Albert said, speaking for the first time. "He's a base kid, isn't it? Your base might be in the middle of a bunch of different kinds of people — I mean *real* different, like *from Japan* kind of different — but all you see are other soldiers, and all the kids see are the kids of other soldiers. Kind of like living on a reservation."

"Yeah," Zach added, "a reservation with running water."

3

I Call Your Name

Though Artie had warned George about going near Summer Barnes, there was no way of avoiding her once she noticed you. "Didn't anybody ever tell you how to dress?" she asked me on the first Friday back as we all headed out to our buses. She generally wore outfits out of the Sunday paper's back-to-school fashions advertisements, and often criticized someone else's lack of style so we could see how *she* was on the cutting edge.

"Well, anytime your dad wants to take me shopping for clothes on his dime, you just let me know," I said.

"It's not about what you can afford," she said, as only someone who can afford things would say. "Someone should have taught you how to dress with what you've got. Okay, I'll take pity on you this once." She glanced at George, then said to me, "Use this kid as your model."

"I'm nobody's model," George said.

"You are today," she said, and then turned back to me. "Unbutton the top button of your shirt. Really, it should be the top two, but whatever, even one will help. Only nerds wear their shirts with the top one buttoned."

"Your dad wears his that way," I offered.

"Because he's wearing a tie, stupid. At home? No tie. And you can be sure *he* keeps the top *two* unbuttoned. You're double nerdy if you want to make that comparison. And somehow you got it all backward. You're always leaving your shirttails out and doing the top tight. Take my advice, *please*. I don't want to see this look for another whole year." She stomped away.

"So, Summer's a friend of yours?" George said to me.

"Listen, George, I want to catch the bus," Artie said. "You coming?"

"Go on ahead," George said.

I took in the way George was dressed, the way Artie was dressed as he fled, and then my reflection in the classroom door's window. No one had, in fact, ever made the observation Summer just had, and I hadn't noticed it either. But as every other kid assigned to our hallway walked out past me, I recognized the truth — top buttons of the shirt open, tails tucked in.

"Can you hang on to these for a second?" I asked George, handing my books off when the last kids had cleared through. I quickly tucked my shirt in, trying to smooth its wrinkles. When it was clear my efforts were hopeless, I unbuttoned the top two shirt buttons. "Better?"

"Why do you care what she thinks?" George said.

"It's not that. It's just, well, look at you," I said. His shirt had been ironed, with creases at the arms. His jeans met his sneakers exactly where they should — not flood pants, and not cuffed like mine generally were because they had belonged to someone else first. "Well?"

"Yeah, you look fine. Here, take your books." We trotted down the front hall, passing Summer, who was waiting out in front of her dad's office. She smirked, seeing that I had taken her advice.

"Thank you so much for saving me from making a fool of myself," I said.

"You're welcome," she said, proud of her community service.

"Not sure how you got into seven-three with that impairment you have, though," I added.

"What do you mean?" she said.

"The inability to detect sarcasm?" I said, and followed George out of the building.

George frowned at me as we walked.

"What?" I said to him, pretending I didn't know.

"That was as bad as what she did," he said. "Do you really want to be like her?"

"No, you don't understand," I said, having dealt with Summer for an entire year already.

"Look, I don't know you, really, and you make your own choices, but me? I don't do things to make life harder on myself. Trouble's going to find you often enough without you seeking it out. Like that, look over there."

In a group nearby, a small kid bent over to tie his shoe, and a bigger kid stepped up behind him, grabbed the exposed waistband of his briefs in both fists, and yanked him a wedgie tight enough to lift him off the concrete. The smaller kid stumbled, stood, and reached behind to free his shorts. When he whirled around and saw who it was, he just laughed it off and walked away, never turning his back.

"And what lesson do you want me to learn from that?" I said. "Make sure I wear my undershorts lower than my jeans?"

"Well, that small kid was asking for it. You don't bend over like that in a crowd this size and not expect someone to give you a snuggie, but —"

"A 'snuggie'? Wedgie, man. You know, like wedged up your —"

"Got it. Usually takes me a little while to learn the 'Local Customs,' as our military moving pamphlets call it."

" 'Snuggie' sounds too nice," I said.

"Either way, you never expose yourself like that — setting yourself up to be attacked, and giving that person a reason to want to do it — unless you want it to happen. Kind of like what you're doing with Summer, rubbing her the wrong way. Anyway, I better get going." With that, we said good-bye, and I headed back to the reservation decompression chamber, aka our bus.

As we pulled out, I thought about what George had said. I didn't want to admit it, but he was probably right. I just wanted to be able to say something back to someone who'd been giving me grief. Power and size can't always win, can they? Either way, pushy or not, I liked that George had nothing to gain by his comments, other than being of help to a friend. It was a first for me.

The next Monday, one of our other early September rituals kicked in. Fire drills *should* be a surprise, but our school lives were so rigid that even our fake emergencies were predictable. We never had fire drills in January. September, on the other hand, was prime drill season. So right on schedule during Monday's end-of-the-day announcements, the familiar siren started squeezing out from the intercom speaker, like the squeal of a robot cat.

On the lawn, I saw the Wedgie King and his victim again. The King was circling, waiting for a perfect opportunity for round two, but his victim countermoved with each new turn, always pretending he wasn't. They kept doing their slow dance until the all clear rang and we went back into the building.

The next morning, after the pledge, Mr. Barnes came on the intercom and cleared his throat. Summer improved her posture, as if he could see us in our classroom.

"Good morning," he growled, in a voice that insisted there was, in fact, nothing good about it. "Now, yesterday, we had the first fire drill of the school year." He paused, sighing before the microphone, sounding like a storm building in the winter. "I would be lying if I said I was a happy man at this moment. The lollygagging you young ladies and gentlemen engaged in suggested you do not understand the meaning of the phrase 'fire drill.' When you hear the alarm, you are supposed to act as if an actual fire is occurring somewhere in the building. Your performance was pathetic, as if a bunch of slugs were commanded to run a footrace."

I imagined he'd heard this line somewhere else and borrowed it for use with us. His voice rose with each new sentence. "From this point on, we're going to have daily fire drills until you get it right. Perhaps I could have *the scent of burning flesh* pumped into the vent systems in your classroom so you'll remember why we're doing this. If we have to keep going into December, so be it. I do not want you to disappoint me," he said, taking the fire drill more personally than any reasonable person should. "You'll thank me later."

"What's up with your crazy dad?" I asked Summer as the bell rang and we shuffled out.

"For your information," she said, entirely unembarrassed, "my dad is a volunteer fireman, which I'm sure no one in your family is brave enough to be."

On cue, all of Summer's friends clucked their disapproval of my insensitivity, as if I could have possibly known this fact before that moment.

"Didn't you learn anything from last week?" George said when we got to our lockers.

"And are you forgetting the principal is her father?" Artie added. "That Mr. Barnes and Summer Barnes are the same Barnes family?"

"Vice principal," I said. "Let's not distribute power unwarranted," I added, imitating our social studies teacher, who went on and on about the Wonders of the American Government System, somehow just skipping over the fact that Benjamin Franklin was partly inspired by the Indian form of government, Tuscaroras being one nation of the larger Haudenosaunee Confederacy. Most Indians I knew, no matter how much they didn't care about history, knew Franklin had said something like: If these savages can make it work, how hard can it be for us to master?

Artie and George didn't laugh. "Remember government class?" Artie said. "Vice principal is pretty much the same thing. If the principal is in a plane crash or something, that's it. Summer's dad is principal."

"I think you're confusing principal with president," I said.

"As far as you're concerned, you should think that too," George said. "Remember, Barnes is the vice principal in charge of paddling."

"Hey," I said to him, "why are you on my butt? I've known

you less than a week, but you keep trying to rescue me from myself. Remember, I've already been here a year."

"And how's that been going?" George said. "Seems like aside from Artie here, and Summer's tutorials, there aren't a ton of people waiting in line to talk to you."

Another valid point, but he was getting kind of free with his suggestions, and it sometimes felt as if, on the giving-unasked-for-advice dial, there weren't too many clicks between Summer's and George's kinds of help. I also didn't particularly like being constantly reminded of all my faults.

"Sorry," he added. "That came out harder than I meant it."

"Truth is, I probably could use some of your 'Local Customs' pamphlets myself," I said.

"What's he talking about?" Artie asked.

"Private joke," George said, and smiled at me.

I smiled back. I don't think I could have told him how awesome a moment that was without sounding like a total dork, but I had never had a private joke with anyone before.

Dear Boy

That I didn't see anyone from the reservation in school was a slight exaggeration, but it might as well have been true. While Carson sat at the back of the rehearsal room in chorus, we never really talked there. He always arrived two seconds before the bell, and once inside, he had a group of worshipful kids who kept him distracted. Since they were other chorus kids, most of them weren't ever going to pull the kinds of pranks he was prone to, so they safely lived dangerously through him.

A fair number of reservation kids also qualified for the free-lunch program, and most took advantage of it. The only problem was that the lunch ladies had to check your name off on a sheet before they gave your personal ticket to you, and the card had "pathetic" written all over it. Tami and I tried to get to the front, grab our cards, and sit with our sections before anyone noticed.

"Scummy Welfare Indians," this kid said as he walked past us in line, not looking, not breaking his stride, barely loud enough for us to hear. I recognized the Wedgie King immediately.

"I can't believe Carson hangs out with that kid," Tami said after he'd left our earshot.

"With *that* kid? Is it really? The one who just called us —?"

"You don't need to repeat it," she said. "Yeah, I don't know what he's thinking."

"Well, does he know that Carson's one of us?" Carson was fair-skinned, and somehow, he could turn his rez accent on and off like a faucet. I'd had to chop my braid off to make an attempt at ambiguity, and my skin was still the color of a brick.

"What do you think?" Tami said. The Wedgie King sat down at the cafeteria's opposite end.

"What'll happen if he finds out?"

"I don't want to be there for the explosion. One way or another, someone's coming out on the bad end of that secret." She shivered at the thought.

I got my card and headed for the seat George saved me with the Manor kids. It was super cool to arrive with my tray and know I didn't have to push my way into getting a seat.

"You coming to the Road to Hell with me today?" Artie asked George as I got there.

"Dear Boy, do you mean Good Intentions?" George asked. Mrs. Thatcher's love for All Things Beatles was so intense that she addressed every male chorus member as a "Dear Boy," after the McCartney song. It was so lame, we couldn't resist adopting the practice ironically.

"Whatever. You're such a candy ass," Artie said.

The place they were talking about was a quarry near the Manor, where those kids went to watch the miners dynamite the rock walls. Artie called it the Road to Hell, but George had some hang-up about swearing, so he had come up with the Pavement of Good Intentions.

"You should come with us," George said to me. "It's neat, but not like dynamite in the movies, with those big flames and people flying through the air."

"Not very interesting, really," Artie added. "Boring, in fact. You probably wouldn't like it. Like dynamite that hasn't had its Wheaties. Just shoving rocks out of the way."

"Someday, maybe," I said. I could take a hint.

"And I got homework to do today," George said to Artie, frowning. I could tell he took the hint personally.

George had asked me a few times to do stuff outside of school. I'd been avoiding it, thinking about the vision Carson had planted in my brain — George seeing my house — but it was a nice, weird little sign that we were becoming friends. I was even almost becoming a Red-Tail Manor kid by proxy, though I'd never stepped foot within its bounds. Artie, while still not exactly warm, acted less and less often like it was an effort to talk to me. Stacey Lodinsky and her best friend, Gloria, ignored Summer's edicts about my force field more often too. It would never be like the reservation, where we knew we'd be together for our entire future lives, but joining a school group for the first time was pretty fine.

These kids were becoming so much a part of my school life that when a new routine emerged in October, I was actually part of it. Unlike Carson, we all arrived early for chorus, and Artie would sit at the piano, playing McCartney's "Dear Boy." George could sing the lead and the rest of us did the backup. In fact, Stacey noted that I'd begun harmonizing parts I was making up. My ma did that when listening to the radio, and I must have learned from her by some crazy singing osmosis. Standing out wasn't exactly among my goals, but if it was for something good, I could totally be on board with that.

Among the other things I especially liked about chorus were the previews of the tape Mrs. Thatcher promised us, about Paul McCartney's death cover-up. The tape said he'd been replaced by a man named Billy Shears, who'd even gotten plastic surgery to make him look more like McCartney. I thought once that if I could find a good plastic surgeon, like the one who worked on Billy Shears, one who might come out to the reservation clinic, maybe I could ask for a few modifications, a pull here and there, some skin bleach, and suddenly, I wouldn't be that kid from the reservation anymore. I would be like everyone else, a Dear Boy.

The one real intrusion on this fantasy was the repercussions of that choice. If Billy Shears really replaced Paul McCartney, sure, he got all the perks of being Paul McCartney for as long as he wanted, and who wouldn't want to suddenly be in the most popular, richest band ever? But the cost of becoming Paul McCartney would be giving up the identity of Billy Shears for the rest of his life, never being a member of the Shears family again. Could I be a Dear Boy and still be an Indian? Was there any way to make an informed decision — any way to find out what would happen without stripping my Indian life away completely first?

"What are you so deep in thought about?" Artie asked as he walked to the piano.

"Nothing," I said, following him to take my place as he played.

"Hey, Artie, you like Wings?" Rose Haven asked him, suddenly also at the piano, leaning over and smiling, pretending I was not there at all. I knew that for most kids my age, Wings was the only band McCartney had ever led, as if the Beatles had never existed — another trade-off.

"Sure, I guess," Artie said. "I figure, since Mrs. Thatcher likes Paul McCartney so much, this would be neat to her. And these 'Dear Boys' all know the song, so it's cool." Artie had heard enough from George and me that he now understood the link between the Beatles and Wings.

"I don't think Stacey's gonna like being called a boy," I said, and he laughed.

"The next time Wings comes to town, you should just ask me," Rose said to him. "I can get you the best tickets. My dad's store is a Ticketron outlet, so we always take our pick of the good seats, even before they go on sale."

"So how come you're not in band if you can play the piano?" I asked Artie. If Rose ignored me, I could ignore her right back.

"I just learned the one song. My brother's in a bar band, and he taught me how to play it. I can't play anything else." Mrs. Thatcher came in and told us to take our assigned seats. Rose left us as Artie stood up. "Where's George and Stacey?"

I looked up and then shook my head. "Dunno. They were in class last period."

"I know, doofus. I was there."

"No need to be harsh, man."

"You sure like to call people names, but you don't seem to like it when it's done back to you," he said.

"Hey, I haven't called you Blimp Head even once this year," I said. "Besides, I was nervous when I made it up. I was in a new situation."

"We were all in that situation," Artie said. "We all came to a new school."

"But you know what, you guys all stick together," I said. Maybe loneliness didn't warrant my lack of awareness, but I also didn't like people pretending our circumstances were even remotely identical. "You're all from Red-Tail Manor, whatever that is."

"What about it?" George said, suddenly appearing behind me.

"Nothing about it," I said. "But you're pretending — well, Artie's pretending — it doesn't make a difference where you come from, where you live."

"Well, we're military kids. My dad, Stacey's dad, Nelson, that kid Harold over there," George said, pointing to a guy with a Moe-from-the-Three-Stooges haircut. "We all live at the Manor. My dad's a career man in the air force, theirs too, I guess. Maybe their moms, but most likely their dads. So Artie isn't *from* there, but I let him hang out with us." Artie punched him.

"Why is that? Why is he different?" I asked, since he was trying to prove me wrong.

"He's not different. We started hanging out because he was friendly to me first. Living in the military, you don't have time to fart around, spending years making friends. Someone's nice to you, invites you over, boom! You're friends. A lot of our decisions come from how fast our lives can change." Then he grinned and added, "Kind of like your argument with Stacey about the Wackies."

I had an argument with Stacey about the Wackies? I thought. My confusion must have showed on my face. Of course I remembered that the first week of sixth grade, when Stacey Lodinsky had been a new kid, she squealed, "Wackies!"

the first time she saw my folders with Wacky Packages stuck to them, and I'd tried out my "Spacey" nickname on her. We had talked about which ones we each owned, which ones we wanted, where you could find the best ones, all of that. I thought I might even have made a friend. Then Summer gave Stacey a crash course on school territory, and suddenly, my force field was up, intact.

"She keeps them on the backing," he clarified. "Saves them in a book like a photo album. She can trade a lamer one for a good one, but since yours are stuck on already, she won't be able to talk you out of them. You know, once you tear them off, they never stick normal again. Like permanent damage."

"Still not sure I follow you," I said. "I'm never going anywhere. The reservation's going to be my home for the rest of my life, so you know, I stick 'em."

"I like that dedication," George said. "But I understand Stacey too. She doesn't have to worry about leaving the stuck ones behind if her dad gets orders."

"Orders?" I asked.

"Stickers and cards are easier to pack than a lot of stuff. Stacey won't admit it to anyone," George said, ignoring my question, "but she has almost a complete *Partridge Family* set."

"They made cards for *The Partridge Family*?" I asked. "Who'd want those?"

"Exactly! She's okay getting teased about it, so that's cool," he finished.

"Do you know if they ever made Beatles cards?" I asked. Those would be cool enough that I might consider saving them in an album.

"Dear Boys!" Mrs. Thatcher scolded us. Apparently, class had started.

She explained in her breathlessly enthusiastic way that we were getting closer to concert season, and that for the next week, she'd be working closely with the individual parts. The other parts could stay in the room if we wished, as silent observers, but she recommended we go to a study hall in the commons, so we wouldn't inadvertently learn the other voice parts.

I found myself occasionally susceptible to this very habit, so I opted for the commons. Besides, I had to work on my show-and-tell assignment for English, which, though it was a babyish idea, I was dreading just the same. As countless others before me had done with stupid school projects, I had decided to recycle mine, hauling out my miniature traditional longhouse I'd made in fifth grade. It supposedly showed how Tuscaroras lived before contact with white people, and it was not of the award-winning variety. Albert had gone with me to the woods to find birch bark to use, scavenging rough last-minute specimens. The door was held on by twin hinges, and the support branches were really stapled together. The bed racks along the inside walls wouldn't even support a family of superhero action figures if they'd moved in. I imagined that my new friends, who'd never seen a longhouse in their lives, would laugh at my pathetic entry. I just wanted a passing grade on this one.

"So what have you got there?" George asked as I stared glumly at the house.

"A traditional American Indian dwelling," I said, in a movie documentary voice.

"My dad would like to see this. Maybe you could bring it over and tell him what it all means," he said. I looked to see if he was giving me any kind of sly smile, but he didn't seem to be. "I think I told you before. He grew up in Minnesota."

"And he knew some Indians there? We're not the same kind."

"It's a little more complicated than that. I'll tell you when we have time, or maybe he could tell you himself, if you come over. He said he'd like to meet you."

"What do you mean, 'more complicated'?" I said. "You can't leave me hanging."

"I'm not leaving you hanging. I've got my own prep." He pulled a scrapbook from his bag. "I give you . . . the island of Guam," he said, imitating my documentary voice. "My dad took this picture and my *Mutti* — sorry, *mom*. That one's going to be hard to break."

"No need to break it for me. Call her what you want," I said.

"Gotta adapt to the new place. Part of my life. So, my *mom* laminated it as an eight-by-ten on the cover." In the photo, he was clearly still a kid, with a blond brush cut. He was leaning on the butt of a baseball bat, smiling, and had a massive, perfectly round welt on his forehead. Both of his eyes had been blacked identically, so he looked like a raccoon. He'd obviously had a major growth surge since, and his hair had come in darker blond.

"It was taken about a year ago, in the middle of our Guam stint," he said. "I got hit in the forehead with a baseball."

"Funny picture — you'll get a lot of mileage out of that. But I hope you have more photos inside the album," I said.

"Oh, I do," he said, flipping the binder open. There was a note about Guam's status as an unincorporated United States territory and one about the military presence being the primary industry, along with Japanese tourism. "This was my school," he said, pointing to a photo of a classroom of kids. "It was a mixed school there, like here, but the cultures were different. I guess I mostly hung out with the other military kids," he said, admitting I'd been sort of right earlier. The last photo was labeled THE BROWN TREE SNAKE, a coppery-looking rope of scales and venom. "This was an invasive species that supposedly stowed away on a military air transport. They think it's responsible for nearly wiping out all of Guam's natural bird populations."

He had a funny expression as we went through it, kind of happy and sad at the same time, but all with enthusiasm. He was going to get an A for sure. I, on the other hand, had no passion about what I'd brought. It was a piece of crap, plain and simple. It was supposed to represent Tuscarora life hundreds of years ago, so I had to pretend it was quaint that the doors didn't fit exactly right, and that there were holes in the roof where new pieces of bark were sewn on as repairs, and that extended family members slept in the same room all together. But it was hard to pretend and be dismissive when all these things were more or less true of our house now.

After study hall, I wandered out to our buses, and Carson slid up behind me, kicking at the backs of my knees with his toes.

"Hey, how come you weren't in the commons?" I said.

"I was skipping with this kid in my section. He stole a couple smokes from his dad, so we went to the lav and hot boxed them, and then we mostly just hid out."

"You blew off the commons?" I asked. I wanted to ask,

Were you with that kid who hates Indians? but I figured I'd probably know soon enough. "Why ditch study hall? It's not like you're forced to work."

"I wanted the smoke and the cheap thrills. You wanna come over today? Car's working, and I can give you a ride home," he said, flicking his eyebrows. Since the reservation had no cops, in families with cars, most kids learned to drive as soon as their feet could reach the pedals.

"You sure your ma and dad will let you?" I asked.

"Pretty sure. I took the car down to Tami's the other morning to get my ma some coffee."

"Still got that guitar?" Some nights, after Albert came to bed, his snoring was so loud it would wake me up, and not even the stereo could drown it out entirely. The one thing that would let me doze back off was thinking about music, and what it would be like to play a guitar.

"Guess you'll just have to come over and see," Carson said, which was typical of him. He would use whatever leverage he could for the smallest of things. He loved the idea that somehow he had tricked you into or out of whatever it was he wanted. "Or maybe you're too busy hanging out with your white friend."

"What are you talking about? You hang out with white kids all the time."

"Only 'cause I'm stuck with them, but *you* actually like it. Don't lie. I can tell," he said, as if I should have criminal charges filed against me for having friends off the reservation.

I thought about his offer. The wind was sharp, and once the sun went down, it was going to be that tear-your-face-off kind that I generally tried to avoid. Still, it would be totally worth the risk if that guitar was still there and it was possible I'd be allowed to pick it up this time. "Sure, I'll come over," I said.

As things turned out, the bus driver would only let me off at a different house if I had a note. So since I got off at home, I didn't have the chance to ask Carson why he hung out with the Wedgie King. There would be other opportunities. Even though Carson seemed to make white friends easier than I did, he still needed me around to be less interesting than he was.

When I'm Sixty-Four

The day before our first holiday concert, Stacey showed up in chorus with Gloria, both crying. We were about to do a dress rehearsal of our lame floor show dance steps, but Gloria handed Mrs. Thatcher the plastic case containing the matching red tie and cummerbund she had given to each of us in mid-November.

"What's going on?" I asked George.

"Gloria's dad got his orders," he said.

"Mine too," Nelson said, looking down at his sheet music. "Gloria's dad came over and told my dad last night. They're leaving in a week, but this is her last day. She has to help pack." The way he said this, I knew he had done this routine himself before, at least once. "I'll finish out until Christmas break, then I'm gone too," he added.

Mrs. Thatcher called the class to order. Instead of sliding around the floor with us, Gloria sat in her usual alto chair, mostly trying not to cry. I had a hard time concentrating on my notes and steps. I had never known anyone who moved, except Marie — the girl Carson nicknamed "Stinkpot" — and she had only gone as far as Niagara Falls, a whole ten minutes from the rez.

"Maybe you'll both come back," I said to Nelson as we filed our music binders away.

"Not a chance," he said, sliding his binder in place.

"How long do you think she knew?"

"Maybe when she got home from school yesterday? This morning?"

"And how long before that would her dad have known?" I asked. Their world seemed unbelievable to me, that one day, you were going to be told you were leaving your home behind.

"Couple hours. Maybe that morning. My dad heard about ours yesterday afternoon."

"And that's it?"

"Yup, that's it."

"And you just go with it?"

"What am I gonna do? Stay behind? You get used to it. Come on, we have to get to the room or we're going to be marked late."

After final bell, we headed out to the bus platform. The bus that carried the air force kids was a few up from the reservation bus, so George and I often stood together, watching as the more eager passengers stuffed themselves through the doors, vying for seats. Gloria stood near Nelson, but they both silently watched their bus. It was as if they had already made their break from each other and us.

"Is that what it's like?" I asked George, pointing my chin at Nelson and Gloria.

"How else would it be?"

"I don't know," I said.

"Okay," George said, understanding I wanted more, but also asking me to drop it. "Are you doing anything over Christmas break?"

"Nah, just staying inside, and probably helping my uncle shovel the driveway if it snows too hard. You know," I said, "like 'when the weather outside is frightful,'" singing this last part.

"You're such a dork," he said, laughing.

"Did you get that word from your dictionary of local slang?"

"I wouldn't need that to know you're being a dork. Still, I guess I'll put up with you."

"Mighty white of you," I said. This was not a nice thing to say, but it just slipped out. It was something you'd hear around the reservation and on TV shows with black characters, making fun of white people acting generously tolerant of others. But I'd never said it, and to the best of my memory, I'd never even thought it. It was as if Carson were somehow possessing me. "I'm sorry. I didn't mean that."

"It's all right," George said, but I could see a wall drop down in his head. "I know what it means to be on the outside — a little. My dad warned me, when we got our orders to come here, that Vietnam was still not popular and we'd be painted with that. Anyway, maybe we can get together sometime during the break," he said. "Both my parents said they're hoping to meet you, since I talk about you at home. Do you, um?" He kicked snow around on the steps.

"Sorry, you're gonna have to give me more than that," I said.

"Exchange gifts? Does your family practice Christmas?"

"Like we wouldn't get it right if we didn't practice?"

"Never mind. It's not important," George said. "Looks like my bus line is pretty short. Guess I'll get on. See you in the morning." He walked away, not turning back.

I was developing a bad habit of deflecting his questions by being a smart-ass. Like biting your fingernails, this was going to be a tough one to break. The simple answer was, yes, we practiced Christmas, but the detailed answer was that my baby-sitting revenue just barely covered the family gifts I had to buy, if I was very careful. And realistically, if he wanted me to come to his house, he would expect that I'd ask him to mine, which would cause my ma to spontaneously combust and take most of the universe with her. Anyway, I'd have no way of getting there in the first place.

"Check your neighbor," Mrs. Thatcher said in a stage whisper in the hallway right before our final concert. We'd already had our big school concert earlier that day, and this one was held at an elementary school, for an audience largely made up of local nursing home residents who'd been bused in. We were supposed to burst through the doors singing, in two lines flanking the audience, then meet in the middle on the risers. If we got it right, we'd conclude "Let It Snow" as the last few people took their places at the risers' ends.

George glanced at me and started smiling. "How come you have such huge cuffs? They look a little like Captain America's gloves."

"It's all I had," I said. I had borrowed dress clothes from my cousin Innis, and my ma said if I folded the cuffs over, my shirt would look fancy. I knew that if I looked down now, I would absolutely only be able to see the giant gauntlets Captain America wore.

"You should have told me. I could have given you a shirt."

"Like we're even close to the same size," I said. "Your shirt would look as bad as this."

"No, I still have a couple shirts from when I was younger, a kid," he said, pretending to sound serious, but a small grin crept back over his face.

"Thanks," I said, punching him. "The next time I'm seven years old, I'll let you know."

"Dear Boys," Mrs. Thatcher hissed, magically in front of us. "Must I separate you?"

"No, ma'am. We're sorry," George said, suddenly at attention and serious, as if this concert for nursing home residents was his most favorite activity in the world. His commitment was sufficient, so she moved along. "Your parents here?" he asked, when she was out of earshot.

"No, other obligations," I said. December was one of my ma's busiest times, and she took on extra jobs for some of her regulars — shampooing carpets, washing moldings, polishing silver, even helping decorate — as they prepared for big holiday parties. My dad, I guessed, was at a bar somewhere, telling stories for beers. "Yours?"

"My dad's on duty, but my mom wouldn't miss it. She's particularly happy that we're doing 'O Tannenbaum' instead of 'O Christmas Tree.'" Most of the farming communities south of the reservation started as German settlements, so Mrs. Thatcher had taught us the German version for the concert, knowing how many of these folks might like it better that way.

"*Yavolt*, Germany," I said, using the only German I knew, courtesy of *Hogan's Heroes* every afternoon on Channel 29.

"Not 'Germany' — Deutschland!" he laughed. "Get it right if you're going to use it."

Before I could answer, Mrs. Thatcher whistled with her pitch pipe, we matched the tone, and then we began our procession, bursting through the doors and sliding our feet on the gym floor, pretending we were skating. It had felt stupid in rehearsal, but the kids gliding in front of me somehow made the illusion work.

Despite all of our practice, I still almost tripped up when I scanned the family seats. Five people away from a ruddy-faced woman who looked a little like George, sat my uncle Albert. I had no idea how he got there, but from the way he was blowing on his raw, red hands, I guessed he walked. It appeared our families were going to meet after all, sort of. I hoped he was having a good day.

When we broke into "O Tannenbaum," wispy-haired heads nodded in approval from the folding chairs. George's ma was smiling and nodding too. I thought back to my days speaking Tuscarora in elementary school, and the way some elders smiled as I'd told my basic story of catching a blue ball in snow. A lot of them, like my grandparents, had been Indian boarding school survivors, and as children, they'd endured beatings, isolation, and hunger as punishment for speaking the Native languages — the only languages they'd ever known. I had just a sliver of understanding of what it meant to them to hear current children learning a Native language in school and being rewarded instead of punished.

Finally, Mrs. Thatcher brought her fingers into pincers one

last time and turned to bow. The concert was over. The audience clapped as we fake skated to the back of the room, arriving at a table under the basketball hoop, where Jingles cookies and 7UP-spiked Hawaiian Punch awaited us.

"Is that an anus cookie?" Carson asked as I bit a licorice-flavored snowflake.

"Why, did you breathe on it before we got here?" George asked, and people around us made disapproving noises. Most white kids tended not to dust it up with an Indian, even with provocation, and just tried to ignore the situation. Maybe George didn't know Carson was an Indian, or maybe he still didn't realize our classmates avoided any Indian.

Carson's ma, Saphronia Mastick, came toward us. The ruddy-faced woman was also closing in, but my uncle stayed in his chair, glancing up every now and then to see if I'd noticed him.

"So you're the friend of George's we have not been introduced to," his mother said, extending her pale hand to shake mine. "I have met the boy Artie, who has been to our home on many occasions, and others, and yet I hear your name often but you have not come for a visit." She smiled, but the way she raised her eyebrows suggested I was required to explain my absence.

"Our car is unreliable, and my ma doesn't like me to put anyone out," I said. "So I only go places I can walk home from." Our car was actually quite reliable. It reliably didn't exist.

"Ah, good manners. For me, this visit will be no problem. I am happy for my son to have such polite friends. Perhaps you could come home with us, on this day, sup *mit* us and I will carry you *nach Hause* in the . . . even. Even-ing."

"Thank you," I said, tempted to say *danke*, but I didn't want her thinking I was making fun of her. "But my uncle's here, and I should probably go home with him." As soon as Albert saw me point to him, he stood up and wandered over, like we'd just run into each other at a store.

"Albert," my uncle said, shaking her hand. "The kids did a nice job, isn't it?" They nodded.

"Albert, a nice German name," George's mother said.

"I suppose so. Never thought about it. My dad thought we should all have regular names to make us fit in better. Guess he might have got inspired by all the gwuh-gwuh farmers around here."

I frowned at Albert. It took him only five sentences to hit reservation slang. He'd used the word we invented for the German farmers generations ago, inspired by the sound their funny shoes made. But then I realized George and his ma would have no idea what it meant.

"George, this is my uncle Albert." They shook hands and Albert mumbled a "good to meet you," then went back to looking around the room. George began to say something, but when it was clear Albert had turned his attention away, he looked down, a little red. I suspected he thought my family would be as eager to meet him, or at least that they'd heard of him.

"Guess you don't talk much about school when you're home," he said to me, and I shrugged.

After we exited the gym, Albert lit a cigarette while George and his ma walked toward their car. Carson and his ma pulled up and Saphronia rolled down her window. "You guys want a ride? There's room back there. You can shove the laundry baskets over."

"We're good," I said. "Parked just over there," which all four of us knew was a lie.

"Okay, take care," Saphronia said. They pulled out, and George and his ma got into the only car in the side lot where our car was allegedly parked.

"Sorry," I said to Albert, since we were now walking home. "I didn't want to be owing anything more to Carson."

"Understood. He's getting to have that kind of streak like his old man, isn't it? Gathering up debts? You can use these if you want," he said, handing me a beat-up pair of cotton work gloves, the kind you might wear to avoid blisters while raking leaves in the fall. "I got pockets." He slipped his hands into the yellow-striped slits in his Hawks jacket as we started along the roadside cinders.

Some people thought Albert was mentally retarded, but that didn't really cover the way his mind worked. He had a bird-shot brain. Some areas were sharper than mine, and others had gaps, disconnections, blank spaces.

But whatever mental abilities Albert didn't have, he excelled in lacrosse. He didn't want to do much when he came home from Vietnam, but my ma and her sister convinced him he should try out for the all-Indian Trans-American Lacrosse League.

Albert passed his tryout, and team members took turns picking him up for practice. He was put on the floor immediately in the first game of the season. The Niagara Hawks won the championship that year he first played, and they all got their signature jackets. They were shiny black leather jackets with patches for the year, their numbers, and the US and Canadian flags, to show we Indians belonged to both and neither at the same time. On the right chest, there was a huge patch of an Indian head, like on the old nickels, which the league teams had chosen as their championship symbol. Albert couldn't afford a jacket, but the other members had pitched in and gotten him one for all that he brought to the team.

Six years later, Albert had been moved to second string, and then phased out because he couldn't run as fast as he used to. But he still wore the jacket no matter the weather. It was a reminder of what was maybe the best year of his life.

"The walk's not too bad once you get going," Albert said. "I see you've kept this haircut your ma gave you. How come? Today's a day you could use long hair like mine."

"You ain't kidding there," I said. "I do wish I still had it."

"I bet you do," he said, rubbing my bristly head. While I'd told him the truth as it applied to that moment, it was hard to admit that my life was easier without the braid, even more now that my summer tan had faded. As much as I hated being invisible in class, I liked being invisible around town. I could be Italian, or even German, and so I didn't get followed around anymore by store employees who just happened suddenly to be doing inventory in whatever aisle I was in. But every time I felt that liking-it feeling, guilt followed, like a garden slug working inside my belly, leaving its slime trail.

We passed the grocery store, and I scanned the parking lot for any cars we might reliably know. No luck. Albert walked to town all the time, but I didn't bother asking him how long the walk would take. Time just kind of drifted for him, getting away until suddenly, he was hours late for some place he was supposed to be.

When we got near the plumbing supply place, a car pulled up behind us, headlights on us. George sat in the passenger seat, shivering with the window down. "My *Mutti* wants to give you a ride," he yelled. "Come on." He opened the door and jumped in the back.

Albert and I couldn't ignore him, but we also knew it was too light out for them to see our house, which showed its limitations even at dusk. The row of trees my grandfather planted in front only obscured so much. "I got an idea," Albert whispered as he pushed me forward, climbing into the backseat with me and George.

"Albert, you sit up here, so you can point out where I am to go," George's ma said. Albert got back out and climbed in front.

"Why didn't you just tell me you didn't have a ride?" George whispered as we pulled out. I shrugged, having no better answer. "That's just weird, you know. My *Mutti*, mom, saw you in the rearview mirror. We were going to do a little last-minute Christmas shopping, but she thought it would be better to turn around and offer you a ride. We can shop another time."

"Thanks," Albert said on cue. "Thanks a lot. I don't mind the walk. Keeps your heart strong, but my nephew here . . ." he trailed off.

"We hoped your nephew might come for a visit," George's ma said.

"Yeah, sounds good," he said.

Like a talented hostess, she introduced questions about his occupation, his life, whatever she could think of, but his vague answers seemed to frustrate her. As we neared the reservation turnoff, Albert just suggested she pull over, which she did, and he got out of the car. Apparently his plan was that we get to the edge of the reservation and walk the rest of the way.

"Whyn't you give me my gloves and I'll hoof it home," he said to me through the open door. "You can have your visit today. Don't worry, I'll tell your ma you're in good hands."

"An excellent idea, but Albert, I am glad to take you all the way to your home too," George's ma said. "It will make it easier to find it again tonight, when I bring the boy back."

"Nah, he can point you in the right direction," Albert said. I passed him the gloves. "You have fun now." With that, he closed the door and started his walk home. Pem Brook was a long stretch with almost no houses on it. I didn't like watching him take that lonesome road, as the dike's shadow blocked out even the weak December setting sun.

"Your uncle is a very thoughtful man," George's ma said as we pulled away and headed to Red-Tail Manor. George grinned next to me.

"Yes, he is," I said, and though I smiled back at George, I couldn't help but feel like I was going across the border into another country, alone.

6

Maybe I'm Amazed

We turned down Tuscarora Road, which, oddly, didn't actually take you to the reservation, and then made a turn near Good Intentions, the limestone quarry where George and Artie watched dynamite blasts. George's ma pulled into the driveway of a very official-looking set of buildings that was flanked by two enormous flagpoles waving equally gigantic American flags. Behind them, a residential area opened up, but it didn't look like any other I'd ever seen.

There seemed to be exactly three kinds of residences in Red-Tail Manor. The first set was a grouping of two-story apartment buildings, but they looked snazzier than the projects where most city Indians I knew lived. There were close parking lots and Dumpsters for each building, and in a lot of the apartments, you could see decorated Christmas trees. Passing through the apartment section, we came to what George called doubles, which were identical L-shaped houses, like the bedroom I shared with Albert, except here, instead of a bedpost, they had a carport dividing their space. Then we turned into a circular road with single-family homes, but even here, each house looked pretty much like all the others, except for the address numbers mounted above the garage. Occasionally one had the garage attached at the opposite side of the house.

George's mom pulled into a driveway. The house was modern and almost shiny, like a place pulled from a Monopoly board, or someone's imagination of what a house should look like. Its size was similar to the double-wide trailers that had been sprouting up all over the reservation, but there were no cinder blocks and axles holding these houses up. They sat perfectly on their neat foundations.

Stacey, Harold, and some other kids we knew were walking the sidewalks together, huddling around, laughing, throwing snowballs halfheartedly at one another. We got out of the car, and as George started to wander over to them, his mother yelled that he had to come inside before twenty minutes were up. He waved to acknowledge he'd heard her, but when we got close to the other kids, we said hi and didn't really slow down, moving along.

"What are we doing?" I finally asked George when we'd cleared them.

"Just follow me," he said as we walked into a building with the letters *BX* mounted above the door. It was like a warehouse. Stereos, televisions, even shoe boxes were stacked high around us, a merchandise maze all around the display models. The place smelled sweet and strange at the same time.

Against the wall nearest the door, a man in uniform sat behind a counter, with racks of packaged candy lining the shelves around him. The back wall was covered with cartons of cigarettes and a gold-trimmed glass case with colognes and perfumes I'd only ever seen on TV.

"They don't really have any records or stuff like that," George said, "but the candy is super cheap, and they carry

Rolling Stone, *Circus*, *Creem*, most of the good music mags. This is where Stacey gets her Wackies. Me too. Prices are lower than a regular store, and no tax either." He picked some Wackies up and the new *Rolling Stone*, and set them on the counter. "You want something? I brought my base ID card, see?" He held out an ID card more official-looking than my rez ID. It listed his name, and his father's name and rank.

"I'm good," I said, failing to mention that I had exactly zero coins and zero bills on me.

"My dad got our new stereo here," George said, pointing to one of the nicer models on display. He took a few more things from the bank of candy packages and looked up at the man behind the counter. The guy had been watching me the whole time.

"Yeah, it's fine," the man said, waving indifferently at George. "I recognize you. You're Sergeant Haddonfield's kid. My paperboy, ain't ya?"

"Yes, sir," George said, "if your paper's the *Courier Express*."

"It is. But you," the man said, looking at me. "You got ID? I don't recognize you."

"I'm not buying anything," I said.

"Don't matter. This stuff is for military families only. Is any of this stuff for your buddy here?" he asked, turning to George.

"No, sir," George said immediately, the tone of his voice changing to a tight, serious sound I'd never heard from him before.

"If you walk out of here and give something to him, you're still violating policies." He pointed to a sign above the door:

MERCHANDISE PURCHASED EXPRESSLY FOR THE CONSUMPTION OF MILITARY PERSONNEL AND THEIR FAMILIES.

"Sir, I was unaware of these policies," George continued, in that strange voice. "Thank you for telling me, sir."

We left the building and George walked face forward, teeth clenched. "Dick," he said quietly, somehow conveying scorn even without shouting. "Don't turn around. I'm positive he's looking and I don't want to give him the satisfaction. People bring in friends from off base all the time and buy stuff. He probably thinks my dad gave him some kind of grief. It's one of the drawbacks of being the kid of an officer."

We made it back to his house and stopped at the door. There was a rough mat on the stoop, where George scraped his shoes over and over before he stepped in. Suddenly, I had a bad feeling about my agreeing to come. I dutifully scraped my boots, but as soon as we walked in, my fears were realized. There was another mat on top of a rubber tray. George stepped one foot on the tray and lifted the other like a flamingo, untying his shoe and depositing it on the mat. He then did the same thing with the other foot. I had to follow suit, but both my socks had holes in the toes. As I took my boots off, I tugged the socks down so the holes were on my soles.

"*Mutti*, we're back," George said as we came into the kitchen.

"*Gut,*" his mother said. "You and your friend can set the table before your *Vater* comes home. What does your friend like on the pizza?"

"Can I order?" George asked as he grabbed plates and gave me utensils to place.

"If you wish."

"What am I supposed to do with these?" I asked, holding up the forks, knives, and spoons.

"Just put them where they're supposed to go," he said, motioning to the cloth rectangles on the dining room table. "What do you think, pepperoni and anchovies?"

Anchovies? Who thought fish on a pizza was a good idea?

"I'm *kidding*," George said. He smiled. "I hate pepperoni." He watched me again and then laughed a second time. "You're so easy. Okay, pepperoni. Anything else?"

"Wings?" I asked.

"We'll get to the music in a little while, but first we have to order the food."

"No, chicken wings, you know. Hot sauce, blue cheese. You order it from the pizza place." Or at least everyone from around here did.

"Is this like reservation food or something?" he asked, waiting for me to crack, laughing.

"No, look, man, I'm totally serious. When you call, you ask — wait a minute, what pizza place do you go to?"

"Pizza Hut, why?"

"Are you kidding? You live in one of the most Italian towns outside of Europe and you get pizza from Pizza Hut?" I recognized I had crossed one of my ma's lines of behavior — not being a good guest at someone's house — and it was doubly bad that I was not even on the reservation. "I'm sorry, I wasn't meaning to be picky," I said. "It's just . . . you're missing out."

"Okay, you're the guest. You can choose, but it's got to be someplace close, because my mom isn't going to want to go far. My dad should be home in another hour. He likes to come in, clean up a little, and then have supper ready."

Even as he said it, I realized I could try something we'd

never done in my family. "Not a worry," I said. "We can get delivery." All local pizza places refused to deliver to the reservation, claiming we would try to rob the delivery guy. Probably someone had at one point. "You got a phone book?" I did the quick pizza research and made the call while George asked his mother if she minded our playing some music. She said no, that she was going into the master bedroom to wrap some presents, so we shouldn't disturb her.

After I hung up the phone, George and I went into the living room. He took out his dad's Beatles albums. "Here, this is the one where you can hear and see the Paul McCartney death clues the most," he said, handing me *Magical Mystery Tour* and putting the album on the turntable. The cover had this psychedelic orange-and-blue background, with a picture of the Beatles dressed in animal costumes in the center. A bunch of tiny, yellow stars formed the name THE BEATLES above them, while more cartoon stars fell around them. The album title itself burst out of a rainbow below the picture, with its own rainbow stripes.

I flipped through the book, looking at the pictures of the Beatles in various outfits and costumes, reading the little comic story that was interspersed throughout, eyeing up the suspicious red stains on McCartney's shoes in the center-fold page, a yard away from where he stood in his socks. You knew *he* never had to deal with socks that had holes worn in them.

"Oh yeah, 'Strawberry Fields Forever,'" I said as the song came on. There was no crackle at all between songs on his record. All the records at our house, even though we were careful, still sounded a little like you were crinkling cellophane anytime you played them.

"Okay, here's the part. Listen," George said. The song faded down and then back up, super noisy, in a part I didn't think I'd heard before, with wild drums and blaring trumpets. "Right . . . here." On the recording, a man mumbled something, but I couldn't tell what it was supposed to be. I shook my head. "John says, 'I buried Paul'!" he shouted. "Clear as day. Here, I'll play it again."

He carefully lifted the needle, then lined the arm back up and flicked the lever again. The sound returned, the noisy music, then the fade and finally the mumble. I supposed it could have been "I buried Paul," but really, I didn't hear it any better than the first time.

The front door opened, and someone scraped away at the mat. A burly man with glasses and a blond brush cut came into the living room. He wore an olive drab jumpsuit with HADDONFIELD embroidered on a chest pocket patch. The suit's legs were stuffed into his boots, which he clearly continued to wear. He looked like a glimpse of a future George, if I could travel forward in time about twenty years to see him as a grown man. They had the same broad, pink, winter-bitten cheeks, blue eyes, and narrow nose.

"Hello, boys," he said, unzipping the jumpsuit enough to pull out the tail of his T-shirt. He wiped his glasses on the white cotton. "Paul is dead, huh?" He laughed. "People never get tired of that. Where's your mother, son?"

"In the bedroom, wrapping presents. Pizza should be here in a little while," George said.

"Well, we don't want to disturb her. Say, you're not Artie," he said, extending his hand, which I tried to grip as firmly as I could. "James Haddonfield."

"Lewis Blake, Mr. Haddonfield. Nice to meet you," I said, trying to stand without revealing the holes in my socks.

"Are you the young man from the reservation?" he said, craning his neck to look at me.

"Yes, sir," I said, these words feeling like LEGOs in my mouth. I'd been trying to learn politeness cues from George, and "sir" seemed to work wonders in dealing with white adults.

"Nice to finally meet you. My boy here talks about you. Says he'd really like to see the reservation. I told him I'd drive him around sometime, but he said he hoped to have a guided tour from someone who knows the place." This was news to me, and George's cheeks flushed red. "Son, what did you mean about the pizza being here in a little while?"

"Lewis told me about delivery. See, they do it here," George said, flipping the phone book open to the page I had shown him. "They said six o'clock."

"That's not the kind we usually get. Did you ask your mother —?"

"She left it up to me, sir. And I asked my friend for advice. You know, sir. Being courteous to guests and all."

Mr. Haddonfield nodded, a frown wrinkling his forehead. "So it's coming at six? I guess I can forgo a shower until after supper." He sat down in the recliner that George had made sure not to leave anything in, though he'd spread album covers everywhere else. "Your mother will kill me if she sees me with these on in the living room. You boys want to help me out here?" he said, untying and pulling off his boots.

He handed them to George, and we headed to the entry to place them with ours. "That's better," his dad said from the living room. "Maybe you'd grab me a beer from the fridge, son." George poured a beer into a mug he'd pulled from the freezer, wrapped a paper towel around the mug's handle, and snagged a cork circle from the counter, then brought them to his dad.

"You take your sip?" he asked, and George shook his head. "Just as well, don't want to set a bad example for your buddy here. Now, you boys can have fun with all this death stuff, but I have in my hands absolute proof that Paul McCartney is definitely alive and well."

He handed George an album, and George switched the records out carefully, never touching the playing surface of either one. When he had *Magical Mystery Tour* filed back in the rack in its proper place, he started the record player.

"Wings," I said, recognizing the opening lines of "Band on the Run," a song that had been on the radio constantly a couple years ago. As soon as I said it, I realized why George had looked puzzled when I asked him if we were ordering wings with the pizza.

"Very good, son," Mr. Haddonfield said to me. I felt my face rush with blood at his calling me that. I'd had so few conversations with my own father that I couldn't remember his ever calling me anything really, and I liked hearing "son" too much for that feeling to be right. "Wings is Paul McCartney's band *after* the Beatles," he added, which I already knew, but I smiled and he nodded. "Just listen to how this song is really like three songs all sewn together perfectly. Just like side two of *Abbey Road*, if you know that. No one else has that kind of genius. Take totally separate songs and put them together in a way that listeners could never think of them apart."

As soon as Mr. Haddonfield said it, I recognized that the medley style was similar. He was right — no matter what the conspiracy folks said, here was absolute musical proof Paul McCartney had survived the most identifiable music group in history. It was a signature you couldn't really deny.

The doorbell rang, and I experienced, for the first time, the miracle of pizza delivery. Behind us, Wings moved into "Jet," another song I loved from the radio. George's ma came out of the master bedroom, looked immediately at her husband's feet, and noticed the socks. Only then did she kiss him on the cheek, while he leaned toward her, singing her the song.

George paid the delivery guy while his ma placed a group of decorated ceramic tiles on the table. When George came in, he set the pizza boxes directly on the tiles. If we had something that fancy, my ma would have propped them on the TV with Albert's and Zach's lacrosse trophies.

"Willy, we need another trivet here for . . ." his dad said to Mrs. Haddonfield, lifting the box of chicken wings off the pizza box. "What is this anyway?" He opened the box and spicy steam blasted his face.

"Those are wings, sir," I said. "They're hot and spicy, but you know that now. I should have warned you not to get your eyes near the steam."

"Like Tex-Mex," he said, smiling. "I've been to Lubbock for maneuvers and I love a good chile relleno." He set the box down and removed the containers of blue cheese. "*Queso?*"

"Do you mean like tacos?" I asked. "No, this isn't like tacos. It's, um, well, you take the wing and dip it in the blue cheese, and then you eat it."

"Maybe I'll just try it without," George's dad said, lifting a wing.

"No, really. See? Like this," I said, taking one out, dipping it in the dressing, and eating it. I felt like one of those royal tasters who took the first bite of the king's food to prove it wasn't poisoned. They all stared at me for a moment, and then George decided he was brave enough to try it.

"It's good," George said, though his expression said the verdict was still out. He had only touched the chicken in the blue cheese, so the hot sauce–covered wing had one small, glowing white spot. I wanted to insist that he make a bigger commitment, but instead I grabbed a piece of pizza.

"Blue cheese, you say," his dad said, doing a similar vague brush with the dressing. "On chicken?" He bit into it, thought about it, swallowed, and smiled. "You might be onto something here, son. A little messy, but good." He reached for more and poured the dressing onto his plate.

The album played through side one as we ate. When it finished, George's dad went to the sink. After washing his hands, he changed the record. What came on was not the rest of that album, but "Here Comes the Sun," which meant side two of *Abbey Road*.

"Now you see," he said, "when we move into this side of this record, you get your songs all connected to one another, like we heard in that first one." He sat back down and dipped another wing in the blue cheese. "Classic McCartney. But kind of sad. They could feel that this was going to be their last work together as a group, so they took all the great pieces of unfinished songs, and that was how they wrote this long, complex piece. Even as they were falling apart, they knew what they'd had was special, and they didn't want to waste any of it."

"I know this album," I said. "My uncle likes this, so I've grown up listening to it." Albert and I agreed on about twenty albums. Any Beatles, but lately, also the Queen album I'd been playing. I wondered why we didn't have any Wings. Maybe Zach took their albums too when he left. "Is 'Listen to What the Man Said' on that Wings album?"

"No, that's a newer one," George's dad said.

His ma smiled. "Papa Smurf likes that song," she said. "Because the soldier boy gets to kiss the girl." She leaned into him, and he wiped his mouth before kissing her cheek.

"'Smurf'? Is that another German word?" I asked.

"Not exactly," George said, standing. "I think they came from France originally, but these days, in Germany anyway, they make —"

"You can show him after you clear the table, *Liebling*."

George sat back down.

"I should get home, Mrs. Haddonfield," I said. "My ma will be wondering where I am." This was about as big an understatement as I could make. Albert would have told her, of course, but her temperature was probably creeping up toward the boiling point even as we ate.

"Then we will have to have you back here soon so George can show you the Smurfs. Would you like to take some of this food home with you?" she asked. "Perhaps your parents would like some. We have plenty here." She grabbed tinfoil from the cupboard.

"That's okay, thanks," I said. If my ma thought I had tried to con some white person out of food, I didn't even know what would happen. A death sentence? Banishment? There weren't many houses on the rez worse than ours, except maybe Bug Jemison's, where there was no electricity. Maybe my punishment would be a sentence to live there forever, or just in our house.

"You must. I would be a terrible hostess if I did not give you food to take home. Family is a most important thing."

I took the bag and weighed my options. Could I accidentally leave it in their car? No, that would be an even worse disaster than bringing it home. I'd figure it out later. "Thank you, ma'am," I said, setting the bag beside the entry mat as I pulled my boots back on.

"Son, you want to start the truck for your old dad?" Mr. Haddonfield said to George, tossing him keys from a fatigue coat hanging in the entry. "Just slip your mother's shoes on there, no one'll see you. Then you have some homework you better get cracking on, I imagine."

Next to George's dress shoes, my boots, and the military boots were a pair of red suede slip-ons that looked a little like Dutch wooden shoes. "If you tell anyone, I'll *beat* you with one of these shoes," George whispered to me as he slid his feet into them and headed out the door.

"He's a good boy," his dad said, laughing a little as he laced his boots back up. "I didn't think he'd do that with you here. He must really trust you. That's pretty hard to come by."

George came back in and kicked the red shoes off as soon as his feet were inside.

"Son, you've got time to show your buddy the Smurfs," his dad said. I unzipped my boots. "Nah, it's good," he said, peeking to make sure Mrs. Haddonfield had gone back to wrapping gifts. "Just go quietly. I'll be in the truck listening to music. Come out when you're ready."

George led me to his room. The space Albert and I shared, because it was small and we each liked to collect things, was filled wall to wall with our furniture and junk. We kept our rack of albums between the dresser and my bed. I had a night-stand with a shelf for my comic book collection and a single slim drawer where I kept private things, which didn't really amount to much — a few school pictures of friends from the rez, some notes, articles I had cut out. Next to that was our bureau, which left a walkway between my bed and Albert's. Most of his clothes were in the bureau, and its top was taken up with our stereo and a spent mortar shell he brought back from Vietnam. In the corner sat his nightstand, where he kept his own private stuff in the drawer. On the nightstand's low shelf, he stored a large stack of magazines he said I was too young to look at, as if I couldn't see the centerfold posters plastered all over the walls we shared.

George's room, by contrast, looked like something you might see in a movie about nuns. There was a single bed, perfectly made, and a nightstand with a radio and lamp on top. A dresser and footlocker took up the other end of the room, and a pennant with the Miami Dolphins logo hung on the wall. Hanging next to the closet was a wooden silhouette of a tree in full bloom. It was a large shallow box with maybe thirty small shelves of different sizes inside. Half of the tiny shelves held figurines, none more than three inches high, of little blue people wearing white, vaguely pointy hats and white pants that looked like pajama bottoms with built-in boots.

"These are the Smurfs," George said.

"What are they?" I asked, getting closer. "Can I pick one up?" One held a bowling ball, one aimed a rifle, one pulled on a slingshot, one in a chef's hat raised a plate with a cupcake on it, and there was even one holding a sudsy beer mug. They looked kind of like elves.

"Sure," George said. "This one is Papa Smurf." He reached into the center box and handed me the only bearded Smurf, also the only one wearing red. The figure was made of a rubbery plastic. "He's supposed to keep all the knowledge and culture for the Smurfs. These guys are big in Germany. There are comic books about the land where they live — you know, the kind of place that supposedly humans can't find — and these are, I don't know, what you might call life-sized. Lots of people collect them. I started getting them, one for my birthday, one for Christmas, every year, a ritual. You always knew what that little box under the tree was going to be."

"Why does your ma call your dad this?" I asked him, handing back the Papa Smurf. One Smurf wore a headdress and held a tomahawk like a TV Indian, but I stayed silent about it.

"Whenever he has a few days off and he's going to be mostly around the house, he lets his beard grow in, and he hairs up fast. It's super blond, almost white, like Papa Smurf's. She teases him about being a know-it-all too. A couple years ago, she bought him a red hat and red wool pants for Christmas. I think he wore them once. Kind of an expensive joke."

"Do you ask for specific Smurfs? Or is it luck of the draw? What do you think you'll get this year?" I did a quick count and realized they did not add up. There were only twenty.

"I don't get them anymore. We stopped when we left Berlin."

"Don't you have relatives in Germany? Your ma's relatives? Couldn't they send some?"

"Yeah, I guess. We stopped. That's all. Germany's over. We live here now." He looked away from the Smurfs, over at his Miami Dolphins pennant. "You better get out there. My dad's a nice guy, but not the most patient. See you in school?"

"Yup," I said, walking out. "Hey," I said, stopping as he put the Papa Smurf back in, "thanks for having me over. It was cool. I really liked seeing where you live."

"No problem. I'm sure you'll return the favor."

I nodded, which didn't seem as bad a lie as an outright invitation. In the driveway, I could hear Mr. Haddonfield's music coming from the car. It was what we'd been listening to in the house, side one of *Band on the Run*. I climbed in. "Just in time," he said.

"Sorry I took so long."

"Don't worry about it. You seem like a conscientious young man."

"Wish my ma thought that more often."

"I'm sure she does," he said. "Okay, listen to this." The song faded and the machine made a grinding sound. Then music started again. "Isn't that something? It's new, a tape deck. You don't even need to flip the cassette. The tape reverses and the heads change inside so you can hear both sides," he explained. "Just go down Snakeline?"

"Sure," I said. "Then left on Dog Street, at the school."

"My boy says you like to listen to music a lot. You're both in the school singing thing?"

"Yes, our last concert was today. That's how I —"

"Right, got it. Shoot, that means I missed all three concerts. I knew there was something I was going to try to get out early for today, but when duty calls . . ."

"Yeah, I know. If there's an extra job to pick up, my ma does it."

He was quiet for a minute. "What does your mother do?"

"She works in Lewiston." I didn't want to tell him at what exactly. It was none of this stranger's business what we had to do to get by. "Here, on the left, that's my driveway there. You can just pull to the side of the road. There's no cars coming." I was ready for a quick exit.

"There?" he asked, pointing to the dark outline behind our trees. "You sure someone's home? It looks awfully dark. Wouldn't your parents leave a light on for you? I don't want you alone on a cold night like this. We could call from our home, keep trying until we get them."

"No, it's good. My uncle lives with us. I'm sure he's home, even if my ma isn't yet."

He insisted on pulling into the driveway instead of just pausing at the roadside.

"Don't go in any farther. You'll get stuck," I said, grateful that Albert hadn't shoveled the driveway. "I can walk from here. Thanks for the dinner and the ride, sir." I opened the door.

"Hold on a second. Do you have a player for something like this?" He pressed a button and the little cassette glided out of the slot. He pulled it out and held it my way.

"No, sir, I sure don't. We have a stereo that my uncle sent home when he was in the service. I guess it's about seven or eight years old now. The only tape there is reel to reel."

"Service?"

"Drafted." I thought that might end any more questions about Albert's military time.

"I see. Well, I know you're in a bit of a hurry here, but if you'd like, I'm happy to lend you the album," he said, sliding a plastic bag from his side of the truck. "I thought you might want to listen to the whole thing. You can give it back to my boy at school, or just bring it the next time you're over. I know you'll take good care of it."

I peeked in the bag and saw an album cover with *Band on the Run* on it, over a picture of what appeared to be a group of nine criminals huddled close together, dressed in identical brown suits, and caught in a glaring spotlight in front of a brick wall. I recognized Paul McCartney as the person in the center of the group. "My ma would kill me if I took this," I said, really thinking George's dad would kill me if I messed it up. Albert and I were careful with albums, but our stereo just wasn't all that good anymore.

"Son, my boy tells me about his friends, and I've met Artie and Stacey and a few of the others, but you're the only person he's really wanted to get to know since we arrived here. I trust his judgment, and I think you'll like this. Please."

"I'll bring it to school as soon as we come back," I said.

"Take your time. I've got this cassette. Maybe we'll see you over the holidays."

I thanked him again and shut the car door, waiting for him to leave before I waded through the snow.

When I walked in, my ma was washing dishes on the dining room table, pouring water from a kettle into the rinse pan. Usually, she did this with the overhead light on, filling the room with light — one of her few luxuries. We weren't supposed to turn that light on unless necessary.

"Was wondering if you were ever going to get home," she said. "What's all that stuff?" I was carrying my school bag, the album, and the leftovers. She stepped from the dishpans to the water pail and began filling it again.

"School stuff," I said, setting the bags on the stairs. "Didn't Albert tell you where I was?"

"Of course. That's why I'm washing dishes in the dark. If those white people bringing you home decided to pull up to the house, this way, they at least wouldn't be able to see in."

"Is that why no outside light either?"

"You've seen how they live now, the way their houses are different from ours. That boy's going to want to come here. Do you understand why he can't?"

"He'd be coming to see *me*, not the house," I said, realizing I did want to have George over and play some of my records for him. I'd taken the plunge I was most afraid of, and I'd enjoyed it more than I could have even imagined. He opened a door for me and I wanted to return the favor. If I wanted to keep this friend, I was going to have to meet the expectations of exchange in some way. But more than that, I wanted to have him here, to show him my world, such as it was.

"Well, you can forget it," she said.

I looked at the places where our walls were covered with plastic stapled to insulation, and at the newspaper under the water pail where we kept drinking water from the hand pump outside — to say nothing of the slop pail in the corner. I heard a dog nosing in the closed-off kitchen at the back, where part of the roof had caved in one bad winter, and I gritted my teeth. The neighborhood dogs had figured out a way to poke their muzzles through the gap in the warped kitchen door frame and wiggle inside. A few were always sneaking in. Some nights,

I ignored their rumblings in the kitchen. But on evenings when my ma wasn't home, and there was nothing on TV, and Albert was holed up in our room, I would hide behind the stove with a basket of Zach's lacrosse balls. I'd see the nose poke in, then the head. The dog would peek in, and though it could probably smell me, the scent of our stove must have been more compelling. I'd wait until the dogs were all the way in, then I'd jump out and whip the balls at their thick-furred hides. They'd turn and squeeze back through the frame, but by then I'd usually gotten some good wallops in. I didn't like chasing the dogs away, and under other circumstances, we were even friendly. I hoped they understood it was just a matter of territory — that I couldn't let go of the idea I had a semi-normal house, however far-fetched.

What was I thinking — that I could have George over to play Whack-A-Mutt with me? I grabbed my things and went upstairs, where Albert was lying on his bed, flipping through a magazine, listening to Deep Purple. I set my stuff down and opened the bag of leftovers.

"You okay?" Albert asked.

"Are you?"

"A little chilly. Those gloves don't work worth a flip in the cold. You guys were good."

"Thanks for coming," I said. "And for, you know, coming up with a plan."

"Plans are what I do best," he said, which was absolutely not true.

"You want some pizza and wings? George's ma sent them home."

"You offer some to your ma?" he asked, scooting to the foot of his bed.

"She'd kill me if she knew I took food from them."

"Probably right. I better eat the evidence," he said, digging in. "I'll throw out the bones after your ma goes to bed. What you got there?"

"His dad lent it to me." I held the album out so he could see it, but I didn't want him getting greasy pizza fingers all over the jacket, even though it was in a plastic sleeve.

"Let's put it on. That first song? It's all yours."

"What do you mean?"

"Just play it, side one." I took the album out the way I had seen George do and put it on.

> *Stuck inside these four walls,*
> *sent inside forever,*
> *never seeing no one nice again*
> *like you.*

Albert grinned. "Now you see why this is your song, isn't it? If there is one place you are stuck, it is inside these four rezzy walls, bare insulation and all, so you better not get used to the kinds of houses your friends live in."

All I need is a pint a day, if I ever get out of here, (if we ever get out of here), McCartney sang.

I wasn't sure what "a pint a day" was, but otherwise, Albert was right: This *was* my song. I fell in love with the album immediately and wanted to learn the subtleties of each song in the way you can only by repeated listening. We spun it loud several times, flipping sides, then starting over again. The way side two ended, with the refrain from "Band on the Run," the first song on side one, made it seem like a continuous loop, encircling us in its world.

Eventually, the lights downstairs went off. I turned the volume lower and gave the record a few more listens until I fell asleep, knowing I would slide it back into its sleeve in the morning and get it to George's dad as fast as I could. The last thing I remember hearing was:

We never will be found.

7

If I Needed Someone

There was a funny freedom in having been to someone's house. I could now picture where George spent his time, and I was no longer locked into talking to him only at school. I hadn't felt this freedom since kindergarten, when Carson and I started staying overnight at each other's houses on a regular basis.

The day after my visit, I had two reasons to call George — to promise I would bring his dad's album back, and this other little thing that had been bugging me. The phone book wasn't new enough to include his family, but my ma was off somewhere, so even though it would show up on the phone bill and I'd have some explaining to do, I called information for a listing: Niagara Falls, James Haddonfield, Iron Loop.

"Haddonfield residence," his ma said, answering the phone.

"Is George home?" I asked.

"I am sorry, who's calling, please?" she asked, suddenly not her cheery self. I had already done something wrong. Maybe he wasn't allowed to have phone calls.

"Hi, Mrs. Haddonfield. It's Lewis Blake, from the reservation."

"Oh, hello, Lewis," she said, switching back to her perky self. "Sometimes, America is confusing in its rules." *You're telling me*, I thought. "In Deutschland, when we call someone, we say, '*guten Tag*,' or if we know the person very well, we might just say '*Tag*' before asking for the party we want. It is like 'good day,' or 'day,' I suppose. It does not translate so well. Since you and I know each other, we might just say '*Tag*.'"

"Okay, sorry, Mrs. Haddonfield. I've only ever called other people from the reservation before, where you just ask for someone." There was silence on the line as we both paused, like we were waiting for some UN cultural translator, but since she was my elder, I eventually said, "*Tag*, Mrs. Haddonfield! Is George home?"

"*Tag*, Lewis! So nice to hear from you. Wait one moment while I retrieve George."

"Hey," George said, picking up the line. I could picture him sitting at the kitchen counter, on one of the stools, near where the phone hung. "Miss me already?" He laughed.

"Funny. Listen, please, please tell your dad that I definitely promise I'll bring his album to school as soon as we come back. I promised —"

"What are you talking about?"

"He lent me *Band on the Run*, and I said —"

"My *dad* lent you an album? He *never* lends out records. You're making that up."

"Yeah, I'm making that up. Why would I do that? Look, just tell him I promise to take good care of it. Anyway, you were going to tell me what you'd forgotten to mention about him and Indians. I keep forgetting to ask. Remember?"

"Oh yeah," he said, and then dropped his voice. "But it's not the kind of thing you can say on the phone, if you know what I mean."

"Come on. I have no idea what you mean," I said, picturing all sorts of bad things I immediately pushed out of my head. What kinds of things could you not say on the phone?

"Well, if you want to know, we'll just have to get together over the break sometime."

"Or you could tell me in school, since you're being so weird on the phone."

"Not really a school thing either."

"My ma doesn't generally take me places I don't absolutely have to go," I said. "She's funny that way." I hated making her sound deranged, but it felt easier than the truth.

"I'm babysitting a couple houses down on New Year's Eve. If you can get a ride that night, my dad will give you a ride home in the morning. After the couple who I'm sitting for comes home, we can walk back to my place and you can stay overnight."

"I don't think —" I started.

"You've got a week to come up with a ride. It'll be totally worth it. The place I'm babysitting has an interesting library," he said, in a way that was meant to convey something other than one with the Dewey decimal system. I had a pretty good idea of what that was. "Look, I've got to go load the ads for my paper route tomorrow. Have a great Christmas if I don't talk to you before then, and hope to see you New Year's Eve." And with that, he was gone.

"Lewis!" my ma yelled later that evening. "Get down here. Carson's here."

I went downstairs. Carson stood near the kerosene heater, rubbing his hands, his boots dripping snow into the old rug. "We just got our Christmas tree," he said. "It's stuffed into the backseat, and my ma wanted to know if you wanna come over and help us with it. We're going shopping first. She said my dad dropped the old box of ornaments, so we have to get some more."

There was no forewarning with Carson, no greetings, no "*Tag*," just life the way I knew it to be, and there was some comfort in knowing the rules. "Sure," I said, since it looked like this was going to be my only chance to get to a store for Christmas shopping.

"Grab a change of clothes. You can stay the night," he added.

"Go ahead if you want," my ma said, reading the newspaper.

I ran up and stuffed clothes into a grocery bag. Albert watched me. I could hear him in my head in that telepathy you get when you've shared a room for years. *You're gonna be sorry*, he beamed into my brain. *All you're doing is gathering more things that kid's going to hold over your head. I don't wanna hear it when you come home in some kind of mess either.*

"You won't," I said aloud.

"Just wait and see," he said, shaking his head and lighting a cigarette as I left.

"What took so long? Let's go," Carson said, grabbing my bag, my coat already in his hands. He flew out the door as I collected my toothbrush and deodorant. By the time I got outside, their car was near the mailbox, blinding me with its headlights as I navigated our snow ruts.

"Get in front," he yelled from inside, which seemed weird. "And hurry up."

"What is your prob —?" I started when I opened the door. Carson sat alone in the driver's seat, glowing in the dash lights. The overhead dome socket hung down empty, the little bulb on the bench seat.

"Get in. You're letting the heat out."

"But —"

"You want your coat back or not? You're not getting it unless you climb in here right now," he said. I could see it scrunched up against the driver's side door.

"All right, gimme it," I said as I climbed in and shut the door.

"You'll be fine," he said, backing out, and then flying down Dog Street. "It'd be warmer if you hadn't left the damn door open. Jeez, what took you so long? I was worried your ma was gonna ask for a ride to bingo, then she'd know I borrowed this car."

"Borrowed?"

"Well, my ma and dad went up to Grand River for the weekend. They're selling beadwork at that big holiday craft show they have in their friendship center. So, it's just me and the brother and sister for a few days. Sheila and Derek are upstairs in his room trying out some new water pipe, so I took the keys and here we are."

"But I really do need to go to the store. It's only a few days to Christmas."

"Don't get your panties in a bunch, Gloomis. We'll go and get Sheila. Maybe she won't be all that baked and she'll take us. But first," he said, flying down the road, "the big lot below the school is all iced and snowed over. Perfect for dog nuts."

In a couple minutes, we were down through the elementary school driveway and into the lot. He hit the gas and turned the wheel sharply. Then he hit the brakes so we slid, and cranked the wheel all the way opposite, pounding the gas again. As I flew across the bench seat with each turn, crashing into the armrest and then the door, I couldn't stop laughing. Sometimes in my force field at school, I forgot about the freedoms of my little world on the rez, where we might lift a car and test the limits of our skills without worrying about being arrested.

As we shrieked in terror and excitement, barely missing the fence a few times, I thought of all the similar things I'd spent my life doing that wouldn't have happened anywhere else. We'd strapped sleds to the backs of cars and flown through fields, dodging cricks and fences and trees, and sometimes simply wiping out. We'd packed cars so heavy, riding in open trunks and on roofs, that their chassis almost dragged. As we got older and stayed out later, we watched friends detonate homemade bombs from afar. They would work on them for weeks and announce the bomb party a few days in advance, and when the day came, we'd hang out, eat, drink, play ball, all being careful not to wander too close, in case the detonator wasn't exactly the most sophisticated. Between Carson's crazy older cousins and mine, it was like living in the same neighborhood as the Road Runner and Wile E. Coyote.

A lot of the things I'd grown up doing might not be considered the safest way of life, but there was no beating the rush in your blood when you were a little less controlled than the rest of the country. Only in hanging out with George in his quieter, regular-kid world did I start to appreciate the weird and rare things I'd taken for granted my whole life.

Carson didn't seem to have a conceptual grasp of the basic doughnut shape. We were making big figure eights in the parking lot, more like crullers. The more crullers we did, the closer we got to the lampposts, and that was when I realized those lights were on, which meant anyone driving by would have a clear view of our activities. Next week, it was quite possible someone might ask Saphronia Mastick why she was doing doughnuts in the school parking lot on Friday night.

Finally, after he almost took us out with a light pole, shaving by with just inches to spare, we headed over to his house, and Carson gave me my winter coat back. "Kick your boots off. They're covered in snow," he said as we walked in.

"You didn't at my house," I said.

"I've seen the rugs at your house. Better just to keep the boots on there."

"Funny. Well, I guess we aren't really getting decorations after all," I said. Their tree was massive, the star on top pressing into their new drop ceiling. I didn't think there was room for even one more ornament, let alone a new box of them.

"Yeah, that was bull to get you out of the house, and to make sure your ma didn't think there might be room to give her a ride anywhere."

I hated that even people my age on the rez knew our business. Of course, when you're patching rides together, even to get to the grocery store, it's not a huge secret. As Carson ran up the stairs, I looked at the ocean of presents flooding from under their tree, spilling out into the middle of the living room. One package, addressed to Carson, was clearly a guitar-shaped box, and it was sitting on another large box with his name on the tag.

"Sheila says she's in no shape to drive," Carson said when he came back down. He saw me looking at his presents. "Yeah," he added, perking up. "You got that right. That there is an Epiphone Casino guitar and an Orange amp, with yours truly on the tag."

"What does that mean, an amp? I've always wondered."

"Well, that piece of crap we got from Bug Jemison was an acoustic guitar. Remember? My dad said if I got good enough on it, he'd consider getting me an electric, which was what I really wanted when he brought that thing home. And an electric has to go through an amp that has a speaker in it. You know those concert pictures where you see that big wall of boxes behind the guitar player? Those are the amps. I bet *you* thought they were just decoration."

I knew they were connected to the sound, but he was right — I didn't know how things functioned. "You're telling me that in five months, you're good enough that you can play songs?" I asked. "I mean, like, real songs? None of that 'Michael, Row the Boat Ashore' stuff."

"Like *you* could play 'Michael, Row the Boat,'" he said.

"'Ashore,'" I added.

"Whatever. I can play one of your favorite songs." He ran to his room, bringing down the guitar I'd seen in August. He sat in a chair, put his left hand on the frets, and did a few moves, pinching the guitar's neck up and down at a couple different places with his full index finger.

"'Smoke on the Water' is *not* one of my favorite songs," I said, laughing. Still, even though the movements he was making were basic, I couldn't have made them if my life depended on it. "So I guess the Bug didn't pay up his wine bill with your dad."

"Nope. Just kidding on the song, though. That's a basic one they teach you to get you excited, because any moron can play it almost instantly. This one, though, *is* one of your favorites, and I'm so good, you *will* believe in yesterday."

He then played the Beatles' "Yesterday" perfectly, as if he'd been doing it his whole life. The only thing missing was the string quartet. And then he started singing it perfectly too, slight fake British accent and all.

"Can you show me how to do that?" I said.

"Just like this," he said, and then played through it again, his fingers moving so fast, I couldn't follow what he was doing. His hands were like small animals, jumping from string to string. Then he stopped and tossed the guitar on the couch, where it made almost a grunt, its strings vibrating. I really wanted to pick it up, but I knew that I hadn't seen any of his positions well enough to recreate them.

"So, listen, I have an idea," he said, dangling the keys. "Hang on a second." He ran back up and came down, grabbing his coat.

"What are you doing?" I asked, following him out the door with my own coat on.

"We are taking you shopping," he said, hopping back into the car. "Sheila and Derek are both crashing, watching TV. They'll be there for hours, and won't even know we're gone. All righty, off to the mall."

I could hear Albert in my head even as I got in the car. We were two freshly minted teenagers with no licenses and unknown levels of driving experience, crossing over into the white world on a winter night. This had "bad idea" written all over it. "I can't afford anything at the mall" was all I could think to say.

"Fine, we'll go to Jupiter," he said. Jupiter was a discount store — perfect, except that it was on Main Street in Niagara Falls. Before I could protest, he laughed. "Gloomis, you're so gullible. How's Towne Pharmacy? I'll take all the back roads. Can you find enough stuff there?"

"I think so," I said.

It was the longest five-mile drive I'd ever been on, seeing imaginary cop cars the whole way. I was glad that at least Carson was tall enough to pass for a short adult. I also had time to think one smart move ahead. As soon as he put the car into park, I snatched the keys, turned the ignition, and pulled them out.

"What the hell are you doing?" he yelled as I stuffed them into my front jeans pocket.

"Making sure I'm not walking home from here," I said.

"The thanks I get."

"You'll get thanks when we're back on reservation land." And with that, I headed into the store and grabbed a basket. I got Albert a pair of gloves — real winter gloves, lined — and my sister Charlotte's family a large chocolate assortment. I already had my ma's gift, a poker set, since another of her few luxuries was Saturday night rez nickel-and-dime poker parties. The only one I had left to buy for was Zach.

I wandered through the store, worried that Carson might have been smart enough to grab both sets of keys from his house. He walked in a minute or so later and seemed to recognize someone. I could hear them talking as I trolled the aisles, hoping to find an idea, and there it was in aisle six: a car cleaning kit with soap, wax, rubbing compound, a soft buff-ing cloth, and a selection of twelve air fresheners, all neatly packaged together, perfect for Zach's Dodge Challenger. I had enough money in my pocket, so I put it in my basket and headed to the checkout.

There I saw Carson talking with the Wedgie King, who was buying a case of Labatt with a fake ID. It shouldn't have worked — he was maybe fifteen — but the Wedgie King was just tough-looking enough to be convincing as one of those wiry men you always see looking for fights at carnival beer tents. Carson said something to him and left while the Wedgie King paid. I stalled, looking around. I didn't want the King to see me and decide he needed to prove his new fake manhood.

By the time I got out to the lot, the only car there was Saphronia's. I didn't see any other fresh tracks, so the King must live nearby in Misty Meadows. Carson sat in the passen-ger's side, with all doors locked except the driver's. I yelled for him to move over, but he just grinned and pointed to the driver's side door. I could see four beer bottles shining in the seat next to him.

"Funny again," I said, digging in my pocket for the keys. "You gonna climb over me?"

"Oh no, you wanted those keys so bad, you're driving us home," he said.

"I don't know how to drive," I said.

"You're getting your first lesson tonight," he said.

"And what's with the beers?"

"If Sheila discovers we're gone, they're bribery. Otherwise, they're our celebration of your first drive. You should be thank-ful. Who else would take you out on a cold December night so you could get presents? Not your ma, that's for sure. And not that white kid you've been hanging out with."

I was wondering when George was going to come up. It was clear at the concert reception that he and Carson weren't likely to ever get along. Carson only liked people who backed down, and George didn't seem to be that kind of person. Now Carson was acting like it was a violation of our friendship that I'd made a new friend who was not from home, even though he had clearly gotten those beers from the Wedgie King.

"If I ditch this car or get pulled over, then what are you going to do?" I asked, hoping his sense of self-preservation was intact.

"I'll say you threatened me and kept me as a hostage in my ma's car. They'll believe me. After all, what kind of fool gets the keys taken away from him? Now put the key in the ignition and turn it the opposite of the way you did when you stole them from me." I did as I was told and the car heaved and rumbled alive. "Now put one foot on the brake and one on the gas, and then you just play the right one."

As little as I knew about driving, I knew this advice was wrong, so I put my right foot on the brake and pulled the gear shift into reverse. Going backward was super disorienting. I'd looked in a rearview mirror before, but had never had to depend on one. Fortunately, the parking lot was empty, and eventually I got us out of it and moving forward down the side roads.

I knew that if any cop saw us, he would be sure to pull us over, and then being lonely in class would be the least of my worries. The wheel felt strange, the slightest move causing us to wander a bit from our lane. And at first, I couldn't step on the gas right. I had us either going five miles an hour or creeping fast up to forty-five. It didn't help that Carson was screeching with laughter and pounding on the dashboard the whole time. But finally I got a decent grip on the wheel and stopped goosing the pedal.

No matter how many times you ride in a car, there is no feeling like the one you have when you're in control. I could see now why Zach would give up almost anything to keep his Challenger. I would too. Still, as we approached the rez, there was a different issue at hand. Being around George had shown me a new way to have friends, one that didn't require you to always be on your guard. When I got to Pem Brook, I hit the blinker to turn left.

"Wait, this isn't where we're turning," Carson said, suddenly serious.

"It's where I'm turning," I said, and headed into the rez, following the same path Albert had a few days before. Carson knew as soon as I hit Dog Street what I was doing.

"If you go home, I'll keep your clothes."

I hadn't been smart enough to sneak them back. "Okay," I said. "If they mean that much to you." I'd had it with his bullshit. The rez was a small place, so I was stuck with him, but it didn't mean I had to be his fool forever.

"Come on, man. Tonight, I gave you your first opportunity ever to drive. How can you do this? I knew as soon as you started hanging out with that white kid, you'd think you were too good to hang with Indians anymore. What are you gonna do, marry him like all these assholes around here who knock up white women?"

"Yeah, that's what I'm gonna do," I said. "Is that what

you're gonna do with the Wedgie King? Oh, wait a minute, he doesn't even know you're Indian."

"Who's the Wedgie King?"

"That jerk you got those beers off of," I said, stopping on the road in front of my house and putting Saphronia's car in park.

"At least pull in the driveway!" he yelled. "There might be a car coming."

"There might be. Guess you'll have to climb over and drive off yourself. Have a good New Yah," I said, and got out of the car.

"I thought we were going New Yahing together," he said, climbing out. "I was gonna pick you up, like we used to."

"Like we used to three years ago? Like when you always stole the best cookies out of my bag when you thought I wasn't looking?" I said. As he scrambled around, I walked up my driveway, not even looking back. I heard him yell, "Asshole!" before he jumped in and took off.

New Yah. I'd sort of been blocking myself from thinking about it. Our ceremonial calendar followed the moons, and it placed the beginning of the year around February, so generations ago, we'd invented a tradition for young people to respect their elders and let them know when the outside world recognized the new year, a full month before us. The young go to all the houses and let them know a new year has come. In return, the elder rewarded you with a treat, something they spent time on as a thank-you.

Running back to the car first and raiding my bag had been one of Carson's personal traditions. I never had any other ride, and beyond his pathetic thievery, I'd still enjoyed ringing in the new year with him, but you can only be burned so many times. When we stopped doing it together, I told him it was because I was babysitting for my sister's kids, but really, it was because I came home every year with half as many cookies in my bag as I'd put in.

"You're home early," my ma said as I walked in with my Towne Pharmacy bag.

"Someone was sick at their house," I said, the lie sliding easy off my tongue. Since I'd started lying a bit to George, it was coming almost naturally, like a developed skill. "Saphronia didn't want to risk spreading it."

I went upstairs, where Albert was still on his bed, reading.

"Thought you were staying the night," he said.

"Changed my mind," I said, setting the bag behind our record rack. "No peeking."

"No promises," he said immediately.

"There never are," I said.

It still seemed funny that, even if I wanted to, I probably couldn't go New Yahing anymore. I could try with cousins, maybe, but they'd begrudge it because their cars were already packed full. Everyone always talked about how New Year's Eve was supposed to be fun when you grew up. Maybe this was my year. I went downstairs to the phone. First I called Zach to see if he would do me a favor, and miraculously he agreed, so I made my second call.

"*Tag*, Mrs. Haddonfield," I said when George's mother answered.

"*Guten Abend*, Lewis," she said. "One moment, please, while I retrieve George."

"Okay, I'm in for New Year's," I said when he picked up. "What time?"

"Eight o'clock would be good," he said. "What changed your mind?"

"Now, that's not the kind of thing you talk about over the phone," I said, mimicking his fake mysteriousness, and laughed.

"Come on," he said, impatient.

"See you in a few days," I said. When I got off, my ma was at the table, baking ingredients spread before her: bags of chocolate chips, flour and sugar, sticks of butter, Crisco.

"Are you really going to miss New Yah this year?" she asked. "I thought you like to go with Charlotte's kids."

I knew this was coming. "All I do is babysit, and then in the morning, when Charlotte and Adam are sleeping off their party, I'm the one who gives out their cookies," I said. "By the time they get up to take us out, all the good cookies are gone anyway. I think I'll have a better time with my friend. Maybe I'll walk the neighborhood with Albert when I get home."

"Don't count on your uncle waiting for you" was all she muttered.

"Guess I'll just have to take my chances," I said.

PART TWO

8

Venus and Mars

On Christmas Eve, I wrapped my few gifts and looked at the tree. In one section, all the yellow and red ball ornaments were in pairs, the yellows in front of the reds on the same branch.

"All right, you know the rules," my ma said. "You put the gifts you bought under the tree and you quit examining the others. You'll open them soon enough. Besides, you're letting all this cold air into the rest of the house."

"Yeah, I know, but what's going on there?" I asked her, pointing to the ornament arrangement as she escorted me away from the tree.

"I don't know. One of Albert's things, I guess. You know how he is." She shrugged and fixed the blankets to get the best seal on the cold front room where we kept the tree.

"How come we don't bring the tree in here and put it up?" I asked, looking around the living room, knowing already there was not really enough space for it. I hated having to run out to the tree, grab a gift, and then run back in front of the kerosene heater for warmth.

"That was where Umps and Umma always put it, so we keep it there to remember them."

When I went to bed that night, Albert was already lying on his. He put on the Beatles' *Something New.* "Think you're gonna like what you find under the tree in the morning," he said.

"How do you know?" I said. Albert never bought presents, since he rarely went into stores, but he usually gave my ma cash for a few gifts. "And what's with the ornaments?"

"Morning comes early on Christmas Day, isn't it?" he said, shutting off his light. His cigarette embers burned bright when he took a drag. I lay there, listening to the album, wondering if I would ever fall asleep. Just as the German version of "I Want to Hold Your Hand" came on, I felt the world grow smaller and smaller, and then, suddenly, Albert was shaking me awake.

"Come on, man. It's six thirty. We gotta get up and see what Santa brung you." I turned on my lamp and grabbed my clothes, still at the foot of my bed. Albert was sliding on a pair of jeans and then boots. "Beat you," he said, clomping downstairs.

"Albert get you up?" my ma said, smiling when I made it downstairs myself. I nodded and she laughed a little. "He's been moving around for the last half hour. I'm surprised you could stay asleep."

"Tough sometimes. How come I can't move into the other room?" I never asked this question — why I had to share with Albert when a perfectly good room almost twice the size of ours was just a curtain push away. Zach and Charlotte had shared it until she got pregnant and married. Then it was Zach's, except for the weekends Charlotte came over after her man smacked her.

"They'll be back," she said. "Kids are like planets. They go around the sun and then wind up exactly where they used to be. Every day is a repeat of an earlier day," she added, pleased with her own cleverness. She *would* think this, having moved us back in to take care of my grandparents. "Zach's having trouble making his bills, and Charlotte's man is just trouble. If neither one comes back by next winter, we can try it out. I thought you liked sharing a room with Albert. What are you going to do for a record player if you move into the other room?"

That had not occurred to me. The stereo was Albert's, and he had taught me how to use it respectfully a couple years ago, when I started paying attention to what was on the radio.

"Come here," Albert yelled. "Hurry up, see what Santa brung you." My ma pointed with her chin at the blanket blocking out the room's cold. I opened it and stepped through. Albert stood in the corner, near the patch of the tree he'd taken a personal interest in. Usually we waited for Charlotte and her family — and this year, Zach — to get here before we opened everything, but we had decided to open one present each early. I took a gift in to my ma. "Yeah, enough about that," Albert said when I came back. I reached down below those red and yellow ornaments and picked up the gift he obviously wanted me to unwrap, turning to go back where it was warm. "No, no, you gotta open it here," he said.

"Okay, okay," I said, confirming on the tag it was from him. It was clearly an album, unless this was one of his weird psych-outs. Sometimes he gave gifts that, when wrapped, seemed like they would be one thing and were something entirely different when you opened it. It was quite possible I was getting a wall calendar.

When I took the paper off, I still wasn't sure, but I understood his tree thing better. In the center of the cover were two shiny balls against a field of black, one dark yellow, the other red. The words *Venus and Mars* spread out from the upper left corner both horizontally and vertically, each sharing the "V." "An astronomy calendar?" I asked as we stepped back into the warmth of the dining room.

"No, dummy. Would I do that to you? Turn it over!" The back was covered in lyrics, proving it was an album. "The latest from Wings." I looked at the song list, recognized "Listen to What the Man Said," and wondered if Mr. Haddonfield had this one. If not, I could return the favor and let him borrow my copy. He could make a tape. "It ain't *Band on the Run*. Twin Fair was sold out, but this is newer anyway."

As I read the unfamiliar song titles, I felt this massive surge of happiness, a different fluttering in my belly from the garden slug of guilt that had taken up residence lately. My excitement was partly because I would be hearing most of these songs with fresh ears. Mostly, though, it was that Albert had made the choice himself. My ma would never have known to choose this gift. If we weren't both so freaked out by physical contact, I might have hugged my uncle in that moment. For his part, he remained his same mysterious self.

We went back in the main room. Albert squeezed the package from me before opening it. "Gloves? Let's see. Winter gloves. Great!" he said, tearing it open. "Champion! Five years for five years," he said, laughing at his string of successes in guessing my gifts correctly. "What time are the others coming?" he asked my ma, who was digging into a box of this nasty multicolored coconut candy she liked.

"Whenever they do," she said, offering us each one of her candies, but we both shook our heads. "Go on. I'll yell up when they pull in." We raced upstairs to our room, and he cleared the turntable while I unwrapped the cellophane on *Venus and Mars*.

"Hey, look!" I said. "Posters and stickers."

"Don't even think I'm taking down any of my posters. You'll have to get rid of some of that superhero nonsense you've got up now, 'cause my lady friends ain't going nowhere. Besides, you're probably getting to the age where you like my posters better now anyway," he said, laughing as I flushed hot.

The inner record sleeve had a ton of those same red and yellow billiard balls decorating it, with dotted lines between them to make them look like constellations. I handed him the album, and he put it on the turntable, stepping back carefully as the needle slid into its groove.

"So I hear you and Saphronia's boy —" Albert said, sitting on the edge of his bed.

"I thought you didn't want to hear about it," I said.

"Two boys steal a car on this reservation and take it off the rez? You're gonna hear about that." I whipped my head around, ready to explain, but Albert held his hand up. "Nothing big around here. You guys returned it safe and sound; I'm sure nothing's gonna come of it. Hell, that kid's old man might not even find out about it for a couple years. There ain't a person out here who hasn't felt the sharp tongues of this rez, but you be careful."

"I know. It wasn't my fault."

"As soon as you got in that car, it was your fault," he said. "Own up to what you do. But that's not really what I want to talk to you about. It's this," he said, tapping the album cover.

"What about it? Two planets, right?"

"Correct. One of these planets is red."

"I know. Mars. Mars, the red planet. I've heard that before, duh."

"The red planet is like the rez here. That other planet, Venus, I guess, that's the planet your buddy comes from. Now he might lend you albums and you'll have pizza nicey-nice every now and then, but these planets are still different. And we ain't got no rez rocket that's ever gonna get you to that other one, even though I know that's where you want to be."

"That's not true," I said, but again, he was using his Albert telepathy, knowing I was curious about that other world. What little I'd seen was a lot nicer than the world I was living in.

"We both know it's true. It's true that it's maybe even a nicer place. I'd argue for here, myself, but I can see how you might like it. But it's just nice for *them*, not you."

"How about we just listen to the new record," I said.

We got through side one before we heard my sister and her kids arrive.

On New Year's Eve, Zach picked me up right at eight. The temperature had dropped quite a bit and the hair in my nostrils froze almost as soon as I stepped outside. "You really gonna spend a night at a white kid's house?" he asked as we headed out. I nodded. "Okay, but you're on your own once you step outside this car. And I ain't picking you up either later tonight or tomorrow morning. I am off to P-A-R-T-A-Y."

"There's only one 'A' in party," I said. "The first one."

"Whatever."

When we pulled up, George stood by his garage, shivering. "What are you doing out here?" I asked him as I got out of the car and shut the door, stomping my feet to shake loose snow from my boots. "It's freezing."

"Waiting for you so you'd spot the house. Your mom drives a Plum Crazy Challenger?"

My brother hit the gas, fishtailing down the road. I ignored the question as I pulled two albums out of my bag. "Now, this is your dad's," I said, passing him *Band on the Run*, "but how long before we're supposed to go? Do we have time to play this?" I asked, revealing Queen's *A Night at the Opera*. Charlotte had given it to me for Christmas, and I liked it just as much as *Venus and Mars*. He nodded and led us into the house, kicking off his sneakers.

"Play the long song at the end of side two first, and sit right between the speakers," I said.

In the living room, George set couch pillows on the floor so we'd be in the perfect spot. "My parents are getting ready to go to the officers' club party," he said. "They'll probably be back before we are. The couple whose kid I watch are younger than my parents, so they tend to stay out later. I'll show you where you'll be sleeping."

He stood, but I pushed him to the pillows. "It can wait. Check this out." As "Bohemian Rhapsody" came on, he didn't know what to make of it at all, but once the piano started, he grinned and turned it up. I figured he'd like this song best because there was nothing else like it, but I was really looking forward to playing him the other side. "You're My Best Friend" was one of the songs there, and even if I thought it was way too lame to say something like that out loud, maybe playing the song would let him know that I felt that way.

Around the time the middle of "Bohemian Rhapsody" came on, with its wild vocals, his ma entered the room in a fancy dress. "What is this music?" she asked, and I handed her the cover, with its regal crest on the front and the small pictures of the band in the gatefold. "These men sound a bit like Wagnerian opera singers. George, we will have to purchase this one." Mr. Haddonfield walked in, wearing a dress uniform, and he held his hand out to look at the album cover, nodding.

"I can leave it if you'd like to borrow it," I said.

"Not necessary, son," Mr. Haddonfield said. "We can pick one up early next week, and we most definitely will. You boys be good and be careful. We'll probably see you in the morning. You have the number to the officers' club if you need to get ahold of me. Did you show your buddy here the room?"

"Yes, sir, I was just about to," George said, standing to escort his parents out the door. After they were gone, we walked to his room, and he showed me the air mattress that had been all made up with sheets, a blanket, and a spread. "That's where I'm staying, and those are for you to use." On George's bed, there was a bath towel, a hand towel, a washcloth, a little bar of soap, and a mini-bottle of shampoo. "Bathroom with the shower's down the hall for morning. I'll show you. But right here, there's a half bath, so if you need to go in the middle of the night, you just go in here."

"I'll sleep on the air mattress, man. I can't take your bed."

"Well, we'll see when we come back tonight. We better get over there. I don't want to be late." I grabbed my stuff and we headed out the door, walking two houses over.

"This is it?" I asked. "Jeez, I didn't even need to bundle back up for this close." He knocked, and we entered a house with a floor plan identical to his. He introduced me to a couple in their twenties. Their daughter was already asleep. All George had to do was check in on her every hour or so to make sure she hadn't awakened. Then, suddenly, the couple was gone.

"What'd I tell you," he said, pointing out a billiards table in the dining room. "You wanna rack while I get us something even more interesting?" I agreed, throwing the balls in the triangular-shaped frame on the table. I'd never racked before, so I put the red and yellow ones together near the front. "All right, come here," he said. He opened a drawer in a little stand and pulled out two heavy short glasses and a couple decanters. He poured us each a third of a glass of what looked like cherry pop gone flat, then closed the decanter and the drawer.

"Okay, now, when we have this, always stay over here," he said, leaning on the pool table. "You take a drink, then put it in the pocket. Remember which pockets our drinks are in and don't aim for those." He held his glass up. "To good friends," he said, knocking back half.

"Good friends," I repeated, and raised the glass to my lips. Though it smelled strange and medicinal, I took a drink, trying to match his. It burned sweet going down, like watered-down cough syrup. I tried not to gag as warmth rushed up my throat and made my head feel as if it were about to take off like a rocket. "What was that?"

"Cherry schnapps! Straight from Deutschland, a taste from my old home. Thought you'd like to know what it's like. That officer's wife is from the old country too. That's how I became their sitter. You want some more?" He walked back over to the small table and poured himself a little more.

"No, this is good for me," I said, still clearing my throat.

"I only take a little, and I've only done it a couple times. No glasses in sight gives you a couple minutes to hide the evidence if someone comes in. I always carry this too," he said, revealing a sleeve of candy violets. "They don't taste so great as far as candy goes, but they're good at masking the smell."

"What would your parents think if they knew?" I said.

"Well, they'd probably be a little annoyed because I'm having it while babysitting, but it's no big deal overseas. If I want a small glass of schnapps at home, on special occasions, they're fine. Just thought you might like it." He drained his glass, washed it, and popped a violet in his mouth. "See?" he said, breathing in my face. The blast of perfume and cough syrup wasn't exactly unsuspicious either.

"Anyway, that's one thing. Now — wait a second." He crept into the bedroom that in his house belonged to him. The drink tasted terrible, but it made me feel warm and more relaxed. I washed my glass, dried it on a paper towel, and put it back in the drawer.

"Okay, she's still asleep. Come on." I followed him into the couple's bedroom as he turned a small nightstand light on, and pulled open the bottom drawer on what was obviously the husband's side. He gently lifted out ironed boxer shorts and set them on the bed. Below them was a stack of magazines like Albert had. "Check these out," he said, handing me one and flipping open another. I went to sit on the bed and he grabbed me by the collar, pulling me up. "Don't be an idiot. They can't know we were in here."

We flipped through the magazines. This might have been exciting a year ago, but it had become routine to me after I started checking out Albert's magazine collection at home, beyond *Rolling Stone*. At the moment, I was more petrified of the couple coming home and catching us in their bedroom.

"Makes you feel —" George said, untucking his shirt so it would hang down in front of his jeans, as if that was fooling anyone. I'd used the same cover-up technique myself before, a couple times when Albert came bounding up the stairs to our room unexpectedly while I was checking his mags out. He would just laugh, busting me.

"Yeah, I know, but it makes me feel more nervous than anything."

"All right, worrywart," he said, taking one last look, then putting them back in the right order and fixing the boxers perfectly on top before leaving. "Let's go listen to that Queen album."

We put it on and he listened intently, but just a couple songs in, he seemed far away.

"Looking at those magazines got you jazzed up?" I said, laughing.

"Something like that," he said, which wasn't exactly the answer I thought I'd get. I'd been joking. "You know Stacey? Of course you do. You've known her longer than I have." I nodded. "She lives in one of the doubles down the circle. I deliver her paper, and even though it's really early when I make rounds, her bedroom light's on. I guess it takes her a long time to get ready. Wouldn't mind getting to know her a lot better," he said, vaguely smiling. "What do you think?"

"She's nice enough," I said. "She was nice to me before Summer told her to stay away, and since you've come, you know, she's been nicer. Not like those women you were checking out in the magazines, though."

"Well, of course not, doofus, but I don't have any chance of going out with any of those women. Stacey, on the other hand . . ."

I tried to think about Stacey in that way, but all I could see were her no-nonsense plaid skirts and sweaters. There was no way I could conjure her propped up on a zebra rug surrounded with candles and satin pillows.

"There's a youth dance tonight here in the complex. I was going to go and try to be near her at midnight. You know, when they do the kiss."

"So why didn't you go?"

"Well, I was going to if you didn't come."

"So I blew your big chance with Stacey?" I said.

"No, I don't mean it like that. I'm glad you're here. I wouldn't have asked you if I didn't want you to come. But you know, she's an air force girl." He didn't call her a kid like he did everyone else. "She knows you have to make friends fast. And I haven't seen her going out with anyone else. I could have a shot," he said. "Look," he added, reaching for his wallet. "She gave me her school picture from last year. She looks better now, but this is still pretty good." I flipped the photo over, and in tiny, neat penmanship, she'd written, *To a good friend from a good friend, From Stacey.*

"Don't read the inscription," he said, snatching it away to put it in his wallet.

"Romantic," I said, and laughed, though he didn't join me the way he usually did.

"You wanna listen to your album some more?" he asked, walking over to the stereo.

"Nah," I said. I felt even dorkier than usual, having planned to play him a song about best friends when he had an entirely different kind of friend on his mind. "Let's just watch TV?"

At midnight, the ball dropped in Times Square on the television. We shot another game of pool after George showed me how to properly rack the balls, alternating stripes and solids, keeping the eight in the middle. In his rack formation, the yellow and red were almost as far apart from each other as possible.

"If your thing is still on, you could go. I can hang in your room," I said after the kid's parents came home at one and we were walking back to his house. I remembered the BX's "For military families only" sign.

"Nah, I'm sure it was over fifteen minutes after the ball drop."

His parents weren't home yet, so we kicked off our shoes and headed to his room. He grabbed some clothes from the dresser and stepped into the half bath. "Be done in a minute," he said from behind the closed door. "Then it's all yours."

I didn't know what he thought I would do — probably just brush my teeth? I took my jeans off, folded them on the floor next to me, then put my socks on top. As I pulled off my shirt and T-shirt together, he stepped out, dressed in a full set of button-down pajamas.

"So where are your pj's? In your bag?" George asked.

"You're looking at them," I said, feeling suddenly as if my white briefs were even smaller and dingier and rezzier and more inadequate than they naturally were on any other day. They weren't even Fruit of the Looms, the big turquoise waist-band line announcing their Kmart store brand, low-budget status.

"You want a pair? I have extras."

"No, this is the way I sleep," I said, and crawled under the sheets on the air mattress, waiting for him to shut off the light.

"If you change your mind —" he said when we were finally in the dark.

"I'm fine," I said. We were silent for a little while. I heard his parents come in quietly and head down the hall, later than

George had expected. There didn't seem to be any stumbling, swearing, or vomiting, so their version of a New Year's Eve party was evidently quite different from the kind that went on at a lot of reservation houses. "You still awake?"

"Yeah, sure," he said. "But morning's going to come early when you're the paperboy."

"All right, never mind. I'll shut up."

"You wanted to talk about that thing with my dad and Indians?"

"I guess, but actually I wanted to ask you something different."

"You want me to put the light on?"

"No, it's better this way," I said. I took a deep breath. "You seem good with people. I'd say charming, even, but I don't want you to get a big ego." We both laughed a little, but we also knew I was taking us somewhere serious. "I hate to admit it, but I didn't have any friends when you got here. Not one."

"Come on, that's not true."

"It *is* true, and you know it as much as I do, but that's not the point here. I know why I picked you for a friend. It turned out that you were cool, and we liked the same things, Beatles, Wackies. I got lucky, but what was in it for you at first? And don't give me any of this I-make-my-own-decisions nonsense either. If we're really friends, you'll tell me the truth."

"Okay," he said, and then lay there silent for a bit. "Okay," he repeated. "What you said was true. We like some of the same things. Isn't that how most people become friends? And you were funny in a way that was different from everyone else. But . . . well, you've admitted you had some reasons for being my friend that had more to do with you than with me, so I guess I can admit the same thing. I mean, I wouldn't hang out with you if you were like that jerk Harold from the other end of the circle. Let's get that straight. The thing, though, the thing that has more to do with me? It really has to do with that thing about my dad."

"This better not be any mystery bull."

"It's not, I promise. My dad's an officer. Even when he's home, he's not home all that much. And remember, I was born in Deutschland, and spent most of my first ten years there. My *Mutti* stayed home to raise me, and since she was from there, we spent a lot of time in the city, unlike a lot of base families. I can speak clean English because of my dad, but Deutsch is still really my first language, and Deutschland the home of most of my memories.

"My dad, though? I don't know a ton about his younger life. I was goofing about it being a secret, just because I know secrets drive you crazy." I had never thought this about myself, but even as he said it, I realized it was true. "This is the first time I've lived in the States, even though I'm legally a US citizen. Both my dad's parents are gone and he hasn't taken me to the place he grew up. But it was sort of on a reservation. Don't you ever wonder about your dad's past life?"

I didn't know much about my dad's present life, so his past was kind of a back-burner issue. This still sounded like a line to me. I'd seen fair-skinned Indians, like Carson, and even blond ones, but there was no way on earth Mr. Haddonfield was an Indian.

"My grandparents were teachers on a reservation," George clarified, "and they lived on a little compound inside. Living there was a requirement, I guess, so all the kids my dad grew up with were mostly Indians. When Artie told me about you, I thought that maybe if I knew someone from a reservation too, it would be sort of like knowing my dad a little better. Make sense?"

"Sure," I said. "Thanks for telling me the truth." As we lay there, I could hear a group of partiers walking home from their event. It seemed like one of us should say something more, but neither knew what. After those people passed, I finally spoke. "You better get to sleep or that alarm's going to be pretty rude." I listened for the steady breathing of his sleeping, then grabbed my clothes and put them on in the bathroom, and then climbed back into the bed on the floor.

I didn't want to think this, but it sounded like his grandparents worked at an Indian boarding school, an idea never too far from my awareness, since my grandparents had been sent to one when they were young. Indian agents from the government had convinced their parents it was the only way they would survive in the changing world with white people. When they got to the school, their traditional clothes were taken from them and burned. They were beaten often, and they would be fed only when they spoke English. The only education they got was training in US customs, in speaking English, and in how to be laborers or domestic help for a future life of serving white people. The United States government had sponsored these schools, where the official motto was "Kill the Indian but save the man." The idea was that if Indian kids were taken from their families for long enough and exposed to a different world, they'd forget their language, families, and reservation life.

My grandparents beat the odds, came home together, reacquainted themselves with our way of life, and raised their children in it. They had almost never spoken of the boarding schools, but I'd learned enough to respect their silence.

I tried to imagine that George was telling me his grand-parents worked in a different kind of school, that I had misunderstood him, that his family hadn't abused mine, but I didn't get a lot of sleep. I had asked for the truth, and I definitely got more of it than I had bargained for. I also felt more and more like I was betraying something of my world for this friendship.

When the alarm went off, George got up. "I have to do the papers," he said, heading to the bathroom. "You can sleep in if you want."

I got up, folded the blankets, and stripped the bed. "I'll come with you," I said when he emerged, fully dressed, and we went quietly out the door. The porch held a wooden crate I hadn't noticed. George unlocked it and loaded a satchel with the papers that had been delivered during the night. "You got another bag? Be faster with help."

We finished in about twenty minutes, and I felt colder than I had during any New Yah trip ever. "That school you were talking about? Do you think it was called a boarding school?" I asked as we were walking home. If he knew, I had to know, for good or bad.

"He hasn't said a lot, in truth, but I don't think so. It sounded like it was on a reservation, but for some reason, the teachers had to live on the reservation too. Does that sound familiar to you? Did your teachers live on the reservation? We could ask him."

"No, ours just live in the area. No need to ask. Some other time," I said. I didn't know what would be worse, asking the question or the possible answer. I wanted to ask Albert what he thought, and I felt suddenly kind of alone, knowing he was probably already bundled up and shouting New Year's greet-ings up and down the reservation without me. The most hardcore New Yahers woke up and got ready while it was still dark, so they could step out and begin as soon as the sun came up. There was sort of a competition among some families as to who made their way around the rez first. Albert had been a lifelong contender for our neighborhood.

"Hey, look there," George said, pointing to a particularly bright star in the sky. "That's Venus. You only get to see it if you're up this early in the winter. Most of the year, really."

"Can you see Mars too?"

"Not now. In the winter, it comes above the horizon just as the sun is rising. Early summer mornings you can see them together. Mars's red glow makes Venus a little more yellow, plain as day. Maybe we'll sleep out in my yard this summer and wake up to see them. Might be better from your place, though. Less light from the city there, I imagine."

"Maybe you'll want to watch the stars with Stacey," I said.

"Come on, man. I was just talking. It was the schnapps, and, well, I trust you. You're my best friend."

"Me too," I said, unable to bring myself to say something that honest. For the first time in my life, I had a best friend, and then he had to give me that one difficult piece of information. I never thought friendship could be so complicated. I almost wanted to be screwed over by Carson again. "You think your dad's up yet?"

"Probably. Why?"

"I should be getting home."

"You don't want to have breakfast with us? I'll even give you the marshmallows from my Lucky Charms," he said, smiling, remembering I had told him there were never enough of them in a box to finish out equally with the cereal. "I thought we might go to the rec center, see who was hanging out around the pinball machines." The sun was coming up and he had a blond corona in its shine, surrounded by a vapor cloud of his breath.

"There's a thing we do on New Year's Day. It's like Halloween — well, not really. You go around and, well, it's complicated and stupid, but it's something I do," I said. "I wasn't planning to. I planned to have breakfast with you. I thought I could blow off this reservation thing, but now I feel like I can't. I'm sorry. And I really appreciate your willingness to skip out on getting a New Year's Eve kiss from Stacey for me. You're going to have to wait another whole year before you get your next shot."

It all came out like word vomit — inadequacy, embarrassment, insecurity, neediness, and an attempt at a joke. But this last fell flat. George didn't even smile, and he kept the same grim face as we got my stuff and climbed in the truck with his dad. We were silent all during the drive to the reservation.

"Hey, isn't that your mom's car?" he said as we blew by the trailer court where Zach lived. Groups of kids, all bundled up, ran from door to door, greeted by people with plates of cookies. We were obviously not slowing down, since Mr. Haddonfield knew where I lived. "What's going on? What are all those kids doing? Is that the thing you were talking about?"

"Yeah, our calendar was geared around the moons," I said. "Starting in February. But these days, our world has to deal with your world." *Like Venus and Mars*, I thought. "We need to know when the rest of the world says it's the new year. So all the kids run to houses and yell, 'New Yah!' and the owner gives you cookies or doughnuts or stuff like that for the news."

"Say, that's pretty cool," George said. "I can understand why you want to get home. We had holiday traditions in Deutschland that I miss since we've moved here. Sometimes, my *Mutti* offers to do them, but it seems lame with just the three of us. Thanks for telling me something about this place you come from, for real."

"That *is* very interesting," Mr. Haddonfield said. "I wonder if it's tied to the German settlements around here. 'New Yah' sounds a lot like 'New *Jahr*,' the German word for year."

"I don't know," I said. "I've never heard that. I can tell you some other things." I wanted to acknowledge George's putting himself out for me, inviting me to share his world, even passing up a chance to kiss a girl he was interested in. I couldn't tell him *all* the truths of my planet, but I could risk a couple. "For one, we don't have a car. My ma cleans houses for a living and we can't afford one. My brother gave me a ride last night, and I had to pay him to do it."

I don't know why I added that last part. I felt oddly mad, and I couldn't even say what I was mad about. Maybe it was the sort of expression they both wore, grimacing, slightly embarrassed for me and my bad manners. Was I really trying to share my life? Or was I just letting George understand the distance as I knew it? I remembered the sparseness of their house and the babysitting house, and the issue about that reservation school. The wall-to-wall-packed room I shared with Albert would never make sense to people who could leave without a trace in a matter of days.

We got to my house and I climbed out, thanking them both. I shut the truck door and they pulled out, heading back to their planet. When I stepped in the house, I could see Albert's winter coat was missing. He was gone, New Yahing without me. Suddenly, it felt a little like I didn't exist in either world, with no rocket to get to George's and no rez rocket to make it home. I had become the Invisible Boy again.

Fixing a Hole

"So I hear you came back kind of early," Albert said that night as I was getting ready for bed. "And you didn't steal my best cookies." He smiled, but it was true. What Carson used to do to me, I would then do to Albert. And this year, recognizing the unfairness of it, I didn't.

"Do you think there are still boarding schools?" I asked.

"You mean like Carlisle, where my dad and ma went?"

"What other kind is there?"

"There's all kinds of boarding schools for rich kids. Not exactly the same experience. But you're safe. The kill-the-Indian-but-save-the-man kind were still around when I was a kid, but mostly gone by the time you were born, I think. Your ma might know better. Why?"

"No reason," I said. His answer didn't really clear anything up. It was still possible that there was an Indian boarding school tied up in George's family's past. I took my T-shirt and socks off, and then remembered one other thing I wanted to ask. "Did you ever wear pajamas?"

"Pajamas? Like *The Brady Bunch*? Hell, no. I only wear

my skivs to bed as a courtesy for you. Pajamas are for kids. You want some?" he said, laughing. "You going backward?"

"No, I was just wondering."

"That white kid wore some, isn't it? Yeah, they live a different life. I guess their kids get to stay kids longer. Or I don't know, did you *ever* own a pair?"

I shook my head and turned off my light as he went downstairs, and then took my jeans off and folded them at the foot of my bed.

For the last couple days of break, I didn't pick up the phone, and neither did George. If we had lived in the same neighborhood, we would have been forced to run into each other on the road or something, maybe ironed out our awkwardness then, and I would have kept up with the news. But by the time we went back to school, George's neighborhood changed, and everyone our age who lived there knew the change.

So on the first day back, I was the only surprised one when George and Stacey walked in from the bus, their gloved hands clasped. Stacey was wearing the scarf George had worn when we'd gone out to do his paper route. I was still at my locker when they came up and stopped at his. Stacey said hi to me, and I smiled and gave her a nod. "Did you have a good Christmas?" she asked.

"Decent," I offered, and then I went into homeroom.

At lunch, they slid over together. She still wore George's scarf, draped like a fashion accessory. Things weren't as tight with Nelson gone, so I could have found somewhere else to sit, but there still wasn't anyone else I wanted to talk to, so I took the seat.

"George said you guys hung out together on New Year's,"

she said. "Too bad you didn't come to the dance. Would have been fun to have you there."

I scooped sloppy Fritos and ground beef up from my lunch tray and didn't say anything, picturing the BX sign again.

"Since you babysat with him, I hope he cut you in on the pay," she added, tickling George's nose with the scarf's fringe. "Maybe we could all hang out sometime. If your mom gives you a ride up to our area, maybe my mom can give us a ride to the mall, and George's mom could pick us up, or some combination."

She raised her eyebrows, smiling at me, which seemed to require an answer. I waited for George to say I didn't have a car, but he made a small, pinched smile, raising his eyebrows too.

"Might be kind of tough," I said. "My ma works a lot." I was pretending that the next six months held so many obligations, I wouldn't be able to squeeze in a trip to the mall. It sounded weak and stupid even as it came out of my mouth.

"Maybe summer, then?" she said, casually eating Fritos off George's tray. George watched her hand as it went from his tray to her mouth. He took a couple of hers too, moving slowly at first, but by the end of lunch, they were taking turns biting pieces off the cookie from his tray.

George's takeover by Stacey felt like the end of *Invasion of the Body Snatchers*, where I'd discovered that the last human in Santa Mira had become one of the pod people after all. He was his friendly self, sort of, at first. He seemed to accept that if we were going to be hanging out, it would be at his house, and I was over there maybe twice a week, or at least once. But more and more, his time was filled with Stacey, though he was too polite to say so. After a while, he halfheartedly invited me only to hang with him and Stacey at their base rec center. I started politely declining, and by March, he quit asking altogether. Sometimes the three of us worked together in the library, but even that I let slide, since they spent the period writing notes to each other in a spiral-bound notebook set between them. Could I blame him? Of course not. How do you blame a friend for his first girlfriend, just because you didn't have the same kind of fortune shine down on you? But it didn't make my school life easier or less lonely.

Loneliness isn't like having a tooth pulled. When that happens, once the dentist yanks the tooth, there's the bleeding hole you shove tea bags into, and you're feverish for a few days, and then, after a while, you start sticking your tongue in there, feeling your body knit itself back together. The pain is like sparks to the touch, but there's less and less as time goes on, and then one day, it's just this gap, and the rest of your teeth close in on it, like they've been waiting for this all along.

No, loneliness is like the feverish tea-bag day all the time. You touch that spot every day, when you walk to your locker and your former best friend looks at you and neither one of you knows what to say, so he goes off with his girlfriend and you go back to the life you knew before, except it's worse than before, because you know what the other side feels like now. And the real worst, worst part? It doesn't fade at all. The scar tissue never grows around the hole.

Artie joined the rest of our section in more or less not talking to me, even as George still made halfhearted attempts to include me. Those efforts seemed like guilt, and there was nothing to be guilty about. It was just the way of things. Unless some Indian girl was going to wind up in my class, one who had to also find me interesting, there was a zero percent chance I'd be going out with anyone. I considered Zach's idea more, that if I started slipping in my grades just enough, I'd wind up in the middle section, where there was sure to be someone I grew up with.

At home, my ma never mentioned my New Year's Eve adventure after I got home, other than to observe that I was earlier than she'd expected me, as she had on that night with Carson. Albert, on the other hand, was never the kind to let something rest.

"You don't play that album I gave you too much," he said one night. "You don't like it?"

"I like it fine," I said.

"You don't like its lessons, isn't it?"

"Don't you have some magazine to drool over?" I asked.

"Nothing new. I know all these chicks," he said, gesturing to his stack. "And the truth? Your Droopy dog face is getting *me* down, so I know it ain't doing wonders for you."

"Well, then quit looking at me," I said. The winter wind pushed small puffs of snow between the upper and lower panes of the bedroom windows. I kept saying we should tape them shut, but Albert said he liked to have fresh air every now and then, even in the coldest winter.

"You're going to have to get back out there sometime. You got a buddy out there, a guide right now. He could help you get used to knowing what that other world is like, without you being thrown right in the middle of it. But if you're ready to come back to our planet, I got a surprise for you tomorrow. If you're up for it."

"What?"

"Well, it wouldn't be a surprise if I told you, would it?"

So, because it was Albert and because I didn't have anything better to do, the next day, after school, we bundled up and walked down the road. "Don't worry, it ain't far," he said. When we crossed the bush line and I saw Bug Jemison had a kerosene lantern on, I had a good idea of where we were going, which was confirmed when we turned into his driveway.

Bug was sitting in his chair near a pool table, a gallon of Rhine wine glowing in the kerosene light. "So this is the guy, huh?" he said, looking me over. "Lemme see your hands." I stuck them out and he grabbed them both, turning them palm up, and then ran his thumb over the tips of each finger. "Kind of small. Might be a hard reach. No experience at all either, I'm guessing. Well, no experience of the kind he needs," he said, and both he and Albert laughed. "Shining your pole might give you calluses on your palms, but where you need 'em for this is on the tips."

I'd had enough dealings with this kind of elder to know he was testing me, and it was my job not to get pissed off. If elders knew they could embarrass you, they would go for it every time. "Depends on your technique," I said, and they both burst out laughing harder.

"All right, bring my gee-tar out," he said, pointing to a case in the corner. He had a wooden leg, and I'd heard he'd gotten pretty used to ordering people around in his house or throwing them right out the door. I grabbed the case. "Okay, now give it here." He strapped it on and played some old country tunes I vaguely recognized. Then he took it off, drew a big slug from the bottle, and offered it to me. I declined, but Albert took a drink from it. "Your turn."

"To do what?" I said.

"Put it on," he said, lifting the strap out for me to slip under. The guitar was enormous.

"The one you —" I started, then remembered there was something funny about that exchange between the Bug and Harvey Mastick. "The one Carson had seems smaller than this."

"It is. It's a three-quarter scale, for travel or kids. Some people say start on those and move up to this. But you do that, you get the fingering all wrong when you switch. Now, you don't want to get your fingering wrong, do you?" I knew they were going to laugh again and this time I just decided to join them. "So you a kid, or you wanna be a man? Which one are you?"

"A man," I said.

"Pretty dood, pretty dood," he said, in his signature alteration of the word "good." "Okay, we're gonna start on chords. The first two you're gonna learn are D and A." He took each of my fingers and lined them up and said, "This is a D. Strum."

I did. It would be awesome to say I sounded incredible, but I sounded clunky and thick, almost like I had dropped the guitar.

"The next one is just a little up," he said, moving my fingers. "This will be easier for you than it is for me because your fingers are small. The A is crowded. Now you're gonna go back and forth between these two until your fingers hurt so bad, you can't stand it anymore. And if you're a real man, you'll go another ten minutes after that. There's only one way to build up those calluses, and it ain't by doing what you've been up to when you're on your lonesome."

We started slowly, with lessons and practice every day for an hour, and for the first week, I could barely play those two chords, it hurt so bad. But I got faster and the sound got cleaner. Albert shot pool while I practiced. Sometimes, nieces and nephews of the Bug's came over. We were sort of half-assed relatives. My cousins Innis and Ace were his nephews from his mother's side, but none of them had any interest in learning music.

As spring came on, and the sun stayed up longer, I stuck around at the Bug's later, playing, learning actual songs, but none I was all that fond of. Whenever I mentioned a Beatles song to him, he'd say I wasn't ready. "Most of their songs sound easy, but there's at least one killer chord in even the simplest arrangements. That's how smart they were. Everyone else took shortcuts," he said. "That was the problem with Hank Williams. Taught everyone how to do what he could do. Suddenly, look at that, he was out of work, and the next thing you know, he's dead in the back of a Cadillac on his way to a gig. He knew he'd given away all his secrets."

"Aren't you giving away your secrets to me, Bug?" I asked.

"Not on your life. You don't have a big enough brain to hold my secrets. But I do think you're ready for the next step tomorrow."

When I walked in twenty-four hours later, I discovered the next step was a duet. Carson was sitting there, in the chair I usually sat in, his three-quarter-scale guitar in hand. We hadn't really hung out since before Christmas, but we were going to be stuck on the same planet with each other for the rest of our lives, so I strapped on the Bug's guitar. "Let me warm up a little," he said, and started playing "Yesterday." "Join in if you want." I could play some of it, but there were still blank spots, holes. I watched to see what he was doing. It was going to be a while before I was at his level.

"So how's school?" he asked.

School sucked, but I didn't want to admit that. One thing I had learned in my daily practices with the Bug was the importance of rhythm. Before a song could have a great melody line and killer words to hang on that line, the backbeat needed to be there. I could do rhythm fairly easily, but I recognized that most people notice it only when you screw it up. Fading out steady is better than shifting abruptly, and when Carson asked, I realized more fully that George and Stacey had largely faded out of my rhythm, or I'd faded from theirs.

"It's fine," I said. "How's it at your end?"

"Fine too."

"Things going okay hanging with the Wedgie King?" I asked, but he didn't respond. "Math is a little hard," I added, "but I'm getting used to it." I'd given up on the idea that I should sacrifice my grades for finding someone from home. School was tough enough without faking it.

"If Lewis can't hang out with his white friends," Carson said, in a dry math teacher voice, "and his Indian friends know he ditched them, who can he hang with? Solve for Friend X." He started strumming the Beatles' "I'm a Loser." "Come on, Gloomis, join in. You know this one."

"There a problem here, you whippersnappers?" the Bug asked.

"No, no problem," I said, stepping back into the familiarity of my old life with Carson. I strummed the chords I knew, leaving empty spaces where he'd moved beyond me and, as usual, wouldn't show me the path he'd found.

No Words

The week after spring break was over, we met the eighth-grade chorus instructor, Miss Fox. I could tell immediately that she would have none of that Beatles nonsense with her Choraliers. I stepped into her office for my scheduled tryout and sat down in the student chair off to the side of her piano.

The audition started terribly and went worse. First I asked her if I could postpone my audition by a week because I had a cold, and she insisted colds do not mask an ability to sing. After a couple failed attempts at some new music, she dug into my current binder.

"Let's try this one from your spring concert," she said, handing me sheet music. It was a medley from *The Music Man*, and she asked me to sing the "Till There Was You" segment. I'd had the hardest time with this song in the spring concert, because I kept hearing Paul McCartney's arrangement of it from *Meet the Beatles!*, instead of the bland, plodding version we had on the sheet music in front of us. McCartney was what streamed out of my mouth now.

"Mr. Blake, I didn't ask you to interpret. Sing the notes as written." But I'd committed the Beatles' version to memory so long ago that I couldn't unlearn it. "You're excused," she said finally. "The results will be posted on the music bulletin board by the end of the week."

I knew my future as I walked out. Sure enough, even before the spring concerts that year, I was listed for Boys Chorus, and both George and Stacey had made Choraliers.

On the same bulletin board with the cut list, there was a sign in bold letters: NEED A SUMMER JOB? BUILD CHARACTER! SAVE FOR COLLEGE! ACT NOW! SPOTS ARE LIMITED! INQUIRE AT OFFICE FOR ELIGIBILITY REQUIREMENTS. I figured, *Why not?* What else was I going to do? If I got one of those jobs, there was maybe a chance of my own guitar in the future. I didn't mind going to the Bug's regularly, but there were nights when I would have just liked to play at home, in my room, alone.

When I stepped into the office, the school secretary, Mrs. Tunny, handed me an application before I even asked. Apparently I fit the bill. If your family was considered low income, you could work for the school as a minimum-wage youth laborer for thirty hours a week through the summer, starting after the July fourth weekend. All I had to do was pass a physical, scheduled at the beginning of lunch period.

After my physical, I got to lunch late and showed my pass from the doctor to the lunch lady. She nodded, but said the free-lunch ticket line was shut down already, so I went to sit down. At the table, George and Stacey sat separated by three other kids, the first time since January when they weren't, more or less, glued at the hip. It seemed weird, the gap so big it was clearly meant to be noticed. The place next to George was empty.

"So where were you?" he asked as I sat down.

"I'm getting a job this summer," I said, "and had to have a physical for working papers."

He leaned forward on his elbows and crossed his arms, like he wasn't listening to me. "Here, I got you something," he said, looking out at the room and rapping the knuckles hidden behind his crossed arms on the table. Lifting his cupped hand, he revealed my free-lunch ticket. I crossed my arms on the table as well, and the card passed from his fist to mine.

"How'd you do that?"

"I just went up and said your name, they slid a sheet of paper with names on it to me, I signed it, and they gave it to me. They don't pay attention. Hurry up. You still have time to eat."

I got up and leaned close for a second. "What's going on with you and Stacey?"

"I thought you were going to say thanks."

"Well, I am. Sorry. Thank you. But I thought my question was more urgent."

"Later. Go get your lunch. Mine's getting cold waiting for you." When I got back to the table, Stacey had rejoined George, so I sat with Artie, who could still be counted on for occasional conversation. George and Stacey seemed to be negotiating something, each trying to be nice and firm at the same time, but in low tones that no one else could hear.

"What's that all about?" I asked Artie.

"You ought to know," he said, dipping a french fry in ketchup. "You're the cause."

"I don't know what you're talking about. I haven't spent that much time with either of them since they started hanging out."

"Going out. They're *going* out, not *hanging* out," he said. "I don't know all the details. George has something he's giving you, but she wants it, and since she's his girlfriend, she's claiming first dibs."

That was the most I was getting out of anyone there, so I ate.

You knew the end of the school year was coming because the new cycle of fire drills began that afternoon. Few things annoyed Mrs. Thatcher as much as fire drills, but she had no choice, and we all trotted outside when the robot cat cried.

"We could leave now," Artie said as we stood around the school yard. "It's not like we're going to do anything in chorus anyway except maybe hear another endless, boring Paul McCartney story. By the time we get back in, it'll be time to gather our junk up."

"But then it's back to homeroom," George said. Even though the final period lasted five minutes, attendance would be taken, and it would be noted if the three of us hadn't made it back.

"We could catch the early explosion down at Good Intentions," Artie said, trying to bribe George by using his "nonswearing" name for the place. "Then we'd get two in today."

Behind me, small annoyed and surprised voices kept bursting through the conversation — little "Ow! Ouch!" notes. I didn't really want to look. Invariably, if you pay too much attention to someone else's troubles, it's like they sneezed their trouble onto you. The disruption to your life starts off minor, like a stuffy nose, but it can easily escalate into catastrophe, like full-blown pneumonia, an oxygen-tent-in-the-hospital kind of difficulty.

As it turned out, I didn't need to move at all. Trouble found me just fine on its own as something whacked me hard on the butt. I let the first hit go by, but after the second, I couldn't pretend I wasn't getting smacked by someone.

I turned to see the Wedgie King just as he was about to deliver whack number three. He hit me in the back pocket instead, right on my wallet. The grounds crew hadn't cleaned all the winter's dead branches yet, and the King held a newly dead one, still glistening with sap at the break. Since it wasn't brittle, it delivered the kind of sting that stayed with you long after the whack.

"Cut it out, asshole," I said as he wound up again to strike.

"You talking to me?" he said, mimicking Robert De Niro in *Taxi Driver*. Pretty much all the tough guys had been saying that for the last few months, since commercials for the movie first started playing on TV. I only understood later, as I thought about this moment over and over again, that he was not really asking me a question. I wondered then if I could have avoided a lot of trouble by keeping my mouth shut . . . but that wasn't what I did.

"Is there any other asshole hitting me with a stick at the moment?" I answered.

"What?" he said. This was amazement on his part, not an actual follow-up question, but I again misunderstood.

"I said, 'Is there any other asshole hitting me with a stick?' " I repeated, then, remembering, added, "at the moment."

Most of the chorus, with their built-in Spidey senses of self-preservation, immediately started backing away slowly.

"I don't think you should be saying those things to me," the Wedgie King said, grabbing the collar of my shirt and twisting it up around my throat.

"If you hadn't been hitting me with a stick, then I wouldn't have had to," I said.

"Let's take it easy here," George said, stepping forward.

"Back off, baby killer," the Wedgie King said.

"Evan, what are you doing with that stick?" Mrs. Thatcher said, wandering over to us.

"Just helping the groundsmen, Mrs. Thatcher," the Wedgie King, evidently named Evan, said, letting go of my shirt. "Wouldn't want them to hit it cutting the school's lawn."

"Well, throw it over into those bushes and be done with it," Mrs. Thatcher said, pretending that she hadn't seen him whacking people with it. I figured that was the end of the incident. The all-clear bell went off and we headed back to the entrance.

"I want to stop at my locker," George said, jogging ahead of Artie and me as we got back to the school building. I crossed the front hallway, the afternoon sun glare on the floor blinding me, when it was cut suddenly with a fast-moving shadow.

Evan landed on my back, squeezing his legs around my ribs as if he'd hopped on a horse, and he began whaling on my face and head. Shadows shifted around us, and I couldn't pick out who was who, but I knew all of my classmates would have kept moving, and all of Evan's friends would crowd around us for some new entertainment. My quickest instinct was to protect my glasses. I was wearing a welfare pair and we would in no way have the cash to get them fixed if they were broken. Once I had my glasses in hand, I spun backward and slammed us against the lockers. This was hard enough to drop Evan, but not hard enough to get him to reconsider his decision to target me.

"Truck!" he yelled, hitting me more rapidly. "This little freak is actually fighting back! What the hell's he thinking? I am speechless! You hear me? Speechless!"

"Better teach him a good one, Evan," the helpful Truck said. "Come on, they announced that we got to go back to homeroom. I don't wanna waste a good afternoon in detention."

Evan delivered one last kick to my butt and stood with his crowd. I put my glasses on and saw satisfaction in all their faces. "Yeah, summer's almost here, but we got a whole long year ahead of us for that lesson," Evan said. "Can you believe it? Fighting back?" he repeated as he left.

I went to homeroom and perched on my seat. My butt still stung from the whipping stick, and I didn't want to touch any of the hot spots on my face and head. I'd been in fights at home before, but this felt different, like the Wedgie King was looking for blood. George wandered in, looking at something in a notebook he'd just gotten from his locker. I expected most of my class to ignore what happened, but how did George not see me get jumped? Was he pretending to be as blind as Mrs. Thatcher? That didn't seem possible, but the garden slug in my belly was back.

"What happened to you?" Summer shouted at me from across the room. "You get sunburned out there? You're all red." She paused. "Red? Oh my God! You really are a redskin today!" Her friends dutifully laughed. Rose repeatedly slapped the palm of her right hand to her puckered lips, making what she thought was an Indian sound, until Summer observed that she was smudging her lipstick. George looked up, puzzled, then frowned, but no one else even glanced at me. They continued their silence through the afternoon announcements, including Mr. Barnes's approval of our fire drill, then the bell rang and most of my class split.

"What *did* happen to you?" George asked as we packed our book bags and left the building. "The last I saw, that kid was getting the message to leave you alone."

"Really? You mean the guy who called you baby killer and you just ignored it? That kid? Is that the one who was getting the message?"

"Hey, you've only seen my dad on good days. He's mostly that way, but the rules I have? There is no negotiating. And not fighting at school is one of them. He prepared me."

"Fighting lessons?"

"Pretty much the opposite. He told me I'd hear 'baby killer' even though he didn't spend any time in Vietnam at all. But he also demanded that I walk away from any fight, and if I get caught fighting? No more Stacey or much of anything else good. Period."

At the buses, Stacey stood with some of her other friends, who closed around her. George, Artie, and I stood together.

"You gonna bruise? I bet you are," Artie said to me.

"Hope not."

"I ain't messing with those Misty Meadows kids. Particularly that one."

"Why not that one?" I asked. "Seems like the same kind of butthead as his friends."

"Oh no. That one is special," Artie said, almost amused to inform me of my new luck. "That kid is Evan Reiniger. He's got a free pass to do pretty much anything he wants."

"Like Reiniger Field?" George said. "Reiniger Scoreboard? Reiniger Concess —"

"I got it, thank you," I said. "Is this one of your Artie stories? Like how you used to say Good Intentions wasn't any fun so I wouldn't come?" I was worn-out, and my hot spots were already throbbing.

"Nope. No story at all," he said, pretending I hadn't said anything else. "That's the truth. Why do you think he never gets called out for all the bull he pulls around school? The whole sports program wouldn't exist without his dad's booster club dollars."

"Well, I don't care," I said. "I'll talk to a teacher. Someone at this school has to operate by rules instead of connections. It'll work out."

"I don't know what planet you live on, but just in case stupid is contagious, I'll be over here," Artie said. "You coming, George?"

"In a minute," George said.

"So you want to tell me what's going on with you and Stacey?" I asked after Artie walked away.

"We'll be getting on the buses soon."

"We could walk," I suggested. "Little chilly, but it's nice enough out. Besides, I gotta walk off these kicks or I'm gonna get a charley horse."

"All right," he said, and then calling to Artie, "If the driver asks, just tell her I've walked."

We sat on the steps and watched the buses load. It was easier to leave after they'd gone, so we wouldn't get caught up in bus backdraft as we made our way along the cinders. "Did that kid really hurt you?" George asked.

"Do you have eyes? No changing the subject," I said, but he wasn't fully in our conversation. His eyes followed Stacey as she laughed with her friends, the same way they'd been following her at lunch. Even when she got on the bus, he watched as she made her way to the back, moving through each succeeding window panel until she disappeared in the shadows.

"So you've got this job?" he asked after the buses pulled out and we started walking. I gave him an overview — when it started, when it ended, what the pay was, glossing over the application's poverty requirements. I wouldn't find out what the actual work was until I showed up for orientation on July fifth.

"What if your job is cleaning toilets?" he said, grinning.

"Then I guess I'll ask my ma for tips," I said. I knew his grin would falter, but if I was going to tell him some truths about my life, I expected him to respect them.

"I'm sorry. I forgot. Work is work, man. A job is a great thing. I've been able to get some terrific stuff with the money I've saved from my paper route. You'll see. Will you be able to keep it in the fall?"

"Hard to say. Some jobs roll over into the school year, but I probably won't qualify for one of those until next year. Lots of kids want steady, reliable work. I'll have to wait my turn."

"Might be hard, like sweeping the cafeteria if your classmates are around," he said.

Maybe he was rethinking having a friend who doubled as a part-time school custodian. "You think I'm invisible now? Look at the color chart on our class, man. I am the only person who falls into the off-white end of the spectrum. People already have their ideas about who I am, and they were in place long before I set foot in that junior high."

"It hasn't affected you that bad. I mean, we're friends," he said. "And Stacey and Artie."

"If you were gone, I'd go back to my old invisible status that moment."

"Well, maybe nobody's just taken the time to get to know you."

"And why do you think that might be?"

"I don't get what you're saying. When I came here, you were one of the first people who talked to me. Well, after I talked to you. Why can't that happen with anyone else?"

"Long story. Maybe you should ask Artie at Good Intentions. I can probably tell you what he'd say, but you wouldn't believe me." We walked along in silence for a moment. "So what's going on with you and Stacey?"

"You think you might want to hang with me on a weekend again? Car situations aside?"

"It's possible. Why? What's up?" I was bracing myself, hoping he was not still angling to come over, though I was pretty sure I'd sealed the end of that conversation on New Year's.

"You think your parents would let you go away? You gotta say yes."

"But you haven't even told me what I'd be saying yes to."

"Three words. Wings over America."

"I don't know what that is."

George reached into his back pocket, revealing a neatly folded newspaper clipping. The top half was mostly a picture of a large, metallic-looking W with wings coming off the outward arms. Paul McCartney and Wings were starting a tour, calling it Wings over America.

"My dad cut this out of the *New York Times*. He gets it delivered no matter where we live. Here," he said, pointing to the fifth concert: Maple Leaf Gardens in Toronto.

"Toronto? That's like an hour and a half away."

"You've met my dad. An hour and a half is nothing to him, particularly if it involves the Beatles in some way. He doesn't even like baseball, but we've been to Candlestick Park for a game because it was the last place they played a concert."

"You sat through a baseball game just to be in the same place?"

"He's crazy. This is the first time Paul McCartney is touring America since that concert at Candlestick. If there wasn't a show close enough for driving, you can be sure he'd hitch on to one of the air transports and catch the tour somewhere else."

"Okay, so lucky for you, Toronto's on the list," I said.

"What'd I tell you about acting dumb, Shoe Box?" He'd taken to calling me that if I made a particularly dense observation. "Lucky for me, *and for you*, Toronto is on this list."

The ad said tickets went on sale on Saturday. "I don't have ten dollars," I said.

"Already taken care of. You can borrow it and pay me back after you've got that job. Rose's dad owns the Ticketron, don't forget. She might not be fond of you, but she likes me fine, so she's saved back three of the best seats. I just bring her money on Monday and she'll hand them over." He smirked, proud of his dealings. "It was a little tricky, since Rose is friends with Stacey, but I don't know what Stacey was thinking, wanting to come. My dad isn't letting his teenage kid spend the night in Toronto with his teenage girlfriend. He's a great guy, but he's not insane."

That explained the lunch-table seat swap, but something still felt off to me. "Couldn't Stacey's dad have gone?" I asked. "And what's this about staying overnight? How much do you think I'm going to make this summer?" George had no way of knowing that my paycheck was dedicated to helping pay our bills and getting me some actual brand-new school clothes for the first time, with maybe a few albums along the way, if I was lucky. And in fantasy land, there was always a guitar to think about.

"We would leave Friday afternoon, stay the night in Toronto, see some sights on Saturday, stay the second night, and then after the show on Sunday, we could sleep on the ride back. My dad will either drop you off late that night, or you can stay at our place and go straight to school with me on Monday. Look, don't worry about the cost of the room. My dad says the room costs the same whether it's only me and him or if we bring a third, and he said there's these awesome sights to see. He's been to concerts in Toronto before, but this is the first time I'm old enough to go along."

"I'll have to check with my ma, but don't get your hopes up too high." I said this to him, but really, I was saying it as much to myself. I'd been wanting to go to Toronto for years, but I figured it wasn't ever going to happen, and now here was the possibility, dumped right into my lap, but with the likelihood of at least two roadblocks. "And Rose won't say outright that she won't sell me a ticket. She'll simply not have enough when the time comes to buy them."

"Don't be paranoid. She said I could have three, and all I would have to do is bring the money on Monday." We got to my Snakeline turn. "So, um, you wanna come over? We'll give you a ride home."

"Nah, I better get home. I'll call you tonight about whether I can go," I promised, not sure how I could convince my ma that some white family liked me enough to be willing to take me to Toronto with them for a rock concert. She was going to wonder how that even happened. "Thanks for getting my lunch ticket today." He nodded and turned. "Wait!" I yelled. "And thanks for not saying anything."

"That's what friends do, man. They can know what's nobody else's business, and it's okay." We shook hands, the way we'd each seen men do in friendship on TV shows, and started walking away again. Then I thought of something else I wanted to ask, so I yelled his name one last time and we backtracked, meeting in the middle.

"Look, if we're gonna keep talking, why don't we go to my place, where we can at least have something to drink and listen to some tunes. I mean, it's been a while."

"No, I promise, this is the last time." I took a deep breath. It had been a while. I guess we were telling the truth. "Why did you ask me? You're smart enough that you could have figured out some way for you and Stacey to go. Be honest."

"My dad didn't tell me I could invite a friend. He said I could invite *you*."

"Because?"

"I don't know. I guess because even though things have been whacked lately, I mean about me spending all my time, um, elsewhere, I've told him you're my best friend. I don't know that I've had one of those before. I don't even like saying it, it sounds so dorky."

"I know what you mean. I never had one before you either, except for maybe my uncle Albert, and how lame is that to count your relatives as your best friends? They're stuck with you, no matter what." They didn't really have a choice in the matter, the way George and I could choose to be in each other's lives or not. "Thanks for being willing to say it," I said. "I have kind of a hard time with things like that."

"Never noticed," he said. I punched his shoulder and he punched mine back. And in that way, we found our friendship again, with neither one of us needing to win, the way Carson always insisted on. I watched him turn and head down the rest of Clarksville Pass. Occasionally, he turned back to wave, and then I started on my own way.

A little while later, I came up by the shack that had belonged to Marie's family. All the snow had melted around the house, but the ground was soft, new grass growing through the previous year's dead stuff. Marie had been nice and someone I enjoyed spending time with, and though I still saw her every now and then, I missed her being in our class. I wondered if she would still be living here if we hadn't called her Stinkpot, or if it would have made any difference if I had stopped all by myself and just called her Marie. Maybe one fewer voice would have changed things, and she wouldn't have to live in the city and deal with a life so different from ours.

When I got home, Albert had Black Sabbath's *Paranoid* blaring, so I went up to our room. He switched it over to the Beatles' *Revolver*, the album Zach had given me for Christmas.

"I have a chance to go see Wings," I said.

"They're not coming to Buffalo. I already checked."

"In Toronto. You think my ma will go for it?"

"Do you have to pay?"

"Only for the ticket, and my friend's loaning me the cash until I get my first paycheck."

"That kid whose house you went to? What is it, ten bucks?" I nodded. He reached into the little drawer above his magazine collection. "Here, pay him up front. Don't owe white people anything. When the time comes, I'll give you some spending money too. You can pay *me* back."

"Well? You didn't answer. Do you think my ma will go for it?"

"I'll take care of that," he said, stuffing the cash into my shirt pocket. "Toronto's cool," he said, grinning. "I played a few games there. Zach did too. Don't you worry. I'll make sure she says yes. You remember, don't borrow any money. You don't need that on your back."

"Thanks, Albert," I said later that night as we each lay on our beds. He nodded, his cigarette ember bobbing in the dark. *Revolver* was still on the turntable, so I hit the Play button and we relaxed, and eventually closed our eyes, floating downstream as it came to an end. It took a long time to fall asleep. I was jittery with excitement as Toronto's skyscrapers began rising, building themselves in my head.

I don't know what Albert said, but my ma agreed that I could go, and on Monday, I handed George my money.

But Rose said, "Sorry, George," when he held out the thirty dollars to her later that morning. "We had a change of plans, and I didn't have your number, so I couldn't call you. Summer, Stacey, and I are going, and my mom, dad, and my brother. The show's sold out, but we have one extra ticket if you want it. We're in the sixth row, on the floor. You can stay with my dad and my brother, while we all will share a room with my mom." She smiled at him.

"No, thank you," George said. He came back to our seats, red-faced. "I told my dad I was going to get these," he said to me. "He trusted me to do a good job, and now we don't have any."

"I warned you this is what my life is like," I said. "Stacey might not have been told all that nonsense about the reservation when she was growing up, but you can bet her friends were."

Stacey came over and asked to speak with George privately. I went to the piano, but I could hear them anyway. "Rose says she could persuade her brother to give his up," Stacey stage-whispered, "if you need two, for you and your dad, but that's the best she could do. It would be *so* fun if we were going together, and these seats are in the *sixth* row."

George grimaced, looked at me, and then asked her if he could get back to her. She smiled and said sure, if he wanted to stop over and see her that night with his decision, that was fine. I sat down as roll call started, feeling that the worlds had gone back into their old familiar alignment: Venus and Mars, impossibly far apart.

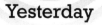

11

Yesterday

Whatever decisions George came to, I wasn't informed of the specifics. He just told me that after school on the Friday of the concert weekend, I needed to be ready to go. I let the Bug know I wouldn't be around for practice, and he warned me not to let too much time go by or I'd have to build up calluses again. I promised it was only the weekend. I had a borrowed pair of pajamas in my bag and my red card in my wallet, along with forty bucks, courtesy of Albert, which I checked my pocket for compulsively. When Mr. Haddonfield pulled up at the end of our driveway, I could see it was just the three of us heading over the border and into Toronto.

"Got your ID?" Mr. Haddonfield asked as we neared customs and immigration.

"Yes, sir," I said, reaching into my wallet. My worn red construction-paper reservation ID card looked even shoddier than usual next to their neat little covered passport booklets.

"What is this?" he said.

"It's my ID."

"Son, you won't be able to get across the border with this.

I'll do what I can to vouch for you, but if they have any questions about who you are, my hands are —"

"Don't worry, sir. I do this all the time. We member nations of the Haudenosaunee Confederacy have a treaty with the US and Canadian governments. Canada isn't a foreign country to us. It's part of our territory, and so we can cross into it with just our ID cards."

I knew I sounded like I was reading a public service announcement on TV, because in some ways, that was what I was doing. Everyone from the reservation learns very young what we're supposed to say at the bridges. I had begun calling myself a Native North American to US border guards at the age of six, and I got my ID card the summer I was ten. It listed my name, reservation address, and clan, and it had a small photo of me glued on and was signed by the Tuscarora Nation enrollment clerk. Some border guards used to pretend they didn't know what we were talking about when we crossed over, but we'd been assured it was now part of their training. We enforced the treaty among the United States, Canada, and Haudenosaunee Confederacy formally once a year, in July. Most kids in my class thought of history and government as something boring and not connected to their lives, but I knew better.

"IDs and places of birth?" the border guard at the booth asked.

"Bloomington, Minnesota," Mr. Haddonfield said.

"Tempelhof Air Base, Berlin, Germany," George said.

"Tuscarora Nation," I said. The guard gave my red card back immediately and then looked closely at George's passport, and then his dad's.

"This your son, sir?" the guard asked, pointing to George.

"Yes, I'm taking my boy and his friend to a concert in Toronto. Paul McCartney, Sunday night, Maple Leaf Gardens. We'll be returning late that night, after the show."

"Do you and your son have anything to declare?" he asked. "Are either of you carrying anything besides personal belongings?"

"No, sir."

"Enjoy your concert and your visit. If you or your son purchase anything while in our province, you'll have to declare it on your reentry to the United States. You may have to pay duty for any large purchases, otherwise, not an issue." The guard handed back their papers.

"Is it always like that when you cross the border?" Mr. Haddonfield asked me as we pulled away. He'd noticed that, once the guard saw my card, all follow-up questions were only directed at the two of them. He knew those questions didn't apply to me.

"Usually it's faster. I've never crossed with white people before. The Tuscarora Nation has a treaty for free passage. Some people from home think it just means that they don't have to pay the bridge toll," I said. "But it really means that the guards can't ask us questions, period. Back there was in our territory. This ahead is in our territory. The way my uncle explained it to me is that we're like those seagulls you see in the gorge, fishing in the river. Sometimes they land on this side of the gorge, sometimes the other. They live on both sides."

"They're animals," George said. "They don't acknowledge laws. That what you mean?"

"We have to recognize some of your laws, but not all. This is one — well, we had elders go through many difficulties to get this treaty enforced again, so we each accept that it's our job, our duty, to be clearly and officially Tuscarora when we cross."

"So when we cross back over —" Mr. Haddonfield started.

"The same thing will happen. They might give me a hard time because I'm one little kid, but if I show them I know what I'm talking about, they'll back off."

"All right, boys," George's dad said, "whatever we call it, Canada or more of your territory, it is Toronto we're headed to." All three of us whooped as we cruised down to the Queen Elizabeth Way, which everyone from the rez called The Queen E. "Lewis, George wanted to see the CN Tower, but it's not open yet. I checked. Is there anything specific you want to do in Toronto while we're there, besides the concert?"

I shook my head. I was just delighted to finally see the city in person. The closer we got, the more impossible it seemed. I'd watched Toronto TV for years, admired its exotic big-city life from afar. Now that we were so close, I could barely stand the anticipation. I read off the highway signs, seeing for the first time all these names I heard on the Toronto radio stations I listened to: Dundas, Don Mills, Don Valley, Spadina. Suddenly, high buildings rose up around us as we flew downtown. I felt my heart racing as we went deeper into this new world.

There were so many cars and streets, directions and lights, I couldn't even tell which signs we were supposed to pay attention to, but George's dad moved us confidently through the lanes. The street stretching ahead looked like those pictures you see of people exploring the Grand Canyon, with small figures scattered among the tall walls of the buildings. In the few blocks I could see, there might have been more people than lived on the entire reservation. I glimpsed something familiar several blocks up.

"Sam the Record Man!" I said, pointing. As far as I could tell from the Canadian commercials, two men ran most things in Toronto: Honest Ed and Sam the Man. Ed ran a store that stretched a city block, full of "a million unexpected treasures" or something like that. Sam switched his identity by adding adjectives before the word "man." He was Sam the Chinese Food Man, Sam the Tape Man, and a few others, but mostly he was Sam the Record Man. "Sam's is supposed to be the best record store in all of Toronto. I see his commercials everywhere!"

"That will definitely be one of our stops," George's dad said as we went by. As we took a right, we had to get to the far right lane to make room for a streetcar passing us, sparks flying from the rod mounted in its roof to meet the low live wires. I'd never seen anything like this in my life, and I was dying to get out of the truck and step into this new world.

I didn't know where to look, every window offering us a different sight, but then up on our left, I saw the marquee. We were passing by Maple Leaf Gardens, and the sign had just seven words on it: WINGS OVER AMERICA SUNDAY NIGHT SOLD OUT. I still didn't know what arrangements had been made for our tickets, but that marquee suggested that if we didn't have any at the moment, our chances of changing that situation were slim.

We pulled into a lot. "There's where we're staying, boys," Mr. Haddonfield said. "An easy block's walk from the arena. Now let's get checked in so we can catch some of the city before it gets too late."

The building, a thirty-story-high hotel with a large neon sign on it, cast a shadow over us from across the street. I tried to watch for cars and run across like I might in downtown Niagara Falls, but George's dad grabbed me softly by the collar of my T-shirt and guided us to the crosswalk on the corner. "You have to be extra careful in a city of this size," he said, nudging us forward when the WALK sign lighted.

The lobby was fancy, with a lot of lights and mirrors, huge potted plants, and oversized furniture where George and I sat while his dad checked us in. We dropped our stuff off and headed right back out, and down the blocks toward Sam's. Everywhere we looked, there were shops selling specialized things. One store seemed to sell only these shiny leather boots with big clunky rubber soles stitched onto them with thick, bright yellow thread. Another just sold incense and incense holders, and yarn hangings like I'd done in art class. One I wanted to stop at — comic books and movie posters — we whizzed right by.

Every third or fourth storefront was a restaurant run by people whose nationalities I didn't recognize. They were mostly darker than me, which was kind of a switch. The food in the windows was equally unrecognizable, such as large wads of meat on sharp wooden sticks, or bright orange ducks with their heads still on, drooped over gleaming stainless steel hooks. Unfamiliar smells exploded in sizzling air as we passed each of these places, where people shouted their orders.

We eventually got to Sam's, three stories high, with massive neon records mounted on the outside of the building, spinning on a neon turntable. We'd walked maybe twenty city blocks. My feet were sore, but I didn't care. I was setting foot inside Sam the Record Man!

We spent over an hour browsing among the racks. George's dad picked up a few things in the import section. He showed us the difference between the British and US versions of the

Beatles' albums. One of my favorite US albums, *Yesterday and Today*, didn't even exist in England, since its songs were just distributed there as singles and on different lineups of *Help!*, *Rubber Soul*, and *Revolver*. It was like an alternate universe. There was an early one, *Please Please Me*, that didn't seem to have a US equivalent, and I would have liked to have gotten it for Albert. But these imports were almost three times as expensive as a regular album, and it also seemed super lame to buy someone a gift with the money they lent you, so I put it back in the bin.

"You hungry, boys?" George's dad asked as we stepped out onto Yonge Street. "How about we get some Chinese here?" He led us into Sam the Chinese Food Man. A hostess in a silk kimono greeted us.

"Kimonos aren't Chinese," George whispered to me.

"Yeah, well, neither is Sam," I said, "so no big surprise there."

When George's dad said we'd have the buffet, she said we could start. George grabbed a plate and started loading it. "Egg rolls," he said, grinning.

I took a plate and moved toward the wings, the only recognizable item in the buffet.

"Those aren't going to taste the way they do in Niagara Falls," George said. "Haven't you ever been to a Chinese restaurant?" I shook my head. He gave me an overview, but with a few items, he said I would have to try them. I went mostly with things that seemed semirecognizable.

"You don't know what you're missing," George teased me, biting into his third egg roll. "Stuffed with bean sprouts. Try them, you candy butt." So of course, I had to meet that challenge, and then went back for three more egg rolls a few minutes later.

We walked back to the hotel, stuffed. George suddenly shouted, "Hey! Hey!" and ran ahead. Stacey, Summer, Rose, and Rose's parents stood in front of our hotel. George gave Stacey a hug, but with grown-ups around, it was the kind of hug you might give an aunt you haven't seen in a while, not quite the sort they usually squeezed in between classes. When Mr. Haddonfield and I caught up, Stacey gave me the same kind of older-relative hug, which surprised me, but I acted quick enough to return it in the same fast-pat-on-the-back style. The other girls mumbled hellos and stared up at the canyons of concrete and glass surrounding us. It was after ten thirty, and the adults decided to meet in the hotel bar after escorting us to our rooms.

"All right, boys," Mr. Haddonfield said in our room. "This bed is mine. I don't want to have to kick one of you out when I come back. That couch is a daybed; you throw the cushions on the floor and use it like a bed when you want. You can take turns — one gets the real bed tonight, one tomorrow, or flip a coin, or whatever. I don't care as long as you're not in mine."

"I'll take the daybed," I said, since I had not contributed at all to the cost of the room.

"Okay, glad we have that settled. You can have the bed tomorrow night. Now, I'll be in the lobby, and you have the number. I'll call periodically," he told us, which we knew in code meant, "Don't even think about any monkey business." He also said Rose's parents would be checking in with the girls. In some delusional adult version of what was happening here, we were potentially double-dating.

"This is cable TV," George said as soon as his dad left. "Let's see what's on." He flipped through the dials. We skipped through, writing down the numbers of channels that looked like possibilities — a couple old monster movies, *The Midnight Special*, and other garbage.

Then we arrived at the channel we knew we'd be keeping it on. A man and woman were in a bed, kissing, sheets rumpled at their waists. This wasn't exactly uncharted territory, but what we couldn't believe was that neither one had a shirt on.

"Holy smokes," George said. "I'm moving to Canada. What is this?"

"Who cares what it's called? Just leave it!" I said, sitting on the bed. There wasn't much of a story line, but we were both riveted, having never seen a movie like this before. Watching this channel also made an action of Albert's suddenly seem logical to me. Almost every night, he would get up after we'd all gone to bed and head downstairs to watch TV. Sometimes, I'd go get a drink and see what he was watching, and it was always the same thing — some game show or nature show. In French.

"Why do you watch this stuff?" I asked him once. "You don't even speak French."

"I'm *learning* French," he said.

"You are not. Come on, spill it."

"Well, if you must know, I heard that sometimes they show movies like my magazines," he said, grinning. "In Canada, they have different rules for TV. Aren't you glad you asked, you nosy little fart?"

So in the Albert World, a French-language TV station equated the possibilities of movies starring naked people. I couldn't wait to tell him I had seen his fabled channel in

Toronto. We watched for an hour, until his dad's key turned in the door. George quickly switched the TV to another channel — a cooking show in Chinese, without subtitles. His dad looked at us, then at the TV, and smirked, saying it was time for bed. Apparently he had watched TV in Toronto before.

I went into the bathroom and came out in my borrowed pajamas, showing I knew how to dress, but they'd already shut the lights off. In the morning, when we got up, they each wore only undershorts. His dad entered the bathroom, and when the shower turned on, I said, "Well?"

"Well, what?" George said, having no idea what I was asking him.

"I borrowed these stupid pajamas because you wore them the night I stayed at your house. I didn't want you offering to lend me some a second time."

"Funny," he said. "That night, I realized my dad was like you and didn't wear pj's, so I thought it was time for me to grow up. You want to be a kid still? That's your choice," he said, laughing hysterically.

"Butthead," I said as his dad came out, toweling off.

"All right, you guys, shower and get dressed. We've got a busy couple of days, which includes the not inconsiderable task of finding ourselves," he said, "one more ticket for the concert."

"What?" I said.

"I guess I forgot that detail," George said, walking into the bathroom.

"Nice time to tell me," I said.

"Don't worry. I've got a few ideas," Mr. Haddonfield said.

We spent most of the day touring the city, continuing to catalogue things I had seen on Canadian TV: the Royal Ontario Museum, the Ontario Science Centre, the Canadian National Exhibition grounds, Ontario Place. Mr. Haddonfield had made arrangements for us to meet the other group in front of the hotel for dinner around seven thirty.

After dinner, Rose's family took a cab back to the hotel, and we chose to walk. Mr. Haddonfield invited Stacey to walk with us, assuring Rose's parents he'd drop her off before he met them for drinks. But Stacey said she would go with the other girls. I felt bad for George as he watched their cab disappear. She was nice, and when they were together, there was more happiness between them than two people could muster separately. It was like "happiness squared" in math class.

It was a little after ten thirty by the time we got back to the room, and we encouraged George's dad to run along and meet his newfound friends in the bar, saying that we were fine and exhausted, ready for bed, but we might watch a little TV, which was not a lie.

"Well, don't watch anything I wouldn't watch," he said, smiling, changing his shirt. "All right, I'm heading down."

We stood outside the room and watched him walk to the elevators. "The girls are on the floor below us," George whispered to me. His dad stopped and told us to go into the room, and we did, but George remained antsy. A few minutes later, he opened the door back up and stepped out. I heard some low, rumbling voices in the hall, and as I got up to see what was going on, George stepped back in, his cheeks red.

"Sorry, my dad totally busted me. I was only going to sneak down and give Stacey a good-night kiss."

"Well, what happened?"

"He figured I might try something like that, and he stayed at the elevators for a few minutes. If this wasn't one of the Beatles, we'd be on our way home now. But he wants to see this show as much as we do. Disobeying just cost me some, particularly since he didn't really have to bring me in the first place." George looked down, embarrassed. "I told him it was only a kiss, but all he could see was disrespect. I'm gonna have some challenges making it up."

I was glad I hadn't glimpsed this sterner version of George's dad he claimed was there at times, since the tone of voice I could hear through the door was intimidating enough. In the room, we quickly changed the TV channel, but instead of the kind of movie we found the night before, this time all we got was a talky drama — the sort I might watch alone, but no one else in my house would tolerate, unless, of course, it was in French.

The room phone rang. It was Mr. Haddonfield. He apologized for his reaction, but reminded George that he knew better. George immediately agreed and assured him we were watching a movie, standing closer to the TV for sound effects. A few minutes later, Stacey called, and George's tone changed to something more leisurely as he settled into the desk chair to talk. He told her he'd been busted trying to sneak down, but after that, they didn't say much of importance, instead just enjoying each other's voices, I could tell. The phone had those multiple-line buttons you saw at the school office, so they knew they would be covered if any of the adults tried to call.

It was impossible to concentrate on the movie with George talking. I slipped behind the curtains and turned the wall-unit heater on, enjoying the hot air blowing up the bottom of my

T-shirt and the hum that filled my ears. All the city lights blossomed below, streetlamps, traffic lights, advertisements, sparking streetcars. Off to the side of the Maple Leaf Gardens, there was a line of tractor trailers up against the loading docks, the Wings over America emblem on their roofs. I thought of telling George, but I could hear he was still talking with Stacey. Behind me, George's voice changed abruptly. "Yes, sir, still watching a movie." There was a pause and then he said, "Yes, sir," again. He switched back to his quiet voice for a minute and then hung up.

A few seconds later, George pulled the drape cords dividing the heavy cloth, revealing me behind them. "What are you doing? Man, it's hot," he said, reaching over and switching the unit to vent. Immediately, cool air blew up under my T-shirt, so I stepped away.

"Just looking out. I've never been up this high before. Check that out," I said, pointing to the Wings trucks. "They're here."

"Neat. But I don't think we should sneak down to see," he said, grimacing a little. "Can you tell me something?" he asked, and then went forward without a response from me. "How come you were waiting by the road at your house when we came to get you? I could have come and knocked on your door. I mean, it *was* raining. You didn't have to get all wet."

"Well, you had this on," I said, pointing to the Miami Dolphins jacket he'd draped over the desk chair. I'd already thought this one up, so it rolled right out. "You know how sometimes kids at school give you grief 'cause it's not a Bills jacket? My family? Whew! Monster Bills fans. I was protecting you from their meanness."

It had sounded perfect and logical in my head, but when it spilled out, it was the stupidest-sounding story ever, on par with that dog that incessantly eats homework. I stared him straight in the eye and he stared right back, daring me to look guilty, but I held on. Neither one of us was willing to flinch. Then, with the slightest shake of his head, he changed the subject.

We spent the morning lying around, and then lugged our bags out to the parking lot, locked them up in the truck, and went walking in the city. By the time we arrived back at the Gardens, the sidewalk was jammed with people milling around in groups, many in wild outfits.

"All right, guys, I want you to stand over there," Mr. Haddonfield said, pointing to the corner. "Don't talk to any strangers, and if you see your girlfriend and the others, flag them down. They're not supposed to be here for another forty-five minutes, but," he said, turning to me, "we've still got to get a ticket."

He disappeared, and I could see the SOLD OUT sign from where we were standing.

"What do you think he's going to do?" I asked George.

"Not sure, but he does this stuff all the time. Trust him. He knows what he's doing."

"Why didn't   ll me I didn't have a ticket?"

"Because y   ave come," he said, which was true enough.   If he says he's going to get something   ne."

"Doe

"Well, if we can't find one, you could always go to the room and watch a *movie*."

"Funny. We checked out, remember? Why don't you give me your ticket and you can watch one, since you're so interested."

"I don't need one as much as you. I have a girlfriend, and we've graduated to some, um, fun things," he said. When I didn't ask for details, his eyes drifted, looking for Stacey. "Hey, you remember when you asked me what hookers were?"

"Yeah, I guess," I said. It had been in one of our very first conversations, about when his dad took him to the club district in Hamburg, where the Beatles had played at the beginning of their careers. I had found George's answer lacking, so I'd asked Albert when I got home. He'd given me a detailed definition, which I guessed had maybe come from experience.

"Well, those are hookers," he said, pointing to a group of women standing kitty-corner from us. They were dressed in small, tight outfits, like miniskirts with tube tops. They looked like the women in Albert's magazines, but they were also familiar for a different reason.

"Hey, there, little brother," one of them said to me, and the others laughed. They had used hot curlers or something to feather their hair and look trendy, but their hair was still long, shiny, and black — Indian women, who recognized where I had come from. "What reserve you in from? Your first time in the big city?" I could tell she was a Canadian Indian when she said "reserve" instead of "reservation."

"Give you Indian price," another one said, and they all burst into laughter again. "Indian price" was a discount you gave if you had a crafts booth for tourist events, mostly beadwork and stone carvings. You had the price you set for others and the lower price you set for Indians.

"Hol-ah! You girls!" another one said. "Leave the little cousin alone. He's with crhee-rhoo-rhitt. Cousin-uh!" she yelled to me. "You going to see that Beatle?" I nodded. "Blow him a kiss for me," she added, and I smiled. "Come here, buy yourself something nice inside," she said, pulling out bills that had been tucked inside her tube top. She held them out to me with long, painted nails.

"Gwaht-ess, nyah-wheh," I said, and waved.

"Little cousin's got manners," she said. "Suit yourself."

"One of you boys got a dad with you?" the first one asked, and they laughed again.

"We gotta go now," I said, leading George away.

"What did you say to them?" he asked as we merged with the crowd.

"I just told them no thanks."

"What was that other word? What did they call me? Cree-roo . . ."

"It's not important," I said. The word they used was the word for grackles, because a grackle pushes eggs out of any nest it finds and steals the nest for itself. I should say, it used to be the word for grackles, but even before I'd been born, it had come to mean "white people."

"Look, I know what it's like to speak a different language in front of people who don't understand what you're saying, and I know why someone might want to do that."

"It was just the word for white people."

"You're lying."

"No, I swear," I said, and then I saw Stacey turning the

corner and I pointed her out. Her group joined us, and a little while later, George's dad showed back up.

"I tried," he said, "but three tickets is almost impossible. Odd number. Nobody buys tickets in threes."

"What's the problem?" Rose's dad asked.

"My son's friend here doesn't have a ticket. I was hoping, because these were such amazing seats, that I might be able to trade someone two for three that weren't as close."

"Rose, you told me your friends only needed four," her dad said. "We had others," he added, turning to Mr. Haddonfield. "I just didn't know. I'm sorry."

"Sorry, Daddy," Rose fake pouted. "I didn't know George wanted to bring his friend."

No one was willing to say out loud they knew she was lying.

"This was the best I could do," Mr. Haddonfield said to me. "A single ticket. There were a few people who had one, someone couldn't make it. You're not as near to us as I'd like, but it's getting close to time. We can swap out for part of the show and you can sit with George."

"Hope you didn't get scalped," Rose's dad said, yanking the top of his thinning hair with one hand and sliding his thumb along his forehead. Rose and Summer grinned at each other, but Stacey and George looked down at the sidewalk.

"How much was the ticket, Mr. Haddonfield?" I asked.

"Don't worry about it, son. I've got it. We better get in."

Inside, we stopped at my seat first and Mr. Haddonfield reintroduced himself to the guy he bought my ticket from. After he assured me he would be back, I sat down. The lights went off and the crowd noise rose. Everyone around me stood, and all I could see were the backs and butts of the people in front of me. The guy next to me grabbed me by the armpit and insisted I stand on my seat. I was short enough that doing this didn't make me much taller than anyone else, but I still crouched a little to even the view for the guy directly behind me. A minute or so later, that guy tapped me on the shoulder and yelled that I was fine standing. He was tall enough to see.

The strangers around me made me one of them. It was almost like being home on the reservation, and I let myself enjoy the surging excitement. I looked down to the area where George and his dad stood but could see only general swaying movement. They were a distance of thirty rows away, half a hockey rink, fewer than fifteen feet from the stage, within eye contact range of the band. I couldn't have asked for a more perfect reminder of the different planets where George and I lived. The feeling was sharp, like a pebble in my boot.

Just then the first guitar notes started, random tuning sounds, and with each note, the crowd decibels inched up until a spotlight warmed center stage. Paul McCartney, in a swirl of smoke, sang the opening lines of "Venus and Mars." The small bright spot lighted his head, which was floating in darkness, only his face and lapels visible as he played alone on stage, no longer one of the Fab Four. I'd never been to a rock concert before, but this seemed on the sedate side, from things I'd heard. Then the band hidden behind him exploded into "Rock Show," and the concert suddenly looked like I had imagined. Brilliant colored lights hit all five members of Wings, plus a four-man brass section. The whole stage was covered in smoke, billowing and drifting around the band. They transitioned into "Jet," and from there, the band played on.

The entire crowd moved in rhythm, like we were all wired into the sound system. The bass notes, Paul McCartney's bass notes, thrummed out of the amps and rocked my rib cage. The lights cascading into the crowd, guys shouting and girls screaming, and the music, perfectly played *and* spontaneously alive at the same time — this whole experience was frying my senses! It was better than anyone had ever described being at a concert before. Somehow we were all part of the show, every one of those eighteen thousand people. Would I be able to capture it for Albert? I tried taking everything in.

A few songs later, George's dad was at my side, bellowing into my ear, asking if I wanted to swap places. I yelled back that I was fine, and I meant it. The show might have been better if I'd been with them, but I was in Toronto, at my first concert, and it was one of the Beatles. I don't think anyone in my situation could have asked for more.

Suddenly, McCartney, from the grand piano he'd been playing, started the frantic opening notes of the Beatles' "Lady Madonna," and we both whipped our heads to the stage, and then back at each other, whooping in disbelief. I knew that "Lady Madonna" had been recorded after the Beatles' last tour, so we were hearing this song performed live on tour for the first time. George's dad shouted again and jumped in the air. I could barely believe the reserved Mr. Haddonfield was, in that moment, not an air force sergeant, and instead was just James, maybe even Jim, freaking out to a song he loved. I jumped from my chair to join him, and he gave me skin, his massive palm slapping mine in a move I didn't think he would have known. I couldn't wait to tell George.

As the song ended, a security guard shined a flashlight on us and asked Mr. Haddonfield for his ticket, expertly gripping his elbow. George's dad reached into his chest pocket for his ticket stub, and I assured him I was okay. The guard led him away, insisting the aisle could not be blocked. "You be right here at the end of the show. Don't move," Mr. Haddonfield yelled back at me as new piano notes started — "The Long and Winding Road," stripped down to just McCartney on the piano. Mr. Haddonfield disappeared into the crowd as the rest of the band joined in.

The show went forward, with explosions and big roiling clouds of smoke rising over the stage. Even though I was far away from the Haddonfields, I didn't feel alone at this concert for the most part: It wasn't like you could talk, the music was so loud, and the image of Mr. Haddonfield lost in "Lady Madonna" cracked me up over and over. I'm not sure I could have leapt the way we had on my own, but his presence had allowed me to feel the epic moment, and the wave carried me through the rest of the show. Maybe I wouldn't tell George or Albert or anyone, just allow it to be a great moment of joy in my life that I couldn't find words to describe.

A little while later, an enormous image of *Band on the Run*'s cover illuminated the giant screen above the band as the opening guitar notes of the song itself played. Sometime during the song, I realized it wasn't a slide being projected over the band, but an actual film, with close-ups of people whispering conspiratorially in the spotlight. As it ended, they all ran out into the dark, leaving only the light and the brick wall. Then it was over. The lights rose and smoke cleared.

Paul McCartney had sung just a few Beatles songs during the show. One of them had been "Yesterday," about longing for an easier, earlier life. On its surface, it was a breakup song. But its perfection at capturing impossible losses made it one of the world's best-known songs. You didn't need to have someone dump you to long for a time when your life was easier. You could fill in your own sadness.

I wondered which life McCartney himself secretly wanted — his new one in Wings or his old one with the Beatles. I'd noticed that on stage, he'd chosen to play a Rickenbacker bass instead of the signature Höfner violin bass that he'd played through most of the Beatles years. Even beyond the solo spotlight he'd started the show with, he wanted to make a distinction. In public, he was someone else now, with a different band, a different look, different songs. He wanted to be Paul McCartney, not "Beatle Paul." In the same way, I thought, I wanted to be just me, Lewis Blake, not "Indian Lewis" like I was at school. I didn't have any objection to being known as an Indian, but couldn't I have my own life as just me? Or like McCartney, was I stuck being expected to play the songs of my first band for the rest of my life? Could you play both, or were you required to make a choice?

Mr. Haddonfield and George came to get me, glistening with sweat and excitement. "Did you see those explosions!" George yelled, winding his way through the crowd. "Live and let die! Boom! Boom! Man, we could feel the heat from those flames!" We traded comments on the show all the way out, and only as we stepped out into the chilly May late-night air did I realize that the others weren't with us. I wanted to ask George if he'd had a good time with Stacey, even maybe tease him about sneaking in a kiss when the lights went down after "Silly Love Songs." But on the sidewalk, he scanned the crowd, clearly hoping to catch one last glimpse of her before we left, and I didn't want his memory of the concert contaminated with my jabbing a joke his way.

At the truck, Mr. Haddonfield tugged the front of his shirt out of his jeans and reached up under it. "I didn't want to get these wrinkled, but I didn't want to carry them around either. Thought you guys might want a souvenir." He handed us glossy oversized programs, filled with concert photos and stories. "They're a little warm from being so close, but I had them between my shirt and T-shirt, so they're at least not sweaty. Looks like they're in pretty good shape."

We flipped through our programs and came across pages in which each band member was featured against a map of their hometowns. Paul McCartney's map, naturally, showed Liverpool. The drummer was apparently from Rochester, New York, about an hour and a half from our home. I knew that to George, the map of my home was just one big blank, maybe a question mark on a sheet of red paper. He could never come to my house, but I was trying to think of other ways to bridge that gap, and I had one idea that might work . . . something to extend the invitation, unfold the map.

12

Heart of the Country

"So, listen," George said during lunch one day in the last week of school. "I know you've got that job coming up, but it's not for a couple weeks, right?"

"Yeah," I said. "What about it?"

"Remember at New Year's? When we were up super early, before the sun rose?" I nodded, thankful he didn't add something like *the morning you bolted like a crazy man*. "Well, this is the season where you can see both Venus and Mars. I saw them last week. So maybe we could camp out in my backyard before you start your job, and I can set the alarm clock. Then maybe we do the same at your house the next weekend. I can bring my tent. It's pretty portable."

"I don't think it's going to be a good time," I said, wishing I'd already planted the seed of my idea so I could head off the irritation that I knew was coming.

"Okay, why isn't it going to be a good time?" he said, suddenly impatient. "It's warm enough now that I won't be wearing my Dolphins jacket. And I know how to be on my best behavior probably better than anyone you know. Look, I just want to see where you live."

No, you don't, I thought. *I don't even want to, but there it is every morning.*

"You see," I said to George. "It's like this. I didn't want to say anything because, well, it's awkward." His eyes slit down. He was waiting for something preposterous, so I pulled out my one big gun, the one that stuns pretty much any white person you point it at. "My ma. She's what you might call a spiritual healer."

This was a terrible lie, because not only did it disparage my ma, who was in no way a spiritual healer — she barely knew her way around an Ace bandage — it also was an offense to real, committed medicine people. I hoped they didn't feel my lie, like a disturbance in the universe.

"Because of that responsibility, she has to maintain a certain level of purity," I said, getting sicker with each shovelful I dug myself deeper into this story. "If a white person comes to our house, it's a huge problem. We have to do a cleansing ceremony. Not that white people are dirty or anything, of course," I added, backtracking. "But their vibe with the spirit world is different. So it would just be —"

"No, it's okay. I got it," he said. "Different religions all have their own thing." I kind of wanted him to be mad at me, or offended that I'd called his spirit dirty or something, but instead, he looked like I felt when I found out I'd been cut from the Choraliers. "We can still camp out at my place, if you want," he said. "Thank you for telling me the truth," he added, sticking his hand out.

I didn't want to shake it because I felt like my hand might crumble into a heap of lying crap if our skin touched, but I took the risk and met his grip. I owed him that, at least.

"Well, let's keep in touch over the summer and see what works out," I said.

As the beginning of summer went on, we talked some on the phone, and he told me what he and Stacey had been up to. I told him about albums that I'd read were coming out soon and other rock music stuff I'd snagged from magazines. I hung around the house and looked at magazines, admittedly mine *and* Albert's, and spent the night at Carson's whenever he chose to drive his field car through the back paths to my house. Carson and I played guitar together sometimes, but since his was electric and he refused to put the volume low, we could only hear him. What the Bug had told me was true, though. I was learning on a full-sized jumbo-style guitar, and Carson's was a three-quarter dreadnought, and there were differences in the way you positioned your fingers. I was learning on a real man's guitar, though Carson naturally attributed my fumbling on his guitar to my incompetence.

The first day of work, I was assigned to the bus garage with Bruce Mac and Rhoda Door, a couple of older rez kids who were already working there. By midmorning, we'd walked through the basics and my summer routine was set. We had to get three buses a day cleaned, and we could work alone or together, as long as we met our quota. It was fun to work with someone else, particularly two kids from home. I was reminded of elementary school, when I wasn't the only Indian in the room.

I was hoping Carson would sell me the acoustic guitar he wasn't using. It was the smaller one, but it would be better than not having one at all. When I asked, Carson said no, because he didn't want to wait five years to be paid in full, so I told him what I'd be making at the garage. Then he said he'd sell it to me for a hundred bucks, but only all at once. No installments. And if someone beat me to it, well, that was the way of things.

Carson offered to have his ma take me to the bank on payday so I could get the guitar first thing, but I had that covered. The garage office manager had a relationship with the bank in Sanborn, and she would cosign our checks so we could cash them. But at the end of the first two weeks, when checks were delivered, only Bruce and Rhoda got paid. There was lag time for paper processing, and since they had worked the rollover, they were still on the payroll. They said the good news for me was that the lag time left me with my last paycheck coming in after the school year started.

"Well, can I see it?" I said to Bruce, when he peeked inside the envelope. There it was, NET PAY, $235.54. "Who's FICA and why is he going to be taking some of my check?" I asked.

"Social security," Bruce said. "Nothing you can do about it." I didn't understand that, but it was social security that paid Albert's disability, so I figured that in some way, I was helping him.

When I got home, I called Carson and told him I didn't get paid after all, explaining the process. "Too bad," he said. "We're going to the Auto Vue tonight, double bill, *Night of the Living Dead* and *The Texas Chain Saw Massacre*. Thought you'd be able to come."

"But at the drive-in, you just pay by the carload," I said. I knew this to be true, since it was my ma's main reason we never went. No car, no way to pay the bargain drive-in rates.

"Well, there's gas, pop, popcorn, you know how these things add up," he said. I suppose he figured that if I could afford to go to a concert in Toronto, I could afford to kick in while hanging out with him. "When *do* you get paid? Maybe there'll be something good at the flicks then."

"Two more weeks, but I already have plans," I said.

"How can you have plans? It's Indian Picnic," he said. Since kindergarten, we met every year at the Picnic and hung out all day. One night I'd stay at his house and the second one, we'd stay at mine.

"Yeah, I know," I said. "Enjoy the chain saws and zombies." I hung up and then took the phone off the hook so he couldn't call back to yell or threaten or con or any of the other Carson techniques of getting his way. Apparently his goal this summer was for me to give him access to my pay.

"You want ten bucks 'til you get paid, so you can go?" Albert said from the living room.

"Quit listening in on my conversations," I said.

"Oh, sorry," he said. "Didn't mean to offer you help." It was hard to tell when Albert was being sincere or a smart-ass. His tone almost never changed, no matter the subject. "If you change your mind, my cash is in the upper drawer of my nightstand, and I'm pretty sure you know how to find my nightstand, since my mags are sometimes in a different order than I left them. And I don't mean the *Rolling Stone* and *Creem* either."

I did a quick look around. My ma wasn't home. I could hear Albert laughing in the living room. "Don't worry, you little pig. I wouldn't say that if she was home. You're still the baby, so she still thinks all you read are your Spider-Man books."

"Shut up, man."

"Just saying. Listen, I hope you don't have real big plans for that money you're going to be bringing in. It might seem like a lot, but your ma's gonna expect you to start carrying your own here. You'll get some, but you know how it is, living here at the end of the month." We received our assistance check the first day of every month, but it was calculated for surviving, not thriving, and any little extra thing, like a slightly higher electricity bill or paying someone to take us somewhere, always threw the budget into chaos.

"You're one to talk," I said, knowing that sounded harsher than I meant. Whatever money Albert received, he tended to use to buy whatever he felt like. Sometimes it included food and contributions toward other expenses, but just as often, he forgot. I didn't know what he did with his money, beyond smokes, magazines, and albums. Most of his clothes, like mine, were used. We had learned to live with his randomness, but it was most frustrating in those end-of-the-month periods. The one thing my ma was always inventive with was food. I'd never gotten used to some of her meals, like one she called Hamburg Gravy, in which she took flour, water, a short loaf of bread, and a half a pound of hamburger, and insisted it was a meal for five.

"Could also be a chance for you to get some new clothes for once," he said, "instead of garage sale or Dig-Digs. Why don't you call your other buddy there?"

I was surprised by Albert's suggestion, but I hadn't talked to George in a few days, so I picked up the phone.

"What are you doing?" I asked when he answered.

"Nothing. My dad was talking about maybe the movies, but the only thing playing —"

"*Texas Chain Saw*? Yeah, I know. Are you going?"

"Well, I haven't been to a horror movie before. That one seems pretty bad. Did you see the ads for it?"

"Of course! Why do you think I want to go?" I changed my voice to sound like the movie announcer. "*What happened was true.*"

"Weirdo," he said, laughing. "You know, since the movie's getting out so late, we could do that sleepover in my yard. Mars and Venus are still in alignment. Be easier if you came for supper and we could set up my tent before heading out. What time can you be ready?"

"Tell you what," I said. "I'll catch a ride to your place so I don't inconvenience anyone, okay?"

"Naturally," he said, the slightest irritation in his voice. "Come when you can. I'll dig the tent out and be waiting."

I hung up, stuffed my school bag with overnight stuff, and headed out to the road, hoping to literally catch a ride. As usual, it didn't take long for a car to stop so I could climb in and get to the border, and the Manor was an easy fifteen-minute walk from there.

Mrs. Haddonfield decided to pass on the movie, but she stuck around for supper. We had pizza delivery from the place I had picked last winter. Apparently it had become a ritual with them, and all three of them had discovered the wonders of the blue-cheese-covered chicken wing.

George and I set up the tent in his backyard while it was still light out, since we wouldn't leave for the show until it was dark enough to see the screen. When I'd shown up without a sleeping bag, he didn't seem surprised. Two were rolled neatly next to the tent and poles.

"Stacey and friends sleeping out too?" I asked as he adjusted the tent poles. "What was it? About four houses away?"

"Girls don't sleep out, Shoe," he said, laughing. I wasn't

sure that dropping the "Box" from the nickname he'd given me was an improvement.

"They do on the rez. Hm, maybe that's why so many girls get pregnant in high school."

"Well, no worries there tonight. But I did manage to stash those," he said, pointing under the shrubs, where there was a white Styrofoam cooler. "For after we get back and my parents go to bed. Two beers apiece, and," he said, reaching into his jeans pocket, "my trusty violets."

We got to the drive-in and George's dad sent us to the concession stand with requests and twenty dollars. "Twenty dollars," I said, looking at the bill. "Are things that expensive here?"

"First time you've seen one of those?" Carson said from behind me, jabbing his toes into the back of my knee to buckle it. "What are you doing here? Thought you were too broke."

"Someone else didn't have a carful," I said, and then realized that George could have interpreted my call as a backup plan. "How'd you see me in all these people anyway?"

"Shoe, I'll go get the stuff," George said, plucking the twenty from my hands. "What do you want? Anything special?" I shook my head. "I'll just get the giant popcorn. We can share."

" 'Shoe'?" Carson said, his evil grin suddenly appearing, and I knew at that second that George's nickname for me was going to spread through the reservation. "I'm sitting there at the concession stand seats," he added. "My dad and the others are up front. I like to be back farther. Besides, my buddy there snuck a fifth of vodka in, and we're pouring it into our Cokes."

I looked over and should not have been surprised to see Evan Reiniger — the Wedgie King — and someone who looked like him, probably a brother, next to an empty seat. "Geez, don't mention me," I said. I was hoping Evan would have the summer to forget who I was.

"Your name ain't likely to come up, Mr. Ego. Or should I say, Shoe? Well, I'm gonna get back to my friends. Enjoy your date."

I'd planned to be scared at the movies, but all the zombies and the crazy people with chain saws on the screen were just flickering images. The possibility of Evan the Wedgie King recognizing me was a lot worse. When we got out of the truck between shows to use the john, I saw Evan and Carson both wandering that way, and also spotted my saving grace.

"Over there," I said to George, heading to the back fence, where a bunch of men stood facing the posts. "That's where real guys take a leak. The men's room is for candy asses."

"But what about washing your hands?" George said.

"Candy asses," I said.

"*Hygienic* candy butts," he said, in his ongoing campaign of not swearing, and went to the building with the bathrooms, while I found a spot along the fence. Despite what I had said, I washed my hands at a hose nearby.

When we got back to George's house, it was after 1 A.M. His dad reminded him he still had to deliver papers in the morning. "Got the alarm on my watch set," George said when we were settled in the tent, showing me a wild gadget, fancier than the elaborate one he already had. "Birthday gift from my dad."

"When was that?"

"Couple weeks ago. No party," he was quick to add. "Getting too old for that. My parents took me and Stacey and her parents out to John's Flaming Hearth."

"Swanky," I said. "Can you actually sit near those big flaming arches in the window?"

"It's blocked off, mostly, but we sat pretty close. Hey, do you ever get to see that girl, Marie, that you told me about?"

"I might, in two weeks."

"What's in two weeks?"

"This thing on the rez."

A real conversation killer these days. And when we were quiet for a little while, I could hear he'd started snoring lightly. I drifted off too and didn't wake until George was nudging me, his watch beeping as he fumbled to shut the alarm off in the dark.

"It's time," he said, and we crawled out, stretching. The air was sharp.

"I have to take a leak."

"Me too. Go up against the hedges here. Then use the hose. Pretend you're at the movies," he said, stepping into the hedges a few yards away.

"Eww, you guys!" I heard a harsh whisper and almost went in my jeans, trying to zip up. Stacey stood there in a hooded sweatshirt and sweatpants, holding three Styrofoam cups with lids. "George told me what you guys were doing — well, not this, but sleeping out, so I thought I'd surprise you with hot chocolate. Only a mix, but it's warm."

She held one out, but I didn't want to fail this test. "Let me wash my hands," I said, reaching for the garden hose. I handed it to George when I was done, and he washed and wiped his hands on his jeans. Then he stuck the nozzle up to his mouth, rubbed his index finger around his teeth, and spat. Stacey handed me a cup.

"Good enough?" he asked her, hopeful.

"I suppose," she said. "Take a drink of this first." She handed him the second hot chocolate, and after he'd swished it around in his mouth, he stepped up to kiss her.

"You could use the hose yourself," he said to her, laughing, and she slapped his arm.

"So where are they?" she asked. "I gotta sneak back in before anyone wakes up."

George and I both studied the sky for a couple minutes.

"Well, that there is Venus," he said, pointing slightly above the horizon. He put his arm around her so she could follow his finger, and left it there.

"And that red one there is Mars," I added, "coming up beneath it right now."

For a little while, the three of us stood there, silent, watching the planets. I would never have believed you could see the difference, but there they were, two slightly brighter, and larger, and more colorful stars. A breeze came up, and Stacey leaned in closer to George, sliding her hand into his back jeans pocket. The sky lightened on the horizon, and the planets lost their colors and intensity in the orange sky.

"Okay," she said, stepping back. "I didn't want to spoil your manly man campout. Just thought I'd surprise you. I'm going back to bed. See you later this morning?" she said to George. He nodded and kissed her again, and then she was gone.

"Thanks, nyah-wheh, for the hot chocolate," I said, and she waved, disappearing down the walkway. "And nyah-wheh to you, for this," I said to George. "It was really cool to see both planets. Even worth it to get up this wickedly early." I looked at the cup. "Nice of her, huh?"

"Yup. You gonna rush off again?" he asked me.

"You talking about Stacey on New Year's Eve? That's why you think I left so quick?"

"Have you given me reason to believe anything else?" he asked. I hadn't. Even now, when we'd mostly been getting along pretty well, I couldn't tell him the complicated nature of the boarding schools in my own family's history.

"So listen. How'd you like to see a game of Fireball this summer?" I said, finally bringing up my idea, hoping we could drop my winter peel-out.

"What's Fireball?"

"Well, it's kind of like soccer, but it's only played at night," I said, then flicked my eyebrows up and down fast. "Oh yeah, and everything's on fire." I grinned.

"Are you making this up?"

"Nope. Well, I guess not *everything*. The players aren't on fire, most times. But the ball and goalposts are, and it only happens one weekend a year. Two weeks from now."

"How come I've never heard of it?"

"It's only on the reservation. My home," I said as the two planets vanished into morning light.

13

Old Brown Shoe

"Shoe, are you positive you really want me to come?" George said when I called to give him details later that week. "I respected the reason I couldn't come to your house once you told me the truth. Is taking me to this Fireball game violating any sacred acts?"

I felt a stab of guilt that he believed my spiritual healer lie so thoroughly. "Look, first, no, or I wouldn't have offered. Second, after the trip to see Wings, I wanted to do something special as a nyah-wheh, a thank-you."

"You don't have to translate. I remember that one. You've said it often enough."

That was, in fact, part of the problem. I was never in a situation to deserve a thank-you, and I hoped that George's trip to the Picnic and Fireball game might reverse that. I'd never done the hosting gig for white people at the Picnic before, never even knew anyone who had, but I had seen white people there, so *somebody* had to have invited them. "So I'll see you at five on Saturday?" I said, and he agreed.

The National Picnic started on the first Friday I was paid. That afternoon, I had over two hundred dollars, but Albert had called it right: When I got home with the wad of bills, I had to hand a hundred and fifty over to my ma. She said she'd hang on to most of my money until we got closer to the time for buying school clothes. Still, when I walked down with Albert for the first night's Fireball game, I had fifty dollars in my pocket, which was unfathomable to me. For the first time, I could buy something to eat when I was hungry, or if I happened to see something really cool at a vendor table, I didn't need to resort to the slow wear-down. I couldn't wait.

As it turned out, I didn't buy much, except some Indian-specific foods that were hard to come by except at a gathering: a bowl of corn soup, some fry bread, and strawberry drink. I finished the last while watching the traditional dance demonstrations and Indian Princess competition speeches, and then listening to a few tunes from the Tuscarora marching band.

By Saturday morning at nine, the pancake breakfast was in full swing, and the vendor booths were open for business, selling everything from high-end beadwork, to plastic tomahawks and vinyl headdresses with chicken feathers glued to their insides, to standard fair foods like burgers, hot dogs, popcorn, and cotton candy, and fresh batches of fry bread and corn soup. The crowd was thin in the morning, but five o'clock was peak time. This was when those local white people showed up — presumably not the ones who used us to scare their bad children.

Exactly at five, George and his dad emerged from the field used for Picnic parking.

"I described what you'd said to my *Mutti*, and she decided to pass," George said, looking at the people milling about, the horseshoe and tomahawk throw tournaments, and the Smoke Dance competition. "Dust."

"Your mother just likes to be tidy," Mr. Haddonfield said. "I've been tasked with being on the lookout for jewelry. Looks like there's plenty to choose from. Anyone you'd recommend?"

I tried to imagine seeing this event for the first time, and I got an idea. "Depends on what you're looking for, but whatever it is, make sure I'm with you. I can get a better price. But before we do anything, I want you guys to come over here in this tent," I said, leading them over to the grouping of picnic tables. They sat while I ran and hit the traditional food stands. As I stood in line, I glanced back to see them sitting alone, the only two people at the table I'd escorted them to. I wondered if I'd made the right decision to invite them. They looked marooned, like people from out of state whose cars overheated on their way to Niagara Falls.

As soon as I got the food, I ran back, trying not to spill anything. "Okay, you made me try Chinese food, and I'm glad you did, so this is food from here." It was almost like having them to my house, or at least my world anyway.

"Fair enough," George's dad said.

"What is it?" George said, examining what I'd brought.

"This is corn soup and cornbread, similar tasting."

"But where's the corn?" he asked, dipping a spoon into the bowl, moving its contents.

"That's the corn right there," I said, pointing to the swelled, white, puffy kernels of Indian corn. "It's prepared differently." Usually, it was best for first-time tasters if you didn't disclose that lye and woodstove ashes were used in the preparation, not to mention pig knuckles.

They tried it, and though their expressions said they hadn't been converted as easily as I had been to Chinese food, they finished everything. They were most enthusiastic about fry bread, which wasn't entirely surprising, since it was like the fried dough you'd find at any fair.

After arranging a time and place to meet later, George's dad excused himself to go look at the jewelry. George and I sat at the table while he choked down the last of his strawberry drink. Since it was, more or less, crushed strawberries and water, it was probably more bitter than he was expecting. I had brought packets of sugar, but I told him those were for kids. Carson spotted us from a distance and made his way over.

"I didn't see you last night," I said to him. It was the first time we hadn't spent a Picnic Friday Fireball game together since before kindergarten. I had even walked both sides of the spectator strips to see if he had chosen a different spot from our usual one on the monkey bars.

"I wasn't here. Was hanging with a friend of mine in Misty Meadows."

I knew that meant Evan Reiniger. "Young Men won last night's game," I said.

"Awesome!" Carson said, much more excited. "Now I'll have to find Bruce. That bastard owes me thirty bucks. Fool bet on the geezers. Probably hiding."

"You did *not* bet thirty dollars on a Fireball game!" I said.

He dug into his pocket and showed me a wad that looked like more than a hundred dollars. Pretty impressive for some-one who didn't have a job.

"So do you play Fireball?" George asked Carson.

"How do you know what Fireball is?" Carson asked, suspicious.

"Shoe here told me. He invited me earlier, but I didn't really believe it existed."

"Ah yes, Shoe," Carson said. Ever since hearing George call me that at the drive-in, Carson had been on a one-man campaign to get it adopted reservation-wide. Somehow when he used it, the name sounded snide, more an insult than a nickname. "We're too young to play. If you see Bruce, tell him I'm looking for him, and that I'll go double or nothing tonight if he's got the nerve." He wandered off.

George and I killed time drifting around, seeing a few people I'd grown up with and whom George was beginning to recognize from the lunchroom. As the sky grew a deep purple and orange in the setting sun, a familiar-looking girl walked up to us and said hi. It took me a few seconds to recognize her, and my surprise seemed to please her.

"George, this is Marie," I said, and her tentative smile broadened when I did not use "Stinkpot." "How's city life?" I asked her. She moved her head in a funny way that was neither a nod nor a denying shake, and finally she just shrugged her shoulders. We caught up a bit, but most of her descriptions of her new life had a careful neutrality, like they'd been rehearsed in front of a mirror for a more convincing delivery — sort of like the mystical home life I had invented to keep George at bay.

"Great to see you," she said, leaning in to give me a hug, a little warm from the sun. "Had to come out for Fireball, but was hoping I would see some old friends. Besides, you know how comfortable your old home is. You just slip it on . . . like an old brown shoe." As soon as she said my new nickname, she started laughing, and we joined her. "Sorry, my cousin Rhoda told me a couple weeks ago, and I just had to use it." I smiled, nodded. "See ya in the winter at the Feast, maybe, Snowshoe," she said, and with that, she disappeared back out into the crowd.

"So that's the girl?" George said when she left. "Seems nice. Why did you say she moved to the city?"

I shrugged my shoulders, an honest answer. While I had my suspicions about the nickname "Stinkpot," I really didn't know for sure.

When the booth lights started going down, we caught up with Mr. Haddonfield, who'd been watching the programming from the bandstand benches. I kept an eye on him throughout the evening. For a white guy, he studied the dancing competitions with great interest. Usually, outsiders quickly grew bored with elimination rounds and wandered off for popcorn or fresh-squeezed lemonade. His interest made me a little less freaked about his past. There would surely have been no Smoke Dance competitions at a boarding school where the object was to get us to ditch the things that make us, well, us.

We wandered across the footbridge to the field, where men were setting up goalposts wrapped with oil-soaked rags. I suggested we squeeze into the center of the crowd, since both ends had a higher potential for audience hazard. It seemed funny not to go to the monkey bars, where I'd sat every year before. From our spot, I couldn't see if the person perched at the top was Carson or not.

"So this is like soccer, you said?" George asked.

"If you take away the refs, shin guards, uniforms, and nets, yeah," I said. "And, of course, light the ball and goalposts on fire."

Shortly before ten, the ball and posts were sparked. Men in their midteens straight through to men in their sixties ran across the field as if their lives depended on it, kicking the flaming ball, sometimes blocking goals by meeting the ball chest-first and even face-first. Sometimes the ball made its way into the audience, and the crowd parted in the firelight, players running as fast as they could to get it back among themselves. You've never seen women with strollers move with more agility than during a Fireball game. George and his dad were mesmerized by the total lack of rules, almost in disbelief at the game.

And then, as suddenly as it started, the ball went out and the game was over.

"That was amazing!" George said. "But is that it?" Everyone, players and crowd, was dispersing already, moving off toward their cars and homes. "There's probably still a little life left in that ball if they just respark it."

"Yup, the rule of the game is to play it for all it's worth until the ball goes out," I said. "Sometimes the game lasts twenty minutes, sometimes two minutes, if it's been raining. There was rain last night, so the ground's a little wet," I pointed out. "But it's a game about celebrating the game, the joy of its existence."

"Fascinating," Mr. Haddonfield said. "I've been to a lot of places around the world, but I've never seen anything quite like that. How do you know who your teammates are?"

"Young Men versus Old Men."

"Age range?"

"Whether you've had a kid with someone or not."

"Oh," he said, startled. Until I'd spoken it in that moment, the truth had never occurred to me before so bluntly: that you became an "Old Man" in our community once there was evidence you'd had sex with a woman. We never said it like that. It was merely a given.

"There are sixteen-year-old Old Men and sixty-year-old Young Men. I'm still a Young Man," I joked, but they both only laughed uneasily. "Did you find any jewelry?" I asked, realizing I hadn't been around to get Mr. Haddonfield the Indian price if he'd wanted.

"Saw a few things, but nothing struck me as exactly right," he said. He sighed. "Looking for jewelry for your wife is a tricky thing. You can't go looking for that one thing. You have to be tuned to the right frequency, and then you know it when you see it. Son, did you find anything for Stacey while we were here?"

"I saw a few things, but decided not to get anything."

"Why not?" his dad asked, stopping. "I'm happy to lend you the money if —"

"No, it's not that. It's complicated. Something from here is maybe not the best gift. I'm not sure it would be Stacey's first choice."

"And why is that?" Mr. Haddonfield's tone shifted suddenly, another glimpse of the sterner version of him I'd sort of witnessed at the hotel elevators that night in Toronto. "Are you telling me your girlfriend has some issues with American Indians? Sorry, Lewis. Now you know, son, how I recognize you're at that age, but I'm *never* tolerating —"

"No, it's not that simple," George said. "It isn't Indians." What I heard in that moment was that maybe it wasn't Indians in general Stacey had issues with, but maybe one Indian, specifically. George knew he was saying it too. "Look, I don't want to talk about it, Dad. It's my personal business. I'll work it out."

I didn't want to get between my best friend and his father, and this was the first I was hearing of George's being indecisive about anything having to do with Stacey. I was beginning to regret having extended this invitation in the first place. Had I screwed things up by accident?

"That girl, Marie?" George asked me, obviously wanting to change the subject. "Is there any chance she'll come back to our school?"

"Not that I can tell. Their rez house has kind of gone to ruin since they moved. Why?"

"You seem to get along with her. Too bad you don't get to see her that often."

It *was* too bad, and now that she'd successfully ditched her old identity, she seemed happier. But I knew we weren't really talking about Marie. I'd seen this shift happening in our classmates, one by one. Boys were negotiating with the girls as to what combinations were going to work better than others. Though "going out with" someone didn't last more than two weeks or so in some cases, in our group of potential pairs at school, there was only one old brown shoe.

The expectations were different on the rez. There were heavy costs for marrying non-Indians, and it was worse for guys than women. If my sister had married a white man, her kids would still have legal status as Indians, but if I married a white woman, my kids would not. How could anyone make that choice, knowing what their kids' lives would be like on the reservation? They'd be treated differently, have to go to a different school, ride a different bus, and for the rest of their lives — even if they attended community events, learned how to social dance, learned the songs — everyone would know their business, and that it was different business. It was the craziest system, but it was the truth as we were bound to it. And since I didn't see any rez girls in school except at the free-lunch line, I sort of accepted that the women in Albert's library were probably as close as I was going to get to dating until high school.

"Is this thing with Stacey something to do with Lewis?" Mr. Haddonfield asked, his voice still edged as we got to their truck. We both wished he would drop it.

"Nothing bad," George said. "She thinks I spend time with him that I could be spending with her, so a souvenir of my being here tonight might not be the best, okay?"

"I see," Mr. Haddonfield said. His eyes softened, but his voice still had this rawer sound, like he was on guard, ready to jump into something messy if he felt he had to. They were going to have a longer conversation once I was no longer with them, and in that moment, I did not envy George his dad. "Would you like a ride home?" Mr. Haddonfield asked me.

I just wanted to get out of there, let them get back to their lives. I assured him I was fine and said good-bye to them at their truck. Then I walked back across the dark picnic grove and the footbridge, and found the smoldering ball of blackened rags, kicking it across the field as I headed home.

14

Live and Let Die

Toward the end of summer, we got our schedules mailed to us. I was still an Eight-Three, still among the smarties. I called George right away to confirm that we were in the same section.

"Of course, Shoe, where else? Stacey and Artie too." He laughed, and it was great to hear his voice. It was the first time we had talked since the end of July, and for once this gap had nothing to do with my saying or doing something stupid. He and his parents had gone to Germany for a week to visit relatives, and then he had spent another week camping with Stacey's family. All of our classes were the same except the final period, when he had Choraliers.

I didn't recognize any of the teacher names on my schedule, so I took my yearly trip down the road with my slip of paper to show my cousin Innis, who was in high school. He told me about which teachers to watch for, and then I pointed to one line on my schedule.

"Hey, do you know why they call Boys Chorus 'Music'?" I asked.

"What do you mean?" Innis asked. Where it should have said, "Boys Chorus," there sat "Music," with the name Miss Ward and a room number. Miss Ward was my homeroom teacher as well.

"That's not chorus. I've taken Music," Innis said, doing the slow nod and cocky grin. He liked passing knowledge on, particularly if it was a little unsavory. "It's, you know, like history, periods of music. I had Miss Ward. That woman's nuts. She left and then came back to the school when I was still there. The older kids called her Miss Mental Ward. Guess she had some big flip-out and her classes had to be subbed for the rest of the year."

"How do you get away with that? How come she didn't get fired?" I asked. That's what happened to anyone I knew who didn't show up for a job when they were supposed to — mostly my dad.

"Don't know. I heard a couple teachers talking about it in the hall. They were calling it something, like expensive leaves. She does bring in a synthesizer and let people play with it," he added. "Pretty much everyone just makes sound effects. You know, it's music class. If any of us knew what we were doing, we'd be in the band or the chorus."

"Are you sure?" I asked. He nodded, and we went out to shoot some hoops.

Less than a week later, Innis was proven right. In eighth period, the kids in band, Choraliers, and the Girls Chorus, including George and Stacey, all stood up in our homeroom and gathered their things to leave. I approached Miss Ward with my schedule as she set her grade book and other materials on the desk.

"Miss Ward, there seems to be a mistake here," I said, holding the slip of paper out to her. "I was supposed to be in Boys Chorus, but my schedule says I have Music here with you."

"Honey, there's no mistake. You're here. What's your name again?" I told her and she pointed to my name on her roster.

"Did I get kicked out of the Boys Chorus over the summer somehow?" I asked.

"No, honey. There were budget cuts this year, and they got rid of the chorus with the fewest number of students. Don't worry, we might sing some through the course of this year. Now have a seat. I'm sure the rest of the students will be here soon."

"The rest of the students?" I asked, turning to see that seven of us remained from my class.

"Yes, because there are so few of you, they combined some sections. The budget again. The students from Eight-Sixteen will be joining us shortly. Their homeroom is on the other side of the building, in the shop wing," she said, seeming disheartened.

"Sixteen?" I asked. "I didn't think the numbers went down that far."

"Yes, sixteen," she said. "They are the last."

The bell rang and I sat down near Steven and Artie in the back. Artie had shot up five inches over the summer and was now almost gangly.

Miss Ward looked at the clock and then peeked out the door, first one way, then the other. She went to the intercom and pressed the Call button. A minute later, Mrs. Tunny, the school secretary, came on, answering a question Miss Ward hadn't even had the chance to ask.

"They're on their way, Miss Ward. We just found them wandering the halls, and Mr. Barnes is escorting them to your room."

Miss Ward thanked her and shuffled her papers some more. A few minutes later, an even dozen of the toughest kids I had ever seen in my life, some of them the size of adults, strolled into the room with Mr. Barnes. Of course, Evan Reiniger was among them.

"Miss Ward," Mr. Barnes said, "there won't be any such lateness in the future, as these students now know where they're supposed to be. And anyone caught in the hall without a pass after the bell rings, that's an immediate detention. Am I clear?" he asked, turning to the new kids. None of them answered as they walked right up to us in the back seats.

"Get out," the kid I knew as "Truck" said to Artie, who shrugged his shoulders and moved up. Evan came right up to me, and I was waiting for him to swing, but he merely gave me the thumbs-out gesture that meant the same thing, and I obliged. *I dodged that bullet after all*, I thought. *A summer of dread for nothing.* Steven stayed put. Maybe his seat was closer to the front anyway.

Mr. Barnes eventually gave up on getting a response from the Eight-Sixteens and left us. As Miss Ward called our names for roll, the new kids pretended they didn't hear, chatting away until she told them directly that she was tired of talking over them. They begrudgingly answered to their names and then took to writing notes, passing spiral-bound notebooks with not even the slightest attempt at being sly. Miss Ward attempted to outline the school year for us, writing her name and highlights on the board, including the enticement of her synthesizer. She told us we were to arrange ourselves in alphabetical order, and the new kids dismissed the idea as if it had been a suggestion. To our shock, she didn't push it, moving on to the topic of our first unit, the blues.

"Now, children, this might seem old-fashioned," she said, playing a few bars on her piano, which sounded like the blues as you might hear them in those commercials advertising Music from the Past record collections. "But it's only a few progressions removed from this," she said, switching to a Beatles tune, "Money (That's What I Want)." "Or this," she added, smiling and playing another one, "I Call Your Name."

"That still sounds old-fashioned," Evan Reiniger said, and as a group, they all burst into grotesque fake laughs, then went back to their own interests. For her part, Miss Ward became willfully blind toward them and seemed more relieved than anything when the bell rang. They exited at warp speed, in direct contrast to their entrance. As they left, Evan grabbed his head and shook it fiercely. "I hate those classroom bells," he said. "They're so loud, they make me *mental*." Miss Ward did not look up from her rosters.

"How was Music?" George said, coming back into the room from Choraliers. "And what are you guys doing up here in front? You're always lurking in the back if there's no assigned seating."

"Never mind, songbird," I said.

The bell rang and we headed out to the building's front platform. George, Artie, and Stacey decided to walk home, so I walked them to the concrete edge and then made my way toward our bus.

Carson was talking with Evan Reiniger, as usual. I hadn't really looked Evan's way in class, not wanting to draw attention.

But out here, I could see that over the three short months of the summer, Evan had gotten even more intimidating looking, which I hadn't thought possible. Maybe it was just that I'd never had to see him up close for very long. He was compact, with a narrow face and wildcat eyes always scanning back and forth, and he curled his top lip to flash his teeth. He wore a tight Eric Clapton concert T-shirt, showing wiry muscles, as if he'd inherited the physique of an adult bodybuilder. I waited until he left before I approached Carson.

"Hey," I said, "anybody interesting in your section?"

"Couple people. That kid over there," he said, pointing with his chin to Evan. "He was before and he's always pretty cool. But if you ever see him talking to me, remember, do *not* mention the reservation. Him and his brother both hate Indian kids." We watched him get on the bus that went to Misty Meadows. "Better yet, if you see him talking to me, don't come up at all."

"If he hates Indians so much, why were you hanging out with him this summer?"

"Gotta have *someone* cool to hang with. Desperate times and all," he said.

"Maybe I should just not talk to you," I said, walking toward the bus.

"If only I could get that lucky," he said, laughing and joining me near the back when we got on, giving me a few head noogies for good measure before settling in the seat across the aisle from me. "Since he's in my section again, I'll be seeing him through most of the day. Better not cause a food fight, though, or he'll be answering to me. No white punk is messing up my digs." Even on the rez-life budget of Carson's family, somehow they always had decent clothes. No Sears Tuffskins on the Masticks.

"He already caused a little trouble this morning in art," he continued. "We got in earlier than the teacher. He broke into the cabinets and poured red paint onto her desk chair. She sat right in it. Looked like she . . . you know."

"What?"

"Never mind. He's going to come up with some name for her. Can't wait to hear what it will be. I don't know why I hang out with you. You're so dumb, you never even get my jokes."

"This seems more like it was his joke," I pointed out. "He in *all* your other classes?"

"Well, I made it to the Choraliers, and he wasn't in that one. I think all the kids who don't sing wound up in a music class. Is that what you have?"

"I was supposed to be in the Boys Chorus, but I don't know. Guess they canceled it." I was trying not to admit I'd failed my singing audition. "Hey, listen," I said. "I had to wait until the whole summer was over, and we got caught up on our kerosene bill, and I got some new clothes that fit, but I finally might have the hundred dollars, just like you said, all in —"

"Too late," he said. "I got rid of that guitar this summer. Remember when I wasn't at Picnic the first night? I was selling it to that kid, actually. He's never gonna play it, but he was willing to give me sixty up front."

"But you told *me* a hundred."

"Well, I needed cash for Picnic that weekend. I'd already laid my Fireball bets, and I knew your pockets weren't gonna be full enough, so when he offered . . ."

"How did he know you had a guitar to sell? If he hates Indians so much, you'd never blow your cover, so I know he never saw it at your house."

"Okay, fine! I asked him if he wanted to buy one. Satisfied? Jeez, you act like no other guitar is going to ever go up for sale. Just look in the want ads. There's tons. So, you wanna come over today? I siphoned some gas from my ma for the field car. I can come pick you up."

"Go pick up your friend, Evan the Guitar King," I said.

The next day, in our third-period shop class, I saw the final outcome of those red paint–soaked pants. Evan was escorted into our class by Mr. Barnes as the period began. Mr. Barnes and Mr. Meyer went through the little door that led to an office inside the classroom. There was murmuring we couldn't make out.

"Who are you chumps anyway?" Evan said, looking at us. "Bunch of losers I'm stuck with now, 'cause Miss Maxi Pants can't take a joke."

Evan left us at our seats and wandered over to the printing presses, tampering with the weights and settings while neither man could see us. A few minutes later, Mr. Barnes left, and Mr. Meyer introduced our new classmate before starting us in on the principles of shop safety.

"When you enter the shop, go directly to the back of the room here," he said, walking to the far corner, "and take one of these shop jackets," pointing out a series of slate-blue coats. "Now, I know they're not snazzy or anything, but they'll keep your clothes from getting stained, and I know you don't want that." He went on from there to talk about general safety, paper-cutter safety, glue safety, and printing-press safety. Danger lurked everywhere in shop class, it seemed. Our first project would be a bound notepad that would use all of the machines. I wondered who was going to slip on their project because of Evan's new press calibrations, perhaps burning the word "notes" permanently onto the back of a hand.

Evan appeared again that afternoon in Music with the other Eight-Sixteens. Now that he was in a bigger group of thugs instead of being among the brainiac shop class, or perhaps among a group with a greater appreciation for his talents, he took a starring role, lifting the lid on Miss Ward's piano and then revealing a bottle of glue I'd last seen in the shop room. He randomly squirted lines of it between the keys, and then quickly shut the lid, shoved the little glue bottle back into his jeans, and sat down next to Michael Truck and Nancy Cannon. Truck cackled with him, and Nancy did for a moment too, but then abruptly changed course.

"Can I borrow your glue?" she asked, flashing a few glossy pinups of some TV show guy. "I want to glue these pictures of Leif on my folders so he can be with me all the time."

I noticed that Nancy had begun developing in ways many of the other girls hadn't yet. The first day, her shirt had been a tube top, and today it was a buttoned Levi's jean vest with nothing beneath it, as far as I could tell.

"Later," Evan said.

"Come on, I don't want them to get ruined and creased," she said, smoothing them flat against the top folder.

"I don't want that bitch to see me with the glue, stupid," he said, flicking her hair back.

"No one's gonna know," Nancy said. "It's just glue. There's no crime in having glue."

"I'll let you use it on the bus, but if you don't turn around right now and shut up about the glue, I am going to punch you in the face and throw these stupid pictures in the garbage," he said, snagging one of the Leif pictures and crumpling it in front of her. He dropped the paper ball on the floor.

"My brother's gonna do to you what got done to your brother if you try something like that again," Nancy said, leaning down to grab her picture. As her fingers touched the floor, Evan quickly stood and stepped on them, not firmly enough to break anything, but too hard for her to pull them out from under his scruffy work boot.

"Mention my brother again, and I *will* crush *all* of them," he said, bending over to grab the crumpled paper. He ripped it into several pieces, and then moved faster than I'd thought possible, snatching the rest of the shiny, clipped pages from her desk and ripping them into tiny pieces as he strolled to the garbage can.

"No!" Nancy screamed as Miss Ward walked into the room.

"What's wrong, Nancy?" Miss Ward said as Evan tossed pinup confetti into the trash.

"Nothing, Miss Ward."

"Well, surely something made you scream," Miss Ward insisted.

"I just realized I had forgotten my . . ." Nancy said, trying to come up with something. "My pen."

"You can borrow this guy's," Evan said, reaching out to the little pen reservoir on Artie's desk and taking what was obviously his only pen. Artie just watched it go.

"I'm sorry, Evan," Nancy said looking at the blank folders in front of her as he delivered the pen to her. "I promise. I won't tell John anything, or Miss Ward. I swear, and I'll get my own glue too."

"That's better," he said, sliding his hand against her jaw, touching her mess of hair.

She smiled. "Maybe I can make it up to you at the bus stop," she said, tugging one of his front belt loops and rubbing her head into his hand like a cat.

Those of us among the Eight-Three crowd watched this exchange, not quite believing Nancy would do the things she was hinting at. I locked eyes with Artie, who bugged his eyes out in amazement, and then with Steven, who frowned. The others just looked down at their desks. These kids were aliens, operating by rules we didn't understand, but we knew they were maybe rules our older brothers and sisters were aware of. After what seemed like hours of odd flirting from Nancy and Evan's grudging acknowledgment, the bell rang, and the aliens left.

"Miss Ward," I said, walking up to her desk in the shuffle, "is there any way I could try out again for the Choraliers? I had a really terrible cold the first time." I had a bad feeling about this class and was looking for any exit.

"I'm sorry. It's not possible. Maybe you can try out again in April, but usually, if you haven't made it once, you're not likely to make it in the future. You're going to have to stick this out, like the rest of the class." She looked at her roster again. "You're from the reservation, right? I have something here that might make you happier. We'll do it tomorrow, I promise."

This alarmed me, thanks to Carson's warning. If Evan didn't know I was from the reservation already, he would get confirmation of that the next afternoon. Given his response to

Nancy, who he was presumably interested in, I couldn't imagine how life might be for someone he *didn't* like.

The next afternoon in Music, Miss Ward started campaigning for how awesome the guest appearance of her synthesizer was going to be. But first, she said, we had to learn respect for instruments. She unlocked a cabinet at the front of the room, revealing percussion instruments on the shelves — maracas, sticks with ridges notched on them, cowbells, and of course, drums.

"While rhythm instruments are perhaps not among the most glamorous," she said, lifting two wood blocks that were evidently supposed to be an instrument, "they are the foundation. The other musicians would be lost without a good rhythm section." She clapped the wood blocks, imitating a horse trot, and then rubbed them to make a whispery sound, to show us their versatility. When it was clear we weren't buying the wood blocks, she went for the big guns.

"Drums play important roles in many societies. Particularly tribal societies," she added, and I knew what was coming. "Now, we have an American Indian in class with us. Perhaps you would like to tell us if drums have played an important role in your life." She didn't look at me or say my name, like she was refusing to acknowledge who she was talking to. I didn't know if teachers weren't supposed to reveal that kind of information or what the deal was, but it didn't take too hard a look around the room to know she was talking to me, anonymous or not.

"No, we don't have any drums," I said, my mind repeating over and over again what Carson had told me about Evan.

"But surely you have used them at different ceremonies," Miss Ward insisted, taking the drum from the shelf with the intention of walking it to me.

"No. I was supposed to be in band, but . . ." I started to say, and then decided I didn't really need my entire class to know why I was not in band. "I didn't feel like it."

"Perhaps you would like to try —" Miss Ward started.

Fortunately for me, the robot cat alarm went off for a fire drill. We stood up to move, as quickly and as orderly as we were able, to the building's front door. "Boys and girls, walk fast, but no running and no talking and no horseplay," Miss Ward said. She followed quickly and then passed us, guiding us out farther from the building.

Once we'd reached the appropriate distance, she wandered over to talk with Mrs. Thatcher. Left unmonitored, our class redivided into its natural groups, like the stuff inside lava lamps. Artie and I wandered over to George and Stacey. Before we could say much, the all-clear bell went off and we headed back in.

In almost a repeat of last spring, I saw the silhouette first, and then there was Evan on my back again, his first hit finding my cheekbone, only missing my glasses by a hair. This time, I rolled with it faster than before, throwing him off long enough to get to our class door.

"I knew there was something about you, but I couldn't remember what," he said, jumping up to see if there were any witnesses to my dodge. "I never forget a face, but it's your ass I remember. You're Mr. Tender Ass." Then he changed his voice, making it higher. "Ow, stop hitting me with your stick." Then back to his voice. "That was you. Or is it Chief Tender Ass? I should have known you were a whiny Indian bitch. I told you. We got a whole new year."

"Let's go, Evan," Truck said, walking in the opposite direction. "I ain't going to detention 'cause you wanna chase this wahoo around. Do it on your own time."

"Yeah, there's lots of time," Evan said, walking backward. He waved good-bye to me.

A few minutes later, George and Stacey came into homeroom.

"You okay? You look really weird, pale, like you're going to faint," George said to me. "And what's that hot spot on your cheek?"

"Put your head between your legs," Stacey added.

And kiss your ass good-bye, I thought. There was no way I could explain what this panic was, that almost five hundred years of my people being wiped out by their people had found its way onto my doorstep at last. They would never believe me, of course, and in some ways, if I said that, pointed Evan's violent campaign out to them, I would be implicating them too. They sat down, and we listened to the announcements and then left when the bell rang.

Carson was all wild-eyed when I got to our bus platform.

"You idiot! How did you piss off Evan? He was crazy mad when he got back to homeroom. Said he was going to kick the ass of some kid named Shoe every day for the rest of the school year." Evan must have heard George call me that in shop and thought it was my name. At least I still sort of had anonymity going for me. "I thought for sure you weren't stupid enough to fight back instead of taking any punches he was handing out."

"That's your best advice?" I asked. "Not to fight back?" Most of the buses had already arrived and kids had piled in, but ours, from a different provider, was late, as it often was. I watched the faces, making sure one dangerous mug in particular was not headed my way, and then sat down on the warm stone risers, knowing it might be a while.

"Dead! Shoe! You're dead! School year's just beginning." I looked up and saw what I had expected. Evan's head and arm were stuck out one of his bus windows in an act of physics that seemed like it belonged in a circus sideshow. I didn't acknowledge him, hoping maybe he'd just forget about me. It wasn't logical, but panic was making it hard to decide what a good plan *would* be.

When they passed, I turned to face Carson, expecting to hear him repeat what an idiot I was, how terrible my life was going to be over the next year, that I should not sit next to him, but instead, by the time I looked over, he was gone. He'd made himself vanish in some way before Evan saw him, and when our bus eventually arrived, he reappeared, as if he'd been there the entire time. I got on and went to our usual seats near the back, but he chose to sit with his cousin Tami, five seats away. I guess half the length of a bus was a safe enough distance from me.

For You, Blue

I dropped my school bag, went upstairs, and stepped into the room where my ma kept Charlotte's old life preserved, waiting for her to resume it. The vanity still sat in the near corner, and I turned on the lamp. Lifting up my Spider-Man T-shirt, I looked in the three-way mirror.

My face would be red today and sore to touch for a few more. Below my T-shirt, though, was another story. There was no denying I was a skinny kid, ribs showing and all — like a birdcage, Zach always said. Now there were going to be knuckle tracks across those slats in the morning. I made a note to come downstairs with my shirt on the next day.

I put my shirt back down, left the house, and headed down the road. My cousin Innis was already in their back field, shooting hoops. He tossed the ball to me without a word.

"So how's eighth going?" he eventually said after we'd played a little one-on-one.

"Not so good. You ever have to deal with someone who hated you for no reason at all?"

"Teacher or kid?"

"What do you mean? Kid."

"You'll see," he said, but offered no more details. "So who's the kid? It's the beginning of the year. How much trouble can you even be in?"

"Some kid named Evan Reiniger." His face told me I was in even more trouble than I'd thought. "Maybe I caused the trouble by telling him to quit hitting me with a stick last spring."

"Nah, you didn't start it. He know you're from the reservation?"

"Yeah, probably, I guess." Then I remembered Miss Ward's big drumming idea. "Yeah, definitely. Miss Ward —"

"Sun dances? Tribal rhythms?"

"Never got to the sun dances, but, yeah, tribal rhythms."

"You will. You watch, she'll ask if you know anyone who has done a sun dance, and when you say no, it will give her an opportunity to talk about it with the rest of the class. That kid, though, that's a bigger problem. You got any huge friends in class?" George wasn't in music, so I shook my head. "That family's bad news, and you can be sure they don't like Indians. Us, definitely. He must have figured out we're related."

He told me that his family was getting groceries late one night, or technically, my auntie Olive was getting groceries and her boys were goofing off in the parking lot, waiting to load the bags into the trunk when she was done. The automatic doors opened, and my aunt strolled through with her extra full shopping cart.

Out of the shadows, this kid came flying, crashing an empty grocery cart right into her and knocking her down. Her cart drifted into the lot. The younger boys grabbed their ma and the cart, while Stan, the oldest and fastest, went for the kid. Evan tried hiding in the shadows, but my cousins caught him, and he learned a lot that night about the tightness of

Indian families — most of it while stuck inside a Dumpster. This was a year ago. I couldn't imagine even dreaming up such violence against an adult at the age of twelve, but then again, I didn't know what to make of Evan at all, except that I wanted to be nowhere near him. As for his singling out my aunt in the first place, Innis had no explanation.

The morning after my beating, I lifted my shirt in the mirror again. The knuckle tracks were neat rows of purple nubs across my ribs, like kernels of blue Indian corn. I grabbed my darkest shirt, maroon, and got fully dressed before I went down for breakfast. My ma was pouring water in the pan so I could wash up. I could smell the iron wetness that meant she'd just gone out and pumped the water this morning. I loved the sweet, metallic taste of water fresh from the pump.

"Take your shirt off to wash up or you're gonna get suds on it," my ma said. "And besides, I told you in the summer, you're to that age where you're gonna have to wear deodorant. Go in the mirror and lift up your arms." I did as I was told, though I kept the shirt on. "Not like that," she said.

"I know what you mean," I said, trying to sound just the right combination of embarrassed and annoyed so she'd leave me alone. I ran upstairs and used the gel stick she'd gotten me. I came back down, neatly washed my hands, face, ears, and neck with a soapy washcloth, and toweled off before she noticed I was done. The bruises should be light enough that I'd be able to wash up properly the next morning and she wouldn't know a thing.

"You gotta wash first, not just use deodorant. You need to learn to clean up better now. You're with white kids, and I don't want them having any excuse to call you a dirty Indian."

"Ma!" I scolded, and headed for the door. "The bus is coming." I wasn't too worried about hygiene. Gym was second period, and I'd shower after. It was such a pain to bathe at home: Heat water, pour it in the pan, take it into my ma's bedroom, wash from feet to belly button, dry, get dressed, heat more water, wash from belly button to face, dry, then heat more water, shampoo, rinse, etc., and finish by refilling the water pail, since I'd used it up.

After gym, George and I walked to shop together. The fall sun blasted bright light into the corridor from the building's back windows. We came from the front, and George said, "Gotta hit the john, and I don't want to have to ask Meyer for a pass. See you in the room."

All I could see were silhouettes along that hallway. I might as well have been in a spotlight. I counted down the doors to the shop room, and as I got close, a shadow flickered in front of me, just like the other day. In the second I recognized the silhouette, I knew I was going to be blasted again. I dropped my books, swinging back after the first punch clicked my teeth on my tongue.

It felt as if Evan had grown extra arms, like the sword-wielding stone statue in *The Golden Voyage of Sinbad*. He seemed to have a sharp memory too, landing punches in every place I was already bruised. I deflected wherever I could, but none of my swings connected. The only thing I could do was push myself toward the light that meant our classroom door.

As soon as I crossed into the room, he vanished. Mr. Meyer looked up at me. I knew my face must be all red, my hair wildly out of place, glasses askew, shirt twisted halfway up my side — and then he did the oddest of things. He dropped his gaze back down at his desk, as if I looked exactly as I should. I stood at the counter and rearranged myself, tucking my shirt back into my jeans, stuffing paper back into the folder it had been knocked from, trying to comb my hair with my fingers.

Evan walked in a minute after me, looking not at all as if he'd just given me an ass whipping, delivering a side kick to my left butt cheek without even breaking his pace. He lingered at some of the machines. I'd hoped he'd sit first so I could find the farthest wooden folding chair away, but then the bell rang and we had to take seats. I chose front and center.

For the first time, the large shade behind Mr. Meyer's desk was pulled up, and we could see into the space beyond it. An office with two desks bridged the classrooms, sandwiched by plate glass. In the opposite room, a man with a brush cut shorter than Mr. Haddonfield's military regulation buzz stood in front of a drawing table. Some guys in that room were from our gym class and from a nearby table in the lunchroom. A few made faces when they noticed the open shade.

"What's that, Mr. Meyer?" Steven said.

"Mr. McKee's classroom," Mr. Meyer said, walking toward his desk, "where you'll be in late October, when we swap. Then those boys will be here, learning what you're learning now."

"What are they learning?" I asked. Mr. Meyer held up a wait-a-minute finger, walked through the door, and closed the blind leading to Mr. McKee's room.

"Shut up," Evan growled into my ear, grabbing fully on to my head of hair — just long enough these days to grab — and yanking my head back so I had a perfect view of the ceiling lights. I reached back in an effort to get his clenched fist out of my hair, but my arms more or less flailed above my head. The rest of the class sat in their seats as if nothing were happening.

"Don't you say another word," Evan hissed, "and don't even think about getting out of this class. You're mine. And gimme your pen." I did nothing and then he yanked harder. "Let me borrow your pen," he said, giving a longer yank of my hair with each word. I reached into my shirt pocket and handed it over. He let go, pushed my head forward, and sat back in his folding chair as Mr. Meyer came back in, about the same minute George did.

"That is the mechanical drawing class," Mr. Meyer explained. "They learn to make blueprints — exact drawings in preparations for projects — so that when you build something, it won't be lopsided, which happens often when people try to eyeball things. Maybe you've seen some disastrous results when your dads have tried to eyeball something in their basement shops."

My dad hadn't lived with us since I was maybe two, never in my memory anyway. And as far as a basement was concerned, one of the floorboards near the slop pail had rotted to the point of giving way a couple years ago. Before we replaced it with a piece of plywood, I caught a quick peek below. Our basement consisted of six to eight inches of space above the packed dirt.

"But enough about that. We have a different matter to discuss today. I'd hoped we'd begin our notepad project, but in first period, I discovered someone had played with the calibrations on the presses. No one came forward in either of the two earlier classes with information, so we sat. I'll extend the same invitation here."

Of course, we all knew Evan did it. I hadn't been the only witness, but apparently I was going to be Evan's example of what happened to kids who crossed him, and nobody else was going to take the risk of joining me.

"I thought not," Mr. Meyer said. "Okay, well, it's going to take me a while to recalibrate all the weights, so you gentlemen can sit here, contemplating your silence. No reading, no homework, nothing. And I'll be keeping an eye on you as I work on the first press."

Mr. Meyer went back to his office and dug through manuals on a shelf banking the courtyard windows. Evan started kicking my back in the space between the chair back and its seat. There wasn't much space for him to get momentum, but he was determined. I stood to move next to George, who had sat in the back row, but Mr. Meyer was like a T. rex — he registered motion in one second. "Sit down," he yelled. "No switching to talk to a neighbor. You're all going to sit and think about responsibility." He came out of the office and glared at me.

"I don't think any of you realize what a dangerous game you're playing," he said, leaning on his desk for effect. "I would have thought my first day's talk about how this machinery is not a toy would have impressed upon you the concept of no monkeying around, but it clearly didn't."

"Does that mean we won't get as much time to work on the presses as the kids who come later?" Evan asked. "I was really looking forward to seeing how all these things worked and making some nice projects for Christmas gifts."

Anyone with half a brain should have seen through this routine. It was as obvious as an after-school special, but Mr. Meyer looked disappointed and apologetic, shrugging his shoulders. "We'll have to wait and see," he said, going back to his office.

By the end of class, Evan's patented method of Get Punches and Kicks in When No Teacher Is Looking, then Look Normal in Two Seconds Flat was perfected. As the bell rang, he gave me back my pen.

"Where the hell were you?" I asked George as we gathered our books.

"Well, at the risk of too much information, when I got to the john, I discovered I had more business to do than I thought."

"Okay, got it. No need for more."

"Good. I wasn't all that keen to share the details. Don't bother with that pen, by the way," George said. "That kid took it apart, blew air into it, shook it, and put it back together loose. Unless you want your pocket covered in blue ink —" He stopped when he finally took in a little better what I looked like. "What happened to you?"

"Tell you later," I said. "This is the only pen I have." When I'd gone to the Towne Pharmacy with my ma for school supplies, they had the single pen in a package, or a package of five for only double the price of one. I explained the simple economics of it to my ma, but she said we didn't have that kind of cushion.

"Here," George said, handing me a Bic. "I have an extra one, but hide it. If he sees you with another pen, the same thing's gonna happen. Why is that jerk in our class anyway?"

I took the pen and slid it into my folder pocket as I walked out of the room. In the hall, Evan immediately re-created the dive he'd taken at me before class, crashing into me and whaling on my head. I blocked a couple blows and tried to swing back, but every time I did, I just opened myself up somewhere else. Finally, I was able to make it to the congested staircase and work my way up quickly against the tide of other kids.

"Hey! Hey!" I could hear George shouting, confused.

"Preston, grab that kid," Evan shouted from six steps behind me. I knew if I got to the top, I had a clear shot at making it out of his range.

Preston, Evan's brother, looked around above me. "Which one?" he yelled back.

"That one in the red shirt," Evan yelled. But he couldn't come up with "maroon," and Preston seemed to have a limited definition of the range of red. I arrived safely to class.

The Eight-Sixteens sat at the opposite end of the cafeteria at lunch, so they went down the opposite cafeteria line and checkout register. I sat down next to George and Stacey at our table. "You're probably going to get a shiner out of that one," George said.

"Ya think?" I said, flinching. Even moving my cheek to speak felt like I'd been struck by a lighted match.

"You'll look like my Guam scrapbook picture."

"You'll never have to worry about getting another shiner," I said.

"What do you mean?" George asked.

"Look at you," I said. "Who would mess with you? *He* wouldn't stand a chance."

"Yeah, well, Evan might not, but if I got caught fighting? My dad would whip my butt into next week. I told you that already. And you've seen his fuse is sometimes quick to spark. What was that all about anyway? Why do you even know that kid?"

"He hates Indians," I said, and knew, as soon as I'd said it, that my classmates would not believe me. I sounded like their parents, threatening them with the scary Indians who hated them, except I was asking them to see it reversed: My daily life in school was the imagined terror they'd had as kids. I'd been dumped off every day among the white people and forced to find my own way out, encountering indifferent teachers, isolation, and now active violence from Evan. Wild Indians on a reservation had nothing on a mostly white junior high in the way of scariness.

George said, "You know, in Guam, base kids had been there for so long, no one made those kinds of distinctions, so there was never really any fighting, since we all had to live in the same place."

"That doesn't happen here either," said Rob Doris, a budding football player. "He's just making the easy Indian claim they all do. Get a group of them together, though, and you're outnumbered, they'll try to kick your ass as soon as look at you. Hear it happens all the time in the high school. It's only when they're singled out that they're running scared."

"Guam sounds like the reservation," I said, trying to defuse Rob's comments. "You might fight — no place is perfect — but even if you do, you're probably going to be friends again before the end of the week. Where else are you going to go?"

"Just like that," George said. My explanation was pointless for most of our table, but it was possible they might hear him, and maybe see themselves in this same situation. "When my dad got this assignment, though, he sat me down and explained the military kids would be a small group in a big school. He said some people here might give us grief, I guess maybe still about Vietnam." He lowered his voice. "I'm not even supposed to say 'Vietnam.'"

"Me neither," I said, thinking about Albert and his reactions anytime he heard the word.

"Anyway, I'd like to help you out," he said to me, "but I've had exactly one butt kicking from my dad in my life, and I don't want another, ever. Maybe if we stand as a group and say we're not —" He was looking out at the group as a whole, but he didn't even finish, given the incredulous noises our table made. "Okay, well, maybe not. But you know," he said, turning back to me exclusively, "if you just stand up to him, fight him once —"

"What do you think I've been doing? What do you think started this? If I looked like you, sure, that might end it, but look at me," I said, lifting my arms up in a muscle pose. George made a doubtful face, confirming what I already knew about the lameness of my biceps.

I really hoped this refusal to back me up with muscle, if it came down to that, was some show he put on for some of the Manor kids who knew his dad, but I didn't think so. In truth, I couldn't fault him, as much as I wanted him to help me. The longer we were friends, the more I understood what Albert told me about the lack of a rez rocket. We were just going to always have that gap and make the most of what we had.

George had come here, maybe trusting everyone, and even seeking me out purposefully, but the longer he lived in this area, the more our limits were defined by the kids in our school district. He'd been with me in the middle of the reservation in the summer, walking around the picnic grove like any of us. But as much as I hated to admit it, if he'd been by himself, he'd be a fool not to be uneasy, after our long history with Niagara County and its citizens. I knew people who, if they found a white teenage guy wandering down Snakeline, would take the opportunity to educate him about borders. He'd know intimately the places where one territory left off and another began.

"What about a different plan?" George offered. "Maybe it'll just blow over. It's early in the school year."

"Does it seem to you like it's going to blow over?" I asked.

"No, not really," he said. "Tell you what. I'll make sure to always walk with you. Maybe that'll make a difference. We usually walk together anyway. When do you tend to run into him?"

"That class and then this afternoon, music."

"Sorry," he said, looking down. "Can't help you there. Choraliers."

"Thanks for reminding me," I said.

At the end of music class, I lingered behind with Miss Ward, instead of going with everyone else to get our stuff to head for the buses right after final announcements. I couldn't see Evan anymore from out the classroom's little door-frame window. Finally, I stepped out of the room for a quick dash to my locker.

"Pounding don't take but a minute if you're good," Evan said, shoving me into my locker. Even with my delay, he had outwaited me. I turned around, and George stepped up. Evan sidestepped him and slammed both hands into my chest, knocking me into the lockers again. He got closer for the next swing as I regained my footing.

"I don't think you need to do this," George said to Evan, stepping between us. "Maybe you should just go along."

"Maybe *you* should go along," Evan said, George's size apparently meaning nothing. "This is none of your business, but if you want to make it your business, we'll get it on."

"Look, cut it out," George said, moving closer.

"You think your baby-killing, tight-ass army dad is gonna like you being suspended for fighting? Whyn't you all go back to killing in Vietnam and stay out of what's not your concern."

George flushed, and his muscles tensed. "My dad's in the air force, not the army, and we were nowhere near Vietnam," he said quietly, almost politely.

"Either way. My dad *likes* it when I get suspended," Evan said. "Shows him how tough I am, that I don't take anyone's bull."

"That's going to get you far in life," George said.

"You know it, candy ass. But I'm guessing things might be different over there in the Manor. So is it worth it to you to help this reservation trash? If it is, let's get it on, and if not, you better step aside."

George stood still for a moment and then did as he was advised. As the bell rang, he stepped aside and took me with him, pushing me into homeroom and shutting the door. Evan glared through the window, but a hall monitor came along and shooed him away. We stayed the few minutes for afternoon announcements, and then he and Stacey walked with me to the buses.

"Where are you going?" I asked as we passed their bus.

"We're accompanying you," Stacey said, as if anyone with eyes couldn't figure out they were trying to protect me.

"You two should go to your own bus," I said. "What, are you going to be my bodyguards for the rest of the school year?"

"No," George said, "only as long as it takes for that kid to take the hint."

"You can't do that," I said. "You even said so yourself. He knows he can take me, and he knows you have to stay out of trouble."

"Well, I'll deal with that if I have to."

That night, my eye grew a bluish, purple ring as George had predicted. Even behind my glasses, there was no hiding it.

"What happened to you?" my ma asked as I was washing my hair in the pans I'd set up on the dining room table.

"Some white kid keeps picking a fight with me every day," I said. To lie was pointless. She was like a lie-bloodhound.

"Take off that T-shirt," she said, and I did as I was told. "Why aren't you fighting back?" she said. "You can't let those white people think they can do this to you, or they'll do it forever."

"Why aren't *you* fighting back?" I said, throwing her own words back at her. "Like when Mrs. D. says at the last minute that she wants you to stay through the evening to waitress a party, though you've been scrubbing her house for eight hours. Why don't you fight back?"

She slapped me then, as I knew she would. I was getting older, but definitely not too old to be taken down with a slap. "You know I do what I can. I need those jobs."

"Do you tell her you have your own family to go home to instead of switching into that outfit she rents for you and putting on your hostess smile?" She looked down. I hated doing this, even got that garden-slug-in-the-gut feeling, but I had to make her understand what was happening. "I do fight back. I do," I said. "It gets worse, every time. It's like that time you told Mrs. D. that you couldn't do the floor on your hands and knees because your knee was all swollen like a softball. Remember what happened?"

Mrs. D., whose house she'd cleaned for over ten years, had docked half her pay, even though my ma had still done the floor with a regular wet mop she'd brought herself.

She just said, "You better figure out something. Have you talked to any of the teachers?"

This seemed like a phenomenally bad idea to me at the time. So as days went by, I spent them being pummeled, and blocking what blows I could, followed by evenings of devising new methods of protecting myself — none of which ever worked. George interfered with whatever moves he could without formally ever acting, knowing he would only be okay with his dad for self-defense. Evan himself must have had some sense of self-preservation, as he would have been no match if George could justify fighting back.

It was unbelievable to me that no teacher ever witnessed these encounters, given how regular and visible they were. Evan didn't even bother waiting for opportunities after a few days. By the end of the second week, he seemed to love the challenge of coming up with new, deadly moves that he could deliver in between classes. He'd figured out my schedule and began showing up after almost every period, as if our twice-a-day tangles weren't satisfying enough. I knew I had to do something different.

You Gave Me the Answer

The next week, Miss Ward brought in her famous synthesizer, an electronic keyboard with dials, lights, and buttons mounted into a header piece. She encouraged us to sign up on the board for an opportunity to play it. After I put my name on the list, Evan erased my name and put his own in its place. I was just as happy, knowing I would do little except make noise on the thing. Most people pressed keys and twisted knobs, generating sounds you might hear on Saturday Afternoon Sci-Fi Theater. Nancy found a couple notes that sounded like the records of one of her pinup boys, and she danced a bit until Miss Ward told her it was someone else's turn.

That someone else was Evan. "Clapton uses this thing," he said to Miss Ward, "where he shoves a little tube on his finger and it changes his guitar sound. He run it through one of these?" He flipped switches and pressed keys. A sound like a December wind came out of the speakers.

"No, it sounds like you're describing a slide, and that is something tied more to the stringed instruments," Miss Ward said. "They work differently. I don't know who Clampton is."

"Clapton. You know, Derek and the Dominoes? *Layla?* The best album ever?" Evan said, frowning. "Never mind. This is stupid." As he walked away, he spotted Miss Ward's coffee on the table, and faked a stumble, spilling the coffee into the keyboard. The synthesizer made a few hums and squeals from its built-in speaker, smoked a little, and then only hummed.

Miss Ward fluttered her arms like a small bird. "Oh no, oh dear," she muttered. Evan pretended to be embarrassed, wiping the keys, but really spreading the coffee farther. I hoped he might get electrocuted, but he seemed as impervious to the laws of physics as he was to regular rules.

Miss Ward dug into her bag for a Kleenex, holding it to her eyes and poking it under her glasses as she told Evan to go back to his seat. She shut the synthesizer off and tried turning it back on, but that just made it hum again, while more little wisps of smoke came from its vents. Then she excused herself, running out the door.

"Oh no, oh dear," Evan kept saying, in a fake woman's voice, waving his hands.

"Maybe Mental Ward will go on another extended leave," Truck said back. "A sub, that'd be cool. Wonder who they'd get."

Evan whipped his head around and stared straight at me. "Oh no, Shoe, oh dear," he said, jumping from his desk. He smiled, shoving desks out of his way, even with kids sitting at them, as he advanced toward me.

Just then the classroom door opened and Mr. Doyle stepped inside. Among the vice principals, I wasn't sure what his job was. We usually saw him at the beginning and the end of the day in the foyer, greeting us in the morning and telling us to have a good evening when we left. I had never seen him without a smile on his face until this afternoon.

"Sit down, young man," he said.

"I was just fixing my shirt," Evan said, smoothing the tails and sitting down.

"You can do that from your seat," Mr. Doyle said. Evan sat immediately, his bullshit-tolerance detector working perfectly. "Now I have just had a visit in my office from Miss Ward, and she is quite upset, and she told me this class was the cause. I of course want every one of my teachers to have a rich classroom experience where they can share their knowledge with students. I also know that not everyone wants to learn, but you, this day, were unwise in your decisions. You have not only upset one of my teachers, but you have also upset one of my very dearest friends in this world." He looked down at his own white knuckles leaning on Miss Ward's table, where the dying synthesizer sat, and you could hear the shake in his voice.

"You think he's gonna cry?" Evan whispered to Truck.

"Who said that?" Mr. Doyle shouted, suddenly scanning the room, trying to find the guilty face. "We are going to sit here until someone tells me," he said, his voice a growl, when the robot cat went off, on schedule, for our continued attempts at achieving the perfect fire drill. We stood on cue, leaving our folders as we were always instructed, and moved toward the door.

"Sit down," Mr. Doyle said quietly, flat. Most of us stopped, stunned. Others, who were so trained to the sounds of the alarm that they didn't even register what he had said, continued to try to exit.

"I said, sit down," he repeated, louder. We looked at one another, no one wanting to make the first move. Was this a trick? A test? A new elaborate wrinkle in the etiquette of fire drills?

"But, Mr. Doyle —" Nancy began.

"I don't care if we burn to cinders and they have to sift through the ashes to find teeth to identify us. You're not leaving this room until I have answers," he said, still not raising his voice at all. Our mystification told us he was serious and we sat back down. In the hall, our classmates shuffled by, whispering to one another and giggling quietly as they passed into safety. Miss Fox, following the last of her students, stopped in the narrow window to our door and made an alarmed face, as if she believed there really were a fire somewhere in the building.

"Miss Ward," she yelled, flinging the door open. "You have to let —" She stopped midsentence, staring at Mr. Doyle.

"Please go on your way, Miss Fox. I have everything under control," Mr. Doyle said.

"Mr. Doyle, I think it's against state fire regulations to —"

"That'll be all, Miss Fox," he said, walking toward her, starting to close the door on her, but keeping his eye on us. "Please get your students and yourself to an appropriate distance from the building." Her eyes scanned from Doyle to us, us to Doyle. "That . . . will . . . be . . . all," he repeated slowly, not even looking at her. The door clicked shut.

Mr. Doyle lifted his knuckles and looked down at the little humming synthesizer. He studied the various knobs and buttons for a few seconds, found the power switch, and shut it off. Whatever had been humming inside the machine continued on for a few seconds, slowly dying down, a sound from inside the machine's guts evidently not synthesized.

Eventually, we heard the all clear and then the return shuffle of our fellow students, many of whom peeked in the window to see what was so special about us. Mr. Doyle, meanwhile, continued to repeat, in slight variation, how much he liked Miss Ward and how we had made rather a bad enemy of him. He might have been more intimidating if he hadn't been borrowing dialogue from *The Wizard of Oz*'s Wicked Witch of the West.

A moment later, Mr. Barnes rapped on the narrow window. Mr. Doyle held a finger up to us, as if silencing himself, and stepped into the hall. Even with the door closed, we could hear a few words clear here and there, "state funding," "heavy fines," "out of control," but the one that got our attention was Mr. Doyle calling us "little shits." While agreeing, I was still shocked.

Mr. Barnes stepped into our room a minute later, called Mrs. Tunny on the intercom, and demanded one of the study hall monitors to come immediately to our room. Mrs. Clemson showed up a minute later, and the dueling vice principals left together, still in heated discussion. Mrs. Clemson looked a little uneasy and just told us to work on our assignments until the bell rang.

Once the Eight-Sixteens left and our homeroom classmates joined us again, Mr. Doyle came back to our room, his neck and face red, a little vein pumping at his left temple. He stood at the front table, unplugged the cords and wrapped them around the synthesizer, then gathered Miss Ward's folders and slid them into a leather bag in the corner, not really speaking to us as Mr. Barnes delivered the afternoon announcements over the intercom.

When the bell came, my class piled out as usual, but I stayed behind, slowly collecting my things. When we were alone in the room, I walked up to the desk. Even if some teachers turned a blind eye to Evan's actions because of his father's booster dollars, here was someone who could maybe understand that, sometimes, people were cruel for no other reason than they wanted to be; that victims could be chosen simply for being in the wrong place at the wrong time; that his friend Miss Ward, despite her best intentions, was selected as a victim. It happens, and clearly he understood it was his job to do something about that kind of injustice if it occurred in this building. "Mr. Doyle," I said. "I'd like to talk to you about something."

"Does it involve telling me who glued the keys together on this piano and who's been writing vulgar notes and leaving them in Miss Ward's bag every day?"

"Well, no. I don't know that," I said, which was a lie. Naturally, I knew about the keys, but I also knew if I revealed the truth about the glue, I would be dead. "But, Mr. Doyle, I've been having trouble with someone hassling me. Someone from this class."

"I'm a little busy right now to deal with a situation like this. You're getting to the age where you should be able to handle people you don't like. What do you think is going to happen when you get out in the real world if you can't fight your own battles?"

It took all I had to resist saying "I'll become Miss Ward," but the reality of my day-to-day poundings was giving me some discipline with my smart mouth, if nothing else. Instead, I said, "You know, I'm pretty sure it's part of your job to deal with students who beat on other students, not just students who hassle your very dear friends."

"Come with me," he said, setting the synthesizer down and grabbing my sleeve, escorting me out. I had to jog to keep from getting dragged the rest of the way to the office with him.

"Mrs. Tunny," he said when we entered the office, "give this young man a piece of paper and a pen, and when he's done writing down his problem, leave it in my mailbox. I'll deal with it the first chance I get." He finished these instructions without breaking stride, heading toward an inner office.

"Won't he miss his bus?" Mrs. Tunny asked as he opened the door.

He stopped and turned to look at me as he spoke to her. "If it's important enough for him to tell me, he can sacrifice the bus ride," he said. Inside the inner office, Mr. Barnes's voice began with a "Jack, what the hell were you thinking?" Mr. Doyle slammed the door and they started a loud discussion I could hear even through the door.

"Here you go," Mrs. Tunny said, sliding a sheet of green paper across the counter at me with a Bic pen on top. I thought for a minute. Eventually, I wrote:

Mr. Doyle:
    Since April, Evan Reiniger has been hassling me. At first, it was just annoying, but from the first time I fought back, it has gotten worse. I mention this only in that your suggestion was to fight back. It has gotten me nowhere except in a worse place. I have tried avoiding him, if that's your next suggestion. I

would like you to do something about this, but please do not put us in the same room together to work this out. That would be a very, very bad idea! Evan is NOT someone you can work with. You might ask your very dear friend about things.

I signed it and passed it over to Mrs. Tunny just in time to see my bus pull out of the driveway. There was no possible scenario in which I could run fast enough to catch the driver's attention, so I went to my locker to get my things and start the long walk home. Turning the corner, I saw two figures near my locker. My first thought was that it was Evan and his brother, Preston, and I was sure I was sunk. Then I recognized Artie's curly head of hair on one of the silhouettes.

"You missed your bus," the taller figure said. It was George, stuffing a folder into a bag.

"So did you," I said, dialing my combination. "I had business in the office."

"You went to the office about that jerk?" Artie said. "Do you just *want* to die?"

"What else am I gonna do?" I said. I was at the end of my possibilities. "So where's Stacey? You guys here sticking around to try out for football or something?"

"Nah, we thought we'd walk home since the weather's nice," George said. "Figured we'd probably still have time to make it to —"

"To Good Intentions, yeah, I remember," I finished for him. "Is it really that fun?"

"It's the best," George said. "You wanna come? Looks like you're walking anyway."

"Not in the mood for fun right now."

"Least we can walk with you 'til we get to that first reservation road," he said. Neither was willing to admit what they were truly doing. If George and I had been alone, we wouldn't have needed this nonsense, but I guess he wanted to protect my privacy — not that I had any in this matter. "Besides, in about three minutes, we won't be on school property anymore."

"Yeah, so?"

"No detention or suspension rules in the real world," he said, flexing his arms like in those muscle machine advertisements in the comics. "Or better yet, I'll teach you some moves like I have with Artie." He instantly put Artie in a headlock. Artie tried working his leg around behind George's, with no success. "He's trying the boomerang, one I learned in Guam," George said. "But I haven't taught him *all* my secrets," he added, letting Artie go. He then effectively performed the move, hooking his foot around Artie's ankle and pivoting on his other foot, flipping Artie straight to the floor.

"Lot of good that's going to do me," I said, shutting my locker. He could teach me any moves he wanted, but I was still going to be a scrawny kid who wore glasses.

"Come on," George said, and we walked past the music classroom.

"You want me to run back in there and get you a drum for spiritual practice?" Artie asked as we burst out the front bank of doors into the beautiful fall air. "You could conjure up an ancient spirit and kick that guy's butt."

"What drums?" George asked as we hit the driveway.

"Had to be there," Artie and I said at the same time.

Right as we were about to the point of my split down Snakeline, a car slowed behind us. George crouched a little and his arms flexed. "It's okay. Relax," I said. I recognized the car.

The Thunderbird's window rolled down, and Mrs. Tunny from the office asked me if I wanted a ride. I told the guys good-bye and hopped in. Mrs. Tunny was a white woman who married an influential reservation man. She was good-natured with us reservation kids, even though our strict way of defining who is Indian and who isn't had a major effect on her family. Her kids had a reservation last name, but they were considered white. They couldn't go to the reservation school with us and joined us only when we reached junior high.

"Nyah-wheh," I said, watching my friends continue on their walk home.

"Jeh. You like those boys?" she said, pointing us down Snakeline.

"Yeah, they're both good guys. One more than the other, but they're both good," I said. "They're in my regular classes. We're Eight-Three."

"I know where all the Indian kids are. That's good that you like them. It's good to have more friends than just those from here," she said. "Not everyone agrees, but I'm glad for you."

"Not like I have a lot of choice, Mrs. Tunny."

"You know it's not Mrs. Tunny when we're not in school," she said. "It's Caroline. What you always called me before." On the reservation, you either went by your first name or a nickname, and you only went by anything like "Mr." or "Mrs." if you were a teacher or the doctor.

"It's easier to remember if I only call you one thing. No slipups at the office," I said.

"Okay, I can understand that," she said. When we got to Dog Street, where we both lived, she went straight down Snakeline, pulling into the lot below the elementary school.

"Have you got something to drop off here?" I asked. "I can run it in if you like."

"No, I want to talk to you about something. I didn't put your note in Mr. Doyle's mailbox. I read it. That boy you mentioned," she said, pausing, "his family, they donate a lot to the school, so they have friends in the school system who know how to change the truth when they feel like it. Because they know that, and have known it their whole lives, those two boys cause trouble all the time, but it always somehow disappears. You'll only be making more trouble for yourself if you see this forward, and they'll just keep going on. Do you understand what I'm telling you?"

Of course I understood what she was telling me.

A) I was an Indian kid growing up on a reservation.

B) The state had taken a big chunk of the reservation because it could, no matter how much we said we were a separate and free nation jammed inside of New York.

C) My family was officially on welfare, and we had to go see a caseworker every month to prove we weren't enjoying ourselves too much at the state's expense.

D) My ma worked off the books, cleaning up after other people in their own houses, and often got told she was working overtime on the day it was going to happen.

E) I had an uncle on disability, who didn't even finish high school and was drafted into the army anyway. He also had to see a caseworker once a month to prove he had not somehow fixed his brain in the previous thirty days.

CONCLUSION: I could believe all I wanted that offering a reasonable explanation to someone in power would set the world right, that rules were in place so everyone was treated equally. But the truth was, no one was ever treated all that equally. The influence Mrs. Tunny was talking about was as real as the influence the sun had over all the planets, keeping them in their orbits.

"Evan'll get bored with you eventually," she said, putting the car into gear and heading toward my house. "And he'll find someone else to bother, given enough time. He will. I've seen it before. Just ride it out, if you can. But in case you doubt me, let me tell you this," she said, and as we pulled into my driveway, she closed her eyes. "One of the teachers — someone defaced her chair, and her clothes as a result. She demanded that something be done, and she even found the paint the vandal used, which had fingerprints on it. Mr. Doyle asked for the jar, and it somehow disappeared, got misplaced. The teacher got a check to replace her pants from the school boosters and was told that was the best they could do. I guess I've told you what you need to know."

I remembered Evan and Carson talking about "Miss Maxi Pants." I thanked Mrs. Tunny again and headed into my house. It was the kind of day I used to love, when I'd get off the bus and meet up with other kids for hoops or cutting paths in the woods, maybe even swimming in the dike if it was a warm fall, still pretending it was summer and that we didn't have home-work and didn't have to get to bed early. With regard to Evan, endurance didn't seem like that fun a plan to me, but maybe George would relent at some point and help me, or I guess I could try to learn what he had to offer in the way of defensive moves. Couldn't hurt. What were they going to do, suspend me for defending myself?

The next morning, I experienced my usual dread heading to the shop wing with George and Artie, but when I got there, no attack, nothing. George raised his eyebrows. Maybe it would be a good day. We sat down, and Mr. Meyer called roll. Still no Evan.

As I was about to start my notepad project, Mrs. Tunny requested, on the intercom, that I report to guidance. Mr. Meyer made a hall pass out for me and sent me on my way. The guidance office was in a suite next to the main office. I had only ever been in there once before, to go to the nurse. The room had a large conference table with several chairs around it, and the nurse's office was one of three inner rooms. One of these inner doors was open a crack when I entered. Mr. Doyle sat at the table and offered me a seat at the end.

"Now, this note you left for me, about this boy who has been bothering you?" he started. "Can you tell me more? I'm all ears."

My handwritten piece of paper sat in front of him. I started with Miss Ward's class, and then backtracked to spring and the initial fire drill. The whole time, I kept hearing Mrs. Tunny warning me in my head, but she must have changed her mind and given him the note.

"Thank you for this enlightening elaboration," Mr. Doyle

said. "These are serious things you're saying. Don't you think we should get this boy in this room to hear his side of the story?"

"No, I don't think so," I said. "Didn't you read my note? I said I thought that would be a very, very bad idea. My exact words."

"Well, this is America, and I know you reservation kids think you're from someplace other than America, but for seven hours a day you live in America, *my* America, where every man gets to face his accusers and defend himself."

"If I thought that was even a possibility, I would have —"

"You would have what?" Mr. Doyle said. "Slashed my tires? Crapped in the toilet's upper tank in the faculty men's room? Ganged up on faculty chaperones at sports nights? This is what other kids from your reservation have done when they've gotten in trouble here."

"I wouldn't have said a thing," I said. "Mr. Doyle, this is a terrible idea. Please do not bring him in here. We could forget I ever said a word."

"Actually, that's where you're wrong," Mr. Doyle said, and I understood the slightly open door twenty minutes too late. "Would you please come in here," he said loudly, as if speaking to the room. That inner door opened wider and Evan Reiniger stepped out from behind it.

"He's lying" were the first words out of his mouth. "All except for that part about my spilling coffee on Miss Ward's little electric piano. That was me, but it was an accident."

His "defense" went on from there. When the bell rang, Mr. Doyle assured me this had been a series of misunderstandings and that we'd become the best of friends. We left the office, and Evan punched my face as soon as the door was closed. I tripped him, using George's move, hooking my leg around his and twisting my hip inward, and miraculously, it worked. I vanished into the crowd.

I headed toward math, then stopped off at the lav. I stood at the urinal until the bell rang and everyone was in class. Then I zipped up, left the boys' room, and walked toward the building's front entrance, the pass Mr. Meyer gave me still in my hand. I stepped through the door as if it was the most natural thing in the world. It was a beautiful day in early October. I headed down the steps and kept on going, not stopping until I reached my house.

17

I Should Have Known Better

The first two days were easy. It was harvest and pruning season, so Albert was gone before my ma. Four days out of the week, she left while I got ready for school, and she was filling her first bucket with suds by the time the bus got to our place. So I cleaned up and got dressed, rushing around like I did most mornings, then watched as she caught her ride.

That first day, as soon as she was out of the house, I called the school office and told them I was being hassled and beaten, that the administrators refused to do anything despite my request, and that I would not be in until I could have a reasonably safe school year. We'd learned about civil disobedience in social studies, so I was applying its principles, and there was no way they were going to take it for anything else. If I was at fault for missing school, then so were Mr. Doyle and Mr. Meyer and anyone else who'd let the Reinigers do whatever they wanted as long as the booster cash came in. Mrs. Tunny dutifully took the message, and the rest of the day was mine.

I spent part of the first day taking a more informed inventory of Albert's library and eventually drifted downstairs to see what was on TV: game shows, talk shows, soap operas, and *Sesame Street*. Watching those shows made me feel a little queasy, desiring a flat ginger ale, since this was pretty much what I felt like on those days I actually was home sick.

After that, I spent some time outside. Usually, I hated the fact that my grandfather had chosen to build our house so far back from the road, but today, that meant I could wander around and not worry about anyone driving by and noticing. A little before three, when it was possible that Albert would come home, I grabbed my book bag and headed into the woods, watching the road. After the bus went by, I walked home to discover I was still alone. Good to know.

The second day was the same, minus TV and lunch, since my ma might notice the fluctuation in our food. She noticed I was eating more at supper, so I had to watch that too.

The third day, Thursday, my ma didn't have a regular house scheduled. I decided that I was going to tell her what I was doing. I recapped the last month for her and declared my independence from school. "I'm not learning anything any-way, except ways to block a punch to my nuts," I said finally. I hoped that bluntness would discourage a repeat chat on this subject.

She stared at me, but did nothing else as I called the school and repeated my standard message. Then she sent me back upstairs — not exactly a punishment, given the entertaining reading material and albums. About the only thing better would be if I had someone to hang out with. I felt like those released hostages you see on TV, disoriented but then delighted to be free. No more tight stomach as I approached the school every morning, no more paying closer attention to my periph-eral vision half the school day, no more blocking punches and kicks. I realized how strange my life had been since Labor Day.

I listened to *Venus and Mars*, imagining the Haddonfields would show up and invite me to come and live with them, to use their shower and flushing toilet and drink water from the tap. I even took my boots off as I lay on my bed to heighten the illusion. The reality, though, was that I'd been missing from school for three days, and George hadn't called the house once. I didn't expect anyone else to — certainly not my cousins, as they tried to make careers out of seeing how many days they could miss and still pass a grade — but could it be that I just disappeared for real? I spent so much time up in my room that I began to get sick of my record collection.

On Friday, my ma went to work as usual, while Albert decided to take the day off. Most farmers drove around the reservation early in the mornings to scout laborers, but no farm trucks had come through by nine. "Later farmers try to pay you for half a day," he said to me. "Totally not worth it. I'm financially better off lying here reading than arguing with some gwuh-gwuh about getting paid by the hour or by the tree. Some of them want to pay you by the branch."

"I know what you're doing, and it isn't going to work," I said.

"What ain't gonna work?"

"Trying to get me to go to school because it's so hard to be a laborer. Not going to work."

"Forget that!" he said, laughing. "I'd prune a thousand trees at a penny a branch before going back to school. I just know how those late farmers are. You supposed to be in school? Isn't this Saturday? Jeez, I wondered where your ma was. Figured she was off shopping. I thought you liked school. You and that white kid you hang with. The Beatle Boys."

"Who calls us that?" I demanded. I'd never heard that name before, but it rang true.

"Nobody. I just made it up. Relax, jeez. So what's the story?"

"There's no story."

"You not in school, and your ma *not* blowing a gasket? Spill it." He tossed his magazine aside to look at me directly. "Unless you wanna start working with me once you get out."

"Get out of where?"

"Kids your age? Not allowed to drop out for another three years. I can tell you that from experience. You don't go to school at your age? They find ways to make you go, even if it means sending you away to a place where the school and the living arrangements are built-in. Just like my dad and ma, even though they don't call them Indian boarding schools anymore."

"They can't do that," I said. "You're making that up, trying to scare me into going back." If white kids' parents chose us as their boogeymen, all Indian parents had the specter of the boarding schools — the beatings, the isolation, the rape. It was a seventy-five-year-old ghost, but still one potent enough for me to listen to Albert. Given what Mrs. Tunny suggested, and what happened with Mr. Doyle, it didn't seem like that big a stretch that someone would come up with a new plan to solve "the Indian Problem," which was the name the US government gave to our refusal to assimilate when they wanted us to. The so-called "Indian Problem" led to the boarding schools in the first place.

"Look," he said, leaning close. "Smarty-pants or not, your butt's not in school. They're gonna find a way to get it there.

Some school's gonna collect its state aid money for educating you, whether you like it or not."

So I told Albert everything, almost word for word as I'd explained it to my ma. I had to convince them, or anyone, that this shouldn't be happening to me. All I had done was tell someone to stop hitting me in the ass with a stick.

"That the same punk who crashed into your auntie Olive at the grocery store?" he asked, trying to piece this story together.

"Don't get any ideas," I said, picturing him and Innis showing up at Evan's house to take care of business, then getting pummeled or winding up in jail. Or both.

"No ideas, just trying to know what is what. Have you tried fighting back?"

"What am I, a moron? Why does everyone ask me this question, as if it had never occurred to me? Do you think this kind of stuff happens to big kids?"

"There's always someone bigger. Hit dog barks the loudest."

"What is that supposed to mean?"

"That kid's probably getting it at home or somewhere or he wouldn't be finding you. Maybe you just have to show him once and for all that it is not worth his time to do this to you. And where's the other Beatle Boy in all this? He's a big kid. Hey, where you going?"

I went downstairs and outside, wanting to go anywhere. I needed a jacket, but that meant going back to where my uncle was suggesting I should feel bad for a guy whose daily goal was to destroy my kidneys. I headed to the woods instead, hitting the paths I'd grown up in, working my way to Snakeline and eventually across it. Finally I came to the reservation border that butted up against Clarksville Pass, across from the school. There was a clearing here, yards away from the bush line cover that kept it a secret. Rocks and burned boards and ashes from old bonfires sat at the center, and the edges were lined with empty cans. I'd been to reservation bonfire parties here before. Some folks would bring beer and pop, while others would lug along a guitar or radio or police scanner, plus marshmallows, a brick of commodity cheese, and a box of Ritz, and everyone would gather dry firewood. This bonfire spot was close to the border, so there were also a few baseball bats under a bush, wrapped in plastic, in case of territorial invasions.

It was another hour before classes got out. Music class would be starting in twenty minutes. I leaned against a tree, realizing I missed being in school. I liked my life as the smart kid, even if I had been a lonely kind of smart kid for a while. But this last year, even the loneliness from those bad situations had passed. Then that troublemaker had decided to take it all away. Was that the cost of calling the wrong person an asshole no matter how true it was? Language skills had saved me, then messed me up, but now it was time for them to save me again. I just needed to speak to Evan in his own language. I slid one of those bats from the plastic and decided to go back to school. It was time for a new lesson, a chat in the language of violence.

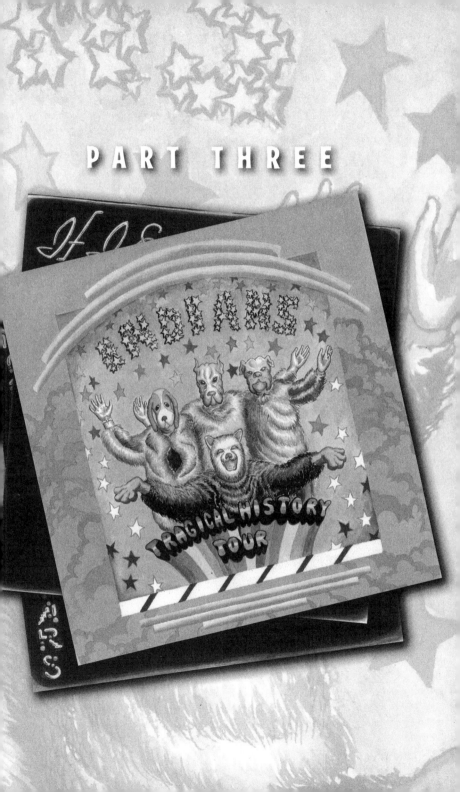

PART THREE

18

Listen to What the Man Said

The outdoor bell speakers allowed me to step inside right as the bell rang. I walked in the front door and strolled past the office with a hundred other kids, my baseball bat maybe looking a little weird, but not enough to draw attention. I realized it was probably the Reiniger PA system I had to thank.

I waited at the corner near our music classroom. Evan would round that corner, laughing and smug, looking for some new target, and there he would find me, ready. He'd be wearing one of his ridiculously tight T-shirts, and I'd target the bump of his sternum and jab dead center with the round end of the bat. He'd buckle forward and I'd bring my knee up, straight to his forehead. Once he was on the floor, I'd throw the bat down the hall and be on him. He'd never have a chance to get up until I was done matching every damned bruise on my ribs with a new one on his. He'd remember my boots after today.

My heart raced and my throat closed. I could feel the bat getting slick in my hands, the closer I got to the inevitable. I was ready to take this jerk out and was finally equipped with exactly the perfect way to do it. It was a relief to know I could do something and make it count.

I thought this right up to the second I felt the hand on the back of my neck. I was suddenly being dragged by my T-shirt collar into the boys' room. I tried to twist but couldn't get clear to swing. He had a firm grip on me, so I quit struggling: Evan was giving me the perfect place for us to chat with the bat. He let go and I lifted it, turning, ready to do what I had to.

"Shoe, what the hell are you doing?" George said, standing before me.

I was frozen, totally disoriented to see him instead of Evan. He locked a grip on the bat and took it away in two seconds. "Where have you been all this —" He paused and leaned in close, sniffing me. "Why do you smell like that?"

I looked down. My boots and the bottom quarter of my jeans were spattered with dark gray muck. It was raw sewage — breaking down, but sewage just the same. I must have walked through a leach bed behind Zach's trailer court.

"And what were you thinking with this? My dad taught me to never have a weapon that you can't handle. It can easily be taken and used against you." He set it down on top of the bank of urinals. "Everyone's been talking about your disappearing act."

"Everyone?"

"Some people." I waited. "Me and Stacey. Artie even asked once. Okay? But we matter. We're your friends. What's going on? A week? Gonna be tough to make that work up."

"Oh, I thought I'd just take a break. Catch up on the soaps," I said. "Why do you think I haven't been here? I'm tired of waking up looking like a cow every day, big, dark spots all —"

"I got the comparison."

The bell rang. "You're late for Choraliers."

"Well, they'll have to start without me."

"Besides," I continued, "it clearly wasn't strange enough for you to pick up the phone."

"Phone works both ways. At first, I thought you must have just been sick, but then —"

The door banged open and we did what any guys skipping classes would do. We unzipped and stood at the urinals, hoping to piss as casually and convincingly as possible.

"Boys, you're late for class." I recognized the voice immediately as its owner walked up behind us — Mr. Doyle, the ever-faithful, very good friend of Miss Ward.

"Yes, sir. Sorry, we'll be on our way in a minute. We were delayed after gym," George said, looking back and nodding. I kept my face forward, hoping he would just move along.

"You there. What's that you're tracking in?" His voice was filled with disgust, but it was like class discussion questions: He felt compelled to ask, already knowing the answer.

"I stepped in a mud puddle coming in from the field," I said.

"Gym class too?"

"Yes, I don't know how it happened."

"And you wear boots and dungarees in gym class?" I turned around. No amount of talking was going to get us out of this. "Ah, Mr. Blake, welcome back. Is that a baseball bat?"

"It's mine, Mr. Doyle," George said, picking it up and holding it casually. "I brought it in for someone to borrow, but he was absent today, so I'm just taking it home."

All three of us looked at the bat in question, dented and scarred beyond practical use, its hitting end blackened from a steady summer of poking bonfires out at the reservation border.

"May I see it?" Mr. Doyle reached out, and George handed it over. "You should get to class. I don't know your name. You might want to keep it that way."

"I should really take my bat?" George said, unable to suppress the sound of a question.

"You can come down to my office and request it formally at the end of the school day," Mr. Doyle said, and George left. "Lewis, come with me," he said, and then stopped. "First, take some paper towels and wipe off your shoes and dungarees." He leaned in the corner, waiting.

"The floor too?" I asked.

"I'll call custodial. You've taken up enough of my time with your shenanigans. Let's go."

We walked toward the office. Through the little door-frame window of the music room, I saw an unfamiliar woman teaching my class.

"Sit there," Mr. Doyle said, pointing to one of the desk chairs lining the walls in the office. "On second thought, stand, and try not to drip. Mrs. Tunny, please call Mr. Groffini and have him come down here." He walked toward his inner office, then turned around. "And tell him he won't have to make that home visit after all."

Mrs. Tunny made the call, and as she did, we looked at each other. Mr. Doyle closed his door. She hung up the phone and motioned me to the desk. "Mr. Groffini will be right down," she said, and slid a piece of paper toward me with "I DIDN'T GIVE HIM THE NOTE. HE MUST HAVE DUG IT OUT OF THE TRASH" scrawled on it. She held on to it, and when I nodded, she ripped it to scraps, stuffing them in her purse.

Mr. Groffini was the guidance counselor assigned exclusively to reservation kids. Before my disappearing act, I had been assigned to one of the regular eighth-grade guidance counselors. Groffini came in, looked at my jeans, and invited me outside for a chat.

"You're in Eight-Three," he said as we stepped into the sharp wind. "You've had great grades since kindergarten. Of course, everyone gets great grades in kindergarten."

"Not true. Hubie Buckman failed the year we were in it," I said.

"Is that really the point here? I'm thinking no. It's not the point, because the point is . . . the point is . . . Why are you ruining your academic career? I don't really think a reformatory would serve you well, but that's what happens if you quit going to school at your age. My hands would be tied. What are you doing?"

"No," I said. "What are *you* doing? Why do you think someone with my grades is dropping out?"

"Why don't you tell me?"

"Anyone else I've told hasn't listened."

"Try me."

"When I was here, I was getting the shit beat out of me every day by an Eight-Sixteen. And who the hell decided that putting hoodlums and smart kids together in the same class was a good idea anyway? That's almost as bad as . . ." I couldn't even think of a suitable analogy for this situation.

"Almost as bad as putting one Indian kid in a smart class with no other Indian kids?" he said. "Part of my job is suggesting placement for reservation kids when they hit junior high. You don't see me much when you're that young, but I'm at the rez school as part of my job every week. I had plenty of people here tell me that was a bad idea, trying to pressure me, saying that I should place you in a lower section to be with other Indians, for your own good."

"It isn't a lack of Indians that's been my problem," I said. "And come on, man. Those other people weren't worried about me. They were worried about the trouble I might cause for the other brainiacs, isn't that right?"

"You sure a lack of Indians isn't your problem?" he said, ignoring my question. "I've been watching you since you were in the third grade, and now you're wasting all the work I did to get you in here. Do you think you'd be better off with your old friends? Would that make you want to come to school?" Groffini crossed his arms.

"You know what would make me want to come to school?" I said. "Not being punched in the face every day by Evan Reiniger. That would make me want to come to school."

"Reiniger? He's a joker, a wiseacre. Come on, you're a smart kid. You can talk your way out of situations. I've seen you. Joke with him, make him laugh. It'll blow right over. What about those fights you used to have with Carson Mastick?"

"Different. We're from the same place. Carson is just a jerk. When he does hassle me on occasion, it isn't because he hates who I am and where I come from."

"You mean he doesn't make fun of what your mom does for a living?" Groffini said. How he knew what rez kids privately said about one another's families was beyond me.

"Different," I repeated. "And if you don't know that, I don't know how the hell you're keeping your job as the Indian specialist."

"Now, you see, it's things like that language that are going to get you into trouble. *I'm* okay with swearing," he said, shrugging his shoulders in his I'm-just-one-of-the-skins way, "but someone like Mr. Doyle, if you say those things to him, whew."

"Well, making a formal complaint didn't do any good. You know what that asshole did? I wrote —"

"Please don't call my supervisor that to me, on school property."

"Why, are you mic'd?"

"I have to document our conversation. It's easier if there's not a lot of vulgarity. Besides, the buses are starting to pull up. Other kids shouldn't hear you talking to me like that."

"Oh yeah, people my age have *never* heard swearwords before. Their ears might split open and bleed. Well, tough. That *asshole*, after reading my request that he do something, brought me in, asked me to repeat it, and then brought Evan Reiniger in from another room — where the asshole *had him hiding*, I might add, so that he could deny everything I just said. And bam. I was gone. Sounds like 'asshole' is the right word to me."

"Okay, listen, I'm going to be square with you. Man to man." He squatted down and waved for me to join him, so I did, as if we were ball players conferring on a play.

"Wait, let me ask you something," I said. "You ever been kicked in the balls?"

"Once or twice," he said, shrugging. "It happens. One of the hazards of guy life."

"Try it every day."

"Ever thought of wearing a cup?"

"Is that on the list of school supplies for Indian kids in all-white classes?" I stood up.

"Okay, here's the deal. Evan comes from a tough family. They're, well, they know a lot of people who grease wheels and who owe them, but that doesn't make them free from pain. And last year, his parents separated. His mom started seeing an Indian guy." He stopped. "I am absolutely breaking confidentiality here, but I trust you to understand what I'm saying, and I think it might help. The guy, well, he's one of those . . . more daring guys. You know the kind."

"Do I know him?" If this guy was from our reservation, I'd have heard about it.

"Different rez. Anyway, the guy dares Evan's brother, you know, Preston?" I nodded. "He dares Preston to put his hand up on the picnic table while the guy goes all the way around it with a pocketknife, stabbing into the table, fast. Says this is a rez bravery test. No flinching."

"Bunch of shit."

"I'm just telling you what I know. The guy wasn't quite as good with his aim as he thought." Groffini stood up. "So those boys have got some room for resentment. I'm not saying it's right or anything but —"

"That has *nothing* to do with me." *Or my auntie Olive*, I thought.

"We're working on it. But in the meantime, you have to come back to school or the law's going to get involved. You should do it for your own sake. Don't blow this. You could go to college. There's even a realistic chance that you could get an academic scholarship."

The last bell rang. My classmates would be out in a few

minutes, no doubt including Evan Reiniger, who was still free to make as much trouble as he wanted.

"At this rate?" I said. "I won't survive long enough to see college. I'm not coming back until you can guarantee that when I'm in school, I'll be going to classes unhassled, *like everyone else*, instead of fighting off some connected psycho every day." I walked to my bus, remembered my jeans, and headed home the way I had come.

Groffini showed up at our door two weeks later. He was, after the electric-meter reader and the heater repairman, the third white person my ma had ever let into our house.

By that time, I'd reread every comic book in my collection, even cross-stacking different titles in the Marvel Universe so it seemed like one big story. The Fantastic Four sometimes showed up in Spider-Man's plotlines, and Wolverine first appeared in *The Incredible Hulk*. I thought it was kind of like the story of my school. If I could organize all the different threads, it might make better sense, but really, doing that just showed me we were all supporting characters in someone else's story.

I then went over the *Hit Parader* back issues Zach left behind for good articles, and became so familiar with the ladies in some of Albert's magazines that a couple of them even got boring. The Bug refused to let me practice guitar at his house until after school hours, as he didn't want to get on my ma's bad side.

"So you can come back," Groffini said. We sat at the table and my ma offered him coffee like this was a weekly social visit. "Here are assignments from your teachers. It's going to be tough to catch up on all this stuff on your own over the weekend."

"I'm not coming back unless something's changed," I said, and my ma made clucking noises like an exasperated chicken.

"He's gone. They've started him in vocational training, apprenticing."

"And how did his influential family take to that?" I asked.

"Can't you just be satisfied?" my ma said.

"He's apprenticing at his father's company, and the district had to agree to his getting apprentice pay, and to paying for it."

"That's it?"

"And he'll get a regular diploma. No GED."

"You were gonna send me to a reformatory, and he's got a full-time job. With benefits?"

"Look, we've accommodated you in ways that we wouldn't do for anyone else. You should be thankful," Groffini said, but there was something insincere in his delivery.

"I don't believe you. What really changed? Don't pretend it was my staying home."

He grimaced, just busted in a guidance-counselor lie. "He jumped someone else. Witnesses. The father complained, heard there was a history. Planned to go to the newspapers."

"White kid?" He nodded. "Anyone I know?"

"I can't tell you that, but it's probably all around the school. Shouldn't be that hard. Now, I want you to keep your word."

"I'll be there, as long as I can get a danger-free education. I'm happy to be there."

With that, he got up and extended his hand to me. It seemed weird, but I shook it.

I went up to my room after Groffini left. Albert was sitting on his bed, pretending to read a magazine. "So I guess you heard everything," I said, looking at my stack of assignments.

"When you go back, don't expect much change," he said. "You won't be getting beat up, but those kids still won't like you. Where was Beatle Boy in all this? You got an answer yet?"

I wanted to explain that George had tried, how he was willing to lie and cover for me when we got busted in the bathroom, but when it came down to it, he never called after the baseball bat incident. I didn't either, for that matter, but what news did I have to report? That Miss July, upon closer examination, looked almost inhuman in her perfection?

"Don't mean to bring you down," Albert said. "It's gonna be bad either way, but I have something that might help." He pulled down his Hawks black leather jacket. "My team gave me this when I needed it. To show me I belonged to them. You and me, we're kind of a small team, but we're a team of two." He paused and pretended to look down at his magazine again. "I got that kid's address. Was gonna teach him a thing or two. I would have done it if that was the only choice. You know that, right?"

"Albert, what good would it be for us if you were in jail?"

"That's what I arrived at too. Anyway, when you go back on Monday, I want you to wear this jacket. It's yours now. Get your grades back up before the school year's out. You take good care of it, make me proud to be on the same team as you."

I slid into it, and though it was too big, I didn't care. Disappointing Groffini wasn't a big deal to me. Since he was the reservation guidance counselor, he was probably used to the feeling. But Albert's giving up the thing he cherished most in the world to help me out — that one act changed something in my heart. I had to go, and I had to rise to the occasion. I couldn't tarnish my uncle's investment in me. I'd always loved him, but in that moment, he was more of a parent to me than even my ma, despite all the ways she tried her best.

Mr. Groffini had offered to pick me up my first day back and drive me in. We both knew that was a lame and not very subtle attempt to ensure that I wouldn't go back on my word. I chose to ride the bus instead with my cousin Ace. When I sat down a few seats away from Carson, he said, "Nice jacket you got, Gloomis. Where's your Harley? Halloween's over."

Carson could have been a poet if he wanted to. He did exactly what my English teacher, Mr. Bolger, said good poets did: He was able to get his point across in the fewest possible number of words. Suddenly, Albert's black leather jacket felt as if I were wearing a shiny security blanket or sleeping bag, or as Carson said, a costume, too big for me. In that moment, it lost Albert's protection.

As each new kid stepped on the bus, I met their eyes, daring them to say anything about the jacket or my absence, but most paid no attention to me whatsoever. When we crept toward the school, the same pulling in my belly began that had been there every morning bus ride since mid-September. I told myself Evan was gone, and I'd be able to walk down the shop wing hallway and not be pummeled. My day would end in music, with a couple songs or a filmstrip about jazz. Still, my stomach was certain I was lying to it, that Evan would reveal himself from behind the concrete staircase in the school's foyer. I leaned toward agreeing with my gut.

The driver pulled into her normal spot. People filed out, some tightening the collars on their coats. The temperature was in the low thirties, maybe even the high twenties. November had settled in, and the sharp winds always blasted through the driveway, picking up power by whipping between the two buildings and riding straight out across the school's front waiting area. Carson walked past me without another syllable. I wanted to remind him how things would be different if his friend Evan had known he was from the reservation.

"Come on. We gotta go in," Ace said. I realized now he probably had instructions to make sure I made it into the school.

"I'm coming. Don't worry about it," I said, slinging my bag over my shoulder. "But if you tell me you're walking me to the office, I am never playing one-on-one with you again."

"All right, you two. Off," said Pinky, our bus driver. "You, shorty, don't you think you've caused enough trouble already? We can't all change our lives because you don't like it." Though she usually told everyone to have a good day, she said nothing else to us, slamming her remote door when we were barely through it.

"She's from Misty Meadows," Ace said. "Probably word has gotten around."

"Gee, really? That hadn't occurred to me," I said. It soon became apparent he *was* going to walk me right up to the main office's door. "I've got it," I said. "I know where it is."

"Look, I promised," he said, "and I promise now, as soon as you walk in that door, I'll go right to my homeroom. I won't stop or slow down or anything. But if your ma finds out I didn't make sure you went to the office, and she tells my dad, well, you know how things are."

"All right," I said. "We're here. See you later." True to his word, he kept on going, and we looked like two kids just walking into school, or at least he did. No one else ever went to the office in the morning except whichever Choralier was going to sing "My Country, 'Tis of Thee" on the announcements. This morning, it was Carson, naturally, and he was doing quiet vocal exercises at the counter, waiting for Mr. Barnes to hand him the microphone.

"Hello," Mrs. Tunny said, smiling her professional smile, handing me a form. "We just need you to sign here, and then you can take this sheet down to Mr. Doyle's office."

I signed it and walked to the inner door. "Mr. Doyle?" I asked, knocking on the frame.

"Mr. Blake, so nice to see you again," he said in a way that clearly meant it was not nice, truly, to see me again. He stood, escorting me into his office. "Let me take your jacket," he added as he lightly pulled the collar band away, halfway removing it before I could say anything. It would be too weird to try shrugging it back up, so I let it slide off, and he took it to an open closet door, pulling out a hanger from inside. He put it properly on the hanger, smoothed it, and hung it next to his own coat, shutting the door as he invited me to sit.

"I was supposed to give this to you," I said, handing him the Resumption of Normal School Activities form, and he took it, setting it on his desk. "Um, I'm not sure why I'm here," I added. "I thought I was just coming to school, and I had to stop in the office before going to homeroom, and then Mrs. Tunny told me I had to take this sheet to you." The bell rang, but distantly. There was an intercom wired into this room, but the bell system must have been disconnected. "And now I'm going to be late for homeroom."

"I wouldn't worry about that. I'll give you a pass," he said, tapping a pass pad on his desk. "So, really, there's nothing you'd like to discuss? No thanks you'd like to offer? We have all the time you want."

"Thanks?" Was he out of his mind? "Can't think of a thing," I said, which wasn't exactly true, but it wasn't like talking to him did me any good the first time.

"Okay, well," he said, frowning, "if you change your mind, and if you need someone or you discover gratitude, you can always make an appointment with Mrs. Tunny. You know Mrs. Tunny." He stood with me and extended his hand. I didn't want to shake it, but I didn't think I could ignore his hand suspended in the air.

"Can I have my jacket?"

"How about if we just leave it for now?" he said, pretending he was offering a suggestion. "It'll be quite safe, I assure you." He put his arm around my shoulder in a let-me-guide-you-this-way maneuver, designed to get me farther and farther from the jacket my uncle had given me as protection. "You can pick it up at the end of the day. I'll be here. I promise."

When we got to the hallway door, he expertly handed me my bag, opened the door, and let me out in the same move, closing himself back in. I looked out the front door and saw the gray November sky, with the barren trees along the bush line where Evan had found his beating stick back in the spring, and I understood why my jacket was being held hostage. Maybe if it was in the forties outside, I could have tolerated the walk home in just shirtsleeves, but there was no way I could make the walk in this temperature even if I wanted to. I realized I didn't have a pass only when I reached my classroom, but I went in late anyway. What were they going to do, throw me out?

Things We Said Today

I stepped into homeroom, and a woman who was not Miss Ward looked up.

"You must be Lewis Blake," she said. "I've been expecting you. I'm Miss Strassburgher, and I'll be taking over for Miss Ward for a while." I confirmed my identity. The bell rang and people began gathering their things. "I'll see you this afternoon?" she asked.

"I'll be there," I said, but even as I turned, I saw Stacey leaving with Harold Russell, and George waiting by the door, his left eye the color of a bad banana. I couldn't picture the events that led to that. Harold must have suckered him. There was no way, otherwise. Maybe that's why he didn't call. He'd been busy dealing with Harold? Fighting over Stacey? Seemed like I had more than school assignments to catch up on. George and I grabbed our books, walked out together, and headed to math class, neither saying much. I handed in my makeup assignments, and was only partially lost in the equations we were doing.

As we left math, we had the daily split: The girls headed to the home ec room while we boys went on to shop. Stacey left

Harold's side, disappearing down that hall, and Harold slid past us, doing a C– version of a suppressed smile.

"So what's going on there?" I asked, now that Stacey was no longer with us.

"Later," George said.

"Look, I can see your eye, so I'm assuming you were —"

"I said I'd like to talk about it later, okay?"

"Okay, but it's not like anyone's around." The guys in our class had, almost as a group, pulled way ahead, so that we walked almost half a hallway behind them.

"You noticed that, did you?" he said.

It seemed that whatever infected me in our class had now spread to George. Instead of his bridging that world for me, bringing me in, I had pulled him out of his own, closer to mine. And somewhere in the three weeks I was missing in action, it seemed like our connection had maybe cost him Stacey, and to an idiot like Harold. None of this made sense. I had a lot of questions, but I said nothing, waiting for his undefined "later."

"We're over here now," George said as I made my way toward the old shop classroom. "Mr. McKee, mechanical drawing." I looked in and saw most of our classmates already at their drawing tables, spreading paper out under the slide rules.

"Yeah, okay," I said. "I'll catch up in a minute. I want to stop and see Mr. Meyer." There hadn't been a packet of materials in my homework bundle from him. This was fairly understandable, as I didn't actually have a drill press at home, but I wanted to let him know I was back, just the same.

"Don't," George said. "Trust me. Do you trust me?"

"Yeah, of course," I said. "But I have to —"

"What do you think you're going to get as a grade for that term?" I didn't say anything. "Do you think you can say anything that will change that?" Again, nothing. "Look, I can't explain now, but I will when we get out of here. Just don't bother going in there," he said.

Before I could finish introducing myself to Mr. McKee, he said he knew who I was already. Then he told me I was behind the rest of the class and it was up to me to catch up. I went to an empty drawing table, and he started class.

"Okay, gentlemen, today is the day you've all been waiting for. I know these drawings you've been doing seem strange, because you can't see what they're supposed to look like exactly, and yeah, I know the paper smells a little funny. Okay, a little like cat piss. Who are we kidding here, men? Am I right?" The group laughed loudly to assure Mr. McKee he was funny and provocative.

"Cat pee, so daring," George whispered to me.

"You can say 'piss.' It's not on your forbidden words list," I whispered back, remembering his weird preoccupation with not swearing.

"Still vulgar," he said.

"Okay," McKee continued, "you remember what we've been practicing, and we've got ourselves a nice sunny day for a change, so let's get to it."

Every other guy around jumped up immediately, grabbed sheets of filmed paper from a table near the back, and laid a drawing they'd already done on top to trace it. There was also some configuration of trapping the drawings inside wooden frames and behind glass. I understood enough to know I was doing absolutely nothing in class today but watching.

They set their trapped drawings on a shelf built next to the windows and went back to their tables. "Now, we've got about fifteen minutes, that should do it, and then we'll give the drawings a bath. If you've done everything right, men, this is what you should have."

He held up a deep blue sheet of paper, a color I'd always liked until I began seeing it too often on myself. While my classmates dutifully let their drawings bake in the window, then washed them in the bank of large industrial sinks at the back, Mr. Meyer came in and walked over to the small hand sink behind me. He wet his hands and began washing them, though he had a perfectly good sink in his own shop. "I see you decided to rejoin school," he muttered at me. "How good for you. Doesn't matter that you've ruined someone else's chance at education. Someone who, I might add, has a very difficult home life, not that these are concerns of yours."

"If you were so concerned about students' educations," I said, knowing now why George had tried to steer me clear, "maybe you would have watched your class, so I wouldn't have been getting punched in the face every day."

"I figure boys have to become men sometime," he said, then paused. "Or not."

"Some boys think their teachers are losers," I said, and then clarified: "They change the calibrations on their machines and then do about as unconvincing a snow job as they can, knowing that the teacher will buy it from them."

His lips pooched out and he narrowed his eyes at me. "And you think that justifies what you did," he said finally.

"What I did? You were pretending nothing was happening to me in your classroom so you wouldn't have to do anything.

I think *that* justifies what I did, which was, um, just leaving." I sighed and stopped for a second. There was likely no changing his mind, but I didn't have a lot to lose here. "I was just trying to do my job, getting an education, in light of no adult supervision. If I'm to blame for someone else not being here, so are you," I finished.

His meaty forearms twitched under his rolled cuffs. "Smart mouth on you. Typical of your kind," he said.

"What kind would that be?"

He wanted to say "Indian," the blame word assigned for any of us, as if our backgrounds and addresses said everything there was to say about us, that we were all intentionally bad smart-asses who hated school. But to say that would be admitting to me what they told one another behind the closed door of the teachers' lounge.

"You know what I'm saying here, smart mouth. We'll see how smart you are next year with at least two Fs on your report card. Maybe four. Can't really see you doing well in wood or metal shop either. Any boy who can't fight his own battles, bound to be incompetent in shop."

Just then George came back with his drawing fresh from the sink.

"Another one. You should be careful who you're defending, son. You wanna blow your good grades over nothing?"

George didn't say anything, pretending that straightening his drawing required tremendous concentration, until Mr. Meyer left.

"The entire day going to be this way?" I asked. "And what did he mean, defending?"

"This was probably the worst, but hard to say. Hang in there," he said.

Shop was indeed the worst, partly because I knew some other guys were as relieved to have Evan gone as I was. They just didn't want to admit it. Lunch was pretty strange too, with most of our section arriving early and putting books around them on the benches, so there was only one small spot on the end of one bench where George and I could sort of sit. Stacey sat with Harold Russell at the opposite end of the other table in our section. "Better not sit near those two," Harold said to Artie. "You look at them the wrong way, *bam!* Somehow they make you disappear from school, like mobsters. You don't want to wind up like that other kid."

"Artie, you gonna pick someone to disappear now?" Steven added. Artie sat with us anyway, but did still act distant. I was confirming a little more that George had something to do with the way my problem had been solved, but no one was really saying how, and I wasn't about to invite more grief by asking. George and I ignored them, and eventually, those kinds of comments stopped. The bell rang after what seemed like hours.

"Is it 'later' yet?" I asked as we stood up to leave.

"No, not yet," he said.

"Will you at least tell me how everyone knows my business? I'm surprised they even noticed I was gone."

He sighed. We were at our lockers, dialing our combinations. "Think about who's in our class," he said. "Who would have information about where you might be?"

"Look, I don't want to play twenty questions. What's going on here? If you're my friend, you'll tell me."

"No," he said. "*Because* I'm your friend, I'll tell you when it's all over. I promise. It's as much my problem as it is yours now. I also promise it's not going to be today, but do you want to come over to my place anyway? One of my parents will give you a ride home later."

"It's freezing out," I said.

"Could be worse. I got a new Queen single. It's not officially out. My dad got the radio copy, but he wouldn't say where. Sound like it's worth the walk? You break out your winter coat yet?" He looked in my locker, which held only books and folders. "Where is your coat?"

"Later," I said.

The rest of the day, I went to classes in the sort of invisibility I'd once grown accustomed to. When I got to music, Miss Strassburgher had broken the class up so everyone sat in alphabetical order. Unfortunately, that left me close to Truck, but he and the other Eight-Sixteens didn't acknowledge me in the least. I was never so happy to have vanished. Miss Strassburgher told us about Bob Dylan; Peter, Paul and Mary; and the protest element of the folk music scene. She played a few tunes, and then it was over. The Eight-Sixteens left, our homeroom class resumed, and finally, the last bell rang.

"So are you walking with me?" George said, sliding on that Dolphins jacket he seemed to live in no matter the weather.

"Yeah, I'll catch up to you," I said. "You wanna wait for me in the front foyer? That way, you won't be freezing your butt off before you have to."

"Well, we can walk together the whole way. Be stupid to wait there. Where did you say your coat was?"

"That asshole Doyle kept it this morning so I wouldn't skip out on any more classes."

"No one said it was going to be easy."

"Thank you, Mr. Cliché. Now, will you please wait in the foyer?"

"Absolutely," he said, and left.

I busted my jacket out of jail with only a minimal exchange with Doyle, then stopped into the guidance area. Groffini was in his office with the door open. I knocked and he looked up, smiling. "First day back. Glad you came," he said, standing to shake my hand.

"Like you didn't check with the office this morning?"

"Well, I wouldn't be doing my job if I hadn't, but I'm glad to see you just the same. So how did it go?"

"Let's see. I'm failing shop, two different kinds, with no options. Most of my class is pretending I dropped out for good, which really isn't that different from the last two years. And they're saying I made someone else disappear. Guess that one's semi-true. Other than that, I got all my makeup assignments in." He was the one person who I thought might take me seriously.

"I kind of thought that might happen," he said, pursing his lips. "You knew there were going to be consequences when you decided to go against the system. I told you that. The best you can do is work as hard as you can to balance out some of those grades not necessarily based on ability and performance."

"Mr. Meyer and Mr. McKee live in Misty Meadows, by any chance? Maybe on the same bowling team as a certain Mr. Reiniger?"

"You know I can't disclose personal information about teaching staff. Most teachers have private listings. Many don't live in the district, in part, I suspect, to maintain their privacy."

"Oh really. How shocking."

"Didn't you tell me that part of the reason this happened was because you were a smart-ass, excuse me, a wiseacre to the wrong person?" I nodded, though I didn't think I'd ever described my situation as such to him. "Maybe you should learn some discretion. It's okay, you know, you and me, but there are times when the old saying still rings true."

I know he wanted me to ask, so I obliged. "Which old saying is that?"

"Discretion is the better part of valor."

I didn't exactly know the definition of "valor," but I had a good enough idea that I got his point. Contrary to what Mr. Groffini believed, keeping my mouth shut was one of my greatest skills. You needed that skill if you lived in a house like mine and wanted others to think you were normal, just like everyone else.

"Okay, well, thanks for doing whatever you did."

"Just my job," he said.

"When did I become one of your responsibilities? When I started being trouble?"

"You might say that."

"So the Indian kids who don't act like the school believes Indian kids are going to act, they don't send them your way." I was beginning to understand I had, in the school's eyes, only *become an Indian student* when I became a problem. Which meant that your Standard Indian Kid could also be defined as your Standard Trouble Kid.

"It's more complicated than that," he said. "We each have a certain percentage of the student body as our responsibilities, so we can give each of them a supportive amount of time."

"Got it," I said, then thanked him again and left.

George was waiting for me in the foyer as promised. When we began our walk, he finally offered me a somewhat clearer picture of a few things that had gone on in my absence.

Apparently Mr. Barnes was the sort of man who took his work home with him, sharing vice principal gossip with the family over dinner. During the past month, I had become a featured player in his ongoing saga of problem kids. I'm sure he kept things anonymous and confidential, but Summer was a smart girl. She was able to connect the missing kid in the story to the missing kid in her class, the Indian who didn't know how to dress.

"So the only way I became interesting to our class was by dropping out, and thanks to Summer, the whole class also knows *why* I dropped out," I confirmed, after George summed up the class gossip. "All of eighth grade or just our section?"

"There's probably some bleeding out. You know how kids talk. On the plus side, not that many people, other than the kids you grew up with, even know who you are."

"Yeah, that's the plus side."

"Or they didn't last month anyway," he said as we walked into his house and took off our shoes. We went into the living room and he pulled out the 45 record. It was the single they'd been playing on the radio, "Somebody to Love." It had an odd gospel vibe to it that you wouldn't have imagined was gonna hit on Top 40 radio, but, man, that plea, that search for someone you could love, working, doing the things you have to do, but still hoping, getting to the point of begging for that somebody — well, who couldn't relate to that?

"Here's what I really wanted you to listen to," George said, flipping it over and playing a song called "White Man," supposedly from the point of view of an Indian. I had to confess, as much as I loved Queen, it sounded preposterous in Freddie Mercury's eccentric British accent. It was all muddy guitars and of course, heavy drums, and angry, acid lyrics. When it was over, George asked me if that was what I felt like.

"Well, for one, I don't know *anyone* who's ever called himself a red man, so that might tell you a little bit of how far off this is." I liked the music, and that the lyrics didn't shy away from the massacres and all the Indians who'd been killed in the long story of this country. But for everything it acknowledged — for all the historical shit that had come to pass on its way to my doorstep — hearing Freddie Mercury use the word "honky" made me laugh more than it provoked anything harsh or outraged inside of me.

"I want to show you something," he said, kind of fidgety.

"Okay, are you going to tell me the rest of the story?"

"No, this," he said, leading me back to his parents' bedroom. He opened the door and stepped inside, nudging me forward.

"I don't want to do that," I said, stopping at the threshold. I hadn't been comfortable invading the space of those people he babysat for, but they were strangers. I knew George's parents, and just seeing the small bottles of unfamiliar perfume and Old Spice aftershave or a jewelry box on top of their chest of drawers made me feel like I was violating their privacy, which, of course, I was.

"Okay, chicken," he said, stepping up to the jewelry box, flipping its lid up.

"It's not chicken. I like your parents. They're the only parents I ever met who act like the ones you see on TV. I'm just trying to be respectful."

"All right, whatever, but you're going to be interested in what I have to show you here."

"Why do you like to dig around in other people's stuff?" I said. "What if people dug around in your stuff? What might we find tucked away in the bottom of your drawers?"

"Jeans, T-shirts, socks, undershorts. Other than that, not a thing. I don't have any stuff," he said. "Why do you think I like checking out what other people have? When you live in the military, you learn to travel light. My clothes, dresser, lamp, clock — that's everything I own."

"What about those Smurfs? Those are yours."

"That's what I have for all ten years in Germany, and the scrapbook is what I have left of Guam. So far, from here? Stacey's picture, our yearbook, that program my dad got us from the Wings concert, my ticket from there, that's about it for me. But speaking of concerts . . ."

He held out a folded piece of paper that looked like it was a carbon copy receipt from Twin Fair. On it were some numbers and handwriting, identifying three concert tickets for Queen, at Maple Leaf Gardens, February 1, 1977. On the last line, Mr. Haddonfield had signed his name.

"It's my Christmas present," he said.

"That third ticket?"

"Yours, of course, bozo," he said, putting it back in the box. It was dated two weeks ago. "My dad decided not to go to Rose's dad for tickets. So he went to Twin Fair, but they had some strange voucher system, so we have to pick up the tickets at the store that Friday before the concert."

"He told you all that? I thought you were maybe snooping."

"Nah, we don't work with surprises. My dad told me when he got them that this was my present. It's a school night, so we won't be staying over, but that'll be cool, right?"

"Was that supposed to be Stacey's ticket?" I asked, again thinking about the dates. Other than the bat incident two weeks ago, George and I hadn't spoken since I quit coming to school, and he and Stacey had seemed pretty serious. It seemed logical to me that she would have been his first choice. But it's not like we'd had much of a chance to talk before Mr. Doyle escorted me and my sewer-soaked jeans to the office. It was possible they'd been having trouble.

"It's supposed to be for whoever I want it to be for. You're the person who introduced me to Queen. It should be yours."

"Did you already ask her if she wanted to go?" I asked.

"Look, I'm inviting you now, okay?"

"Did she break up with you about this thing with me? The thing Summer's been broadcasting?"

"It's —"

"If you say, 'complicated,' I'm going to punch you in the gut."

"Well, it is," he said. "Things change. Come on, man. We're going to be in high school soon. It's not like we were getting married or anything. She decided she likes Harold better now. Good for her, good for him."

I didn't believe it for one minute, but in some funny way, I think he felt he was telling me and himself the truth. He had some way of just accepting the end of things when it came, drawing a line between before and after. But that kind of attitude made me want to know even more what happened, and it wasn't like anyone else was going to tell me.

I had figured out that he was the kid at the junior high who Evan Reiniger had jumped after I did my vanishing act — the white one whose dad got Evan removed for good. The details, though, didn't add up. When Evan hassled other people, they were always kids like me, shorter, smaller. Coming after George was going to cost him one way or another. "When are you going to tell me what happened? Why did Evan Reiniger give you a shiner in front of a bunch of witnesses that mattered?"

"Why do you care? You're back in school, things are right in the world, and we're going to see Queen in February. How much better could things be?"

Things in my life could be a lot better, but he didn't need to know that. "Come on, let's listen to the A side of that single," I said, leading us back into the living room.

"I haven't been listening to that song too much," he said.

"Remind you of Stacey?"

"Do *you* want to get punched in the gut?"

"You could still ask her, try to make up. A concert ticket would be a pretty successful way." He didn't respond, so I put on "Somebody to Love," and got to hear it for the first time through a decent set of speakers.

"Hey, boys," Mr. Haddonfield said, coming in the door. "Your mother home?" he asked George, who shook his head. "Didn't think so, or you guys wouldn't have had this up so loud. How are you doing, Lewis?" he said, as if we'd seen each other just a few days before instead of a month. "I understand you're going to see these guys with us. Terrific. You sticking around for supper, or you want me to run you home before I unlace these?"

I couldn't tell if that was a hint that I should go or stay or just a plain old question. But I was pretty sure Albert would want to know how my first day back was, and then my ma would quiz me when she got home too, so it was probably better that I take the offer now. George wanted to stay home and catch up on his assignments, and by the time we hit the reservation, I decided one other person might tell me the truth.

"Mr. Haddonfield, what happened with George and that shiner?"

"You don't know?"

"I wasn't there," I said, shaking my head, and he frowned, I guess thinking about what he wanted to say.

"I don't suppose it's anything to worry about. Some things, son, take care of themselves. You trust that the right things happened. The rules are in place to keep us functioning as a society, and sometimes, people find their ways around the rules, but it always catches up with them at some point. That is the beauty of order. Things work out one way or another," he said.

We both knew he wasn't answering my question with any kind of meaningful detail, but I suppose we both also knew that he wasn't planning to either, no matter how I might rephrase the question.

"The holidays are coming up in a bit," he said as we turned onto Dog Street. "Are we likely to see you again this year?"

"Ride situations —"

"No need to worry about that. We can arrange something. It's nice that George has someone other than his mom and dad to be around. One thing I always worried about, once we knew we were going to have him, was the high potential for loneliness in our lifestyle. There's no getting around it."

"He's got all of Red-Tail Manor to hang out with."

"Maybe he has discerning taste."

"Mr. Haddonfield, George told me a while back that you had spent some time around Indians, at a school where your parents worked," I said. George might not tell me for sure if there was a boarding school involved, but maybe his dad would directly. As appreciative as I was, I couldn't find a reason on earth that this family had decided to include me in so much of what it did. But if there was a boarding school in his past, it might make a difference at my end. I knew Mr. Haddonfield couldn't pick his parents any more than I could pick mine, but I still needed to know, if only for the ghosts of my grandparents.

"A long time ago, yes," he said. "Kind of hard not to, if you live in Minnesota. Scandinavians, English, and Indians. Some French. That's your stock up there. My parents did work at a reservation school, and while they did, we had to live on a compound in its bounds." We pulled into my driveway. I wanted to know the rest and I didn't want to know, again. As I reached for the door handle, he said, "So will we see you? Christmas? New Year's? Anytime you and George decide you want to spend time together, you two just let either his mom or me know. One of us is bound to be available with enough notice." I nodded. "Either way, though, you put February one on your calendar. You've got an obligation in Toronto, and we'll see you then if not before."

I got out of the truck in my driveway and waved good-bye as he pulled away.

Junior's Farm

Though I would have liked to take Mr. Haddonfield up on his holiday invitation, I got kind of caught up in things at home. To be on the safe side, George had suggested that we exchange gifts on the last day before winter break. Then if we could get together, great, and if not, we would at least have shared the holiday in this way. I'd gotten him the new Queen album, *A Day at the Races*, and he had gone over-the-top on mine, with the triple-album set *Wings over America* — a recording of one entire concert from the Wings tour we had seen. Anytime I wanted, I could close my eyes and listen, and it was like being at the show. I felt guilty that I hadn't gotten him something more, but a single album was what my budget could afford.

Over the break, I made some cash for the concert trip by shoveling snow with Albert and watching my sister's kids. On Christmas Day, there were only two gifts under the tree for me. First I opened the one from Charlotte. She was keeping a tradition going and gave me *A Day at the Races*. The other gift was a bizarre package that looked like a gigantic letter *T*. I peeled the patchwork wrapping off, but even when it was mostly gone, I was still at a loss. The *T* had been made up of three boxes, taped and stapled together, with a long one in the middle, flanked by two smaller ones. I cut through the tape, finally, and lifted the top, and I could not believe what I was seeing. A full-sized, deep sunburst guitar lay inside.

Somehow this had to be one of Albert's psych-outs: I'd remove the guitar from the box and then he would reveal it was some kind of prank. It would take my family years of saving to come up with enough extra cash that a guitar would seem like a reasonable gift. Still, I just had to touch it. I carefully lifted it out, feeling the slick finish on the neck, the nubs of the frets against my fingers. I could see six tiny versions of myself in the chrome tuning pegs, each one grinning the same insane, lock-you-up-in-an-asylum-because-you're-smiling-so-wide grin.

"Psych!" Albert yelled, laughing crazily as I reached up to play a D chord. I inhaled sharply. "It took me hours to get that right! Stapling those side boxes on so you wouldn't know what it was, man — that was totally worth the look on your face. Well, go on, play that chord. I already tuned it. The Bug taught me how to do it and I can show you."

"This isn't his —" I said, alarmed. No matter how much I wanted one, I could not take a guitar away from a one-legged man with no electricity and a piss bucket for a bathroom.

"You kidding?" Albert yelled again, spitting coffee. "The Bug give up his guitar? He'd sooner give up his other leg, isn't it?" He could not stop laughing and pointing out the way he had attached the smaller boxes to the cardboard box the guitar came in. In the extra boxes were a strap, picks, a polishing cloth, a set of strings, and a couple beginner guitar books.

My ma said, smiling at her own cleverness, "Remember the money I hung on to from your paycheck after school clothes and supplies? In case we needed it for the heating bill? Well, we did pretty good this year, so I didn't need to use too much of it, and we even had heat in October."

"I noticed that. It was nice to not have to wait until after Halloween," I said.

"Well, I took what you had saved and I started saving myself since summer, not going to bingo much, just cutting corners where I could, so I matched you dollar for dollar. Then the Bug and Albert and I went to Heavenly Music and got the best guitar we could with the money we had. I was going to get one of the smaller guitars, but the Bug said you knew your way around a full-sized one, and this one would be good enough to last you until you grew up or lost interest."

"I won't be losing interest," I said, playing the D, and it rang beautiful and true. "Watch."

"You might want to bring it in here and let it warm up first," Albert said, stepping back into the warmth of the dining room. "Wait about an hour, maybe two." I didn't want to wait, but I did as I was told, wanting my guitar to last. I set it down gently on the daybed. While it warmed, I flipped through the books, but I kept looking up, admiring the guitar's deep red-to-black finish, like an ember burning, waiting to spark. There was a whole tab book of Beatles songs, arranged for a beginning guitarist. They still looked pretty intimidating, but it was something to work toward.

"Who picked these books out?" I asked my ma. Some part of me was waiting to wake up, to discover I was still in my bed.

"The Bug. He looked to see which ones were a bit beyond what he was teaching you so you wouldn't get bored. He also said not to bring it to his house until winter was over, so if you're still going to do lessons there, you can use his. How are you paying for those anyway?"

It had never occurred to me that we were supposed to be paying for the lessons, but it made sense as soon as she said it.

"I'm doing his lawn and his driveway, and he needed some shingles done," Albert said.

"But you're afraid of heights," I said, not knowing any of this had been going on.

"Can't let your fears get the best of you, isn't it?" he said. "Gotta live the best way you can."

"Yeah, I hear you," I said. I wanted to thank them, but I knew my voice would be thick with the tears I was holding back. It was never in my family's nature to get emotional about anything. I don't even think I saw my ma cry when we buried my grandfather. "This is amazing," I finally said, my voice cracking in exactly the way I didn't want it to. "Thank you. Thank you, so much." I wiped my nose on my sleeve, and my family, all around the table with me, just said, "You're welcome." Charlotte's kids looked but didn't touch, and even Zach held off on being a smart-ass — a true modern Christmas miracle if ever there was one.

As the day went on, and I was finally convinced the guitar was mine and going to stay, I wanted to show George. But since there was no way I was taking the guitar out in the winter, and of course no way he could come to our house to see it, it would have to wait for spring. I flipped through the Beatles book to pick a song that would be a cool one to play when I finally showed him.

I didn't believe George when he'd said that people's memories would fade, that no one would dwell on all that shit with Evan once we came back in the new year. I would have a clean slate, he insisted — and he was sort of right. It wasn't like I was transformed into Mr. Popularity as 1977 began, but in home-room, when people swapped stories about what they'd gotten for Christmas, a few people besides George asked me. I mentioned *A Day at the Races* and George's gift, but I had to keep silent about the guitar, for fear of waking up George's hope to visit again.

January blew by, and I was glad we'd gotten caught up on our heat bills at home. This had been a tough winter so far. Even in school, it was freezing, like the furnaces couldn't keep up with the nosedive the temperature took each night. At home, I almost lived in front of the kerosene heater's blower, even sneaking down in the middle of the night after my ma had gone to bed and while Albert explored his French-Canadian TV shows.

One morning I got up early to watch TV for the list of school closings. The previous evening's snow had started heavy and got worse throughout the night. But our school wasn't on the list, so I got dressed and ran for the bus, almost missing it because our driveway was already two feet deep, wind blowing off our lawn, making a dense layer I had to punch my legs through.

By the time we got to fourth period, the sky had become nothing but a haze. The kids who sat near the windows complained that the wind was blowing on them, and they were allowed to retrieve their coats. Just before the bell rang, the fire-drill robot cat went off across the PA. Surely Mr. Barnes had lost his mind if he thought we were going outside to wait for the all clear, but Mr. Gorker's face suggested this winter bell was a first in his twenty-year career.

"Please stand, class," he said, his voice fluttery and nervous. But before we could leave, Mr. Barnes's voice boomed over the speaker.

"Attention, please. Buses are in the driveway for early dismissal because of the weather. You should proceed to your lockers and then your buses in an orderly fashion. Be cautious to bundle up, and walk hanging on to others from your bus route. I am serious. The wind has gotten *extremely* dangerous."

Dangerous wind? I'd never heard that particular announcement before.

"Weird, huh?" George said to me. "But great for us. My dad's taken the day off and he's going to swap that voucher out for the tickets. If he's still at the house when I get home, do you want to go with us to pick them up?"

"Sure," I said. "I've got some cash from shoveling, and that new David Bowie album came out a couple weeks ago." Albert had recently gotten *Changesonebowie* and I liked it.

"Bowie? That guy who was in that alien movie and who wears dresses sometimes?"

"Yeah, that's him," I said, disappointed George had gone for the more unusual elements of Bowie's story, which I'd read myself in one of Albert's more recent *Rolling Stone* issues. "Have I steered you wrong yet? Besides, you should like this new album, *Low*. It's supposed to be influenced by Berlin, where it was recorded."

"Whatever," he said. "Okay. For you, I'll give it a listen, but no promises. It's bad enough Freddie Mercury's wearing ballet tights now. I'll call you as soon as we're ready to pick you up, or, well, I'll just call you when I get home and let you know one way or the other," he said as Stacey and Harold walked by. Reaching the foyer, they grabbed on to each other and ran.

A half hour later, I was shoveling the roadside end of our driveway while Albert worked on the house end. I'd made a path one shovel wide from the house for my feet. Even with a hat, gloves, and scarf, the wind tore in everywhere, and I wondered if it was such a wise thing to head out for the tickets. But Mr. Haddonfield was in the military, and I trusted his judgment in knowing his surroundings. By the time George and his dad arrived, I had a wide enough patch for a car.

Mr. Haddonfield pulled in slowly and stopped, his bumper inches from the drift I was working. "You fellas want a hand with that?" he asked, leaving the cab and holding his hand out for my shovel. "Go faster with four men."

Albert trudged down my path, almost dancing in its narrowness. "We only have the two shovels," he said. "We'll manage. When Lewis gets back, he'll help again, and then he'll have some cash for that trip you're planning to take." He looked into the wind, squinting. "If this keeps up, you're gonna have a challenge getting to Toronto next week, though. Tuesday, is it?"

"Yes, Tuesday. Does it seem like the kind of storm that might blow over by then?" Mr. Haddonfield asked. "I grew up in Minnesota. We got some bad ones, but these snows with the lake effect — never seen anything like this before."

"Me neither," Albert said. "We started shoveling this when your boy called. Even in these few minutes . . ." He didn't have to finish that sentence. The path he had come through a minute ago was already disappearing. Snow blew across our wide front lawn and filled in any place there was a drop. "You better get going before the roads get too rough," he said. "Glad you're at least from the north. You know how to drive in the snow. Not like some people."

"Yes, Minnesota winters gave me plenty of practice," Mr. Haddonfield said. "Albert, right? Lewis talks fondly of you. Would you have any objections to coming with us? The four of us can squeeze in the cab. Maybe you want to grab some groceries in case this gets bad."

"My sister's not home and I want to make sure we have at least a path for her," Albert said, not taking his eyes off the sky. In the wind, the flakes were snow spikes, hitting our faces.

"I understand, of course," Mr. Haddonfield said. "It's just that, if we get stuck anywhere, it might be good to have another driver so I can get out and push. These boys are too young." Albert looked at the truck doubtfully, and he frowned more than the wind would account for. "It's a standard, though. I forgot to mention. Can you drive a standard?"

"You know, I never did learn," Albert said, his frown blown away as if the wind had knocked it off. "Sorry. You better get going." Mr. Haddonfield motioned me in through the driver's side door and climbed in after me.

But when he put the pickup in reverse, we spun our wheels, digging ruts that were going to be a pain to shovel out. Albert pounded on the hood, held one gloved finger up, and ran back toward the stand of trees that obscured the view of our house, disappearing around them. He came back a few minutes later, dragging two big plastic garbage bags on the ground.

I recognized them as bags of old concrete mix that had been sitting in the tractor shed since before my grandfather died. Mr. Haddonfield got out and met him halfway up the drive. The two men lifted the bags into the truck's bed, and then Mr. Haddonfield extended his hand to shake before getting in. To my relief, Albert shook it and then watched us as we pulled out, our back end now giving us more traction.

The road was slower going than I had imagined it would be. When the school let us out, we thought it was some lucky delusion of Mr. Barnes's, but who was going to argue with an early dismissal? By the time we made it to the reservation's edge, though, I was pretty sure Mr. Barnes had been right, and that we were the delusional people. Sometimes I could feel the truck floating over the snow as if it had rocket boosters on the bottom, like the Jetsons' air car. Then Mr. Haddonfield would make some maneuver and it would feel normal again.

"Nothing to worry about, boys," he said, monkeying the clutch. "Sometimes, we're losing a little traction. We'd be in a lot worse shape without that concrete. We'll make sure to give it back when this is over. I don't imagine your uncle's got plans for it over the next couple days."

"Well, since he hasn't in about seven years, probably not."

"Seven years? Has it gotten wet? Hardened?"

"Maybe. The tractor shed's not in as good shape as it was before," I said. We used it mostly to store old mementos and firewood.

"Your uncle has a tractor?" Mr. Haddonfield asked, looking at me, puzzled. "He should get a plow attachment for the front. Would make your shoveling job a lot easier."

"We don't have the tractor anymore," I said. "My ma sold it after my grandfather died."

"Didn't you tell me your uncle mostly does farmwork?" George said. I nodded. I wondered how Albert was managing with the snow, and if my ma's ride had given any thought to how they were going to get up the hill from Lewiston whenever their employers let them go.

"Didn't he like your grandfather's equipment?" Mr. Haddonfield asked.

"It's complicated," I said, not wanting to go into the whole history of Albert's inability to drive and my family's debts, and relieved that we were finally arriving at the Twin Fair in Niagara Falls. The parking lot was filling faster with snow than the hired plows could clean it.

"Families often are," Mr. Haddonfield said as we parked. He handed George a piece of paper. "Boys, here's the ticket voucher. I'm going to get some groceries. It looks like a lot of people had the same idea." We stepped out and he ran to Twin Foods next door. As we followed, I yelled to Mr. Haddonfield that the buildings shared an interior door, but he couldn't hear me. A massive gust of wind blasted us with a wall of snow, blowing partly from the sky and partly from the plow blades. I felt like I was going to take off into the air.

Finally, we made it inside Twin Fair. A few staff people looked at us, two kids covered in white, and I recognized the look from a mile away: *Aren't you supposed to be in school?* Customers were loading up on antifreeze, windshield washers, rock salt, stuff like that, as if they'd suddenly realized that morning that it was the middle of winter. Marie's mother, Deanna, was working the ticket counter. I hadn't seen her since they moved. She either pretended we didn't know each other or she flat-out didn't remember me. She looked carefully at

George's ID, noting that his name did not match the name on the receipt. He explained where his dad was.

"Here they are," she said, sliding three tickets onto her counter so we could see them. "If you want to go get your father, he can pick them up. I can't give them to you. The signature's gotta match, and I'm pretty sure neither one of you can do that."

"Deanna, it's me, Lewis Blake, from Dog Street. I went to school with Marie," I said, hoping that wouldn't backfire.

"Oh yeah, thought you looked familiar. So you're Vera's kid. Your uncle Juniper, the kind of funny one, he still live with you?"

"Juniper?" George said, totally confused.

"He always hated being called Junior," Deanna clarified. "Nicknames can be tough. Who are you, kid, anyway, and where's" — she looked at his ID again — "Iron Loop? That's not a rez address."

But before George could answer, an obnoxious beep came over the store's intercom system. "Attention, Twin Fair shoppers," a harried voice said from the speakers. Every person around us stopped what they were doing, like a storewide game of freeze tag. "The National Weather Service has announced blizzard conditions with up to sixty-mile-an-hour winds for all of western New York. It's declaring a weather emergency and advises that road travel is extremely hazardous and that lesser-used roads may soon be impassable. If you must get somewhere, you have approximately half an hour to an hour to successfully reach your destination. Because of this unheard-of circumstance, we are closing in ten minutes. If you have purchases you need, please take them immediately to the front registers."

The frozen faces around us had grown wild. These people knew that stores never shooed you out the door when they thought they could make a buck. I glanced over at the TV section of the store, where Tom Jolls gave *The Weather Outside* on channel 7. The caption said it was Tom, but static from the storm reduced him to a vague shape, like a ghost holding a microphone.

"Go on, kid," Deanna said, forging the signature of George's dad on the receipt and passing us the tickets. "I don't think you're getting to that show, but just in case, take your tickets." She turned up the volume on one of the store TVs, where Tom was explaining that Lake Erie had frozen over in the very cold early winter, so there was already a ton of snow on it. Now, in addition to the snow falling from the sky, near hurricane-strength winds were blasting the snow off the lake, and it was heading right for us, a wall of white.

"Thanks, Deanna," I said, just as our names were being called to come to the customer service desk up front. We ran and met George's dad, who was covered in crusted snow, and the three of us hit the door immediately. Everything was dark outside, as if it had somehow become night in the fifteen minutes we'd been indoors. The TV was wrong, as far as I could tell. The storm wasn't coming. It was here.

21

I've Just Seen a Face

"We should be good here, boys," George's dad said as we fish-tailed into the thruway onramp right near Twin Fair's entrance. "Sorry I was so long. It got worse in just the time I took to load the groceries, and then there was thunder and lightning."

I'd lived here my whole life and I'd never seen lightning in a snowstorm, period. Even on the thruway, we still crept along at twenty miles an hour. I could barely see the car in front of us, despite the fact that we weren't more than a car length behind it.

"Turn on the radio — AM," George's dad said. "Find me some news."

News was more or less on every station I could get. "Repeating," the announcer said. It was always a bad sign when they were repeating. "The governor is asking that the area be declared a state of emergency. The thruway, from exits 50 to 55, is closed. Buffalo city schools are closed. The Grand Island Bridges are closed." We were just north of those bridges. "The Niagara section of the thruway is closed. This snow is very dangerous and deceptive. You may pull onto a ramp, thinking it's clear, but the thruway is becoming impassable in the blowing snow. If you're already trapped, don't panic. It's okay to be scared. It's appropriate to be scared."

"A little too late for that information," George's dad said, sighing a small, shaky breath. "All right, shut it off. That's not doing us any good." Snow growled beneath us as we crept into the left lane and passed some slower-moving cars — shadowy hulks along the path. "We've got a higher suspension, so we're in better shape than those sedans."

Still, I knew that grinding sound was snow caking on the chassis. If we stayed on the road much longer, we'd be driving through snow higher than the grille. But we had to see this trip through. The first opportunity to exit would be Clarksville Pass, the road that led to the reservation and Red-Tail Manor. If we got stuck before that, the only option would be to jump the guardrails and walk toward Misty Meadows, which we all wanted to avoid.

The trip should have taken us five minutes, but we finally got to the ramp after a half hour. Weirdly, it was clear. The wind tunnel created by the overpass blew snow completely away from the ramp, the road down to bare asphalt. As we stopped at the bottom, we were in a small bubble of clear air, but in front of the truck, even just five yards, the world began to disappear.

"I don't think we're going to be able to make it back to the reservation just yet, son," George's dad said to me. "I assume those roads are even less clear than these." I nodded. The state was, by treaty, required to maintain our roads, but they were a little loose in defining the word "maintain." I'd been behind the salt truck in the winter once as it passed the borders in and out of the reservation, and I watched a full road treatment dwindle to whatever trickled out of the spreader vent as soon as they crossed on to our land. They opened the vent wide again as soon as they crossed back out, distributing the least amount of salt they could while still legitimately claiming they'd done our roads. "I'm sure we'll get a break from this in a few hours," he added. "Or maybe tomorrow. You've stayed the night before. We can call your mother when we get to the house."

As we reached Historic Heights Elementary School, traffic came to an almost complete stop. We could see solely the car directly in front of us, and then only because their brake lights were on. The rest of the world was a glowing and blowing blue swirl, like we were caught in the Icee machine at Kmart. Occasionally, I saw flickers above and heard rumblings that confirmed the lightning Mr. Haddonfield had seen while we were in the store. The car ahead inched forward and we mimicked it, but the longer we stayed still, the more the snow around the truck filled the road. If we didn't keep moving, the grille would soon be fully caked.

We saw more regular light pulses: police-roof bubble lights. An officer with a bright orange flashlight and a parka emerged from a car, stopped briefly to speak to the driver in front of us, and then came to our truck. "Hello, folks, where are you trying to go?" he said, breathless.

"Red-Tail Manor," George's dad said. "Have to drop my boy and his friend off. I was supposed to be on duty at the base a half hour ago." I glanced at George, who gave me a funny, crinkled-nose expression for a second, confirming his father had lied.

"I'm pretty sure you're not flying anywhere tonight, sir. If the roads ahead aren't impassable now, they will be in about a half an hour. We're having everyone go to the fire hall down Clarksville here. Follow the car ahead of you." The trooper started walking toward the next car behind us, but Mr. Haddonfield called him back.

"I'd like to try for Red-Tail. It's not that far. My wife is home alone."

"Sorry, sir. We're instituting a driving ban. There are already cars up ahead abandoned in the middle of the roads, and we need to keep these stretches as clear as possible for emergency vehicles. Please go to the fire hall. It's not a suggestion." He pointed ahead of us, where, barely visible, there was another trooper with another powerful flashlight, the sort that show up in disaster movies where the brave landing-strip man guides airplanes in for a rocky landing. He was flicking it faster and more impatiently the longer we sat here.

"There's a bank of pay phones at the fire hall," I said as we lurched forward.

"And how do you know that?" Mr. Haddonfield said, his voice flecked with frustration.

"I've played bingo there with my ma and my uncle. There's a big kitchen too, a bar, some pinball machines, and a big room. They hold weddings, reunions, stuff like that there."

"Looks like we'll be finding out firsthand," he said as we followed the line of cars into the fire hall's driveway and then down to the back parking lot.

We opened the doors and wind blasted in at us, almost tearing the door out of my hands. Suddenly, there was a man holding his hand out, telling me to take hold and follow his arm to the man next to him, then on down the chain until we got to the building. I told him I was okay, that I had been here maybe fifty times over the last few years, but he told me not to trust my eyes and to just hang on. As I looked up, I realized I had no real idea where the building was.

"Okay, boys, grab my belt loops and put your other arms around my back," Mr. Haddonfield said. "I'll hang on to the chain of people here. Don't let go, no matter what."

And with that, we began making our way in the blue haze of snow. The temperature had plummeted, and my nostrils felt like they were full of broken twigs when I tried to breathe in the frigid air. As we passed each man in the chain, Mr. Haddonfield reached out and touched their shoulders, shouting thank-you so they could hear him in the wind. They would nod and we kept going. They were all bundled haphazardly, and I wondered if people inside had given up what they had on to those who volunteered to guide others into the building.

When we made it in, several women dusted off the clotted snow encasing us and brought us into the main hall. We were offered hot chocolate, coffee, and doughnuts, instructed to show our hands and faces to make sure we hadn't been frostbitten, and then told to sit anywhere.

Mr. Haddonfield and I made our way to the pay phones and stood in line. Every couple minutes, a volunteer fireman would remind people that the phone company had requested that phones be reserved for emergencies or checking on family members. Casual conversations were supposed to wait. Mr. Haddonfield's phone opportunity came first, and he called his wife.

My phone came open, but the man behind me stepped up and cut in front of me.

"I was waiting for that. I was in front of you," I said. He pretended not to hear me, picking up the receiver and throwing a coin in until I repeated it louder.

"You heard the man," he said. "No casual conversations. Your little girlfriend can wait."

As he turned back to the phone, Mr. Haddonfield, suddenly off his phone, put one hand on the man's shoulder, and with his other, pressed the hang-up button. The man's dime fell into the coin return.

"I believe that young man was ahead of you," he said.

"You wanna take it outside, buddy? I don't give a shit if it's snowing. Let's get it on."

"I don't think we need to do that. Why don't you just let this young man call his family, and then you'll have your turn." The man shrugged and lifted the phone to his ear again. Mr. Haddonfield leaned in. "Do you really want me to point out to the authorities here that you prevented a boy from calling his family, and that you jumped in line to do that?"

"Do whatever you want, man. I know these guys. Every one of these guys. They'll throw you out on your ass sooner than they will me, so you go tell whoever you want, just so long as you get clear of me so I can make my call."

"Here, kid, you can use my turn," a woman said. Mr. Haddonfield let the man go. The man shrugged again, as if flicking away a wasp, and began his call, a cocky grin on his face. "Hey, baby, me and the boys ain't home yet," he said, as if the person at home couldn't have figured that out.

Everyone chose to look elsewhere. I thanked the woman and called home. My ma answered. "You're home," I said, relieved.

"Yeah, Mrs. D.'s husband came home early, and when he saw how bad it was out, he gave me a ride. Where are you? Albert said you went to Twin Fair three or four hours ago."

"On the way back, they blocked the roads. We're at the fire hall with a hundred people, maybe more. Every couple minutes, new people are coming in the doors. Okay, I'm not supposed to be on here long. Just wanted to let you know where I was and that I'll get home as soon as I can." I hung up and thanked the woman again, walking back into the main room as the jerk told the person at the other end of the line how he made some army pinhead back down.

Mr. Haddonfield stood in the bar entrance, offering to relieve someone on the line to the parking lot, but the volunteer fireman told him the number of new arrivals was trickling down. They'd blocked the roads and were going out to stranded cars to make sure no one was caught inside. So we went into the main room, where George had saved us seats.

"What's the matter?" he asked, reading his dad's face.

"Oh, just some jerk who cut in line, said he knows everyone in here and should therefore get to do whatever he wants," he said. "Hard to imagine they can't put that attitude in check even in a crisis like this. What an asshole." I hadn't heard him swear before, and George had said he did it only rarely. George had developed his avoidance of swearing in imitation of his dad's choices. "Said he was here with someone else."

"Well, I'll give you two guesses about who those others might be," George said, pointing with his chin to a table about ten yards away from us. There sat Evan and Preston Reiniger, staring at us. Even in a room this size, with this number of people, Evan had noticed me immediately.

"So," I said to George. "You think it might be a good time to tell me what happened in October?"

Too Many People

"It's complicated," he said, but there was no smile on his face.

"What is it, boys?" Mr. Haddonfield said. "What's going on?"

We watched the pay-phone man come in, reach between two people in the food line, and grab three doughnuts by sticking fingers into their holes. The people in line frowned at him and he stared back. "Some problem with my getting food for my sons?" he said, leaning into one man's face, never flinching until both people he'd bumped turned away, pretending nothing had happened. I could see a lifetime of this man doing such things. He smirked, strolled over to Preston and Evan, and dropped doughnuts in front of them, stuffing the third one into his mouth.

"You know those boys?" Mr. Haddonfield said, connecting the dots for himself.

"Dad?" George said. "You remember when you came to school after I'd gotten a black eye, and I was the one who was being suspended for fighting, though I hadn't swung even once?"

"Are you telling me one of those boys is the one who clocked you? Which one? Neither of them is even close to your size."

"I remembered what you told me about fighting," George said.

"So you just let that guy sucker you?" his dad said. Evan Reiniger and his brother were all muscle, but George could have probably taken both out in a fight unassisted. "Boy, you know better than that. Self-defense, defense in general, that's what I . . . Why do you think I'm in the military? You could have pounded —"

"That's where the complication comes in," George said. "I never told you, but that period in the fall when Lewis wasn't coming over? It wasn't just because Stacey and I were seeing a lot of each other. He wasn't in school because of that kid." I thought his dad knew all along what had happened, but he was obviously hearing this for the first time too.

"Folks, may I have your attention?" a fireman said over the PA. "We've been asked to cut our natural gas consumption as much as we can. The gas company's declared a call for conservation, since there are cars abandoned from here to the Pennsylvania line and no one knows when the transport routes are going to be clear. So we're going to turn the heat down a bit, but we're going to try to keep it comfortable." Another man stepped up and spoke into his ear. "If any of you have blankets in your cars, tell Franklin here. Franklin, raise your hand for the folks, so people know who to come to" — the fireman did — "and we'll get them before it gets too bad. The sheer number of bodies in this building should help, but the first thing we're doing is shutting off the heating vents to the back hall and the restrooms. It's going to be a little chilly to use the facilities, but on the plus side, we're well stocked with toilet paper." The crowd laughed nervously.

"You told me once," George said to his dad, as if our conversation had not been interrupted, "that sometimes, the rules don't work right, and you have to find ways to work within the system. That's what I did. That kid had been jumping Lewis since September."

"You didn't fight back?" Mr. Haddonfield said, turning to me.

Even here, with someone who knew me and seemed to like me, the immediate thought was that I had somehow failed in self-protection, self-preservation. "Of course I did, sir, but look at me," I said, standing and raising my arms. Not even Albert's leather jacket could hide the fact that I would never be a big guy. "George might be able to take them, but who's going to be intimidated by me?"

As I dropped my hands, my cousin Innis noticed me across the room and waved. I realized that if I could catch a ride home, then George's dad wouldn't have to deal with our roads, which were sure to be worse than anywhere else. Innis stood and walked toward the bathrooms. "Excuse me, Mr. Haddonfield, I want to talk to someone who might make this a little easier," I said, standing.

"Sure, you do that," he said, not taking his eyes off George. "I'm interested to hear what else my son has to tell me about this fall."

I wanted to hear that myself, if only to try to take whatever heat there was off George, but I needed to catch my cousin. "Innis," I yelled, stepping through the double doors as he disappeared into the men's room at the end of the hall. It felt at least twenty degrees colder in the corridor already. As I got halfway down, the double doors banged open behind me and I heard footsteps running toward me. I knew I had to turn and deal with this.

Five seconds later, Evan ducked his head like a football player, plowing directly into my gut. I pounded both fists on his back, but I was already in the air, Preston having kicked my feet out from under me. "You're gonna wish you got lost in the snow," Evan said, giving me a couple quick kicks to the side as I tried to get up. Preston grabbed the waistband of my jeans, tugging me down, and then suddenly he was gone.

I saw Innis had dragged him off with a headlock. In that moment I was delighted the Reinigers had been equal opportunity offenders. Then Evan grabbed on to the pocket slits of my jacket and ripped a long and jagged gap from pocket to waist. "You asshole!" I yelled. "You tore my jacket!" It wasn't even along a seam. If it could be repaired at all, the scar was always going to show.

"That ain't all I'm gonna tear," he said, coming at me again, fists swinging from the side.

Instantly, I understood how time sometimes did strange things. I'd seen movies in which they went all slow-motion, like the end of *Bonnie and Clyde*, and it seemed fake. But now it truly felt like Evan slowed down. My skin flushed cold from the top of my head down, the way the temperature had dropped that afternoon, and an idea materialized out of nowhere.

His arms came around me, like a horseshoe zeroing in on my ribs, and I knew he planned to knock the wind out of me. I'd be done if that happened. So I crouched like I had in the past, spreading my feet to firm them, and I clasped my hands together, the way you'd help someone get on a horse. Right as we made contact, I thrust straight up and slammed my locked fists into his nuts as hard as I could. As he buckled down on me, I stood up straight with all the spring my legs had, so the back of my head connected with his chin, and I heard a loud *click* as his jaw slammed shut. He fell backward, and I kicked him a couple times as he scuttled away. Each time he almost regained his footing, I boomeranged my leg around his ankle and twisted my pelvis again, knocking his feet out from under him with the trick George had shown me five million years before in the junior high music wing.

"Lewis, look out," I heard Innis say as Preston crashed into me. I lost my balance, and by the time I stood up, both brothers had taken back off down the hall and reentered the main room.

"Thanks," I said to Innis, who helped me up.

"Man, are those two ever going to smarten up?" He thought for a minute. "Probably not. Sorry, I held him as long as I could, but he got away from me."

"I was coming to ask you if I can catch a ride with you guys, even just to your place. I can probably walk from there."

"A ride? How'd you get here in the first place? That old guy with the buzz cut you were sitting near?" I nodded. "Who is that anyway?"

"My friend's dad."

"Oh, that kid with you too, duh. I'll ask my dad, but I can't picture it being a problem. Might have to sit on someone's lap, but you're pretty scrawny."

"Funny," I said, pushing at him, but not moving him one bit. He laughed and said he still had to take a leak. One of the doors opened then, and I tensed, waiting to see who came through.

It was George. "What just happened in here?" he said.

I must have looked worse than I thought, and then I remembered my jacket. Evan had torn one of the sleeves at the seam too, but that was going to be an easier repair than the side. "Evan Reiniger and his brother just happened in here," I said. "What happened out there?"

He shook his head. "We are definitely *not* done with that conversation, but as I told my dad what happened, I got even more clearly what you meant about people automatically believing you were lying. The look of doubt on his face . . . I almost never see that directed at me. I mean, I believed you before, because of something that happened at the mall while you were missing. But when I saw my dad's face, I knew it fresh in a different way. People don't believe you about something, even when they should, because the truth involves them too."

"Someone just give you a hearing aid?"

"Guess I deserve that. When you said that most of our class lumped you into one category because of where you came from . . ." He paused, looking down. "I'm sorry. I didn't understand," he said, and then he paused again. "No, I mean, I didn't believe you. *Really* believe you. We get some grief for being in the military and Vietnam, but the military, that's who my dad chose to be."

"I don't get what you're saying here."

"You didn't choose to be from the reservation."

"Hey, I'm happy being from the rez," I said. "It'd be nice if others didn't have an issue."

"That's not what I meant. Man, I hate to tell you this, 'cause you're going to think it confirms everything you believe. And maybe it does."

"Do you think anything you can say to me could possibly be worse than this fall?"

"While you were out, gone," he said, and then let out a deep breath, "Summer was saying all those things I told you about, and I didn't think anything of it. That was Summer being Summer. But Stacey — someone who knows you, someone who got up before the sunrise to meet us — she caved to the pressure of Summer's saying no self-respecting person in our section would hang out with you. Stacey told Summer she'd been doing it for me, and kissed me, and then later, in private, told me she only said that to keep her friends. So I let it go. I said fine, keep them. And we started hanging out at the mall with them. I'm sorry. Can we go back? It's freezing out here." George grabbed the door.

I put my hand on it, keeping it shut. "Girlfriends get chosen over friends all the time. It's part of life. I've never had a girlfriend and I *still* know that. Tell me the rest. Finish."

"We were all at the pizza place in the mall, crowded into a booth, and we decided to order wings. I said it was too bad you weren't there, since you introduced me to wings. I don't know how I didn't grasp the way that would be received. I was missing you there, I guess. Summer did one of her melodramatic eye rolls and said it was your own fault. You were working a system, according to her dad, singling out a white kid for harassment. Summer said most Indian kids just beat up whoever they want to attack, but you were doing it the way a smart kid would. She added that she knew you were trouble immediately, by how shabby and backward you always dressed, and everyone else there cracked up, buttoning their shirts to the top like you used to. She finished saying I'd better watch out because you'd turn on me at the first slight. Look, man, it's not Stacey's fault, but . . ."

He stopped again, and this time I waited.

"Even if she wasn't saying anything, if she was just going along to get along, it still meant she'd been changed by the way those jerks in our class see you. At first, it was in the expression she made when those others started talking about you. It was like you weren't even Lewis to her." He pursed his lips and his chin dimpled, his eyes red and narrowed. "Now can we go in?"

"Not until you tell me what you did."

"Jeez! Wasn't that enough? That tore my guts out."

"I know. I appreciate it, I do. I wish I could say I'm stunned, but I'm not. Tell me."

"Fine! After that, I finally got that everyone was dismissing what you said about Evan because of who you were, or maybe who he is. I kept seeing Stacey's face in my head, a face she didn't even know she was making. I guess — no, I know, the big change for me happened when we were alone. We were out behind the rec building, making out in the shadows, and she stopped, and said she feared for her own safety. 'What if Lewis gets mad at me?' she said. And then she said that if we were going to stay together, I had to really think about who I spent my time with.

"After that, I needed her to know what you'd been through, thinking it would change things. We talked about it, but she didn't get it. So I figured I could force the school to face up to it by making him fight me, and then she would see what I could finally see. It was a matter of waiting for the right moment, when Evan and I were both in front of the office between classes. It took a while, but I had to wait for all the elements to line up. I finally got it, said what I knew would provoke him, and wham, straight to the face — eye, then jaw. He's got a pretty powerful right-left combo."

"Think you're telling me something I don't know?" He shook his head. "But how did you know you could get him to swing?"

"You, actually, and a little information Artie gave me about Evan's brother. He's not very good at controlling himself when someone says something he objects to."

"So you said?"

He smiled sort of an embarrassed smile. "I said: 'Hey, asshole, did your brother get picked for the bravery ritual because you're the bigger candy ass?'"

"You lie! You did not! *You* swore?"

"Yes, I swore."

You wouldn't think that was a big thing, but in that moment, in his willingness to break one of his own weird personal rules for my sake, I was absolutely convinced I'd been right in calling him my first, true, best friend.

"Cheap, I know, but I had to get him to respond. He might be in Eight-Sixteen, but he's not stupid enough to be caught twice. And who isn't going to defend his own toughness?" I shook my head. "My dad's not too happy with me right now. He was willing to go to the newspaper when Doyle tried to suspend me and not do anything to Reiniger, saying I was the one who started things. My dad went to Doyle, said he knew there were witnesses to an opposite story. Doyle at first just offered to erase my suspension, but my dad about went ballistic when he refused to do anything to Evan, saying it was a school matter."

"All this over a fight? I don't believe you," I said.

"We kind of went through one of those big plate-glass panels in front of the office. They're Saf-T-Glass, by the way, like in cars, so you don't get cut. Doyle was trying to charge my dad for replacing it, and Evan's dad."

"No way! Through the glass! I guess your boomerang move can be pretty effective."

"Anyway, now that my dad's seen the size of that kid, he knows I set up the situation. I mean, look at me."

"That's what I'm doing," Evan's dad said as he pushed through the double doors. We backed away quickly, and he closed the doors behind him, leaning against them, preventing our escape.

"So you're the two. My boys told me some guys jumped them just now when they came out to see if they could help in the bar. You're that Indian kid, but who the hell are you, boy? Should know better than to trust this kind. Stab you right in the back. What every Indian sees when they look at you or me? They see Custer, plain and simple. I trusted one. You know where he is now? Teepee creeper's in the sack with my ex."

Just then the door behind him moved a bit. He dug his boots in, but after a brief pause, the door opened a crack. Mr. Reiniger pushed back harder, but a steel-toed boot sat in the gap.

"Boys?" George's dad said, not loud, not alarmed.

"We're going to need some help, sir," George said. Mr. Haddonfield squeezed an arm in, and then, no matter how much pressure Mr. Reiniger put on the door, it slid steadily open. Eventually, he leapt away from it, and Mr. Haddonfield stumbled in, shutting it behind him.

"So you were going to manhandle two boys in the middle of a blizzard?" he said calmly. "In a fire hall full of people who can't get home?" I had expected him to come in ready to pound, but he just stood firm. "What is wrong with you?"

Evan's dad snorted. "I'll take you out, and I've got easily fifty witnesses in there who'll testify, in court, that you got yourself up in my business, that I don't even know who you are. Let's get it on."

It was clear that violence and covering it up was a way of life for this family, that they were a group of people who knew their way around a real truth and a truth as verifiable in court.

"I don't doubt that you might have fifty buddies in there," Mr. Haddonfield said, still unmoving, but with the sharpest edge I'd ever heard in his voice — easily double the harshness I'd heard at the Picnic last summer. "And maybe you're good in a bar fight, scrapping with drunks, but I've had years of regular combat training. If you threaten my family, trust me, I know how to protect them. Most people understand real family responsibilities. Boys, go on inside. I'll be back in a minute."

Neither George nor I moved. I felt like any motion would cause this all to explode, like I was in front of a cobra whose hood was flared. "Now!" Mr. Haddonfield yelled, and George elbowed me, neither man moving as we made our way to the doors. When we reached them, Evan's dad stepped aside without taking his eyes from Mr. Haddonfield's. "Go on now, keep walking," George's dad said, and as the door closed, he said to Evan's dad, "You might want witnesses, but I don't need . . ."

His voice faded to a muffled rumble as we went to sit back down. Evan and Preston were in the same seats I'd last seen them in, and their eyes flicked to each other, and then back to us. They were not exactly in the situation they'd planned.

A few minutes passed, but when the doors opened, Innis was the person who came through, looking a little confused. I motioned him over and asked what he saw. "I didn't really see too much," he said, crouching down to whisper. "But I was on the john, and I heard all this scuffling and grunting coming down the hall. I knew it wasn't kids, so it couldn't be you. I flushed and then, when the noises got to the john, I put the lid down and hopped on the toilet seat, so it would look like no one was in there. Then, I'm not sure, but I swear it seemed like one man was giving another man a swirly in the next stall. Under the partition, I could see two pairs of men's legs kneeling in front of the bowl, scrabbling around, and you could hear some struggle, then, you know, *blub blub blub* and splashing. Grown-ups? Do they give swirlies? There was this one time, after basketball practice —"

"Innis!" I said.

"Oh, right. Anyway, then they were gone. I don't know where they went. Hey, look, there's Big Red and Squash coming in. I better go ask my dad if you can come with us."

"What do you mean?" I asked, still watching the doors.

"My dad and a bunch of the other guys got the idea to call Big Red and offer to pay him. You know, he's got those plows he does driveways with, and we're only a quarter mile from the reservation. He's supposed to bring two plows here, then we're gonna follow him back to the rez." And with that, Innis ran over to the section of the fire hall where all the other Indians were sitting, so it looked like a mini-reservation.

Mr. Haddonfield came back in, his coat and brush cut clotted with snow, his hands and face red and raw looking.

"Forgot my gloves," he said, sitting down. "Son, will you get me a cup of coffee and a napkin? My nose is running."

George got up as Evan's dad came in, with dark maroon, hectic flares covering his cheeks. He looked like he'd tried to brush all the snow off him, but there were patches where it was frozen on, and he had icy streaks in his hair. He sat down with his sons, and when they asked him what happened, he told them to shut up. Then he scanned the room, defying anyone to speak, or maybe searching for his friends.

I told Mr. Haddonfield about the convoy plan and that it would be easy for me to get a ride home. He asked where the people from the reservation were, and I pointed them out. He took the coffee from George, holding it in both bright pink hands, and told us to sit still. "And don't you worry about our friends there," he added as he got up. "They won't be bothering us again."

He walked across the room, snow still melting off him in drips, and shook hands with a few people, including my uncle Frank and Big Red. When he gestured to where we sat, Frank waved to us. There was more talking and then he came back.

"Have you got a dime?" Mr. Haddonfield asked me, putting on his gloves. I nodded. "Call your family. Is your uncle likely to be home?" Again, I nodded. "Ask him to listen for us and then to make his way out to the end of the driveway when he can. There are enough cars here that we should be pretty loud."

"I think I can make it from the end of my driveway to the house," I said. "Why are you going? I can get a ride from someone going that way, like my uncle Frank."

"Son, do as I say, and hurry up. I don't think we have a lot of time." Everyone from the reservation was standing and gathering their things, adults bundling up themselves and their little kids. One of the firemen approached them. There were some exchanges that looked like arguments. Eventually, a fireman got back on the PA system as I made my way to the phones.

"Folks, remain seated," he said as others watched everyone from the reservation clearly getting ready to leave. "These people live very close by and they've arranged their own plows to help get them home safely." A wave of grumbling went through the room, people wanting to know why they couldn't be escorted home by private plows and so on. "Folks? Folks! The reality is that just a few yards from here, where these folks live, it's not New York. They have different laws, and if they've chosen not to close their roads, that's their business. For the short distance they're using our roads, we're letting that go." More grumbling. "Folks," the fireman said, suddenly irritated. "The fewer people here, the more resources. Think about it. We have freezers of food here, but we don't know how long this storm is going to take." And instantly, those remaining quieted down and went back to whatever they were doing.

I quickly called Albert with the CliffsNotes of what had been happening, and Albert said that he'd be waiting. I pushed back through the doors to find everyone from home huddled at the far doors. "Good riddance," I heard Evan's dad shout at us, but no one joined him.

"Okay," Big Red yelled. "We got dual plows up front, and we're gonna overlap one behind the other, trying to clear a path. We're hitting sixty-mile-an-hour winds, with snow, so you can't hardly see nothing." He sliced his hands in front of him like a referee indicating an invalid play. "Pay attention and watch the roads. It sounds like I'm making this up, isn't it? But you might not be able to see even your house. Look for any-thing you might recognize before your place: mailbox, cherry tree, anything that's going to give you a clue. That's when I want you to put your blinkers on and flick your high beams so the people in front and behind know you're getting ready to turn off. And you might not be able to make it into your drive-way, so just goose it a bit as you get in. That way, even if you're stuck, you'll be stuck at home. Got it?"

He looked into the adult faces to make sure they under-stood what he was asking of them. "I been doing this a long time, and I never dealt with snow this tight packed. It's like driving on one big snowball. And if you slide 'cause of the ruts, or you drag behind, turn your headlights off and on to let the driver in front know. No matter how you cut it, we're in for a rough ride.

"Now give me five minutes to clear enough of this so you can get to your cars. I'll honk when I'm ready for you. Try to organize yourselves so the ones closest to home are nearer the beginning, if you can, so we can keep track. We've got a third driver here," he said, holding up my uncle Frank's arm, "who has agreed to bring up the rear to watch you."

"How come Frank's doing it?" someone shouted.

"He's got the right equipment, a four-wheel-drive truck, a CB radio, and four healthy boys to help push him out if need be," Big Red said, and people laughed in a nervous burst.

Big Red and Squash stepped out the door, and a murmur went through the crowd from those who had glimpsed the out-side. The two plows scraped through for a few minutes and then they honked. The doors opened, and as it turned out, the descriptions hadn't even come close to matching to the reality. The snow was at least halfway up most cars, and only pickup trucks, Jeeps, and combination trucks like Broncos had a competitive edge.

"Same as before, boys, belt loops and back," Mr. Haddonfield said. "Hang on."

We stepped out, and even in our sturdiness, we were blown down three times before we made it to the truck, helped back up each time by whoever walked behind us, as we helped those who fell in front of us. This was the way it was going to work. In the couple minutes it took us just to get to the truck, my face and hands ached and my nose ran like it was attached to a hose.

"All right," Mr. Haddonfield said, nearly breathless as he started the truck. "We made it. We're going to climb in, and then, son, as soon as we drop your friend off, we're going to work our way home. The Manor's not that far from the reservation. There should be at least one lane clear enough for us to get there."

We got the high-beam flash and Mr. Haddonfield shifted us into second gear to get a better grip in the strange, dense, wind-driven snow. As we moved along the first few yards, we felt ourselves rise up and fall, rise up and fall, as the snow shifted beneath our tires.

We crept toward the reservation. Cars were pointed along the road in wild directions, like in those day-after-the-atomic-bomb movies where all the humans vanished. Big Red's trucks kept us to one lane until we crossed the reservation border, and then the first truck veered into the oncoming lane and the one behind rose to meet it.

We plodded along, tires jerking wildly. Sometimes, it wasn't even the ruts in the snow, just the wind bumping us over in massive gusts that made the windows shift in their frames.

Cars occasionally turned off into driveways, but all I could see around us were the vague, glowing dots of headlights behind and taillights ahead. It felt like we were in a reverse snow globe. I hoped Albert wasn't out waiting already. It was going to be a while before we made it to my house.

23

The Long and Winding Road

As we crossed the bush line at our yard, Mr. Haddonfield turned on his blinkers and flashed his high beams. A few yards before we got there, two shapes appeared — my ma and Albert, shoveling as fast as they could. We had just enough room to pull in.

"Thank you, sir, now go, go!" I yelled, jumping out. "Don't get left behind. Stay with them." The car line made its grinding creep onward, and I was sure they'd do all right, until Mr. Haddonfield stepped out and waved my ma and Albert to the back of the truck.

"You're probably going to need these," he shouted to my ma in the howl of the wind, pulling out several bags of groceries. "We were at the store, and I thought, as long as I was there . . ."

My ma took the bags from him and stacked them on the snow, where they didn't sink at all. She yelled to Albert, asking if he had any money in his pockets. He shook his head.

"I'll be right back with some cash," she called to Mr. Haddonfield, taking the bags and climbing the snowbank, almost losing her balance. He shook his head, stacking more bags at the bank's edge as she disappeared. The convoy had passed and even the last taillights were no longer visible. We could hear them if the wind dropped a little, but even that sound was fading.

"Do you want a hand carrying these to the house?" George's dad asked.

"Thank you," Albert said, shaking hands with him. "We can handle it from here. If you don't move it in the next couple minutes, the wind's gonna get rid of all what Big Red just did."

Then my ma arrived back, offering cash to George's dad. "It's fine," he said, not taking it. "Another time." She thanked him again and told him he should be on his way.

He nodded and told George to get in the truck. They waved, and though none of us had spoken, we understood that the concert in Toronto was a distant dream. I wondered if it would even go forward. Maybe it would have to be rescheduled and our tickets would still be valid.

The Haddonfields climbed in and started to back out, their tires spinning. My ma and Albert and I leaned into the front bumper, then lifted, then pushed again, as Mr. Haddonfield rocked the truck back and forth, all of us in rhythm, and we got them out in less than a minute.

"That your friend's dad?" my ma asked as their taillights became vague red glows, like twin cigarettes being smoked in the dark, until they disappeared. I nodded. "Not bad for a crhee-rhoo-rhitt," she said, handing me one bag, Albert two others, and taking the last two herself.

"They're not all bad," I said as we made our way to the house, entirely on top of the packed snow. It was strange to suddenly be a foot taller, like I'd instantly become an adult.

Inside, she had us set the bags on the dining room table so she could see what we'd brought in. "Did you ask him to do this?" she said, unloading steaks, hamburgers, stuffed pork chops, bread, rolls, frozen french fries, frozen pizzas, cheese wedges, and several boxes of Ritz, among other things. "This looks like your handiwork. What is this anyway?" she asked, holding up a box of egg rolls.

"Chinese food, and, no, of course not," I said. "Don't you think you've been clear about what I can and can't accept?"

"Then how does a man I've never met before seem to know all of your favorite foods?"

"Well, for one," Albert said, "who wouldn't consider this their favorite foods? Come on, Vera, this is just good food, plain and simple, isn't it? When was the last time you had a stuffed pork chop? I'm firing up the oven." He put his coat and gloves back on and pulled out the socks that we used to seal the kitchen door shut.

"Have you met him before?" she asked him.

"This morning. Nice enough guy, for choosing a life in the service. You know me, nervous in the service." Albert pulled the door open. The kitchen's back door was almost entirely blocked with snow from the inside, and icicles crept in where the rotting boards met the sky. The plastic tarp covering the hole in the kitchen roof must have blown off sometime during the day. Albert dug out his lighter and the paper towels he'd wadded in his pocket and shut the door behind him.

I went out to the cold front room and grabbed a shovel. We were going to need the outside path clear, at least to the pump and the kerosene tank, but more than that, some part of me refused to allow snow to pile up inside our house. And that meant I needed to begin shoveling out the kitchen.

Given the wreck we lived in, it probably didn't matter, but I remembered when the kitchen was rainproof and warm, when some cupboards held food and daily dishes. Others stored my grandmother's fancy dishes — something she called carnival glass that, when you let it sit in sunlight, gleamed like a rainbow. After my grandfather died, and we went further to the fringes without his retirement and social security, those things gradually changed or disappeared altogether. First was probably the fancy glass stuff, which vanished slowly, sold piece by piece to antiques dealers. The leaks got worse in the kitchen, but we just let it keep raining in, knowing the water would run out the gap below the kitchen door, since the floor was sloped.

When part of the roof in the kitchen caved in with snow weight two years ago, we moved everything we could into other rooms. The fridge went into the front room, the cupboard and washstand in the dining room corner. The rest of the house was heated by two kerosene heaters, but we kept the old wood-burning stove, just in case, wrapping it in plastic to keep the moisture out. The one thing we'd never been able to move was the cooking stove, because it would have required a changing around of the gas line, and we couldn't afford to switch the hookups. So mostly we pretended the kitchen didn't exist anymore, and we went in there only for cooking.

"You're digging a clearing in the kitchen?" my ma asked as I walked through with the shovel. I nodded and got my jacket and gloves secured. "You still didn't answer my question."

"What question was that?" I asked. I was tired, cold, freaked out, and beginning to hurt from the fight with Evan. I just wanted to finish shoveling enough to clear the paths, get in bed, and listen to some music, maybe dig out my favorite old issue of *The Amazing Spider-Man* again.

"I wanted to know how this man knows every one of your favorite foods, including, apparently, something called egg rolls that I have never even heard of."

"Ma, really? Is that your question right now? I'm standing here with a puffy lip and a ripped leather jacket, and I've been stuck at a fire hall for hours, and I had to come up with my own ride home 'cause we have never once had a car in my entire life, and that's your question?"

"I don't care what kind of day you've had! I won't have you —"

"Fine! He knows all my favorite foods because, in the last year, I have probably sat down to more meals with that family than I have with my own, 'cause mine is too busy picking up after rich shit heads in Lewiston," I said, and she grimaced at the truth of her life. "And if they ever invited me, I might even consider moving in with them, but I don't think I'm ever getting out of here, so don't worry about it." I opened the kitchen door, where Albert was fiddling with the oven, and slammed it again behind me.

"Shouldn't have said those things," Albert said.

"Shut up, man. Leave me alone," I said, instantly hating everything I'd just said. It wasn't even true. I held my hand out for his lighter, ignited some newspaper, and stuck it in one of the holes in the oven's floor. The flame ring rumbled to life and I shut the door. "What should I do with this?" I said, holding the shovel while more snow blew into the room. There was no way to stay on top of the snow, maybe even no way to get the door clear at all. "Well?"

"Didn't you just tell me to shut up?" Albert said.

"You know what I meant."

"Yeah, okay, I did. But still, you never used to talk to me like that. What's going on?"

"Nothing. Nothing that hasn't been happening for the last two years anyway."

"I told you you'd change once you seen how that half lived," he said. "You didn't believe me before. I hate to tell you, but that road only goes one way. You can't turn around."

I stood in silence for a moment.

"There were things I had a hard time dealing with when I was drafted, but the hard living that broke most of those suburban losers? I had that kicked. You had hard living down too and you didn't even know it. But now you do, isn't it? You know our life is rough." He sighed. "Just spread that snow over here, near the stove. As it melts, I'll mop it up. We've gotta be able to get to the pump, no doubt about that. Hey, wait," he said, shaking the large kettle. "Full, but pretty icy. Light this burner."

The thermometer on the wall said it was hovering around twenty in the kitchen, which meant it must have been zero outside, and twenty below with the windchill factor.

"Heat this water, pour it on the snow. That'll melt enough to get ahead of it. Can't be any worse than it is now," he said. Just then my ma yelled for me. "Go ahead, see what she wants. I'll let you know when I've got enough cleared that we can open the door."

In the dining room, my ma sat in her chair. She looked at first like she was laughing, but then I understood it was crying. I'd never noticed your body moves in the same way when you're doing either of these things. They even sounded a little similar to each other.

I had made her cry with the things I'd said, something she hadn't done even when my grandparents passed. Still, I didn't know exactly what I'd actually said to cause her tears, or what it was about white people in general that triggered them. Had working for white people, cleaning up after them all the time, so destroyed her that she couldn't see them as human? Was she so sickened by the idea of them that my friendships caused her this much grief?

If so, I was terrified. It meant we weren't going to have the same life. White people were going to be in my life, and not just as my bosses, particularly since I'd been thinking about maybe going to college one day. I wish I knew how to tell her they weren't all like the rich jerks she worked for. I wanted to try to navigate both planets, make choices within both worlds, not have to choose one to love and one to hate.

On the table sat a baking sheet holding all six stuffed pork chops, with a neat line of egg rolls surrounding them. I guessed she was planning to conserve the bottled gas by fixing a lot of the food at once, but we were still going to have to reheat the leftovers on the stove.

"Turn on the outside light," she said. I did, but all we could see out the window was snow whipping by, like the contents of a shaken can of 7UP. I flicked the light switch back off. "No, leave it on," she said.

"We can't see anything."

"It's not for us. I called Zach. Snakeline is closed." She was trying to tell me something in that way she did whenever she had information she didn't want to say directly. "No cars in and no cars out. Take those upstairs," she said, pointing to a stack of sheets. "I'll deal with it later."

"Deal with what?" I said.

"You know, for being so smart, sometimes you can't add for shit. Snakeline is *closed*," she repeated. "There," she added, pointing her cigarette to our bank of front windows. "Is it any clearer now?"

A glow filled the windows near the driveway. A car had just pulled in, and then its headlights blinked out. A couple minutes later, someone was knocking on our door, and we both had a pretty good idea of who it was.

The one fear my ma had expressed when I started hanging around with George had come true: He had come to our house, and there was no way to deny him entrance. He'd come, and we would be proven to live in this scandalously broken place we'd always kept a secret from any white person we'd ever met.

"What should I do?" I asked.

She stood and smoothed her apron around her, then pushed some stray hairs behind her ears. "What do you think?"

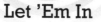

Let 'Em In

George and his dad stood on our porch as I opened the door. "The road's closed, drifted over," Mr. Haddonfield said. "I got as far as the corner, and then I tried the way we'd come, but it's gone in impassable drifts already."

I was stuck in place, looking at the two of them. The wind whipped through George's hair and even made the little bristles of his dad's brush cut vibrate like tuning forks.

"I know it violates some ceremonial protocol, but I thought maybe we could use your phone," Mr. Haddonfield said, "in this one emergency exception?"

I stepped aside so they could come in. They kicked snow off their boots before crossing the threshold. Mr. Haddonfield started unlacing his boots, and George followed suit. "Don't bother," I said. "You're going to want to keep them on." I brought them in, sure they noticed that the front room was maybe only thirty degrees warmer than the outside. It was like being outside, minus the wind.

"Phone's through here," I said, pulling back the blankets from the door frame so they could pass into the dining room. "It's warmer too. You can sit here if you want." I cleared Mr.

Haddonfield a space at the desk we kept the phone on and put stuff on the daybed next to it. No one regularly slept on it, but my ma kept it around as a just-in-case.

"Why don't we go into the living room," my ma said, her polite face back on. "Lewis, find out what's going on with this storm on the TV. The radio just keeps repeating the same information over and over." She escorted us in and then slipped into the kitchen to put food in the oven while no one was looking. We'd never had a white-people-in-the-house drill, so we were improvising.

I looked out the west windows for the first time. I thought the snow had just blown against the window and stuck there, but at the north windows, drifts were building. The one coming around the corner would already be above my head if I were outside. "It's warmest over there by the stove," I said to George. "That spot on the couch. I sit there when I watch TV. Sometimes even that other chair. Not as comfortable, but I can stick my feet in closer to the stove's hot core. Sorry, it's, well, I was going to say messy, but that doesn't exactly cut it."

George sat where I suggested. He didn't say anything, but I could see he was taking it all in: the smoke-darkened walls, the extension cords, the plastic on the windows, our sagging furniture, and, totally out of place, Zach's five thousand lacrosse trophies. I wished I could read his expression. If pressed, I'd have to say disbelief with a little bit of fear. I realized that, to some degree, my house looked a lot like the one where the crazy cannibals lived in *The Texas Chain Saw Massacre*, minus the meat hooks and skeleton art, of course.

It wasn't hard to find TV coverage of the storm. Every channel was All Blizzard, All the Time. We'd been declared a national emergency. A reporter said the plows had to return to base, because the wind was so bad, they couldn't see their blades.

They were beginning to use "storm of the century" type language, and continued to urge minimal natural gas usage, saying we were in the middle of a shortage already, and for those on bottled gas or kerosene (that is, us), they could not give a definitive answer as to when they would get delivery trucks out again. The streets were officially closed to everything but emergency traffic through all of western New York. Wherever you were, that was where you were staying, for an undeterminable amount of time.

"I'll be right back," I said. In the dining room, Mr. Haddonfield was still on the phone, telling his wife they were safe, which, under other circumstances, I might have found funny.

"Wait a minute," George said, growing red. "Is your mother really a spiritual healer?"

I realized what he was looking for, and that there were no kinds of traditional items up anywhere in our living room. My ma didn't want us to hang out in the white world, but she wanted her house to look as close to theirs as it could. Traditional stuff just reminded her of everything we'd lost.

My silence was its own answer.

"So that was a lie. For what? What was the reason I couldn't come to your house? Because you think your place isn't neat enough? And if you say it was my Dolphins jacket —"

"No, of course it wasn't your jacket," I admitted. "But, um, a lack of neatness? That doesn't really cover our house here."

"You think because my mom's German, we're clean freaks? That's friendship?"

"Look, I'll explain in a minute," I said, heading for the kitchen. I had to tell Albert what the TV had said. But George followed me, and Mr. Haddonfield hung up as I tried to open the kitchen door. It was stuck, no matter how much I tugged, so Mr. Haddonfield stepped up, wrapping his gigantic hand around mine, and yanked harder than I could. I heard someone slip on the other side as the door flew open.

George and his dad could see right into the kitchen. My ma was bent over the oven with the food, and Albert was sprawled on the planks where the linoleum had rotted, his legs out. His right arm was buried in one of the drifts creeping across the room. The drift covered a third of the kitchen floor, a blinding, pure wedge of whiteness almost as tall as those outside. More snow blasted at us through the hole in the roof. A dog barked and whimpered just beyond the back door, scratching to get in. Mr. Haddonfield and I had opened the door to the place where my family really lived, the other planet none of us ever talked about to anyone.

We all froze, staring at one another.

"The TV said we have to conserve gas. I was coming to tell Albert to shut it off," I said to my ma, who still held the baking sheet.

"What the —? Did the storm collapse the roof already?" George's dad said, rushing forward to help my uncle up, entering the Land of the Dogs. I don't think I'd ever seen anyone's jaw literally drop, but that was George's expression totally, chin down near the collar of his shirt, eyes bugged out — not a look I wanted to see again.

"Please, just go into the living room," my ma said, her teeth chattering a little, sending out a jagged vapor cloud. She hadn't put on her winter-cooking getup of overcoat, boots, and a scarf, so I knew she must be freezing. She took a couple seconds to quickly get the sheet into the oven and close it before letting all the heat out. "Supper's going to be a little late. The oven's having a hard time keeping temperature. It gets like this in the winter." She was trying to pretend this was just a minor inconvenience, which for us it normally was. But with white witnesses, I could hear her voice cracking in a way I never had before.

Mr. Haddonfield took her by the arm and led her back into the dining room. To my surprise, she went with him. I shut the door from the other side. Albert and I stood looking at each other as more snow poured in. "I told you," he said, and then he stopped and went back to pouring hot water on the snow. He'd made a decent dent in it and was using an old scoop to fill a canning kettle with more snow. "One more dump of hot water and we should have this door open."

I poured the warm water onto the snow pile and shut off the burner. Though it was a slushy mess, we could now open the door that led to the porch, kerosene, outhouse, and pump.

"Digging out the path would go a lot faster with some more hands," I said, and Albert shook his head vehemently. "It's not like they're going to forget what they've seen already," I added. "And besides, I don't think anybody's going anywhere for a while. I'm getting them."

I pushed the door open. George was standing near the dining room kerosene stove, listening intently to his dad, who sat at the table with my ma. She was expressionless, staring into the stove's small window, where you could look to make sure the flame had not gone out.

"Mrs. Blake, listen, please. I know this isn't the optimal way I would have liked for this, but . . ." He stopped, not knowing what to say. "Lewis, how old is this house?"

"I don't know. I think it was pieced together at different times, like most houses here."

"Why is that?" George asked, bewildered. He had thought he could take my life when he saw that our house was on the run-down side, but the kitchen was something else entirely.

"The first part, those two rooms, or what's left of them, are older than I am," my ma said. "My dad built them when he was getting ready to ask my ma to marry him. He wanted to have a place to carry her over the threshold. That threshold is gone, like them now. Then we added this room, then those two, and then the upstairs, and finally the porch."

"No mortgages, is that right?" George's dad answered. My ma nodded, and he explained to George, and to me as well: "The land here, it's reservation land. Can't be taken away, the way a bank can foreclose for lack of mortgage payments in the outside world. So you might sell it to someone else on the reservation, but it can't be used as collateral, which means you can't use it to get loans for home improvements or a car" — and then he looked to me — "or college?"

I shrugged. This had always been our house. I'd never given that much thought to how it came to be or its history, more aware of the frustrations its condition caused me. But now I saw the kitchen — that sunny space from my childhood that I thought I was saving, preserving, protecting from the rez dogs — was an eternal source of mortification for my ma. She knew, even more than I did, what the house had looked like in its prime, and now she was cooking in the literal ruins of the house she grew up in. I wondered how she did it every day, and generally with a smile.

"Do you know so much about Indian life from the years you spent on that reservation, Mr. Haddonfield?" I asked. This was a calculated gamble, since I was almost certain it at least wasn't a boarding school, and maybe my ma would find the situation a little more bearable if she knew he was already familiar with rez life. "I still don't quite get what your life was like there, and George has been kind of vague about it. And you've pretty much seen all my vague answers at this point, except for how you're going to be using the bathroom and washing up."

"I'm familiar with how to use a pit latrine, son. My boy here might have some challenges, though." George blushed a little. "And the reason he's been vague is I've never really told him everything myself. He knows I grew up near a lot of Indians because my parents worked at a reservation school. That's true in the most general sense, but there are many more details to the story than that. It never mattered much when we lived in Guam and Germany, but I told him a little when he was younger, and some more when he first mentioned you."

Albert came through the door at that moment, carrying the baking sheet and setting it on the grill on top of the kerosene stove, and I remembered I'd abandoned him outside. "Where's the plates?" he said. "Let's get this food on the table. We've got work ahead of us."

George and I got out plates and glasses and I grabbed the pitcher of iced tea from the fridge. Both our guests looked kind of scandalized at drinking iced tea in a blizzard, so I guess that was another of our eccentricities I hadn't been aware of.

"We might as well eat in front of the television," I said, "to find out how long you're going to be stuck here. Was Mrs. Haddonfield all right?"

"We'll eat here, at the table, together," my ma said, serving the food Albert brought in. She sat down at the table, and we all began to eat.

"She says she's missing us," Mr. Haddonfield said. "But my neighbors are a good family. The wife is from Germany too, so she and my wife share a longing for their home country. Makes it a little easier for her. In the same way being here, with generous people like yourselves, is making it easier for us. It's nice here to me."

"Nice place to visit," my ma said, a jagged laugh in her throat.

Mr. Haddonfield looked down, of course hearing the rest of the implied sentence. "Really," he said, staring at his plate. "It reminds me of almost every house I spent my youth in."

"I didn't know your wife was from Germany. Lewis doesn't tell me all that much about his friends," she said, like she ever really asked about anyone from off the reservation. She lit a cigarette in the corner, so she wasn't blowing smoke while people were eating.

"Yes," he said. "And I did mean it about liking this place. This truly reminds me of where I grew up. As Lewis mentioned, my parents were teachers in a government school for American Indians."

"One of the boarding schools?" Albert said, his eyes narrowing to slivers, reddening like the laser beam Cyclops used to destroy enemies in *The Uncanny X-Men*.

"Quite the opposite," Mr. Haddonfield said. "But I heard stories from survivors of the schools, which was why I was hesitant to explain them to my son." He stopped for a minute and leaned back, looking up at our ceiling, blackened with years of kerosene soot and cigarette smoke.

"The place where my parents worked while I was growing up was built as part of the wave against the boarding schools, once they were recognized for the criminal idea they were. This school was right on the reservation, like yours here, but the area of Minnesota the reservation exists in was pretty isolated then, so the government, as part of the treaty, I suppose, provided on-site housing for the teachers. We lived in a little gated area, so it was kind of a reservation within a reservation. I couldn't go to school there, because it was funded through the treaties," he added, and I thought of Mrs. Tunny's kids, and some others who lived on the reservation but were not allowed to go to our school with us.

"There weren't that many teachers, just a few, and my family was the only one with a child. An only child at that. Me. So I did what any kid would do. I made friends with the kids I met, all the kids from the reservation around us. I spent more time in reservation houses than I did in my own, and I got to know the culture, a little. They used to call me a name in their language, and I always asked what it meant. Eventually they confessed it was a word they had for albino rabbits, because my hair was so fair and my ears and eyelids so pink."

"Do you remember it?" I asked.

"I never got the pronunciation right. They laughed at the way I mangled it, no matter how hard I practiced. So since I never had it right in the first place, it's surely lost to me now. I asked if that was my Indian name, and they said no, white people don't go through those ceremonies. They weren't mean, just setting me straight, as they had about the realities of boarding schools, and they weren't shy. The beatings, the denial of food at the schools — I heard details I don't even want to think about now. There were probably things they didn't tell me, things I've learned about the corruption of power since —"

"Vietnam," Albert said.

"Yes, since Vietnam," George's dad confirmed. "But I appreciated that they were honest, that they thought enough of me to tell me the truth." As he said that, George looked at me with the same X-Men glow Albert had given Mr. Haddonfield a little while ago. "I did attend a few ceremonies, those that were open to the public. Some of my best memories are of those years."

"Are your parents still there?" my ma asked.

"My parents are passed on," he said. "But, no, that ended. They never would speak to me of what happened until I was much older. Something happened with one of the other teachers, I don't know what, but there was an internal affairs investigation. And they discovered my parents *had* worked at a boarding school before we'd arrived at that school, before I was born.

"I don't know any other details. I didn't want to know. Even as they told me, when I was planning to visit the old reservation as an adult, I couldn't believe the ways they had lied to me. They insisted they left the boarding school when they discovered some corruption. I'd like to believe that's true, but I have no way of knowing for sure." He looked down. "Because they'd been in the government work system, after their stint in Minnesota, my parents had the option of taking a new assignment or leaving the system entirely. Times were tight, so they took another job, and started teaching at a US military base in Germany, teaching the kids of Americans stationed there."

"Is that how you and *Mutti* really met?" George said.

His dad smiled a funny little smile, like he had just bitten something sour, a fresh lemon.

"I know we always told you we met while I was stationed there," he said. "She was a village girl from the rural areas outside of Berlin, who made her living cleaning houses for officers at the base, and some of the teachers as well. She came to our house, looking for work, when I was fifteen. My mother always believed in cleaning up after herself, and declined, but your mother and I decided to meet for coffee." He sighed, paused, then continued.

"She was the reason I enlisted. We — your mother will kill me if she knows I've told you this," he said to George, who shook his head to commit to his silence. *More cover-ups*, I thought. "We had to get married. I was only seventeen when that happened, and she was eighteen. She didn't want to leave, and it would have been hard for me to get a real job in Berlin.

"Your grandparents weren't too happy that I decided against college. But the military still had the draft then, so I was unusual in requesting to enlist, and I got an agreement for Berlin to be my home base, unless there were defense reasons I had to be shipped somewhere else. We got a good twelve years." I could see George figuring something in his head, but before he could call his dad on it, Mr. Haddonfield clarified. "We lost that child, but eventually, we had you."

"So *did* you go back to that reservation after you knew the truth?" my ma asked. "My folks never wanted to see Carlisle again, but it seems like your situation was different."

"I did. I rented a car one afternoon when I was on maneuvers in Minnesota and drove up. Our old house was still there. Looked like someone was living in it. The gates were torn down, naturally. The old school looked like it had been made over into tribal government offices."

"See anyone you knew?" Albert asked.

"Nope. Drove around. Some things had changed. Some roads where I used to have friends had barriers up across them, saying only tribal members and those with permission could enter. I was neither of those things, so I turned around and left. My life is in the military now, with my wife and my boy. I'm a career man."

"I'm sure your wife misses you. I wish we could find a way to get you home," my ma said.

"Ah," he said, all blustery, "she's maybe just a little bit glad to have the opportunity to give the house the required thorough scrubbing without her messy men getting in the way." George shot me another look, as if somehow I had done a little ventriloquism act on his dad to prove that they were uptight in their obsession with cleanliness. But I hadn't really heard anyone use both "required" and "thorough" before concerning the cleaning of a house. "She has our neighbors too, as I said. Good people. It's one of the things about being in a community of connected people. You can count on everyone around you, but I imagine you folks know that."

My ma nodded. I don't know what it was about the things he was saying, but she seemed to finally relax a bit.

"Mrs. Blake, do you do beadwork? One of the things I was hoping to do when I went back to Minnesota was to get my wife a piece of beadwork, but there was no store or stand or trading post anymore. Things change, I suppose. I looked at your National Picnic this summer, but nothing struck me. I want something that'll be perfect for my wife. I haven't found it yet."

"My ma doesn't do beadwork," I said, not wanting to get into that subject. My grandparents had come back from Carlisle and reconnected with home, but they dragged some school ideas with them, like extra suitcases. My grandmother once threatened bodily harm to a reservation teacher for trying to teach my ma and her siblings how to do beadwork in school.

"Okay, well, it was worth a try," Mr. Haddonfield said.

"I want to thank you for taking the time to pick up food for us," my ma said. "We have some, naturally — we'd get by, we always do — but it would not have been like this."

"Reminds me, I still have our groceries in the truck. Probably should bring them in."

"We can do that," I said, looking to George. "Do you need it done now? If there's anything that shouldn't freeze, we should probably get right out there."

"Finish your supper," George's dad said. "That'll be enough time."

On TV, we saw shots of city streets in downtown Buffalo, where snow crept past windows like it had here. One clip showed drifts almost up to the crossbars of the power lines. The announcer said people were losing electricity left and right, but so far, ours held. They would bring the weather guys on occasionally to cover technical information on why this storm was so impossible and unpredictable, but even when they went back to the regular anchors, it was still full-time weather with no end in sight.

My ma eventually pulled out two cans of government-commodity canned peaches, with their bland drawings of a peach on the can, so even an illiterate person would know what was inside. She opened the cans and dropped the peaches, heavy syrup and all, into a large serving bowl, proclaiming they were dessert.

After supper, the five of us worked: back and forth to the end of the driveway for groceries, then digging workable spaces around the kerosene tanks, the pump, and the outhouse. In between, we'd come in to thaw out around the stoves and hear that the storm was getting worse. After the late news, we watched the beginning of *The Tonight Show*, which I almost never got to see, and then we had to figure out sleeping arrangements.

My ma decided our situation warranted opening the Charlotte and Zach shrine, and at some point, she swapped out the sheets that were on the beds in there for fresh ones. She poured a mix of cold water from the pail and boiling hot from the kettle into the wash pan in her bedroom, and invited first Mr. Haddonfield and then George to clean up if they wanted. Mr. Haddonfield came out a few minutes later, holding the pan with milky soap water before him.

"Where do you get rid of this? I can toss it out on the slush mound, if that's all right." He shrugged on his coat and stepped out into the kitchen, coming back with fresh water for George to use. While George was behind the curtain, scrubbing with the washcloth my ma had set out, the rest of us sat at the table. Albert was in our room doing something vaguely noisy, but I couldn't tell what.

"Mrs. Blake?" George's dad said, after a little while.

"Vera."

"Okay, Vera. James. Jim, really, but Willy, my wife, she likes the formality of 'James.' Are you the only house using that well?"

My ma nodded, but she really didn't like talking about our situation. "Lewis, why don't you show Mr. Haddonfield the room they'll be in as long as they're here?" she said, standing. "I want to check the weather to see if there are any updates."

"Did I say something wrong?" Mr. Haddonfield asked when we reached the top of the stairs, where they opened to our room, and I saw my bed was, surprisingly, neatly made.

"My sister cleans the houses of others for a living," Albert said, stepping from around the corner. "Doesn't bother me how we live. Been here my whole life. Haven't even been inside too many other houses, except for those we were required to check in the jungle, and those, well, I wasn't really visiting." He leaned in the doorway. "But for Vera, it's sort of like being shown a picture of a car, and then being asked if she would like it, and when she says yes to the person holding the picture, they give it to her."

Mr. Haddonfield had been listening intently, but that last part he didn't understand. I had a pretty good idea, knowing how Albert's brain worked, so I translated the best I could.

"Albert means the picture. They give her the picture. Not the car. My ma spends half her day working her butt off cleaning beautiful houses that are all decked out, and then the other half resting up from being on her knees all day, here, in *this* house."

"I understand," Mr. Haddonfield said.

I pulled back the curtain on the shrine. "Here's the room," I said, "obviously." It wasn't like there was much of a tour to give. "Hope you're not allergic to cats. I think Fat Cat and LeKittia are up here somewhere. If they crawl up, you can just boot them if you want. No door besides this curtain, so there's really no keeping them out of the room."

"Am I kicking you out of your room, son?" he asked, looking around.

"Albert and I share the other room up here, the one you just saw some of."

He nodded. "Maybe you boys would like to share a room. It looks like we're going to be here a while," he said, pulling back the heavy winter curtains and looking out the window. I wondered if he noticed the snow gathering on the windowsill inside the glass, stiffening the bottom of the cloth, but really, how could he not? "I don't want to bump your uncle here, or invade his privacy. I could stay on the couch."

"No, that's a great idea," Albert said. "The guys could stay in here. I don't mind giving up my bed for your boy, but you might not like what's up on my wall."

Mr. Haddonfield leaned into our room and saw one single centerfold. Albert had taken all the others down, and in his convoluted logic, one totally naked woman up on his wall was far less scandalous than ten of them.

Just then George came up and joined us. "Dad? What did you do with your dirty water?"

"I'll take care of it," Mr. Haddonfield said. "I was just telling Albert and Lewis here that you guys should be in one room, and I'd sleep somewhere else, but Albert thought I might be uncomfortable with his wall decorations if you stayed in here." George looked at the centerfold and then looked down, his ears reddening. "I was about to say it wasn't an issue, since I was *pretty* sure you'd encountered such pictures before." He grinned.

George flushed red all the way, then looked at me, maybe remembering that I'd acted like I'd never seen the likes of these pictures that New Year's Eve. He was still tallying all the ways

I'd deceived him, and there were a couple more he might find over the course of the storm.

"So you boys going to be okay in there?" Mr. Haddonfield asked, opening the curtain to the sibling shrine as we stood near the window, watching the snow fly by. When we nodded, he suggested it was time for bed.

"You can have Lewis's bed," Albert said to George's dad. "Way more comfortable than the couch. Don't worry. I changed the sheets earlier. Fresh and clean, no kid tracks."

"Thank you. I'm going to take care of that bathwater, and then I'll be up, so I won't disturb you too much. You know, I was looking at that tarp. I think if we get even a little letup from the wind tomorrow morning, like they're saying on TV, we can get it back up in a flash. At least keep the snow from accumulating in the kitchen."

"Sounds good," Albert said, turning my bedside light on. "Hope you don't snore."

"No guarantees," Mr. Haddonfield said, heading downstairs.

"There never are," Albert said, shutting his own light off and turning over.

George and I silently undressed and crawled into the shrine's beds. George's dad came back up, and within half an hour, the sounds of two separate, low, buzzing snores came through the curtain. I recognized both — Albert's from every night and Mr. Haddonfield's from Toronto. All I heard from the other side of our room, though, was the wind trying to lift our roof off.

"You awake?" I murmured.

George grunted an acknowledgement.

"Look, I'm sorry." I got out of my bed, put my clothes back

on, turned on the lamp next to my bed, and wandered over to the vanity next to his, leaning on it. "It wasn't you. It was my ma. You understand, don't you? You and your dad are the fourth and fifth white people in here, *ever*. And number three was the guy who told me I was headed to a reformatory."

"You wanna sit down?" he asked, clearing a spot near the foot of the bed.

"Thanks. You gotta trust me. This is all new territory for me."

"Trust you," he said, fake laughing.

"You know what I mean. It's one thing to tell people what life on Dog Street is like, but it's something different to watch your face when you see the reality."

"But you *never* told me. You never told me *anything* except some nonsense about the spiritual harmony of your house. Your mother really isn't even some ceremonial leader, is she?" he asked a second time, sitting up higher, pushing himself away. I shook my head. "I knew it. I would never do this to a friend. To you. As long as I lived here, my place would be open to you."

"Look, I said I'm sorry. I hope you can forgive me. Isn't that what real friends do? Here on the reservation, we kind of have to forgive each other, because none of us is going anywhere. But out there, if you want to walk away from someone else's life, you can. In your world, there aren't any guarantees," I said.

"Like your uncle just said, there never are," he said. "*Anywhere*," he added.

I went back to my sister's old bed, undressed again, and climbed back in. Another half hour passed, but his breathing remained the same. We were in that spot between the two planets, maybe building the rez rocket Albert said didn't exist, maybe without all the essential parts. But I hadn't gone through all of this craziness to give up on our friendship when pretty much everything I'd been hiding was now stripped bare and torn away.

"You never answered me," I said. "You going to forgive me or what?"

"It's what friends do, isn't it?" he said, not moving. "How good are you at forgiving?"

"Pretty good, I guess."

"Have you ever really been put to the test?"

"If you're asking if I'm ever going to forgive Evan Reiniger, the answer is absolutely not. He wasn't ever my friend, though, so that's a different situation. Know what I mean?"

"Yeah, okay," he said. "You know what? I finally got to see the Wacky Packages on your headboard. Didn't think it was going to take quite that much patience." We laughed, and for the first time in a while, it was a real laugh, without strain.

"Good things come to those who wait," I said.

"Doofus," he replied.

"One good thing?"

"What's that?"

"You don't have to get up early tomorrow to deliver papers," I said, and he laughed again. Small, but real.

"One good thing," he repeated. A little while later, his breathing evened out, so though I'd thought of other things I wanted to say, I kept quiet and fell asleep myself.

Across the Universe

In the morning, Albert and George's dad shrugged on their clothes and stomped downstairs as Albert and I did every morning. I cracked the curtains and looked outside, where the blizzard roared on full blast. George was still asleep. I quietly grabbed my guitar and stood on his side of the room, then launched into the Beatles' "Good Morning Good Morning."

"What are you doing?" George said, grouchy, pulling the covers over his head. Then, a couple seconds later, he whipped them back, his eyes open wide. "You got a guitar? When did you do that? Is that the one you told me about, the one Reiniger had?" He jumped up and started getting dressed. "Let me see it? What else can you play?"

"A few things," I said, handing it over. "Of course it's not Evan's guitar. I just got it for Christmas, but I started taking lessons when —" I started to say, *When you fell in love with Stacey*, but I didn't think that was quite the right thing. It wasn't even the truth. "When we were spending less time together. So, you know, about nine months ago."

"Less time," he said, strumming chords. "I wasn't exactly the best friend to have either. I could have made more time, but

Stacey's the first girl to ever like me in the same way I liked her. The first girl who let me kiss her and who wanted to kiss me back. Was kind of a big thing."

"On the bright side, now you can come over anytime your dad's willing to bring you," I said, but his expression was kind of funny. "And pick you up, sorry."

"No, it's not that," he said, pausing like he was going to say something serious. But he just started strumming the first song off *Let It Be*, "Two of Us." We both knew the harmonies on this song, so I joined in. He was still the better singer, but he never pointed this out. "My dad taught me some songs over the last couple years," he explained, handing the guitar back. "He said that's the easy version of the song, but there's a truer one where the progression is harder."

"I didn't know you had a guitar at your house," I said.

"Well, it's only used for spiritual ceremonies," he said, and I punched him.

We went downstairs to see what was happening on TV, and shovel the outhouse path. George decided he didn't have to use the john. He might have moved around the world a couple times, but he'd apparently never had to do anything that personally exposing.

"Okay, the trick is to wait," I said on Saturday afternoon.

"What do you mean, 'wait'? Wait for what?"

"Wait until you really, really need to go. That's kind of the tricky part. If you wait too long . . ." I said, letting him fill in the blanks. "You should have gone a couple hours ago when the wind died down. Anyway, you wait until you have to go, then you run, drop your jeans — I'd recommend no lower than midthigh in this weather — do your business, with paper already prepared —"

"You some kind of outhouse scientist?" he said.

"Look, I've been doing this for ten, eleven years? We won't count the diaper and potty-training years. I'm telling you, if there is someone who knows what he's talking about, it's me."

"Good to know an expert, I suppose," he said, looking glum.

"Right. So to continue, you drop them, sit, and — now this is the important part — make sure you're over the hole and that you're pointing in the right direction, or you're going to piss all over your jeans. And then do your business and run for the house."

"It's just a hole?" George said, his brow wrinkling in dismay.

"It's like a bench, inside that little building. You know those school bus shelters people build for their kids by the roadside?" When I first noticed those shelters near mailboxes at some white people's houses, I could not believe that those fools had built their outhouses so close to the road. My family laughed about that for years. "They're built like that, except the bench has holes cut in it, where you park your butt."

"Well, where does it all go?"

"That's the problem in the summer. It doesn't really go anywhere. It decomposes, so the smell's not too good, but it's all frozen now. This one has two holes."

"People do this *together*?" he asked, scandalized.

"No. Did *you* grow up in a shoe box? You alternate holes so neither one gets too full. If you time things right, you might not have to clean it out for a couple years." It felt odd to be silent for so long and now suddenly lead a complicated workshop on the finer points of outhouse usage, but while he wasn't ready to commit to a trip out there yet, he did seem less freaked out and more intent on learning efficiency tips.

We passed time by keeping on top of the new snow swamping us. Every couple hours, the paths needed work, so they'd be passable. The outhouse path grew steeper and steeper walls as we pushed the hardpack snow up and out. It eased the trip, actually, because there were sections of the path where your head was literally below the drift level, which cut out the wind. When we took breaks from working, George and I played my albums and showed each other the songs we knew on the guitar. When our fingers hurt too much from playing, we watched the blizzard news with the adults, wondering when anyone was going to report a letup in the storm.

"All right," George said, standing up suddenly, late on Saturday night, in the middle of listening to *Revolver*. "I'm going."

I knew immediately what he meant. "Take the flashlight, and keep the paper tucked in your jacket so it doesn't get wet," I said. "One more thing. When you sit, there's going to be a blast of cold air that's likely to take your breath away. There's no getting around it. Don't jump up in shock or, you know, the directional spraying issue." And with that, he was down the stairs and out the door.

He got back in under four minutes, which I thought was a pretty impressive first attempt.

"As bad as you'd imagined?" I asked as he huddled near the stovepipe.

"Worse."

"That's just the way things are sometimes, man," I said. "But you've done it now. It won't be so bad the next time."

"I'm hoping there won't be a next time."

But of course there was a next time. As the day became days, we listened to more music and each became better at the songs the other knew. Mr. Haddonfield's beard started growing in, transforming him into Papa Smurf. All he needed were the red hat and wool pants.

By the third day, the winds died down to gusts of forty miles an hour instead of seventy. The ban on driving was still in effect, with wild fines for anyone caught on the road. We saw footage of other houses where the whole building was under drifts, just the peaks and tunnels for the doors visible. One picture showed a couple people standing on top of the snow and reaching up to touch a traffic light. That was how high and how firm the snow was. The news even had a scientist on to explain the "broken snowflake crystal problem," but I didn't get it. The bottom line was that they had to use front loaders and trenchers to break the snow. Regular plows were just stopped dead by the walls of snow they rammed into.

As February first approached, it was obvious we weren't going to Toronto for the Queen concert. The streets might have been cleared in Toronto, but we weren't even supposed to leave the driveway, let alone the country. That night, we sat at the table, looking at our unusable tickets, and listened to the concert warm-up on CHUM from Toronto. The station promised to play Queen songs throughout the evening, and then as soon as the show was over, they would do the instant concert replay, in which they played, in order, all the songs in the band's set list.

Halfway through the evening, they announced they would play all of *A Day at the Races*, without interruption. I had it already, of course, and could listen anytime I wanted, but there was something about hearing it on the radio, knowing it was reaching thousands of people simultaneously. Attending a concert was like being on the reservation in a funny way, a place where everyone gathered there shared the same experience. And even though this was just shared through our speakers, it still felt like that kind of belonging.

"I'm really sorry, boys," George's dad said. "I thought there was possibly a chance the roads would be clear enough. I bet it was a terrific show."

"Maybe we'll catch them the next tour," I said, and neither responded, but a look passed between them. Any other Queen tour was easily a year and a half away, and I didn't want to think about the possibility that they might not be around, but I knew it was a part of their lives to always take that chance into account.

The morning of the sixth day, the plows finally came through. One headed west and then, a few minutes later, a second one came through to the east. It took us a while to dig the Haddonfields' truck out, but we eventually had them packed up and cleared out, and we waved as they took off down the road. Before they left, I asked Mr. Haddonfield if he would show me the truer chord progressions for "Two of Us." He was happy to, but they *were* tougher. Maybe the Bug could show me some technique to make the transitions better, I thought.

The next day, when school finally resumed, everyone compared notes. George and I took turns telling stories about the worthless concert tickets, the fire hall, and my house, both selectively offering details. Summer told us how she and her family had heroically taken in twenty strangers, going out into their road to find trapped motorists, and even having a birthday cake for one. I had a hard time believing her — she lived on a dead end, which she insisted was called a cul-de-sac, where the only people who drove on it either lived there or knew people living there — but I decided not to call her on it. Maybe that was a story she needed to tell.

One day the following week, I came home and our dining room had been changed substantially. The beat-up dresser on the kitchen wall was gone, and in its place was a counter with a built-in sink and drawers off to one side. Next to this was a large tank with tubes coming off it, disappearing behind the whole new cabinet-sink thing. And on the opposite wall, the ratty daybed had been replaced by our old, familiar cooking stove, transplanted into the dining room.

"What's going on?" I asked Albert, who sat in the corner chair, taking in all the changes.

"Oh, your buddy's dad, Captain Air Force, the superhero," he said, making a face. "Coming back to save the day. I guess him and your ma talked about it sometime while they were here. Said he wanted to repay her generosity. You know your ma, but when he pointed out that she saved him and his kid from the storm, she was okay with it. Not exactly great, but okay."

"Did you help him?"

"Of course, what else was I gonna do? He brought the gas company guys and everything to switch out the line from the tanks to here and test it for leaks. Works fine. I tried it already."

"What's that?" I asked, pointing to the new counter.

"A sink. What's it look like?"

"I know it's a sink," I said, walking toward it to get a closer look.

"Don't bother trying it. It's not hooked up. They can't work on the lines until the spring thaw, but he's got all that covered already. He said they'll be gone before the well people come, but he left the paperwork there on the desk. It's all taken care of, paid in full."

I glanced at the paperwork — instructions to install a motor-ized pump, run a trench to the house, insulate it, and close it all back up again — but my attention was focused on something else. "Wait a minute, what did you say? Before who's gone?"

Albert didn't say anything for a minute. "Thought you knew," he said finally, reluctant. "Captain Air Force seemed to think you knew."

I called George's number immediately, and when he picked up the phone, I dispensed with the greeting. "Are you moving?"

He hesitated, so I rephrased. "Are you leaving western New York and going to live some other place?"

"In a week," he said, and let out a deep breath. "Lubbock. That's in Texas."

We were silent, each listening to the other breathe little pissed-off breaths.

"I didn't know how to tell you."

"So you were going to just not show up one day?"

"No, I was going to tell you ahead of time, of course. I just didn't know how far ahead. Usually it's easier with the least amount of time, so we don't get dragged out in good-byes. On Guam, we had a tradition where best-friend families escorted the leaving families to the transport plane. Glad to be done with that tradition. Was superhard. About tore your heart out." He paused. "I was going to tell you at the concert, but then we didn't go."

" 'Usually,' " I said, wondering if he was compiling a scrap-book even as we talked. "Do you have your new address yet, so I'll be able to write to you?"

"No, not yet. Sometimes families don't know until they arrive in their new towns. They stop at the base HQ and are told which place to pull into."

"I can't believe you didn't tell me this the whole time you were here," I said, thinking of all the things we'd talked about. There had been plenty of opportunities.

"You're not exactly in a place to talk about holding infor-mation back," he said.

There was another long stretch of silence. I tried to picture my world beyond the next week, and I found that I couldn't. I discovered that I had imagined him into my future, like I had all my reservation friends.

"Look, don't make this any harder than it is. I guess this is why I usually only make friends with other base kids. But in fairness, you knew. You had to. You saw Nelson leave, Gloria leave. Leaving is what we do. It's our way of life."

"It's what you do," I repeated. It was a truth of his life I never understood, because my own situation could best be summed up as *Never leaving is what we do. It's* our *way of life.*

"Listen," he said, kind of awkward. "I have to meet with the kid who's taking over my paper route. You gonna be home later?"

"Where else would I be?" I said, and we hung up, disconnecting.

26

Letting Go

There wasn't a lot I could do but accept that my best friend was moving away. I looked on a map to see where Lubbock was, and seventeen hundred miles seemed an impossible distance. He might as well have been moving back to Germany, or off to Venus.

As unlikely as it seemed, my ma asked me if I would like to invite the Haddonfields over for dinner on the night before they left. They arrived promptly at six thirty. My ma was cooking at the newly relocated stove as I escorted them in. Mrs. Haddonfield must have been briefed on our protocols, read a "Local Customs" pamphlet designed by George just for her, as she didn't take off her shoes, and reacted as if our house looked like hers instead of the increasingly jumbled, wall-to-wall-furnished smoky ruins it was. Albert had disappeared before I'd gotten home from school, and I had no idea where he went.

To acknowledge the occasion of our reunion, my ma made stuffed pork chops like she fixed the night of our first dinner together. But she also had a side serving of some sausage I'd never seen before, covered in a foul-smelling concoction she said was sauerkraut. I'd heard of it, but thus far, had been lucky enough not to encounter it in person. She had done something to the potatoes that made them unrecognizable too, so I decided I'd try to get my fill of the pork chops.

The linen cloth Ma spread on the table was covered in intricate embroidery patterns, with plants growing on long, ropy vines. The whole pattern was in white, so mostly you saw the design as light cast shadows on the threaded texture. Our plates were the mismatched dishes we always used, but she'd set out knives and forks and spoons in orderly arrangements around the plates, which I had only ever seen at George's house and on TV before.

"Such beautiful linen." Mrs. Haddonfield touched the tablecloth, tracing the patterns.

"Lewis's grandmother made it," my ma said. "She learned the skill at school and she kept it up until she passed away. It's the last piece we still have, and we use it only for special occasions."

These occasions were so special that I'd never seen it before in my life. As we were getting ready to sit down, the whine of a snowmobile grew louder in the driveway, idled for a few seconds, and then took off. Albert came in, carrying a big covered pot. "Sorry I'm late," he said, setting the pot on the counter. "Hasenpfeffer!" he shouted, lifting the lid. "I snared and dressed Mr. Rabbit here, but all I know how to do is boil 'em. So I took it to one of the German farmers I work regular for and asked the wife if she would prepare it like in Germany, in trade for some labor when they need something."

Mrs. Haddonfield leaned over the pot and breathed in deeply, smiling at the aroma.

We spent our last evening together eating and talking around the table. Eventually we knew they had to leave, and as George and I cleared the dishes, my ma went into her bedroom and brought out a shoe box. "Oh, look, a little model of you," George said, and I punched his gut. Everyone laughed, but just a little. The clock was ticking away on us.

"Open it," my ma said to Mr. Haddonfield. Inside were three neatly wrapped gifts. "Something to remember us by."

George and his dad had gotten identical beaded belt buckles with a picture of a dog in beads, and below it, also in beads, DOG ST. 77. Mrs. Haddonfield's package revealed one of the little beaded waving-flag pins that were so popular down at Niagara Falls Prospect Park. Women from the reservation sold probably thousands of these little flags to tourists every summer, which I always found a little ironic. Instead of an American flag, though, this one had bars of black, red, and deep yellow — the German flag. Mrs. Haddonfield put it on her blouse. As she looked in the mirror, her husband slid her coat over her shoulders, saying it was time.

"Thank you so much," he said, "for everything. I'm sorry we have to go. We still have some packing to do, and we have to be out by midafternoon tomorrow." He took my mother's hand in both of his, shaking it some formal way, a kind of warm embrace for people who don't naturally hug others. Mrs. Haddonfield made a similar gesture, and George copied it as well. They all thanked Albert, and I grabbed my jacket and walked them to their car — the sedan Mrs. Haddonfield had picked Albert and me up in, a thousand years ago, after the chorus concert.

"Mr. and Mrs. Haddonfield," I said, and stopped. For being the Tuscarora language whiz, I really wasn't all that good with speaking when I needed to say something monumental. "Nyah-wheh. Thank you for inviting me to your house, for allowing me to spend time with your family. I wish I could tell you what it means to me."

"Lewis, it was good," Mrs. Haddonfield said. "When we left Deutschland, I was worried George would be without my big family, and Guam proved my fears." She reached out and patted my hand. "I am glad he was able to find a larger family again here, with you."

"Lewis," Mr. Haddonfield said, shaking my hand in his monster grip, enveloping my hand in both of his. "Thank you for giving me and George, and now Willy, a chance to glimpse my childhood again. I'd hoped, in meeting you and bringing you along for the concert, that I would be repaying some debt I owed for my parents. Instead, I find myself in deeper gratitude. You've given me back something I'd lost. It's been an honor to have known you, son. And to have met your family. They're nice people, and I hope you know that."

I nodded. I did know it, and I knew it now more than ever. George's parents got in the car and started it. George and I stood in the snow, glowing in the running lights, a sharp wind cutting through the evening.

"I guess this is it," he said. "The real good-bye. I'll be in school tomorrow, but we're leaving right after. My dad's got the route planned to the minute, surprise, surprise."

"Get an address yet?" He shook his head. "Listen, you're going to think this is super dorky, and I don't even do this with my ma, but a handshake and a punch on the shoulder? I don't think they're going to cut it for me."

"Even with my Dolphins jacket on? Won't you explode or something?" he said.

"Yup, I'll risk it," I said. I guess we knew for sure then that this was it. He was leaving. So we hugged, and it wasn't the chest-bumping hug that football players gave each other when they score a touchdown. It was the clunky embrace of two friends who didn't have any other words to express the loss we felt as our worlds drifted into different orbits. We didn't even pat each other on the back. It was a real hug, straight and true.

"I better go before they flick the lights on me. I still have to finish packing."

"See you tomorrow?" I said. He nodded and turned, getting in the backseat.

They backed out, and I walked to the front door in the wash of their headlights. We waved one last time, and I watched their taillights disappear around the bend, and then I waited a little more, until I couldn't tell the sound of their exhaust from the wind and winter and everything else in my life, blowing apart.

"Who did you get to make that beadwork?" I asked my ma when I got back in the house.

"I made it," she said. "Where do you think I get money for Christmas presents?"

"What about all that talk of my learning the language being a waste of time?" I said. "That tradition was dead? And I have never seen you pick up a piece of beadwork in my life."

"When you find a way to make money on the language, you go right ahead," she said. "Until then, you've probably got a lot of catch-up work to get your grades back to where they were. You've only got a few months to do that before the school year's over." She put water in the kettle to wash dishes. "As far as you ever seeing me do beadwork? You don't know everything. I wait until late at night. My hands are less swollen then, my fingers more nimble. I give the work to Ruby Pem and she sells it for me down at the falls. Only takes a little cut. Less than others."

The next day in school, George didn't say much, though he pretended to pay attention, dutifully writing down assignments he was never going to complete. And then, in the middle of seventh period, he was called down to the office for early dismissal. I had hoped to walk him out, but his parents must have arrived early. He stood up, shook hands with Artie and me, patted my shoulder, and handed me a small cardboard box before he walked to the door.

There was no way Mr. Bolger was going to give me a pass, so I couldn't do anything but watch him leave. All through the lecture about dangling modifiers, I imagined the Haddonfield family pulling out of the school driveway, heading down Clarksville Pass one last time, hitting the on-ramp, and vanishing.

As we left school that day, Artie walked out with me.

"That was hard, huh?" he said.

I nodded. "Hardest thing ever."

"What's in the box?"

"I haven't looked."

"Hey, when it gets warmer? When the seasons change? You want to start coming with me to Good Intentions?"

"That's not Good Intentions," I said. "It's just the Road to Hell and nothing more."

"Come on, don't be that way," Artie said, smiling. "If we call it Good Intentions, it'll sort of be like he's still here. And you and me, we're still here. And Stacey."

"Yeah, we are. Okay, thanks. I appreciate your extending a hand, man. I do."

I rode the bus home, and when I got to my new room — the former shrine, which I just stayed in after the storm was over — I opened the box. Inside, wrapped in tissue paper, was the little red-dressed, white-bearded figure from George's display — Papa Smurf. I wondered, when he unpacked, what he might put in its place, or if he'd just leave the space empty.

For about a month, every day when I got home, I asked my ma if any of the mail was for me, and every day she said no. Eventually I stopped asking, and as it warmed up, I did some-times go to the Road to Hell with Artie. Sometimes I felt sharper stabs of the loss if I tried to use George's name for the place. Stacey hung out with Summer less and less in school, and eventually, I could almost forget the things she'd said, or come to forgive them. One day in May, she was at the Road to Hell with a few people we both knew. She walked over and offered me one of her Suzy Q's from the BX.

"Half?" I said, so she extended it and I tore part off.

"Have you heard from him?" she asked.

I shook my head. "You?"

She shook her head in turn. "The difference?" she said. "You expected to. I knew when they got their orders, that was it. He'd be moving on. Sometimes you write to your old friends for a little while, and then it stops. Some of us make the cut cleaner. He broke up with me, but maybe more for me, since I'd been kind of listening too much to Summer's nonsense. I'm sorry. I didn't know. He explained it better, later. And anyway, when we broke up? He knew he wasn't going to be here much longer."

"You knew in November that he was leaving?" I couldn't believe he'd kept that information from me for so long.

"Yeah," she said. "His dad's an officer. They get more notice than my dad would."

"Thanks for the Suzy," I said as she joined her friends a

few yards away. Carson and Tami were there too, since Tami was going out with Artie now. She had somehow penetrated the white dating fortress, and Carson apparently used that as a way to cultivate a new set of friends.

"You want me to see if my mom will give you a ride?" Carson asked when Saphronia picked them up. I shook my head. He shouted that he'd give me a call to hang out in a couple days, and I knew I'd probably answer the phone and probably say yes.

"I'll see you tomorrow," I said to Artie, and started my walk home. Once there, I went to my room, but I didn't know what to listen to. Nothing seemed right.

About a week later, when I got home from school, there was a package on my bed with a note from Albert in his terrible handwriting:

CAIM 4 YU 2DA

There was no return address, but the cancellation stamp was Lubbock, Texas. I tore it open. I had a pretty good idea of what it was, or at least what kind of object. It was a shape and size I knew well.

Inside was an album that had been released in the last week, after years and years of having sat in storage: *The Beatles at the Hollywood Bowl*. It had a gatefold sleeve of concert pictures, images of the program, and fake torn tickets as part of its artwork. I went back through the shipping carton, and there was nothing else in it. No note. No card. No mailing label. Nothing.

I put the album on and played it through several times on the record player my ma had found at a garage sale in April.

Almost half the time, the band was drowned out by screaming fans. Mr. Haddonfield had said he'd seen them in Bloomington, Minnesota, at Metropolitan Stadium, and he was always disappointed that the Beatles had never released a live album, so he could hang on to the experience with more than his memories. He said memory was sometimes unreliable, and made things better or worse than they really were.

I had to wonder if this was the idea behind George's giving me that *Wings over America* album for Christmas. He knew he was moving by then, and maybe he even knew he wasn't going to write. So he gave me something to hang on to, if I wanted. And maybe this too: We became friends through the Beatles, but there weren't any new Beatles albums, and there never would be any new Beatles albums ever again. But the old songs would always be there, sounding as magic as ever — and now George had helped me remember that was true. Friends are always worth the moments of joy you share, even if they don't last.

I kept replaying one song, "Things We Said Today." Eventually Albert stepped into the room. "Why do you keep putting the needle back to that one, over and over?"

"It's about two people who know that everything always disappears, eventually."

"I don't think that's right," he said. "I think it's about two people who find each other again, their memories keeping them connected, even when they don't live near each other anymore. Two people who each want the other to remember them."

"I guess people hear things differently."

"I guess they do," he said, about to turn, but then he stopped. "I noticed there wasn't any return address. Is there a letter?" I shook my head. "Which one do you think sent it?"

"Not sure," I said.

"Can you hear what he's saying, whichever one?"

"Yeah," I said. "I can. Now leave me alone, will you? I've got some studying to do."

"Sure thing. Nice place for that, by the way," he said, tapping the Papa Smurf. I had taken some of the looser boards from the tractor shed and built a small box shelf to fit into a hole Charlotte had kicked in the wall when this had been her room. It was slightly off kilter, since I didn't know how to do a blueprint or conduct exact measurements, but lopsided as it was, it suited our house. I covered up some of my poor construction with new Wacky Packages, left on their backing to keep them firm.

"Nyah-wheh, Albert, for all the stuff you did," I said. "And for knowing when to keep your mouth shut and when not to."

"What uncles are for, man. Got to get you in training for treating Charlotte's kids right. They're gonna be a handful, isn't it? And you and Zach are the uncles who gotta stick around and watch out for them. That's your job. Why don't we hear that new album one more time, and crank it a little? Your ma's not home yet."

I triggered the turntable again, starting the album on side one. This time, I let it play all the way through to the end, and when the needle arm lifted after it was over, I watched it swing back to its resting place. As it shut itself down, I picked up the guitar my family had sacrificed to provide for me, and I tuned it. There was no one to sing the harmony part, but I started playing "Two of Us" anyway, using the tougher, truer chords I'd learned from the Haddonfields.

PLAYLIST & DISCOGRAPHY

Each part title is a riff on a song, as noted, and each of the chapters is named, in alternating order, for a Beatles song and a Paul McCartney post-Beatles song. Below each, I have listed the album most commonly associated with the song's release, contemporarily. Some were singles that were never released on an album, which was the culture at the time, so a few of these albums are compilations. I have also identified other songs that are referenced in each chapter, with occasional repetitions and notes concerning live versions as opposed to studio versions, as identified in the narrative.

Links to online versions of these songs are available on my website at www.ericgansworth.com/IfIEverGetmusic.

The radio program mentioned in Chapter 2, "Paul McCartney Is Alive and Well . . . Maybe," was broadcast several times on WKBW (1520) in Buffalo, New York. It is available for streaming at www.wkbwradio.com/paul.htm.

Part One
If I Ever Get Out of Here (Paul McCartney & Wings: *Band on the Run* — title song)

Chapter 1

"With a Little Help from My Friends," The Beatles: *Sgt. Pepper's Lonely Hearts Club Band*

"Uncle Albert/Admiral Halsey," Paul & Linda McCartney: *Ram*

Chapter 2

"Man We Was Lonely," Paul McCartney: *McCartney*

"Yellow Submarine," The Beatles: *Revolver*

"Hey Jude," The Beatles: *Past Masters, Vol. 2*

Chapter 3

"I Call Your Name," The Beatles: *Past Masters, Vol. 1*

Chapter 4

"Dear Boy," Paul & Linda McCartney: *Ram*

Chapter 5

"When I'm Sixty-Four," The Beatles: *Sgt. Pepper's Lonely Hearts Club Band*

Chapter 6

"Maybe I'm Amazed," Paul McCartney: *McCartney*

"Strawberry Fields Forever," The Beatles: *Magical Mystery Tour*

"Band on the Run," Paul McCartney & Wings: *Band on the Run*

"Jet," Paul McCartney & Wings: *Band on the Run*

"Here Comes the Sun," The Beatles: *Abbey Road*

Chapter 7

"If I Needed Someone," The Beatles: *Rubber Soul*

"Smoke on the Water," Deep Purple: *Made in Japan*

"Yesterday," The Beatles: *Help!*

Part Two

Moon and Stars (Paul McCartney & Wings: *Venus and Mars* — title song)

Chapter 8

"Venus and Mars," Paul McCartney & Wings: *Venus and Mars*

"Komm, Gib Mir Deine Hand," The Beatles: *Past Masters, Vol. 1*

"Bohemian Rhapsody," Queen: *A Night at the Opera*

"You're My Best Friend," Queen: *A Night at the Opera*

Chapter 9
"Fixing a Hole," The Beatles: *Sgt. Pepper's Lonely Hearts Club Band*
"I'm a Loser," The Beatles: *Beatles for Sale*

Chapter 10
"No Words," Paul McCartney & Wings: *Band on the Run*
"Till There Was You," The Beatles: *With the Beatles*
"Paranoid," Black Sabbath: *Paranoid*
"Tomorrow Never Knows," The Beatles: *Revolver*

Chapter 11
"Yesterday," The Beatles: *Help!*
Concert: Paul MCartney & Wings: *Wings over America*, full concert album, with selections noted: "Venus and Mars," "Rock Show," "Jet," "Lady Madonna," "Yesterday," "The Long and Winding Road," "Band on the Run," "Live and Let Die," "Silly Love Songs"

Chapter 12
"Heart of the Country," Paul & Linda McCartney: *Ram*

Chapter 13
"Old Brown Shoe," The Beatles: *Past Masters, Vol. 2*

Chapter 14
"Live and Let Die," Paul McCartney & Wings: *McCartney, All the Best*
"Money (That's What I Want)," The Beatles: *With the Beatles*
"I Call Your Name," The Beatles: *Past Masters Vol. 1*

Chapter 15
"For You, Blue," The Beatles: *Let It Be*

Chapter 16
"You Gave Me the Answer," Paul McCartney & Wings: *Venus and Mars*
"Layla," Derek and The Dominoes: *Layla*

Chapter 17
"I Should Have Known Better," The Beatles: *A Hard Day's Night*

Part Three
Tragical History Tour (The Beatles: *Magical Mystery Tour* — title song)

Chapter 18
"Listen to What the Man Said," Paul McCartney & Wings: *Venus and Mars*

Chapter 19
"Things We Said Today," The Beatles: *A Hard Day's Night*
"White Man," Queen: *A Day at the Races*
"Somebody to Love," Queen: *A Day at the Races*

Chapter 20
"Junior's Farm," Paul McCartney & Wings: *McCartney, All the Best*
David Bowie: *Low*
David Bowie: *CHANGESONEBOWIE*

Chapter 21
"I've Just Seen a Face," The Beatles: *Help!*

Chapter 22
"Too Many People," Paul & Linda McCartney: *Ram*

Chapter 23
"The Long and Winding Road," The Beatles: *Let It Be*

Chapter 24
"Let 'Em In," Paul McCartney & Wings: *Wings at the Speed of Sound*

Chapter 25
"Across the Universe," The Beatles: *Let It Be*
"Good Morning Good Morning," The Beatles: *Sgt. Pepper's Lonely Hearts Club Band*
"Two of Us," The Beatles: *Let It Be*
Queen concert album from this era: *Live Killers!*

Chapter 26
"Letting Go," Paul McCartney & Wings: *Venus and Mars*
"Things We Said Today," The Beatles: *The Beatles at the Hollywood Bowl* (Live)
"Two of Us," The Beatles: *Let It Be*

ACKNOWLEDGMENTS

If you're reading this book for class, you can skip this page. There will surely not be a quiz on any of this information. Each book I've written has begun in a strange way, most often erupting spontaneously out of multiple threads colliding in my life when I had no expectation. This one was no different, and the people to thank are both familiar and new. This novel could not have been written without these contributions.

As always, thank you first and foremost to Larry Plant, co-dreamer, first reader, multiple-draft reader, and charter member of the Band on the Run. I promise not to mention the Beatles for six months. Okay, a couple weeks . . . maybe. Let's not get carried away. Thank you to the following people, who discussed or read drafts or parts of this book, and offered valuable insights: E.R. Baxter III, Susan Bernardin, Mick Cochrane, Joyce Carol Oates. Thanks to my old college friend Melisa Holden, librarian extraordinaire, who, despite her irrational hatred of the Beatles, pointed me in some very useful directions early on. Thanks to two friends for providing gifts at the most strangely useful crossroads. Jeffery Richardson found "Wings over America" tour footage on a Paul McCartney

DVD before I knew I wanted to see it. Brittany Gray, a former student, put a guitar back in my hands after many years of absence, and then led me to discover that the Topps Company had recently published a wonderfully demented retrospective book on Wacky Packages. These stickers taught me to think critically while simultaneously corrupting my youthful landscape. These gifts have infused this novel with some of their flavor.

Thanks to three old friends, whose spirit gave this novel the foundation it needed: Jeff Ewing, for driving a couple hours, several times, to reminisce and provide extremely helpful details about his life in a military family and to remind me of the wealth that small kindnesses give — also for digging up that photo; Steve Hasley, who bravely shared some of his own experiences while I was working, informing and confirming some of the major patterns here; and Chuck Collins, wherever he landed, for changing my life, plain and simple.

Nyah-wheh to Debbie Reese (Nambe Pueblo) and her essential work at American Indians in Children's Literature (http://americanindiansinchildrensliterature.blogspot.com/) for her courage, kindness, activism, and generosity, and for introducing me to my editor at Arthur A. Levine. Thank you to Cheryl Klein, that very editor, for actively seeking out indigenous writers, and investing in my work over the long haul. Cheryl took time out of her busy schedule to teach me some explicit lessons in this new territory for me, hoping I might be able to grow in a new direction as a writer. She also had faith in this project, from its original, two-sentence description, to the book it became, in all its incarnations and idiosyncrasies. Thank you to Canisius College for its support, specifically the

Joseph S. Lowery Estate for Funding Faculty Fellowship in Creative Writing.

Nyah-wheh forever to my family, always recharging my batteries, even when they don't know it, and for their memories of the Blizzard of '77. And finally, thank you to the Beatles, the family of my soul, and to Paul McCartney specifically, who took sad songs, and made them better.

This book was edited by
Cheryl Klein and designed
by Christopher Stengel. The text
was set in Sabon MT, with display
type set in Rockwell. The production
was supervised by Starr Baer. This
book was printed and bound by
R . R . Donnelley in Crawfordsville,
Indiana. The manufacturing was
supervised by Irene Huang
and Angelique Browne.